DESOLATION OUTPOST

Terry L. Vinson

DESOLATION OUTPOST

A DOUBLE DRAGON PAPERBACK

© Copyright 2010
Terry L. Vinson

The right of Terry L. Vinson to be identified as author of this work has been asserted in accordance with the Copyright, Designs and Patents Act 1988

All Rights Reserved

No reproduction, copy or transmission of the publication may be made without written permission. No paragraph of this publication may be reproduced, copied or transmitted save with the written permission of the publisher, or in accordance with the provisions of the Copyright Act 1956 (as amended).

Any person who does any unauthorised act in relation to this publication may be liable to criminal prosecution and civil claims for damages.

ISBN 978-1-78695-509-8

Double Dragon
is an imprint of
Fiction4All

This Edition Published 2021
Fiction4All
www.fiction4all.com

Cover art by Deron Douglas
www.derondouglas.ca

Dedication

To my wife and best friend of twenty-five years, Kum Hui, who is the inspiration for all that I create.

Someday, I may yet pen that elusive love story just for her.

Prologue I: Look to the Skies

Peeking through the parka's narrow, tunneled space was much like staring through a child's spyglass, only with the added handicap of having one's tightly squinted eyes pelted by tiny specs of ice and oversized snowflakes.

Forced to avert my sights elsewhere, I look down to see my boots have practically vanished amid the growing drift now reaching past my ankles. The dizzy spells have subsided a bit, no doubt aided by the frigid night air, though there is still present a stout sense of bewilderment I could only imagine one might feel after waking from a lengthy coma.

"What... time is it?" I mutter aloud, turning to press my elbows against the warmth of the cruiser's hood, the engine humming beneath providing a faint, soothing massage to my overly chilled bones.

"Jeez, Counselor... you scared you're gonna miss a dental cleanin' or what? I'd wager it ain't no more than about three and a half minutes since the last time ya asked."

Considering the source, I ignore the good-natured ribbing. Besides, I know I'm being a pain. It's just nerves after all... natural apprehension when faced with such an otherworldly scenario. It's so much easier for them. After all, they've experienced all manner of bizarre goings-on. It's how they've made their living. I should be allowed a considerable amount of slack for enduring such madness. In reality, I should be cited and congratulated for not gouging out my own eyes by now.

"In eighteen seconds it'll be exactly twenty-three hundred hours," came the answer via an exasperated huff.

"That's eleven o'clock p.m. to us in the civilian world, right?" I respond, an admittedly pathetic attempt at humor, but at least it allows me to work off still another bout of the involuntary shakes. You'd have thought I was standing stark-naked with my bare feet submerged in the piled snow instead of wrapped snugly inside a comfortably thick, well-insulated parka.

"Sharp as a tack, Counselor... can't get one past this boy," chimes in the lone female voice, and I twist about to spot her through the fur-lined hood, which I've shaped to resemble a one-eyed binoculars of a sort.

"Anything?"

"Nothing but the passing blizzard. Won't be for another ten minutes or so anyhow, that is if the calculations are on the bean."

"They will be," I tell her, quickly scanning the desolate, ice-capped surroundings before re-joining the others in our group stargazing efforts. As cowardly as it sounds, there is indeed a part of me, however minute, that hopes the aforementioned calculations are incorrect and that what we're expecting to appear streaking through the night sky will never materialize. That said, the larger portion of my psyche aches to witness the purest form of retribution, even to the point of contributing whatever I can to see it through.

"You sound more confident than you act, Counselor."

"Just nerves, that's all. This... kind of thing isn't

exactly my specialty... unlike the rest of you."

She regards me with a wink through the wide chasm of her own parka hood and I feel a twinge of arousal, as has usually been the case whenever she and I share a personal moment not tied to some sort of charted itinerary.

"No sweat. I gotcha covered. Besides, if women's intuition counts for anything, I'm thinking this is gonna be a cakewalk."

"Lord, I hope... pray you're right. After all, I'm an advisor by trade, not a brawler."

She laughs then, and I feel a rush of warmth bathe my insides. It's a genuinely positive sensation, something that's been mighty rare these last twenty-four hours.

Moments later, someone behind me gasps, and I whip my head about in all directions, almost toppling over from dizziness in the process.

A false alarm apparently. Three minutes past eleven. Seven measly minutes to go... approximately. So many lives at stake... so much sacrifice doled out already. It has to work. It simply... has to, as the alternative is far too grave... far too gruesome to contemplate. Thus, we not only need to win... we simply have to. Ignoring Mother Nature's wrath, I stare westward into the tar-black, stormy night and wait for the light.

Prologue II: Raging Bull/Probationary Conditions

"Honestly, Chief, I... think you might've had enough. What say you head on back to the barracks and take in a ballgame? I hear the Bears 'n Packers are about to tee it up on that there frozen tundra... " the bartender chided good-naturedly, though being extra cautious to keep several feet of space between himself and the bar.

"Appreciate the concern, Pete... it certainly does ya justice," came the gruff reply, only slightly slurred. "Now quit playin' nursemaid and pour me another Jack and Coke. Hell, on second thought, hold the Cola. I hear all that carbonation turns the gut linin' into Swiss cheese."

"You're the boss," the bartender replied sheepishly, dispensing a double shot over freshly placed ice while eyeing three new arrivals who had sauntered up so quietly as if to purposely catch his client off-guard.

"Get something for you, gentlemen?"

The first man, and easily largest in stature of the trio, waved him off with a gloved hand, the overhead strobe lights reflecting off diamond gauntlets. The other two backed away several steps and struck textbook 'at ease' poses. Adorned with matching crew cuts, stocky, muscular physiques and equally sour dispositions, both were dressed in identical uniform garb complete with silver insignia name tags sewn above the right pockets and spit-polished steel-toed boots.

"No thank you, good sir. Unlike *some* present,

true professionals such as my companions and I abide by the set rules of the facility, most notably the one damning the consumption of alcoholic beverages while on duty."

Purposely ignoring the statement while looking past the speaker, the man emptied his glass in two quick gulps before sliding it approximately halfway down the bar in the bartender's general direction.

"There ya go, Pete. How's about a Southern Comfort Breeze this time around... and oh yeah... omit the breeze."

Wiping the building fop-sweat from his forehead with a bare forearm, the bartender flinched as though he'd been slapped across the backside with a drenched, tightly wound towel.

"Uh... um... Chief, I don't think I... can... I mean... not while... um... ."

"See to your other customers, Mister Chapman," the spokesman for the newest arrivals announced calmly, taking the seat directly to the left of the man previously being served. "We'll take care of the chief here. Make sure he gets back to the barracks without harming either himself or anyone else along the way. Isn't that right, Chief Thomason?"

"Tell ya what, blockhead," Ben Thomason snarled, intertwining his freakishly oversized fingers and applying just enough pressure in order for the explosive retort of cracking knuckles to drown out all surrounding sound, to include the pop music tune blaring overhead.

"I've got a better notion. How's about you and the butt-munch twins there mind your own Ps and Qs and leave your superior officer to his midday meditation? I'll only ask once, that is... I'll only ask once... *politely*."

The other man scooted closer, leaning down and in until his cowl-covered visage was mere inches from Ben Thomason's left ear.

"Now, Chief, there's no reason for baseless name-calling or physical threats. We're just... concerned for your well-being. Then again, there is the matter of the nonprofessional behavior on display for all... shall we say, lower-ranking patrons to see. Not exactly the example we want to set, now is it?"

Snorting aloud, Ben then tossed his head back and howled in baying coyote fashion, causing the other man to flinch as if warding off an impending slap.

"Concerned for my well-being? I'd lay ten to one you've had me on electronic report since strollin' into the bar. Ya really oughta think about officially changin' that hero moniker from *Eighth Degree* to *Narc-Man* or maybe *Captain Squeal*? Be a helluva lot more accurate. Now, for the last time... I'm requestin'... no, make that a di-rect order... step away and depart my personal space."

In response, the twin brutes visibly tensed while the larger man hardly twitched, the corners of his mouth upturning ever so slightly in sardonic glee.

"What exactly are you proposing, Chief?"

"I'm proposin' you adhere to a superior's command or prep for pain, asshole. Your choice... just remember while yer suckin' peas and carrots from a straw that I gave ya one. Same goes for Frick and Frack standin' back there sniffin' your shorts."

Cocking his head as if to ease a particularly bothersome crick, Ben then slowly rotated his neck until three distinct cracks were heard.

"All BS aside, I ain't in the mood for this lame-ass power play. Now you three be good little correctional spies and hop the hell on outta here before I forget my manners and retrieve your yellow-tinted spines by pullin' 'em out yer collective bungholes."

Though Jarod King, AKA 'Eighth Degree' stood at least a foot taller and was twelve years Ben Thomason's junior, the lack of an immediate response and the shaky grin he struggled to maintain in the wake of such a blatant challenge spoke volumes to how seriously he took the immediate threat.

"Only a matter of time and federal decree, and you'll be addressing the lowest-ranking CO on this burg as a superior," he whispered, though not nearly from as close a range as mere moments before. "Your pal the warden can't protect you anymore, Force. Once the board puts the case file together and initiates court-martial proceedings, you're toast."

"No thanks to you, right, asslick?" Ben replied without turning, instead facing front and staring directly into his own slightly warped reflection from a wall mirror mounted directly behind the bar.

"It sickened me, Thomason," the other man continued, gnashing his teeth as his naturally pale complexion flashed a shade of maroon almost as dark as his cowl and matching leotard. With a single, fluid movement, he flung his silken, dark blue cape over one shoulder as to provide additional free movement if needed.

"Arriving here and being forced to take orders from a vulgar, drunken buffoon such as yourself, when I am clearly your superior in every way, most notably from the standpoint of *basic* intelligence. Luckily, you've been so very cooperative in digging your own grave, as it were."

Turning in the direction of the bartender, who had taken up residence at the far side of the bar with several equally timid patrons, Ben began thumping the bar with his oversized digits as if tickling the ivories on a phantom baby grand.

"Hey, Pete, how's about a triple shot of Comfort on the rocks? Just pour it in a doggy cup and I'll take it with me. It reeks in here all of the sudden. Fact is, somebody's breath stinks just like *freshly... kissed... ass...* "

The larger man giggled and stood up, gesturing with a nod for his twin cohorts to join him in departure. Meanwhile, the half-dozen or so patrons inhabiting the bar, including Pete the server, seemed to cringe simultaneously as one, as if expecting an impending explosion.

"Go ahead, *Chief* Thomason... talk it up... and booze it up while you're at it. Being that those are clearly the *lone* talents you possess. See you at the weekly staff meeting... seven a.m. sharp. Meanwhile, please excuse your assigned assistant chief while he goes and cleans up your latest mess."

"Four words, pal: *Eat shit and die*," Ben mumbled, tossing a mock salute airborne and almost falling off the bar stool in the process.

The twin brutes having already departed the tavern through swinging glass doors, Eighth Degree hesitated, halting in his tracks in order to fire a final tally, though all the while refusing to turn about while spreading his cape in true 'Count Dracula' style.

"By the way, heard from Leah lately, Force? How is your former assistant chief and loving spouse? Ahhh, bad news, I take it. Well, such is life. Women: can't live with them, can't live without them. Guess you can *run* them off, though. Drive them away with boorish behavior, a laughable lack of discipline and doltish, drunken escapades, correct? By the way, if you do happen to speak to that adorable little Asian killer, tell her Jarod says hey, and that he'd hire her sweet Oriental self to be *his* assistant chief at the drop of a fortune cookie."

Pausing a moment longer as to await a response, Eighth Degree then shrugged in apparent dismay and took a lengthy stride forward, only to halt in mid-step as a hard slap stung his left shoulder.

"Freeze, pal," a husky voice whispered, the very air around the assistant chief correctional officer suddenly thick with whiskey vapors.

"Got an amendment to that last order, Assistant Chief King."

Tensing as if to endure an impending blow, Eighth Degree nonetheless remained conspicuously silent, grinning devilishly even as the grip atop his shoulder increased to vice-like proportions.

"Meet me at the lower level sweat and strain in fifteen, and come alone. Leave the fug-ly twins in their cages, got it?"

"The inmate gymnasium? Why, whatever for, Chief Thomason? Can we not discuss matters *here,* in front of so many... intrigued witnesses?"

Shoving severely chapped, trembling lips practically flush against the cowl's open left earhole, Ben spewed forth a fine mist of spittle that the mask quickly and effectively absorbed upon contact.

"You'd like that, wouldn't ya, cheese dick? Sorry, but it ain't goin' down like that. We're gonna handle this here personality conflict like men. That is, if ya actually own a pair. Personally, I've always had my doubts."

"Why, since you put it that way, *Chief*," Eighth Degree growled, jerking his shoulder free and shoving the twin glass doors ajar with open palms, "see you in fifteen."

He cleared the swinging doors just as they'd descended inward, only to be flung back through headfirst in an explosion of shattered glass and warped metal frame.

"On second thought, *here and now* will do just fine-witnesses be damned," Ben growled, slinging the larger man airborne in a circular whipping motion by the ends of his cape, which was rolled like tightly coiled rope at the tail.

Releasing the cape following numerous rotations, Ben cried a warrior's howl, the metallic buttons of his uniform shirt popping off like spent ammo shells from the expanded bulkiness beneath.

Sailing the length of the bar, approximately thirty feet from the entrance, Eighth Degree skidded across the slick bar top directly into a mirrored wall and partially through the thick oak boards backing it, filling the air with a fresh tidal wave of glass and wood shards.

"Oh, great landing there, *Jet Li*... reeeeaaal

graceful," Ben quipped, tearing away the remainder of his shredded uniform top with a muted ripping sound. "Thought you martial arts geeks were supposed to be light on your feet. Guess in your case, it's more like light in the *loafers*."

As the few patrons present hurriedly departed for safer climes, Eighth Degree crawled from the wreckage, his cowl sprinkled in whitish debris.

"Y-you... you s-son... of... of... b-bi... bit-"

Stepping forward, Ben jumped the bar in a single bound, all the while rearing back a right first the size of a medicine ball.

"Now, is that any way for a subordinate to babble to a superior? Truth be told, I guess it's all I should rightly expect from such a back-stabbin' horse's ass."

The fist shot forward like a fired piston, landing with a muffled thump atop the masked man's forehead and sending him flailing into a virgin section of wall that instantly collapsed as if constructed from rotted balsawood.

"Seems to me some serious counselin' is in order. Too bad I never was the 'talk it out' kinda boss... fact is, Hoss... "

Ducking into the dark, dust-filled gap his target's flailing body had created, Ben reached inside and gripped a pair of wriggling ankles.

"... I never was much for paper-pushin' in general when dealin' with uncooperative employees... soooooo... what say we skip all the jawin' and time-out sessions and move directly to the ass-kickin' phase?"

Yanking up and out, Ben swung the larger man's semi-limp form about at chest level, smashing loose a large chunk of the marble-based bar in the process, before flipping him airborne with a decided spin.

Tearing through a half-dozen tables and adjoining chairs like a mini-funnel cloud forged from flesh and bone, Jarod King's second forced landing was, if anything, even less gentle than the first. In a groggy, ill-advised attempt to minimize the level of destruction and/or personal injury upon descent, he'd managed to tuck his body into a rotund crunch, resembling a drunken diver executing a rather clumsy splash dive. The results were of the human cannonball variety, as not only the outer but inner walls were torn through like nets constructed from soggy papier-mache, leaving only a jagged-edged, perfect circular chasm in its wake.

Wiping glass fragments from his bare biceps and forearms, Ben surveyed the damage with a deep frown.

"Geez, it's a damn good thing the cellblock walls are made of stouter stuff. Looks like this joint was put together with string, straw and mud pies."

Leaning down onto one knee, he was unable to detect either sound or movement within the smoking hollow.

"Damn. Looks like I've done it again. Try and talk yourself outta this one, bonehead," he sighed, his flaring nostrils picking up a faint burning metallic scent.

"Might as well start preppin' the resignation speech."

The sound of thundering boots echoed from outside the demolished saloon double doors, from which only a small portion of the outer metal frame remained.

"Too late, Einstein-here comes the Calvary, and me without a white flag."

Rising to strike an at-attention pose, Ben quickly altered his stance to that of the combat type once the pair of sprinting, all-too-familiar figures swam into clearer view.

"Shoulda known... it's just Frick and Frack comin' to the rescue of their beloved... "

The two men, seemingly joined at the hip upon entry, quickly separated as the space narrowed between themselves and Ben, whose crouched, slightly tilted back position remained unchanged save the tucking of both arms across his chest. Crossing his hands at the wrists yogi-style, he appeared to be displaying an ancient prayer ritual of sorts.

Now charging from either side while rapidly closing ground, the pair meant to converge in a classic 'scissors' maneuver, wherein the intended victim would be impacted from above and below. Holding his ground until the very last millisecond, Ben continued to stand statuesque as each executed their final dives, both leading with their upper bodies as if to initiate twin headbutts.

Just as his attackers released similar growls, Ben uncoiled both arms like twin springs, his balled, wrecking ball-sized fists swinging out from his body with immeasurable torque.

The left landed squarely atop brute one's squared forehead, temporarily suspending the man's skull even as his floundering torso sailed forward from the clothesline effect.

The right pummeled the whole of brute two's

face from the bridge of his horrendously pulped nose to the tip of his equally shattered chin, his body going limp almost instantly even as it levitated forward at warp speed.

Hopping back a step, Ben watched in grim bemusement as his would-be attackers slid across the slick tile flooring in opposite directions, their flaccid shapes cutting similar paths while tossing various tables and chairs aside like bowling pins.

"Nothin' personal, boys. Can't help but admire your sense of loyalty, if not a woeful lack of combat savvy."

Following a quick status check of the knuckles of both hands, a few of which had cracked and bled in lieu of the blunt trauma endured, Ben lumbered over to each of the fallen men and gripped them by their uniform collars. With a single thrust, he hauled each up and over a separate shoulder and headed for the bar's demolished exit, which looked as though it had been blasted open with heavy explosives. Several former patrons, including Pete the bartender, peeked from afar, watching Ben's progress from the end of a twisting hallway leading to a trio of elevators.

"Least I can do is haul your ignorant carcasses to the infirmary."

Ben had just pulled even to the exact spot where the double-glass door entrance had once been when a flurry of blows to his lower back and upper thighs sent him plundering forward in a wild lurch, the comatose bodies of the twin brutes flying from his grip as he landed face-first in a pile of jagged debris.

Spitting glass and metal fragments from

between bloodied lips as he arose, Ben whirled about just as Jarod King planted a solid right front kick directly into his exposed midsection, followed by a perfectly executed backhand to the chin, and finally a looping left hook that landed squarely on the right cheekbone.

Unable to alter his backward momentum, Ben fell back into the narrow hallway and began a series of clumsy rolls, only to recover somewhat by ending the trek with an impromptu backflip that at least served to land him upright.

"How about picking on someone closer to your own size, Thomason?" King bellowed, stepping slowly forward while performing a series of calculated martial arts movements. Even with his cowl hanging comically off-kilter and his cape in virtual tatters, he appeared otherwise unaffected despite the previous battering.

"Son, I gotta tell ya... that *Kung-Fu Grip* shit only goes so far," Ben replied flatly, holding out both hands in a pleading gesture. "Personally, I'm suggestin' we drop it as it is and report to the warden to take our medicine."

Blinking rapidly, King's anger-charged grimace suddenly transformed into a expression born of pure, unadulterated befuddlement, complete with mouth hanging agape and wide, bugged-out eyes.

"Take... take our... report to the warden to... take our... our medicine? Not to sound openly critical here, and I truly hope you don't take this wrong... but, sir, are you out of your rock-filled, dementia-laced mind?"

"Hey, I'm sayin' don't *push* it, Hoss. Pullin' punches don't come easy for this boy. Back off or pay the price, that's all I'm sayin'. I can't and won't promise any leniency just 'cause I got ya outgunned in the power department."

As Ben retained his stance of mock surrender, the man known as Eighth Degree, infamous for the seven separate martial arts belts he had so effortlessly mastered, continued a gradual progression forward through carefully orchestrated half and sidesteps.

"I'm not intimidated by your bad-ass rep, Thomason, nor those overrated wrecking balls you call fists. Never was... never will be. To me you're nothing but a loud-mouth ignoramus with oversized meat-beaters."

Ben smiled despite himself as King paused to straighten his damaged cowl.

"Touche, pal. Not bad at all. Didn't know ya possessed the inner crudeness. Now, let's just make peace and let the warden decide on a fair and reasonable punishment."

"You practically snapped my spine and now you want to make peace?"

Dropping his massive hands to his sides, Ben bowed his head a tad and stared menacingly into the taller man's cowl-shaded eyes. As was the case when booze begat violence, he could feel his formidable buzz decrease with every passing tick.

"Damn it, King, you're the one who took the shot at Leah. I warned ya once, hell, several times, about crackin' wise on that particular subject. Even three sheets to the wind, I can still take a board-snapper like you without strainin' a single testicle."

"Is that so, tough guy? Well, as the old saying goes... *the proof is definitely in the pudding*," King cracked, enunciating each syllable of the final sentence in a mocking, purposely sluggish, garishly faux southern accent.

"So shut the hell up and *prove* it already."

Tossing up his hands in frustration, Ben then gestured in a reluctant 'come hither' motion just as the hallway to his rear grew crowded with the sudden arrival of a half-dozen armed guards, all of which were donned in full SWAT gear.

"Chief Thomason... Assistant Chief King... what the... what's... going on here?" the lead guard inquired through a dark-tinted faceplate, the five men at his back tentatively shouldering the stun-rifles they'd previously held in firing position.

"We... we got word of a brawl of some sort... Chief?"

"Just a slight misunderstandin' between me and my backup, Sergeant Clifton," Ben replied, straightening up as best he could while rotating his gaze between King and the guard supervisor. "We... I had a few too many and... things got a tad outta hand.

"Assistant King and myself were just on our way to the warden's office, ain't that right, Assistant Chief?"

Ignoring the guard unit completely, King shuffled forward an additional step while maintaining exclusive focus on his intended target.

"I won't let you BS your way out of this one, Force. The charade that is your so-called reign of leadership ends right here and now. I alone must take a stand to expose you for the drunken, irresponsible lout that you are.

"Nobody, and I mean *no one* or *thing*, sucker

punches Eighth Degree and simply waltzes away. Besides, it's no secret whose side The Guardsman will take, no matter how many eyewitnesses to your cowardly assault speak the truth."

Once his peripheral vision captured the sergeant unsheathing an electrocane from his utility belt and the other men following suit, Ben flashed the guard unit a textbook 'hold your position' gesture. Seconds later, still more back-up personnel arrived, including a specially trained three-man team commonly referred to as the 'Confronters'.

"Hell of a speech there, Bruce *Lie*. Always knew you were a closet politician at heart. All horseshit aside, Jarod, what say let's drop the school play dramatics and handle this in-house... by the book."

"By the... by the book? Did... did you really just say... " King howled, briefly dropping his guard before resuming the same mantis-styled fighting stance, "Oh, always the comedian, aren't we? You never even read the *book*, Thomason. Enough with the faux professionalism already... to use a certified redneck quip straight from the master... that being *you*... enough with the jaw-jackin' already and *let's do this*!"

"Chief Thomason, do you wish this man restrained?" Sergeant Clifton asked, holding the now extended shock cane in a defensive pose, the dozen or so men at his disposal equally braced. In his four-plus years on staff, Clifton had shared both many a hearty laugh and cold brew with the man he called boss. More so, the two had stood side by side as loyal teammates on numerous occasions in more trying times. Certainly there had been a strong level of respect for the man's past, almost legendary deeds in the civilian sector, but over time Ben Thomason had cultivated his rep as a tough but fair, even fun-loving supervisor amongst the assigned guards. Oppositely, Jarod King was considered a selfish, bullish mini-dictator whose self-centered ways and blatant disregard for his men (save the two he'd personally hand-picked as his personal pets) had led to the nickname 'King Prick' throughout the ranks. In his brief, six-month stint as Ben Thomason's second-in-command, Eighth Degree had managed to alienate inmates and staff alike while cultivating an aura of cockiness and mean-spirited arrogance.

Thus, if taking sides in such a case were an issue, there would exist no dilemma amongst Clifton and his men on which to choose.

After little more than a three-second pause, Ben repeated the stand down gesture.

"Not necessary, Sarge. The man wants a piece of me this bad, I guess he's entitled. However this ends though, the next stop for the both of us is the warden's office, understood?"

Sergeant Darrin Clifton, a fourteen-year vet of the corrections trade, stiffened as to salute, tapping the cane against his heavily padded thigh.

"Affirmative, Chief."

"'Course, I'll need witness statements after the fact."

"Yes, sir, that's a given."

Eighth Degree speedily closed ranks, sidestepping ahead until there was less than three yards of open hallway between the two. In response, Ben struck the pose of a classic twentieth-century pugilist.

"Alright then, Chop Suey, have it your way. Just remember what they say... be damned careful what ya wish for."

"You may be stronger, Thomason," King concluded, ripping away what remained of his tattered cape before circling Ben at a decided angle, "but it's been proven throughout the history of recorded combat that skill, determination and courage can overcome brute force."

Sidestepping to keep King directly in front of him, Ben kept his main focus on the man's constantly shuffling feet, which he'd learned long ago was the main weapon of choice of all martial arts types.

"Uh-huh. Whatever you say, Jean-Claude... it's your dance. Jeez, and they say *I* talk too much."

Weaving in and out like a striking cobra, King tossed several dozen, mostly ineffective jabs Ben's way, the majority of which were easily slapped aside.

Maintaining an exclusively defensive posture, Ben staved off a series of front and sidekicks by either sidestepping from their path or using forearm blocks, though a select few did make minimal contact with his shoulders, left side and upper chest.

"Wearin' down yet, Segal?" Ben chastised, backing down the looping hallway and forcing the guard units and scattered witnesses to do the same.

"Just warming up, boss man," King spat out angrily, his frenzied pursuit growing increasingly reckless. "You have no idea how long I've waited for this-dreamed of the day I would be allowed the opportunity to test the waters-go toe to toe with a living legend... even if it was a *self-proclaimed* one."

A wildly aimed roundhouse kick sailed well over Ben's head, instead removing a large chunk of the synthetic stone wall. Flashing a wide grin while back-stepping furiously in the opposite direction, Ben seemed on the verge of hysterics.

"Oh, that hurts, Jackie Chan. So now not only am I a worthless sot *and* shitty supervisor, but a card-carryin' egomaniac to boot. Gotta tell ya, boy... that cuts... deeeep."

Still another clumsily executed roundhouse missed its mark, King's steel-reinforced bootheel ripping a foot-long section of stucco free, its jagged remnants littering the hall like gravel-laced confetti.

"Stand still and fight, you damned... lummox!" King croaked, his voice crackling like an enraged preteen, inducing Ben into a barely subdued fit of muffled giggles.

"L-Lummox? What... what the hell nineteenth century Thesaurus did ya pull that particular gem out of? Gottta tell ya, Jarod, you're soundin' gayer by the minute."

Enduring a surprisingly solid jab to the ribs, Ben then caught a hard right to the left temple and staggered back, gripping a steel railing for support and ripping it from its post in the process. A front kick to the solar plexus ended the mad flurry, and he soon found himself staring up into the hallway's bright fluorescent lighting, the bent railing lying across his chest like banding straps.

"How'd you like those marbles, Force? Still feel tickled, do we? Where'd all the laughter go, big mouth?" King bayed, bouncing about in a victory dance that included an impromptu moonwalk aimed directly at the guard units.

"Ben, um, Force, um... Chief Thomason, might I inquire how much longer this... session is going to take?" Sergeant Clifton inquired stoically. Having previously folded and put away his shock cane, he stood with his gloved hands atop his hips.

"I mean, not to overstep my bounds, but we do have active cellblocks being woefully undermanned due to this... distraction."

Tossing the rod iron aside, Ben rolled to his feet and began casually brushing shattered pieces of carpet lint and stucco fragments from his ample chest hair.

"Gotcha, Clif- uh, Sarge. You're right as rain... guess the booze clouded my good judgment. Send everybody back to their posts save you and... let's say two others to help haul 'Happy Feet' to the warden's office."

"Getting a shade cocky for a man who's getting his lunch handed to him, aren't we, Benjamin?" King gloated, still jerking and hopping around in a semicircle, his damaged cowl having again slipped free and threatening to fall away altogether.

"Small wonder such a fine, classy lady as Leah packed up and made tracks. My god, how did she tolerate you to begin with? For that matter, how could *any* woman with good sense? Hmm, perhaps that classy lady part needs to be amended to dumb as a stump... "

"Whoops, there ya go again," Ben replied in a hoarse whisper, having instantly stiffened once the subject had been broached. "See, here's where cold hard reality sets in, Jarod, old buddy, old snatch."

As Ben took a lengthy stride forward, cutting the space between the two men roughly in half, King's premature celebratory jig noticeably slowed.

"Hey, I'll give ya credit where credit is due. Eighth degree black belt in seven forms of martial arts... it was all confirmed by the hiring panel before they officially brought you aboard as my... new assistant chief. Damned impressive combat resume to boot. Gotta confess though... I had some serious reservations about ya."

Still another stride and predator quickly became quarry, as King leapt back several feet to maintain a safe distance. Meanwhile, Ben trudged forward, his clenched fists pinned against each bulging thigh.

"Nothin' substantial as far as powers go save what your file listed as 'minimal' superstrength. Hate to sound prejudiced, but after all, how effective are a few karate chops, headbutts and knee-jabs gonna be if one of *these* inmates manages to bust loose? After all, we ain't talkin' run-of-the-mill convicts, but superpowered baddies just itchin' to pound the nearest correctional employee into plasma fragments."

Finally holding his ground, Jarod King's raised fists visibly shook as his bloodshot eyes grew wide and spastic with apparent fear.

"All that aside, I took ya under my wing as best I could," Ben sighed, halting less than two feet from the other man's position while staring down at the carpeted floor with his arms still hanging loose at his sides.

The hallway grew deadly silent-no murmuring or shuffling of feet-no whispering or movement of any kind-as if a universal mute button had been employed. Even the familiar hum of the air regulators seemed to pause in reverence to the incident at hand.

"Endured your insolence... ignored the backstabbin'... overlooked the lack of respect for my authority... but there's one thing, Hoss... one thing that I flat refuse to take from a snivelin', traitorous punk such as yourself... "

As Ben peered gradually upward through tightly squinted eyes, he bared his teeth like a predatory beast prepping to feast, his jaw muscles flexing in timed intervals.

"... you will not take the name of my lovin' wife in vain... and remain upright... "

Lunging forward just as King flinched back, Ben never felt the flurry of punches that ricocheted off his forehead and nose, effectively breaking the latter with a loud crunch.

The stiff left hook that lifted Jarod 'Eighth Degree' King from the carpeted floor and bounced him off the granite wall like a human pinball hardly registered when compared to the ferocious uppercut that followed, wherein the two-hundred-fifty-pound man was pummeled the length of the hall, landing a full twenty feet from the spot the blow had originally impacted and forcing two of the remaining three guards to duck and cover in order to avoid being crushed upon his floundering descent.

Moments later, Ben Thomason stood over the prone body, flanked by Sergeant Clifford and his men.

"Go ahead and cuff the stupid bastard, Cliff," he said as softly as his naturally husky voice would allow, "and while you're at it... "

He turned to the sergeant and extended his own bare wrists.

"... do the same for this stupid bastard as well."

"But, Ben... Chief... " the sergeant mumbled, actually backing away from his superior's offer.

"I started it, Cliff. I was drunk on duty... am legally drunk *and* damned disorderly. Shithead that he is... Jarod's in the right. Yeah, he pushed my buttons like he always does... like only he knows how... but in the end, I tossed the first haymaker... not just the last."

The three guards, all having lifted their glass-shield masks, exchanged a worrisome glance. Reaching up, Ben laid an oversized mitt atop the sergeant's shoulder.

"Hell, it's okay, guys, really. I've... had this comin' for a while now. Take us to the warden, Sarge... and that's an order."

Adhering to the command, albeit somewhat hesitantly, Sergeant Clifton then instructed his men to carry Jarod King forward as he brought up the rear a few steps behind Ben, the small group half-stepping their way through a handful of awe-struck witnesses.

"Oh yeah, call the med boys and get Mills and Clark prepped for the infirmary. I get the feelin' they'll both need more than a band-aid and a handful of aspirin."

In the fourteen and a half minutes it took to reach the outer hallway leading into the warden's private office, Benjamin Kyle Thomason had a chance to rethink his actions of the past month. The word disgraceful came to mind, as did a sickeningly familiar term used most often by peers and enemies alike whenever his name was brought up in even casual conversation: Loose cannon. In a lifetime of blown chances, he deduced solemnly, this last bit of ridiculously bad judgment might well have taken the mythological cake. The best job he'd ever been entrusted to was more than likely history, just another negative footnote on a resume littered with such unsightly incidents. As for his marriage, he felt a sense of overwhelming nausea that it too would soon follow suit.

Chapter One

Welcome to the Jasper Hyatt: The Memoirs of Counselor Darrin Jackson

On the very day, January 18th to be exact, that our newest class arrived for indoctrination, I was awarded the prestigious title of Assistant Counselor. I recall psyching myself up with constant mental reminders of all I'd went through to gain the confidence of my peers, a well-respected, veteran group of professionals with, unlike yours truly, nothing further to prove. At the top of the list with a streaking bullet was Chief Burton Jay Hanover, who had served as my advisor and mentor for just under a year.

A big, hearty, bull of a man who'd once served as an Army Ranger before discovering his true talent lay not in doling out pain but in helping mankind repair severely injured minds, Burt was a multidegreed, confirmed genius whose genuine modestly and lack of ego concerning same was perhaps his greatest gift. Former war vet and vice-chairman of the Joint Chief's Top Secret '*Spandex Brigade*', Burt had advised such luminaries of the superhero trade as Reed Richards, Leonard 'Doc' Sampson and even Charles Xavier. This, of course, I found out not from the man himself, but from secretly procuring his personnel file a few days after being relocated to the Reclassification Counsel at the Jasper Ridge Outpost, which just happened to be my initial assignment as a recently knighted counselor's aide. I never quite reached the level of courage necessary to ask such a man how he'd ended up at such a desolate, remote place. Rumors had been plentiful among the staff, but nothing verifiable. I finally came to the conclusion that if Burt had wanted me to know, he'd have surely volunteered the information. As for the aforementioned staff, there were a total of four, not counting myself or Burt, all experienced counselors hand-picked from gritty urban areas where it was assumed they'd literally seen (or at least heard) it all. More on them as I trudge forward. First things first-that being the place we'd all call home for the better part of a year.

The *Jasper Ridge Outpost* (named for a tiny township three miles *east* of the facility) had been constructed with government funds in June of 2004, originally as a detoxification center for high-ranking military and government employees. Basically a series of concrete and brick buildings connected by dome-covered walkways, the facility sat atop the second, and slightly lowest, of what is referred to by the Oregonian locals (residing in both Jasper and nearby Boulder Valley) as the Three Tops, a trio of off-the-map boulder and shrub-infested Cascade Mountain Ranges that overlooked the entire valley like looming guardians. To state the painfully obvious, there wasn't a whole lot to see once off facility grounds, as Jasper and Boulder Valley's (two and a quarter miles to the *west* of the Outpost) combined population barely topped two thousand, and the eighty-plus mile trek to Corvallis might as well have been eighty thousand once the winter temps turned brutal and roads unpassable in the aftermath.

The landscape between was as bare and barren as any stereotypical Sci-Fi flick moonscape; a "never-ending rock quarry as far as the eye can see" a former client once proclaimed-the absolute perfect description, it was mutually agreed. With its barren sand dunes, jagged, stalagmite-like stone formations and hideously gnarled shrubbery, it seemed no small miracle that the local population of prairie dogs (plentiful no matter the harshness of the season) could even survive, much less thrive. At times, it truly felt as if we inhabited an insolated stretch of Mars, especially when the clear night sky was star filled and a thin layer of fog would entomb the compound in its arachnid-like webbing. Strangely, those were the times I felt the most at ease, more... at home. Never quite sure when or why such a feeling was birthed, there was a stout sense of comfort in the isolation I'd never experienced in the city. Perhaps I was just a closet extrovert at heart. Whether or not I was in the minority with such feelings was never in doubt. Most openly... verbally and nonverbally... despised such blatant seclusion, and weren't exactly shy to share such opinions.

To say the very least, our initial class of specially endowed types were no exception to the rule.

As for the compound itself, no one was going to mistake it for the Pentagon. Building one of the 'Jasper Hiatt Regency' (as so famously pegged by a former client and highly respected Army three star general with a nasty gambling habit) contained personnel records, the communications room and a small clinic (the latter two located at the rear of the building near a glass doom walkway) referred to by staff as sickbay from *Star Trek* lore. The front end of this building also served as the administration branch, where in-and-out processing was completed and classes were held. Though I never spotted any actual blueprints, I would speculate the entire structure to be no more than two-thousand to two-thousand five-hundred square feet. As for content, enclosed were five separate admin offices (The main office reserved for the chief reclassification counselor; a second for his/her personal assistant, a third for the lone medical officer, and the final two offices shared by four assistant counselors) and a single but spacious conference room complete with fully stocked coffee station and snack bar. Once in-processed, our clients would find little reason to occupy the admin building until their personal graduation day arrived.

Building two, roomier by far at approximately four thousand square feet, served as a combination dining hall/recreation area-gymnasium/supply building, with each wing separated by thick stone walls that were virtually soundproof. The mess hall and connecting kitchen were overseen by a staff of five rotating cooks/kitchen workers, all of whom resided in nearby Boulder Valley. Three complete meals were served each day, starting with a daily breakfast menu served only from five to five thirty a.m. The 'snooze and you lose' policy was strictly enforced, though the practice of *sleeping in* had never been a problem, at least with the military crowd we'd grown used to accommodating. We learned a quick and painful lesson regarding hero types, a few of whom seemed to think being mollycoddled was an unwritten constitutional right. The recreation area's interior included a playroom with electronic dartboard, two regulation pool tables and a trio of antique but fully serviceable pinball machines. The larger gymnasium section included half-court basketball, a sizeable weight room, and a single racquetball court. Again, this had been constructed with civilians in mind. There was also a separate TV room (local channels only-no cable service) that contained a large screen, high-def plasma model, a roomy leather sofa and matching easy chairs, along with several bookcases filled with both fiction and nonfiction reads and haplessly outdated magazines of all types. Perhaps more vital than what *was* furnished in terms of passing free time were the items conspicuously absent, such as wet bars, video or disc tape capability, cable programming (though Chief Hanover was allowed limited Dish Network access in his private quarters) or Internet access (the lone computers on-site were located in the chief's office as well as the counselors' offices, respectively). To list one of many similar mission credos, once officially garnered B&B status (booked and bedded) inside the Jasper Hiatt, thc outside world was purposely placed off-limits.

As for the last of the compound's trio of shelters, it contained both the staff and clients' living quarters, complete with a pair of spacious unisex community bathrooms and a tiny clinic stocked with basic first aid supplies. The client quarters were of the old military barracks style, thus preventing the ease from which certain clients could withdraw ever further from their fellow man. It was all about unity at Jasper-unity, understanding, and most of all... healing. As for the aforementioned staff, the private rooms we inhabited were roughly the size of your typical phone booth, though complaints were few and far between despite the lack of living and/or storage space. After all, there was the privacy factor, the luxury of which made up for any and all negatives. A single door at the rear of the building led to the Outpost's lone underground space; that being the generator/electrical room, a locked, restricted area privy to maintenance types only.

Given the panhandle area's harsh, unforgiving landscape, scorching summers and tundralike winters, it was little wonder the location was the prime choice for a government program whose main focus would be isolation and lack of societal distractions. It wasn't until the fall of 2009, near the conclusion of the Iraqi conflict that the powers that be decided a major facelift was in order in terms of the Outpost's assigned mission. Thus, treating and reassigning military personnel was out, while government-assigned hero types were in. It seemed a rather disturbing trend had begun to develop within the plentiful ranks of the specially endowed, or at least those certified and licensed to accept government contracts with their alter ego's secret identities still intact. There had been a sudden glut of inappropriate behavior associated with the usual suspects who had dogged mankind for ages; that being the use and abuse of alcohol and illegal drugs, and/or depression-related conditions leading to uncontrolled bouts of unbridled rage and brutal overkill. In other words, *specially gifted* or not, these folks needed similar guidance as an ordinary, average Joe Blow. Hoping to nip this dangerous (not to mention quite expensive in terms of potential lawsuits) trend squarely in the costumed bud, the joint chiefs quickly shifted the facility's mission, assigning Burton Hanover as the lead counselor. As old Burt was often overheard to say, "Sometimes even the good guys go bad over a long spell of crime-fighting... it's our job to help 'em find the white hat they misplaced along the way."

Talk about tall orders, it's one thing to counsel and advise battle-weary grunts straight out of some distant war zone. Such sessions were usually fairly cut and dry in terms of identifying the core problem. Battlefield stress and the booze and/or dope related addictions that were often tied to same. It's quite another to attempt similar naval-gazing with globe-hopping supertypes or shape-shifting mutants whose very existence was often hard to accept from a logical, thinking man's perspective. Nevertheless, while still termed as being in the experimental phase, the program kicked off in earnest, and we as staff welcomed our first class of such beings on January 18, 2013.

Weather conditions in and around the Outpost, especially once past the Thanksgiving and Christmas holidays, served not only as a yearly wake-up call for whatever annual brutality Old Man Winter had in mind, but also as a vital scheduling tool. The effects of global warming within the spacious confines of the Cascade Range had been less gradual than an overnight transformation, affecting not only a once bustling tourist season but moreover those tasked to work anywhere near the vicinity of the Range's nucleus.

Just days away from the season's initial series

of glacier turf episodes, the compound welcomed four separate hovercraft to its landing pad that chilly, overcast afternoon, dropping off an equal amount of passengers toting the mandatory limit of one duffel *slash* piece of personal luggage each. As for *emotional* baggage, well... the sky was indeed the limit.

***

January 18, 1310 Hours
Personal File D-132:
Subject: Tate Wayne Fletcher
Trade Name (*Government copyright*): Scar

Pegged the original Bionic Man for reasons we'd soon delve into with great depth, Tate Fletcher was a four-time United States Army heavyweight boxing champion and demolition expert. A recent file photo had provided a full-frontal view of the man in licensed/copyrighted hero garb: Half-face mask marked with red, white and blue striping all the way around; camouflage parachute pants; matching muscle tee; size fourteen black (steel-toed) combat boots; gold-plated wristbands constructed from titanium; studded utility belt housing various weapons of combat.

Fletcher struck quite the imposing figure upon initial viewing, what with his regulation buzz-cut hairdo, steely eyed gaze and deeply creased mug seemingly chiseled from the mightiest of stones.

"So I take it this is the portion of the show where I state name, rank, social, and the mental deficiency that led to this... involuntary incarceration?" he'd asked the board upon greeting, his raspy tone and deliberate pronunciation not nearly as intimidating as the cocked eyebrow and tightly clenched jaw that accompanied it. We'd all studied and discussed each client's individual personnel file days before their arrival on site, and 'Scar' Fletcher's easily rated as one of the more fascinating case studies. Dressed in full camouflage garb and spit-polished black boots, he looked every bit the grizzled supersoldier. According to his file, Fletcher stood six-four and weighed upwards of two-hundred seventy-five pounds, a lean, mean khaki-donned machine whose battlefield fighting prowess was matched only by a tenacity and ferociousness some viewed as borderline psychotic. The latter, of course, was what we as a group were there to determine.

"Not at all, Mister Fletcher," Burt countered calmly, a familiar twinkle in both eyes; a twinkle I instantly recognized as security barrier number one. Burt possessed several such self-control barricades, each stouter than the last. Thickest skin in the business, I'd venture, and definitely a *mandatory* trait in such a profession.

"This is merely the intro phase of in-processing. All incoming clients will meet the Outpost staff in the same manner. You being the first to arrive, well, you've earned the initial honors."

The conference room's cozy interior had felt unusually chilly that midmorning, despite the heater's incessant hum. Perhaps it was simply an offshoot of Fletcher's demeanor. With his squared noggin (sporting the aforementioned 'high and tight' buzz cut), squinting eyes and frozen grimace, he appeared far less than thrilled to be awarded such an honor, as Burt had so eloquently put it. Jay Peterson, an experienced counselor though new to the Outpost, sat to my immediate left, adjusting his glasses in almost precision-timed twenty-second intervals (yes, I did indeed count), while Jessica Lewis, a veteran counselor and former school teacher, took up position on my right. Burt and Dave Gonzalez, the Post's assigned medical technician, sat directly across from myself and Jay, respectively, while the lone chair at the head of the lengthy conference table was reserved for whatever client was being indoctrinated. In this case, the man once dubbed the 'G.I. Cyborg' by his military handlers, took center stage.

"Can't tell you how special that makes me feel," Fletcher replied blandly, his unblinking gaze seemingly transfixed on the puke-green colored walls directly over our heads. According to his file, Fletcher had been federally licensed since March 14, 2002. Consequently, said license had been duly suspended on November 27, 2012 for striking a superior officer and *severe deviation* from assigned mission.

"Please then, let us commence with the in-processing ceremonies. If you don't mind, I'm a little bushed from the trip and would appreciate the opportunity for some downtime."

Burt nodded amiably, appearing to drop his guard a bit. Despite the sarcastic lilt of Fletcher's haggard tone, it appeared a sincere request.

"Not a problem, Mister Fletcher. I understand your weariness. I can imagine Newark by hovercraft is indeed a fatigue-inducing trek. Allow me, then, to introduce my staff.

"To my right is Doctor David Gonzalez, the post physician."

Dave nodded without speaking. Slightly balding and potbellied in his middle age, my dealings with the man had been few-seemed a nice enough chap, though his tentative manner and stilted dialogue were a bit unnerving at times.

"Across to the left is Miss Jessica Lewis, counselor extraordinaire, and beside her is Jay Peterson, another veteran of the analytical wars. Next to Jay resides our newest resident and recently designated assistant counselor, only don't let the peach-fuzz complexion fool you... Mister Darrin Jackson is as sharp as a tack."

Jessica, an attractive brunette in her late thirties and thrice divorced, had indeed proven herself as a force to be reckoned with having an impressive resume that included recent stints at several state mental health facilities. Jay Peterson was the youngest of the senior counselors, having just recently turned thirty-two. A self-proclaimed *West Coast Romeo* who once acted professionally in several off-Broadway stage plays before changing careers, the man's egotistical smarminess had a way of wearing thin at warp speed.

"I, as you might have already surmised, am Burton Hanover, chief counselor as well as site manager. Now, if you will be so kind, please state your name, age, place of birth, and whatever else you wish to volunteer about yourself."

"Tate... Wayne... Fletcher. Before you ask, Papa Fletcher was a big Duke Wayne fan. Media hounds refer to me as Scar for... obvious reasons.

I'll be forty-five years young this coming March. Born in Casper, Wyoming, but grew up in Vegas. As you've probably deduced from my dossier, I've done a bit of traveling since."

Of course we'd read the man's file-as fascinating a history as I'd ever had the pleasure to peruse, surely as entertaining a suspense-thriller as any Tom Clancy novel, only twice as awe-inspiring since it wasn't the least bit fictional.

As a proven, effective way to break the ice with newly assigned clients, Tate Fletcher was first asked a series of pointed, rather off-the-wall questions. Though not at all considered mandatory, most clients had no problem with the queries, save perhaps the last.

Burt Hanover: "Mister Fletcher, what is your favorite color?"

Fletcher (humorless): "Without a doubt... khaki green."

Burt (smiling): "What is your all-time favorite movie?"

Fletcher (scratching his head): "Don't get a chance to catch too many flicks, you understand, but I'd have to saaaaaaay... it's a toss-up between *Soldier* and *Full Metal Jacket*."

Burt (his smile having grown wider still): "Predictable enough. Along the same lines, television program?"

Fletcher (appearing increasingly perplexed): "Um... not much of a couch potato either... but I'd say either... *American Gladiators* or the *A-Team*. I know I'm dating myself something fierce. They... um... sure don't make 'em like that anymore... (titled his head quizzically) ... do they?"

Burt (laughed): "I'd say probably not, though the *A-Team movie* was quite entertaining, I've heard. Um, what would you say is your favorite song?"

Fletcher (sighed deeply): "Finally, one I don't even have to think about... *Don't Fear the Reaper*, Blue Oyster Cult. Words to live by in this business."

Burt (grimly) "I... see. Tell us, what is the one thing about yourself you'd change if such alterations were in your power? This can be from a physical sense or character-driven."

Fletcher (thoughtfully): "Well, my Willy could use a tad more girth... (peered toward Jessica, who glanced away in apparent disgust, though obviously straining to conceal the tiniest of smiles) ... just yanking your collective chains a bit for levity's sake. I'd say my dedication to task is a bit questionable these days, a tad... over the top. I'd like to be able to tone it down in times of duress... just back off and better evaluate a situation before going balls to the wall on instinct alone. Maybe you folks can help me regain a semblance of self-control. If not... well, you just might see me flipping burgers at your local Mickey-D's."

Burt: "I... seriously doubt it, Mister Fletcher. You'll find we're all about positive thinking. Lastly, please entertain us with a confession, if you will. This can be an embarrassment of some type you've never before revealed to anyone, much less a roomful of complete strangers. This can cover any time frame, from childhood to the present."

Fletcher (wincing): "I take it this is the mutual trust phase of the intros."

Burt: "Aptly put, Mister Fletcher, yes."

Fletcher (following a lengthy pause): "Well, lemme see. Um... (snaps fingers) ... well, as a kid my big sister did catch me playing with her, uh, Barbie doll once. Think I was six or seven at the time and she was nine or ten. Of course, it was all a part of a larger G.I Joe scenario, and I had the doll tied to a bedpost being tortured by a perverted SS officer. Joe never even got the chance to jump in and rescue her before Mom was beating me over the head with a whisk broom and chasing me outta my sister's room. Not sure I've ever quite lived that one down."

While Burt somehow, miraculously, managed to maintain his composure, the rest of us laughed unabashedly and without shame.

"Thank you for indulging us so, Mister Fletcher," the chief resumed once we'd all gotten our jollies. "Now, if you have no reservations, please explain the extent of your... powers, for want of a better word, and just how you obtained said skills."

Fletcher shifted a bit, briefly rolling his eyes as if mildly perturbed by the request. His weary, battered tone, however, told a different story; simply that of a man taxed by having to repeat the same passage ad nauseam. Again, we knew the details, but it was a prerequisite within the intro sessions that the individual themselves verify said facts.

"Sure. Not a problem. Short and sweet then... same way I like my women."

Everyone shared a nervous laugh as Fletcher took a deep breath as if he were preparing to submerge in a deep pool of water, all the while using the forefinger of his left hand to gently massage one of the deeper scars adorning both cheekbones. I later found in speaking to the man face-to-face that there was simply no way *not* to focus on the veritable roadmap of creases and cracks found there, though it was also painfully apparent he wasn't the least bit self-conscious.

"I'd just got my corporal stripes a few weeks earlier and damned if orders to Saudi didn't follow soon after. Desert Storm was wrapping up by the time my unit arrived to provide area security. Three of us were tooling along down a Medina back road when the Humvee rolled over a booby trap of some sort, more than likely stuffed down into a pothole just minutes before. I don't recall a whole lot, just one hell of a jolt and then total darkness. I was later told the sarge and private I was riding with didn't make it. Sad thing, but I don't even recall their names, since we were plucked from different units that same morning. Anyway, I have blurred memories of waking up in some field hospital and realizing I couldn't feel a damn thing below my waist. To this day I ain't sure what was real and what wasn't. I do know they had me doped to the gills, so anything's possible. Finally woke up, four days later they tell me, at a VA hospital somewhere outside of San Antonio."

Fletcher suddenly raised a finger airborne, the same one he'd earlier used as a massage instrument. Unlike the initial few moments of dialogue, his eyes seemed to sparkle, losing a bit of their bland dullness.

"But... this wasn't just any VA hospital, no sir. This particular sawbones facility couldn't be found on any known map, government or otherwise. This bad boy required a minimum level two top secret clearance just to stroll in and wax the floors. It wasn't until the staff was near three-quarters of the way through with my personal 'treatment' that I was even given the slightest clue concerning the extent of my injuries. By the time I did, it was too damn late to object."

Placing both hands palm-flat on the tabletop, Fletcher leaned back and sighed. I'm fairly sure it was at this point that he'd decided to jettison any technicalities involved and get down to what such men refer to as the brass tacks. Like so many of his ilk, Tate Fletcher was notorious as being a man of few words. If this were indeed the case, he might well have already been on the verge of utter exhaustion.

"Well, eighteen separate surgeries and another ten months of rehab *slash* physical reindoctrination later, I was unceremoniously shoved off the assembly line and listed as fit for duty.

"Fast-forward nearly two decades later, I sit before you, *lady* and gentleman, still the first of my kind, but most assuredly nearing the dreaded expiration date no doubt engraved on my inner workings. Career-wise, the stats speak for themselves as being fairly impressive, if I do say so myself. Three-hundred twelve successful missions, most of which were performed abroad amidst total secrecy. The kind of secrecy that dictates said missions were never even attempted, much less carried out."

After a moment, Fletcher shrugged good-naturedly and began drumming his fingers atop the table while refocusing his gaze onto the back wall.

"Your service record is undoubtedly remarkable, Mister Fletcher, and certainly not in question here. To continue, please expand on the nature of those... inner workings, Mister Fletcher," Burt chided after several more rather awkward ticks.

"Oh... that. Sorry. By all means, ready those pencils, people," Fletcher replied with icy indifference before pushing his chair back with a noisy screech. I don't recall outwardly flinching at the sudden, frenzied movement, though if it were possible for one's entire skeletal mass to leap from its fleshy shell, mine would have done so without reservation.

"First off then... let's talk replacement parts," he barked gruffly, initially striking an 'at-ease' pose while standing a scant few feet from the head of the table before unbuttoning and subsequently exposing his right arm up to the upper bicep.

"This arm consists of synthetic flesh stretched over tinsel-wound muscle bladders and held in place by an exoskeletal framework. It has a lifting capacity of just over one ton and punching power upwards of four-thousand pounds per square foot. If you think *this* bad boy looks lifelike, I hear the latest models can not only tan with reasonable likeness, but also regrow body hair at regular monthly intervals... without artificial transplants."

Recovering the arm, he bent down and began rolling up his left pant leg, halting at just below the knee.

"This here drumstick and attached foot are similarly constructed, only enhanced with rotor-boosters that allow for a much greater ratio of pounds per square footage, as in a two-ton leverage capability. To put it in layman's terms, I'd never keep a job as a football placekicker for fear of decapitating the poor slob unfortunate enough to stick his head in the line of fire."

After squatting to reset his pants, Fletcher leapt up and quickly backed to the far wall.

"Last but not least, the majority of this pumpkin-shaped noggin is cocooned in a thick titanium-based helmet. They somehow managed to layer my own skullcap over it, thus the grayish-shaded spikes so gloriously on display are truly my own, unlike those manufactured plastihairs injected into my leg and arm.

"As for the helmet's purpose and/or usefulness, behold... "

Whipping his head back in a furious jerk, he rammed the back of his skull into the combination wood/stucco wall, flashed a wide, mischievous grin and slowly took a half-step forward. The outline left behind, crushed inward as if struck by a wrecking ball, was so neatly drawn it was even possible to make out the vaguest outline of the man's slightly pointed ears within the shattered carnage.

"You can see where it might come in handy in a battlefield scenario. I've had more than one hollow-point round bounce off the old armor-skull, yes sir. Plus which, it makes for one hell of a headbutt if need be."

Wiping drywall fragments from his head and neck, Fletcher gracefully reclaimed his chair as Burt cleared his throat for an impending response. As was the case countless times over the next several days, I didn't envy the man his job. Truly, such tasks were why he garnered the big bucks, such as they were.

"Impressive, Mister Fletcher, if not wholly unnecessary. There is no need for such dramatic show-and-tell sessions here at Jasper. Believe me when I say, *whatever* such information you tell us, we'll take it as gospel."

Lowering his head a shade in what appeared to be sincere regret, Scar Fletcher shrugged his massive shoulders and nodded.

"Sorry, boss. Force of habit. Won't happen again. Put that section of wall on my bill if you must... well, Uncle Sam's to be more exact."

"He signs our checks as well, Tate," Burt said with a playful wink. "We'll write it off as a training expense. Drywall's pretty cheap in these parts."

Wincing, Fletcher briefly appeared the quintessential troubled youth sincerely relieved to be let off the hook, as it were.

"Appreciate that."

"Not a problem. Now, on the personal side, I see here you're listed as divorced."

Fletcher nodded solemnly.

"Numerous times. I've been single for the past several years."

"Children?"

"One daughter. She's currently attending the Air Force Academy."

"Well, you must be quite proud."

The big man then flashed a rather weak, acutely sad smile.

"Um, well, actually I haven't seen nor spoken to Marie in over three years. Found out about her yearning to become a flyer from some of my Lowry contacts... ur, that's Lowry Air Force Base in Colorado. They handle assignments."

Burt seemed to hesitate before delving into the next query a bit timidly.

"I... see. I have heard a soldier's life isn't very agreeable to what most consider a blissful marriage."

"True. But then again, neither are alcoholism and the drunken rages that followed. Happy to say I've kicked the booze habit. Been sober one year, three months and sixteen days as of my arrival here. Like they say in AA... it's a daily challenge, but then again, so is life in general, right?"

"Very, very true. Well, now that we've covered the formalities of what qualifies you as a client, we can discuss why exactly you've been sent to us."

Breathing heavily, Fletcher squirmed a bit.

"Makes perfect sense. Nothing too complicated there."

Turning back to the group, Burt nodded Jessica's way before leaning back and folding both hands behind his balding plate.

"Mister Fletcher, allow me to read the official statement regarding your presence here with us."

"Yes, ma'am, by all means," Fletcher replied almost shyly, again lightly drumming the tabletop with the fingers of both hands.

"Last November 8th while assigned to the Army's Pacific Tactical Search and Destroy Unit in the Republic of the Philippines, you were accused of physically assaulting a superior officer. Please explain."

Briefly lowering his head to stare into his own

lap, both the man's expression and demeanor had dramatically altered upon resetting his gaze in Jessica's direction. With a creased brow and tightly squinting eyes, he appeared to be suffering intense internal pain.

"You got it, Miss. Fair warning though... it ain't the least bit pretty, and I'm not about to sugarcoat a single detail. I love my country like no one before... proven as much countless times, but I'm not about to take a fall for something I deem wholly justifiable."

Jessica nodded amiably. A former lead counselor at one of the more infamous psychiatric units in the State of Texas, I would've presumed it took quite the dicey scenario to shake such a woman.

"We wouldn't expect you to, Mister Fletcher. Please proceed."

As he commenced, Tate Fletcher fixed the aforementioned gaze on each of us, and I noted the slightly milky shading of his left eye and secretly pondered its usefulness. His folder had said nothing of vision loss, but there was a deep, pronounced scar that ran from the brow to just beneath the eye itself. Regardless, it made for a chilling stare indeed, and couldn't help but enhance the overall sense of dread in the story he so effectively regaled us with. Sounds juvenile, but I couldn't help but think that all we were missing was a dark, stormy night and a campfire to crowd around.

"I'd been sent to Manila to track Juan 'the Jackal' Baliar, the leader of a people-trafficking syndicate out of Columbia. Baliar and his boys had recently launched some sizeable expansion plans that included southeast Asia and even a few U.S. border states. They'd also added heroin and coke distribution to their resume, though international prostitution, slave labor and the buying and resale of newborns was still their main stock and trade."

Pausing to pull a badly crinkled cigarette pack from his left shirt pocket, Fletcher then produced a small pack of matches before tossing both items atop the table.

"Anyone mind? Damned if I can ever get through this story without a healthy dose of nicotine."

We seemed to nod as one without speaking, and he proceeded after a long, drawn-out drag, wherein thick plumes of smoke puffed from each nostril like duel exhaust pipes.

"Appreciate it. Well then, long story short, I was hired to search out and eradicate the bastard and as many of his sicko cronies as I deemed fit along the way. Took me and my crew, that being three veteran paratroopers and a still wet-behind-the-ears second lieutenant Navy Seal named Masterston, all of forty-eight hours to accomplish Phase One. Found the slimy jackasses holed up in a jungle fort about forty clicks east of the capital city. Well-guarded as it was, we found the Jackal's hired security personnel woefully lacking in effective preventive techniques in case of an actual breech. Translation: we cut through the lot of them, perhaps two dozen bodies or thereabouts, without breaking a sweat in rainforest humidity.

"Eventually, I found Baliar and his twin bodyguards cowering inside a concrete bunker a few hundred yards from the main compound. While the Jackal commenced to whine and cry like a spooked second grader, the twins proved to be loyal to a fault in trying to protect their precious dictator. I snapped the first one's neck with a single twist and practically decapitated the other with a solid front kick to the jaw before training my sole focus onto the international monster I'd been paid to dust. After dragging him out of that hole by the ankles, all the while being bribed and begged in at least three South American dialects to spare his miserable life, I clamped a gnarled claw around his scrawny neck and slowly began to squeeze. Don't get me wrong, people... I'm no 'path, socio, psycho or otherwise, but on those not-so-rare occasions when my government has employed me to play the part of assassin, I cannot risk a moment's hesitation in completing said job without endangering the mission as a whole. Not to sound egotistical, but I'm... *was* damn good at what I do... um, *did*. Juan Baliar was a murdering rapist who sold his fellow man like so much bagged trash. The way I saw it, I was doing society as a whole one hell of a favor, and didn't feel a single twinge of guilt in doing so."

Taking a final draw from what little remained of his cancer stick, Fletcher blew out the blackish remnants before casually mashing the butt into the palm of his right hand.

"Baliar had just begun to gargle his last when I became aware of the barrel end of a still-warm M-16 being shoved against my left ear. Seems I'd been so lost in the bloodlust of the moment that I'd gone completely stone deaf to the verbal orders being screamed my way.

"I then heard Left-tenant Masterson order me to

release the Jackal or else the steel helmet protecting my precious gray matter was gonna resemble Swiss cheese. Fact is, he repeated this same order several times, and at a higher decibel level each time."

Fletcher paused to light yet another smoke, and I couldn't help but focus on the 'bionic' hand which had so effortlessly flicked the lighter to life. From the five to six-foot distance between the man and myself, there appeared no distinction between either the flesh-and-bone hand and its wholly artificial counterpart. From my point of view, however naive, the man named Scar was a true scientific marvel come to life, though according to official Department of Defense records, the technology used to enhance his damaged limbs was easily a decade out of date. Small wonder he'd ended up in our care, as had so many other old soldiers tossed onto the governmental scrapheap.

"So, I take it you refused to follow said verbal order?" Burt asked, snapping both a rather uncomfortable silence and my own personal daze.

"You already know, Chief. Not only did I complete the job I'd started on Baliar courtesy of a short right jab that drove fragments of bony cartilage from his nose directly into his brain, but also managed to backhand the good left-tenant airborne, breaking the jackass' jaw in the process. Officially, I was made to apologize for so brutally roughhousing a superior. Unofficially, the little prick should feel fortunate I didn't plant my size thirteen atop his pigskin-shaped noggin and pop it like an eggshell."

The big man paused, grinning devilishly from ear to ear.

"Needless to say, myself and the left-tenant hadn't exactly seen eye-to-eye from day one of the mission.

"After a... short struggle, I stopped short of engaging the rest of my team in mutual combat and allowed them to take me into custody peacefully, though to a man they weren't the least bit thrilled to do so."

"Why did you... snap so, Mister Fletcher?" Jay Peterson inquired between chews on a number two pencil.

"I mean, why not allow the lieutenant and the rest of your team to take the Jackal into custody to stand trial for his crimes? Why risk your career or reputation? Surely you'd dealt with such scum before."

"Good question, my man," Fletcher countered, his hazel-shaded eye pulled wide and ablaze with color, "and a damned fair one at that.

"You see, the reason I simply could not allow such a man even a semblance of freedom outside that jungle compound was due to the... abomination I'd bore witness to less than a half-hour before our initial raid. Balair, you understand, was somewhat infamous for his taste in young girls, most of which he'd either bought or snatched right off the streets to sell into prostitution, but not before... testing the waters himself, so to speak."

"So what you're saying is, he practiced rape on those he imprisoned as a means of... breaking them in for prospective clients?" I asked, in retrospect perhaps sounding a bit too enthusiastic for such grisly, perverted subject matter.

The milky eye having turned my way, I felt the

first of what was to be several icy chills trail the length of my spine.

"Ah, much more than just that, young counselor. The Jackyl liked to play rough. Sure, it started with rape and assorted physical assaults, but as with that particular day, often ended on the most fatal of terms. Maybe he was... overstocked and simply didn't feel obligated to feeding them all. Perhaps he'd deemed certain ones of too low quality... not valuable enough to maintain as... as inventory. Regardless, as we neared the compound from thick jungle cover, we discovered a small bamboo shanty. Nothing more than a shabbily constructed lean-to really, we figured it to be a supply hut of some sort. I caught the stout whiff of death just as I'd peeled away a back wall. Thirteen bodies all told, stacked like cordwood on a country cabin's front porch. All were female and painfully young, as in the ten to thirteen age range. Some had been dead for a spell, as long as a week or more, while several more had been fresher kills. One appeared to have just been added to the stack, perhaps even that very day."

I heard Jay swallow hard just a millisecond before both Jessica and Doctor Gonzalez noisily cleared their throats in almost perfect harmony. I myself felt chill number two take the fast track from my butt-bone all the way to the base of my neck, where tiny hairs were suddenly standing as erect as any porcupine quill. Though I cannot speak for the rest of the staff, I wasn't at all used to such grisliness. Drugs, drink and sex additions were more my speed, not child molesters *slash* murderers.

"Some had been neck-tied... um, had their

throats slashed. Others had endured head shots from small arms fire, while several possessed the bruising and telltale marks of choking victims. Most had bled profusely from the anal region. Doesn't take an atom-splitter to figure that one out. Yep-per, old Juan was a real card all right. Equal opportunity mass murderer, pedophile and master of torture. A real triple threat, he was."

Fletcher paused just long enough to stare each of us down individually, and I found it a tall order indeed to maintain eye contact.

"Folks, I wasn't about to allow such an inhuman creature to cop a plea somewhere down the line. That was their plan, you know. The CIA had already pegged the Jackyl as the ultimate south-of-the-border stool pigeon, and hoped the maniacal bastard would do them the colossal favor of clearing the board on their most-wanted list. So before you ask if I regret snuffing out their prize catch... don't bother. I sleep just fine, thanks. End of story."

"Well, not quite, Mister Fletcher," Burt injected without pause, seemingly unfazed by the man's gruesome yet undeniably captivating tale. Again, it was crystal clear who was the superior among us and exactly why.

"There is the matter of why you've been sent to our little mountainside community. According to your file, there've been several similar rebellions against direct authority since the Philippine incident. Care to elaborate?"

Again, Fletcher eyed each of us while responding, though his expression was notably less menacing; his tone borderline apologetic.

"Wish it were that simple to explain, Chief. I

mean, there is a certain amount of surliness expected in my line of work. I don't kid myself. No delusions of grandeur here. I'm a paid brawler; strictly brawn for hire-government muscle. Of late, however, this particular lapdog has found it nigh on impossible to effectively reel in the incisors. Since my so-called superiors saw fit to make a deal with the worst kind of Devil, I've seriously mulled over retirement, but financially it just isn't feasible, and I've burned far too many bridges to even think about freelancing. I'm just an old-school puncher with a US of A bar code tattooed on his ass for the duration, I guess. I either accepted this little forced TDY or packed it in for good. In all honestly, I'm still not sure this choice was the correct one. Only time will tell, if you'll pardon the moldy cliche."

"We appreciate both your candor and honesty, Mister Fletcher," Burt concluded blandly, though I could recall little else of what was said during that particular session, my thoughts thoroughly imprisoned by horrid images of stacked, mutilated bodies constructed mostly of preteen arms and legs protruding from a single, bloated midsection. Try as I might to shift focus onto something, *anything*, less stomach churning, the act of shaking Scar Fletcher's outstretched synthetic hand, however lifelike the warm flesh, did little but enhance the nauseating vibe. From a mental diversion standpoint, I was more than ready to proceed with the day's second of four such intro sessions.

***

January 18, 1420 Hours

Personal File D-133:
Subject: Cassie Jane Wilkes
Trade Name (*Government copyright*): Jekyll-ene

Rumor had it that the woman federally licensed to fight organized crime (since September of 2007) under the rather enigmatic moniker of *Jeyll-ene* had obtained her powers through some sort of involuntary chemical alteration. Her file photo, which had been labeled July 2011, had displayed a much bulkier version than the woman sitting before us, her shoulder-length locks streaked in blonde, her expression an open-mouthed, eyes-pulled-wide expression of pure, unbridled rage.

The costume consisted of an eye-cover only mask and dark maroon spandex tights, black calf-high boots with what appeared to be gold-shaded serrated spurs at each heel, and an ankle-length black cape flashing a flaming yellow skull at its center. As far as costumes went, this was nothing special or even remotely unique. What was shockingly off-kilter about the photograph, taken against a backdrop of what appeared to be an inner-city skyline, was the facial appearance of the individual showcased. Apparently I wasn't alone in my confusion, as I noticed even Burt giving the same photo a twice-over between curious glances at the subject now sitting before us. In studying each, it was hard to believe it was indeed the same person, though to be fair it was difficult to gauge with such dispiriting expressions to compare. Still, the costumed figure's forehead and jowls appeared longer and thicker, respectively, with a vastly different contour than the young woman present within our midst. Perhaps it was simply a matter of timing, much like an overly bulked-up weightlifter can appear almost normal-sized away from the gym while donned in street clothing.

Most fascinating amid the many tidbits of interest surrounding Miss Wilkes was the origin of her chosen trade name, which centered around the three distinct personalities she claimed to inhabit. These were outlined as such, along with a brief listing of skills for each persona:

Personality one (*Cassandra*): Intelligent, analytical and wary within the company of strangers. Skill: First-degree blackbelt-Shaolin Kung.

Personality two (*Cassie*): Crude, cynical, brash. Skill: Third-degree blackbelt-Taekwondo; superstrength to equal that of five to seven average-sized males.

Personality three (*Jekyll-ene*): Unthinking brute fueled solely by combative rage. Skills: Basic brawler-possesses the approximate strength of twenty average men.

Suspended from active federal duty since November of the previous year, it seemed Cassie Wilkes claimed a similar temper issue as that of Tate Fletcher. As we were to discover rather quickly however, *any* and *all* similarities between the three Miss Wilkes and anyone else on our current client list ended right then and there. As it turned out, there was only one among said trio whose claim to fame was that rather infamous character in classic fiction, and meeting that certain persona face-to-face would prove a virtually impossible task. As it was, identifying which personality had initially greeted us wasn't nearly as difficult.

"Before we delve into the usual layer of bullshit amenities, let me state two things for the official record: I ain't down with this Doctor Phil skull-fuck program you're running here... obviously nothing more than a bunch of second-rate mind-massagers attempting to justify what must be one hell of a paycheck. Secondly, this girl don't cotton to criticism from strangers, so you'd be wise to button that lip if I appear even the slightest bit perturbed at whatever psychobabble advice you're dishing out. Fair warning: with or without the juice, I can dish it out as well as I can take it... and then some."

Thus concluded our rather unique introduction to the second of the three listed entities, Miss *Cassie* Wilkes, a Caucasian female aged twenty-three.

"So start analyzing me already, but do me a colossal favor and make it snappy. I'm bleeding like a stuck pig this month, and in dire need of a diaper change, if you catch my rather feminine drift."

Before initiating the session, Burt shot us a quick 'here we go, troops' glance. Can't speak for the entire group, but I was still coming off a rather dizzying adrenalin rush from Fletcher's interview and wasn't about to be so easily defused by nothing more than a few well-staged obscenities. Besides, Wilkes' personnel file clearly targeted this specific personality as the outspoken malcontent.

"We'll... do our best to adhere to your wishes, Miss Wilkes. First off, let me introduce you to the staff. To my left, we ha-"

"Skip it, Doc," Wilkes broke in with a raised hand and severely creased brow. "All in due time,

I'm sure. What say we excise the dead air and tear into the meatiest portion right off the bat?"

Ever the calm, cool, collected professional, Burt maintained as only Burt could, shrugging his shoulders while pillaging through the young woman's surprisingly thick file.

"Fine, Cassie. Please then, indulge us by answering a few pointed, rather personal questions. This is used merely to break the ice... "

"Fire away, if you must."

Burt: "Please state your favorite color... "

Cassie (rolled her eyes in apparent disgust): "You've gotta be yanking my leash, Doc."

Burt (sternly): "Cassie, if you please."

Cassie (frowning): "All right... all right then. Black... darkest, deepest Africa black... coal mine black... black-hole black... you get the picture."

Burt (clearing his throat): "Um, yes. Please state your all-time favorite movie."

Cassie (wide-eyed, mouth hanging agape): "Favorite mov- here and I thought this little session was gonna get deep. All-time favorite flick... lemme think (pauses)... *Mary Reilly* comes to mind, for obvious reasons. So close to my heart, that one, and of course Malkovich's a master. Played the duel Jekyll-Hyde roles with equal skill; not too wimpy as the former and with just the right layer of insanity as the latter. Still, pretty little Sally Field gnawing the scenery like a big ol' greasy porkchop as *Sybil* will always be King... um, Queen Dysfunctional in my book. That flick never fails to uplift, after all, chick had about four-hundred whacked-out personalities to deal with, right? Sure makes my situation pale in comparison, and that's a *good* thing."

Burt: "Understood. How about a TV show?"

Cassie: "The boob tube ain't never been my thing, man. Always had better things to do."

Burt: "Nothing ever caught your eye and... kept you interested?"

Cassie: "Nope. I did catch a few episodes of the *X-Files* back when it was the hot ticket. Not bad, but damn if it wasn't too talky for this girl, especially when they were tied up in all those farfetched alien-abduction theories. Other than that... well, I used to think the game show network was an okay distraction if I had a minute or five to kill between missions. Now, you have to understand I'm speaking solely for myself here. Those other two nitwits I share brain space with might be TV crazy, though I just can't see big sis number two cuddling up to a network sitcom without eventually aiming a bootheel toward the screen. Next?"

Burt: "What is your favorite song?"

Cassie: "Shit, that's too easy, professor... *Cult of Personality* by Living Colour (pauses). Well, what did you expect, Barry freakin' Manilow?"

Burt: "Alright then, tell us something you'd like to change about yourself if it were in your power. This can be a physical trait or personality... um... I, uh... or something concerning your daily behavior or attitude. I, uh, didn't mean... that is... "

Cassie (laughing): "Aw, don't sweat it, Prof. Bad choice of wording, that's all. No harm, no foul. As for the question at hand, it oughta be fairly obvious. How about the permanent jettisoning of my two alter egos? Case closed. Nothing else even rates."

Burt: "Duly noted. Lastly, tell us of an embarrassing episode in your life you've never previously shared with anyone else. This can cover any period... from childhood to present day."

Cassie (smiling mischievously): "Well, if you're gonna be that way. I could lie and say none come to mind, but that just ain't this girl's personality, so to speak. I... uh, well... you might say I found myself in an uncompromising situation with a former teammate a few years back... the tender teenage years to be precise. Long story short, I... um, almost... *almost* mind you, gave in to my lust, despite the fact I don't normally, um, roll that way."

Burt (looking comically befuddled): "Could you please specify a bit, Cassie... "

Cassie (rolling her eyes and looking away as if extremely embarrassed to continue): "The chick's name was Marlena, code name *Shadow Cheetah* (grins)... hey, I didn't name 'em... just ran around with 'em. Anyway, Marlena was one hot tamale of the Spanish persuasion who was... now how can I say this without sounding grossly homophobic? She preferred raw fish to cooked wieners, dig?"

Burt (clearing his throat): Understood. Continue... "

Cassie: "We'd just wrapped up a particularly trying mission and had shared a bottle of wine over dinner. Once we got back up to our hotel room... she... um, let's just say Marty broke the unwritten rule amongst female supergroups and got... well, frisky with yours truly. Can't say deep down I wasn't flattered, and I never was one for holding my wine too well. Long, potentially disgusting story short, I did... we did lock lips for a few ticks before I came to my senses and backed away. For the record, that little episode has nothing to do with... well, what came later and why I'm here. I was barely eighteen at the time and didn't know my rear end from a gopher hole."

Burt: "Um, very interesting, Cassie. Very... insightful. Now, if you'd please tell us more about yourself and the issues that *did* precede your name being added to our current client roster."

"By the way, Doc, call me Cass, rhymes with *ass*," she replied with a sardonic wink before folding her heavily tattooed arms across a narrow bosom. Decked out in a sleeveless, black leather ensemble with matching calf-high boots and dark maroon, spiked locks streaked in yellow, she appeared the atypical biker chick, only with a healthy dose of Goth tossed in for good measure. One couldn't help but be amazed at the physical contradictions from the photo of her alter ego. Still, I had to admit she'd filled out that skintight spandex get-up quite nicely indeed.

"Again for the record... it really chaps my cheeks that I'm forced to flap my gums stating facts you people are already privy to. Really, why bother? Haven't I divulged enough warped personality traits already?"

Raising both palms in a gesture of peace, Burt was extra careful not to sound overly condescending; If anything, he sounded increasingly parental, like a concerned elder explaining the virtues of right versus wrong to a wayward youth.

"It's nothing personal, Cassie, simply a way for

us to... feel you out, so to speak. Please continue."

"Sure, Doc. I hear you. Feel me *out*... feel me *up* is more like it," Wilkes scoffed, pressing each thump tightly to her dimpled chin and in the process displaying a trio of silver-plated skull-rings attached to the middle three fingers of each hand.

"Great... *what... ever*. But again, this is under strict protest from yours truly. Shit, I should've told those ungrateful ass-clowns to catch the nearest bullet train straight to hell."

Reiterating his 'we're only here to help' stance, Burt allowed the young lady a few moments to stew within her own hateful juices before commenting. It was genuinely frightening how quickly this spate of anger had arisen, and seemingly from nowhere in terms of a justifiable trigger. Then again, it was far too early in the game to attach the bi-polar label.

"Your comrades... um, teammates were very concerned, Miss Wilkes. Their... intervention in your behalf proves the sincerity of their actions. I was told they desire nothing more than your return to their ranks as soon as the problem is resolved."

"You think, Doc? Personally, I took their kindly intervention as a permanent pink slip from the so-called ranks. They dumped me here as an example to those who follow. Made a textbook example out of me as to better enforce their inane rules. Do you have any idea how many times I saved each and every one of their ungrateful asses over the past two and a half years? And *this* is the thanks I get? Shipped to and subsequently marooned in this concrete-and-steel bandbox out in the middle of ab-so-lute-ly nowhere? For sure, Doc... I can almost smell the love."

Perhaps for no other reason than to avoid triggering a similar rant, Burt refused to respond either verbally or otherwise. As was normally the case, his strategy worked to perfection, as Wilkes eventually caved in to the classic silent treatment and begrudgingly conceded with the planned itinerary.

"Ah, the hell with it. I'll play the game... for now. It ain't like there's much else to occupy one's time here on the dark side of Mars.

"I dropped out of school when I was fourteen... ran away from home a few months later to escape my old man's vodka-laced tirades. Drunken bastard had run my mom off a few years earlier and had happily turned his rage onto me soon afterwards. Point of order here: haven't seen hide nor booze-soaked hair from that worthless SOB since... may he and his metal-buckled leather strap unhappily rot in hell's steamiest pit for all of eternity. Anyhow, after a few short months on the street I found survival one unmerciful, unforgiving bitch.

"Needless to say, I was hungry, cold, and damned near suicidal when a fellow homeless urchin introduced me to the jollies of the Institute for Voluntary Human Research. For three warm meals and a leakproof rooftop overhead, the terminally down-and-out could count on the kindly staff at the VHR Institute to transform them into the most pathetic examples of human guinea pigs since Uncle Adolf attempted breeding German Shepards with Polish homemakers. Allow me to raise a hand high as one such ready and willing rodent. Young and dumb as a marble stone, I realize, but then I didn't exactly have a lot to lose at the time."

Listed at five-seven and one-hundred forty-five pounds of taut muscle and very minuscule body fat, Miss Wilkes appeared to shrink as her dialogue continued, perhaps some sort of physical manifestation from reliving past events that were less than memorable. It was truly amazing to witness as her entire body seemed to be gradually imploding, much like a slowly deflating balloon.

"I left the Institute some three and a half weeks later, the entire experience nothing more than a hazy blur that the passing years have done little to clarify. Both arms were badly pockmarked at the crook of the elbow, so there was little question who was playing the part of human pincushion. It wasn't until around a month later that the first side effects kicked in... about the time I was getting settled at my aunt's. If nothing else, the Institute had paid my way East via Greyhound, while also kicking in a few greenbacks for good measure. Whoopee shit... right? Guaran-damn-teed if those Nazi assholes had even a hint of what they'd accidentally released into the world, I'd have never again seen the light of day outside their laboratories."

"What had they released, Cassie?" Jay asked in a throaty whisper, leaning up and adjusting his designer eyewear while tilting his head just slightly.

"Well, I'll tell you, Slick," came the growled reply, delivered through highly glossed, tightly gritted teeth that might easily have been mistaken for bared fangs.

"I started to experience lengthy blackouts from which I had no memory whatsoever. Come to find out that during these sessions, some of which were several days in duration, an alter ego was birthed.

An alter ego who simply abhors the nick 'Cassie' and insists on being called Cassandra. Never had the displeasure of actually meeting the bitch face-to-face, you understand, but I gather she's touted quite the academic egghead; a real whiz with higher math, biology, physics, chemistry... the works. I even hear she fancies herself some sort of hotshot amateur psychologist, so you folks might wanna gird your loins 'less you find yourself mentally outmanned. As years went by, Cassandra began to dominate the... our existence more and more, usually leaving me hung up in some kind of purgatory state I can only describe as a dark nothingness.

"Do you realize my high school memories consist solely of a half-dozen fistfights and a single backseat groping session with some pocket-protector wearing, Clark Kent lookalike computer geek? Sad but true... while Cassandra graduated with honors, Cassie found herself permanently incarcerated behind some kind of brainstem firewall that only allowed for a furlough whenever there was a desperate need for physical prowess.

"People, you ain't known frustration 'til you've spent years in forced imprisonment; locked away by a judge whose face is all too damned familiar while staring at you from the other side of a mirror. You ain't known frustration 'til you realize the judge dolling out the sentence was created and/or handed the keys to the kingdom by your own segmented mind."

While Cassie took a short hiatus for dramatic sulking purposes, Jessica seized the opportunity to spout the painfully obvious.

"So what you're saying is, you're the brawn, and this... Cassandra entity is the brains."

"Sharp as a serpent's tooth, you are, lady, though I ain't the drooling retard that comment insinuates," Cassie retorted with a tight smile; flashing a brief yet tangible seductive power behind those bright hazel eyes that I'm positive every male in the room couldn't help but take notice of. Personality glitches and severe mood swings aside, this young woman was a fireplug of considerable wattage; a potentially lethal dynamo who for all the world reminded me of a young *Joan Jett* in her rock-and-roll prime-sexy sneer and all.

Jessica inhaled deeply to reply when Burt, probably wisely, intervened with a request I'd never have had the testicular fortitude to ask.

"Cassie, how exactly do we go about... meeting with Cassandra?"

Tossing her head back with a hearty laugh, Cassie tossed up both hands in apparent disbelief, though her tone was openly light.

"Bored with my act already, are we? Figured as much, but damn! That didn't take nearly long enough."

Feeling my chest tighten a notch, I'd expected a fiery, obscenity-laced tirade, as Cassie's file had reiterated ad nauseam how enraged she normally became at such a request. Fortunately for the group, everyone but Burt appearing a bit piqued, she seemed nothing more than slightly annoyed, and even then I couldn't be certain of the level of sincerity involved. Perhaps the young woman was doing some testing of her own, taken from the pages of a hidden agenda we as of yet had no knowledge of.

"Okay then, if banal, analytical dialogue and android-like tendencies are what you truly desire, far be it from me to play the stubborn bitch." Placing a sharp-nailed forefinger against her left temple, she stared into the ceiling thoughtfully. "Come to think of it, *that* is a role I play quite well.

"Simply present me with a textbook question I couldn't possibly answer and we'll play a round of *Final Jeopardy*. Usually does the trick, from what I hear. I do have one condition though... "

"What might that be?" Burt asked with a cocked brow.

"If I do happen to spew out the correct answer, you brainiacs lay off in forcing Miss High-n-Mighty smart ass to the head of the consciousness class, so to speak. In other words, I'm allowed to roam the reality circuit for a day or two before giving up the crown to her snooty ass."

"Um, agreed then. Give us a moment to converge and come up with a suitable problem."

Clapping her hands in childish excitement, we witnessed an all-together too brief glimpse into Cassie's lighter side.

"How about something sports related, huh? How about porn trivia? I'm a whiz at all things filth.

"Just none of that chemical equation shit, okay? Trying to cipher that crap gives me one humdinger of a migraine."

We nodded as one while converging to the back of the conference room, whispering like schoolchildren sharing the juiciest of secrets.

"By the way, folks," she added solemnly just as we'd formed an impromptu huddle as to create a sound barrier of sorts.

"I'm sure your crib notes forewarned about the possible consequences of pissing off little Miss Smarty-Pants, right? Like the man once said, you don't wanna see her angry... 'cause you sure as shit wouldn't like her angry."

"We've... read the file, Miss Wilkes," Burt retorted calmly with a casual wave. "We'll... be careful not to fray any sensitive nerves."

Cassie Wilkes bowed halfheartedly before leaving us to our brainstorming.

"Appreciate it, Chief. You can't know how aggravating it is to wake up covered in hives and open sores that take weeks to heal. Much as I despise Professor Cassandra, that other crazy bitch has one messed up complexion... and it is, without doubt, a *hereditary* thing."

"But... " Jay intervened, spastically waving one hand, "doesn't it normally take an act of extreme aggression to... awaken Jekyll-ene?"

Cassie beamed seductively.

"Normally, yeah, but lately I've heard it takes nothing more than the wrong combination of unflattering words to evoke that loony chick out of hiding, so... choose 'em wisely, sport, or prepare to test the limits of whatever health insurance you're carrying."

Needless to say, the subject of sister act three was thereby dropped like a two-ton anchor.

In the six to seven minute span that passed, all but the good doctor tossed in suggestions, but eventually it was Jessica's idea that held the most merit.

Cassie had lowered her head and appeared to be

napping as we retook our seats.

After several throat-clearing attempts to revive her, Burt finally broke the silence verbally.

"Um, Cassie, are you still with us?"

"Yep," she croaked between yawns. "Right here, Chief. Just rereading the crib notes I'd attached to the inside of the old eyelids," she replied sheepishly, the fatigue evident in her hangdog expression. "Fire when ready."

"Alright then, Miss Wilkes, please list the first ten U.S. Presidents without breaking the correct order."

Slapping her forehead with the flat of one palm, Cassie Wilkes' mouth hung ajar in comic shock.

"Jeez, is that all you got? And you call yourselves intellectuals... "

"By all means, Miss Wilkes, please commence, then... " Burt chided, happily calling her overtly cocky bluff.

"No sweat, boss," she began, flashing a raised finger with each corresponding answer. "Washington, Adams, um... Jefferson... Madison, Monroe, Jackson... no... no... no! Strike that... Monroe, Adams, John Q., then Andrew Freaking Jackson, ugh... umm... gimme a sec here... shit! Just a tick and I'll have it wrapped up."

Leaning back with her face cupped in both hands, Cassie grumbled, moaned, and gyrated as if the chair beneath her was receiving sporadic electric shocks.

"Ahhh hell... I wanna say Polk or Van Duran, but I cannot for the life of me recall which one of those two old fossils served first... damn it all to... shit!"

I heard Jay unsuccessfully stifle a giggle at the 'Van Duran' remark, to which Jessica and I exchanged mischievous grins.

"No, damn it! I'm not letting you in! I know this!" Cassie shrieked, suddenly gripping the sides of her skull through her spiked coif while nodding violently from side to side.

"Back off, *bitch*! I said... I know this one... just... j-just give me... give me a fair shake, that's all I ask... back... the hell... off for... just this... once."

As this young woman squirmed, shook, and struggled in apparent anguish, I couldn't help but ponder the drama queen possibilities, but as her body language grew increasingly animated and a thick layer of perspiration coated her bare arms and neck, my initial skepticism quickly abated. In briefly checking my colleagues' reactions, I noted similarly mixed expressions, that is, all save one. Burt Hanover's creased brow, tightly pursed lips and hard, unwavering gaze left little doubt that the man in charge was buying the transformation act hook, line, and bleary-eyed sinker, thus providing instant credibility from my own personal outlook.

As if to as sinuate such a belief, Cassie Wilkes' hands left her face to grip the sides of the tabletop in a steely death grip, her pasty, sweat-coated complexion surely beyond any and all Oscar-caliber performances from cinema's past.

Most disturbing, however, were the state of the woman's eyes, which had literally rolled back into her head and were showing only the ivory whites.

"Wow, she's really tripping," I heard Jay whisper in awe-struck wonder as natural reflex forced me to initiate several hard swallows.

Suddenly Scar Fletcher's war stories were looking pretty tame by comparison.

Emitting a throaty hum that caused the tiny hairs about the nape of my neck to stand out like steely quills, Cassie's head eventually collapsed forward onto the table with a muffled thump, her formerly spiked do having unraveled about her moistened shoulders like soggy seaweed.

"Doc, you think you should che-" Jessica began, only to be cut off by an all-together alien voice originating from a familiar source.

"Van Buren was eighth, followed by Harrison and Tyler. Just for the record, Polk was eleven. I can continue if you insist... " blurted out this new addition, one that looked if not sounded remarkably like Cassie Wilkes, but most likely would only answer to the more formal Cassandra.

"No? Then you'll have to excuse me for an inquiry of my own. Just who are you people and where exactly are we?"

Twenty-five minutes of explanations and reintros later, Cassie Wilkes' smarter, infinitely calmer sibling seemed at least partially content with the whys, whens and hows of her presence at the Jasper Hiatt.

"So what's the itinerary, if I may be so bold?" she finally asked coolly, her pristine posture and elegant body language the exact opposite of her tightly coiled twin. Despite the overly pasty complexion and 'Medusa' locks, there was no doubting the utter turnabout in personality from mere moments before. Joan Jett had left the building, replaced by a yet-to-be determined entity from which there was little resemblance.

Burt hardly hesitated before taking the lead, no doubt fearful one of us might indeed utter some of the unflattering words Cassie had mentioned and thus birth the most troubled, not to mention potentially dangerous, of the trio.

"Well, Miss Wilkes... Cassandra, our goal is to help you regain a... portion of self-control that seems to have been misplaced in the past several months, at least according to your former teammates. Once we feel our therapy has reached the desired results, you'll be cleared via government waiver and given the green light to resume your career."

"Now, let me make sure I understand this correctly," she stated serenely, striking a thoughtful pose with the tip of her chin resting atop extended thumbs. "If I'm... if *we're* a good little girl, Uncle Sam will reinstate us for duty. May I ask which of my former mates pushed this little rehab session? Only curious, you understand, since there are so many potential suspects among the roster of back-stabbing ingrates I left behind in Miami. The cloak of jealousy was thickly sewn back at the old HQ... thick and malice-filled. It's a real shame it had little to do with yours truly. "

"As for specific names, I'll have to decline an answer at this juncture, Miss... um, Cassandra. Needless to say, your coworkers showed great concern and wish you nothing but the best."

"Hmmm, sounds a bit like a pink slip sayonara to me, Chief Hanover, but then again... beggars such as I surely cannot be choosers, yes?"

Burt scooped up Wilkes' personnel file and began to casually skim the contents.

"I've... we have read your file, of course. It seems you had similar issues with the initial group from which you held a roster spot. Please correct me if I'd wrong."

"Ah yes, the long-ago disbanded *Teen Queens*. Five painfully young, naive, immature tweeners possessing powers far beyond their scope of control. That was easily the most hectic, frenzied half-year I've had the displeasure to experience; a constant catfight with no end in sight. It would've served as the perfect blueprint for today's influx of reality-based TV programming. I would venture to guess you've been filled in on the incident involving our Hispanic representative, Shadow Cheetah?"

"As a matter of fact, we have," Burt conceded, though refusing to elaborate as to avoid getting hopelessly sidetracked.

Pushing her chair back to allow a crossing of black leather-covered legs, Cassandra briefly glared at the gaudy jewelry adorning the majority of her fingers with a look of comical disgust.

"I figured as much. Well, this was all pre-government employment of course, before it was mandatory to hold a federal license to practice the hero trade. For the record, I refuse to accept any of the credit for that particular... forced resignation. To explain in laymen's terms, Cassie simply refused to... play nice with others. In retrospect, it truly is a miracle Jekyll-ene didn't make a *daily* appearance, though that one ugly incident where she *did* surely made up for any and all absences. It's probably a good thing the government stepped in to regulate. No way such a loose-cannon group of malcontents could ever hope to be licensed and bonded in this day and age."

"And what of this latest series of confrontations within your present group, *The Alfa-Dames*, more specifically the team member known as... Bull-Dyke Devil?" Burt inquired with a cocked brow, pushing the file aside as if to dismiss its officially documented content. How the man kept a straight face while mouthing the words *Bull-Dyke Devil* was anybody's guess. Personally, I had to pinch a knot into the meaty portion of my left thigh to refrain from guffawing aloud. No doubt sensing the selfsame juvenile reaction having swept over the group like a synchronized stomach cramp, the chief continued to dominate the questioning for the next several minutes.

Cassandra Wilkes responded following a deep, pained sigh, and one couldn't help but notice the color slowly returning to each of her cheeks, even as the dark bags beneath each eye grew miraculously lighter. It was truly as if the young lady had been reborn and was only then beginning to heal from the grueling aftereffects of the transformation.

"Good *grief*, you would think the holder of a Ph.D. and two BAs would be beyond such juvenile subject matter.

"Alright, in a crudely package nutshell then: from what I've gathered, Cassie accused Jenny, um... BDD of hitting on her on numerous occasions, which of course didn't set well with BDD's better half, Tamara... um... a rather attractive Brazilian named Witchhaven. Quite embarrassing and awkward for all involved, I'm sure, though I have no clear recollection of the brawl that ensued. My personal opinion leans toward Cassie not only inviting such behavior, but purposely instigating the incidents which followed. Sick kicks, I've heard it referred to."

I swear I detected a twinge of excitement in Burt's next query, a rarity for a man infamous for cloaking such emotions.

"Personal opinions aside, Cassandra, please clarify 'hitting on'... are we speaking of a sexual nature or more a physical altercation?"

"To use the vernacular, Bull-Dyke was hot for Cassie's bod and, supposedly, let her know it in no uncertain terms, usually whenever copious amounts of alcohol were a factor. Cas, in her usual tactless manner, proceeded to protest via a combination left jab to the midsection and overhead right, the latter of which sent BDD sailing through a plate-glass window with a fractured jaw. Once Witchhaven hopped into the fray, I'm told it was only a matter of moments before Jekyll-ene surfaced and, to use a rather tiresome cliche, all hell broke loose in a veritable avalanche."

"You... have no memories of these incidents, correct?"

"Affirmative... not a blessed clue until I awoke with various bruises and blood spatters about my person."

"So... others must have reported them to you? What transpired I mean... "

"Yes, which is why I've made it a point over the years to search out and secure a roster spot on whatever gal-team would accept my special... symptoms."

"So we are to understand that she... this... that

the Jekyll-ene persona is two to three times stronger, in a physical sense... than the Cassan-... Cassie... than Cassie," Jay babbled red-faced, trailing off while averting his eyes from Cassandra to his own rapidly tapping fingers drumming atop the table. It was surreal seeing the self-proclaimed 'Doc Valentino' so openly uncomfortable in the presence of the opposite sex. Surreal, and not the least bit unpleasant. To wit, I noted Jessica's glued-on smirk as she studied Jay's glowing cheeks with apparent amusement.

"No, sir, in fact I'd call that a blatant underestimation," Cassandra responded without a hint of good humor, all the while scanning our individual reactions. "Cassie is no pushover by any means, but the progressive stage is akin to a speeding semi with cut brakes... bull elephant stout with the disposition of a rabid wolverine."

With that, I broke in with a query of my own, barely avoiding raising my hand like a curious grade schooler.

"The progressive stage meaning Jekyll-ene?"

"Yes, though I personally think of it as the *regressive* stage, from Rhodes Scholar to mouthy brawler and finally bloodthirsty Neanderthal, complete with frothy jaws and hairy knuckles. By the way... " she paused with a forefinger raised airborne, "you folks don't happen to keep an ordained exorcist on staff? If so, I hereby officially give permission to play the part of guinea pig."

"Sorry, Cassandra," Jessica answered, eying the good doctor with a sly grin, "unless our resident sawbones is willing to try for yet another merit badge."

To which Doctor 'man of few words' Gonzalez simply shook his head without reply.

Removing a brass skull ring from the aforementioned forefinger, Cassandra's expression turned instantly grave, so much so it seemed to literally suck all previous good humor from the room even before her grim, tight-lipped response.

"Then you good people definitely have your work cut out for you. More than you'd ever know, I'm afraid. I may be somewhat of an easy mark, but good luck clearing contestants two and three for further duty.

"You have no idea what I'd give for the chance to go solo... permanently."

Rotating both arms in a 'give the lady a hand' gesture, our leather-clad guest suddenly appeared a decade older; a haggard, bone-weary victim of mental fatigue and untold misery.

"Hey, a girl's got to have a conscious dream amid all the unconscious nightmares."

"Not to worry, Miss Wilkes," Burt said in his best comforting, noncondescending tone. "We're here to help... all of you regain your livelihood. It's our job, and more than that, it's our calling. You save lives with heroic acts. By the same token, we attempt to salvage *psyches*."

"Sounds like a plan, Mister Hanover. Though I can only speak as a third party, I'd surely appreciate the effort," Cassandra responded demurely, managing to drudge up a small, pained smile while replacing the skull rings she'd earlier removed.

"One final question, if you're up to it."

"Please. I'm never less than intrigued, no matter the level of fatigue."

"If, in future counseling sessions, we *are* introduced to the entity referred to as Jekyll-ene, what advice can you offer in how we should precede with treatment?"

Leaning forward on both elbows until it looked as though she might actually be attempting to crawl full body onto the tabletop, it briefly appeared as though Cassandra Wilkes' was about to give us the opportunity firsthand. Her wide-eyed, unblinking gaze pierced like twin lasers. For the second time in a half-hour, I felt my spine birth a fresh growth of icicles.

"Simplicity in itself, I'm afraid. Don't try to reason with her, Mister Hanover, and for God's sake don't attempt to stand your ground and go toe to toe. One word, Mister Hanover: Run. Correction... make that three words: *Run... like... hell.*"

***

January 18, 1522 Hours
Personal File D-134:
Subject: Nickolaus Delbert Parione
Trade Name: (*Self-Proclaimed*): Dejà vu

"Pleased and honored to make the acquaintance of each and every one. I have to admit to a certain apprehension, though I'd wager such feelings to be completely natural. Regardless, in the few moments we've spoken, I now feel an overwhelming sense of relief in knowing I've been placed in such qualified, capable hands."

These were the first words uttered by client number three, one Nickolaus Parione, officially designated by the feds as a Mutant and better known in the hero trades as 'Dejà vu', a human time machine of sorts, at least according to his file. It was said the young man possessed the power to alter time, more specifically to... reverse situations (with limitations, of course) and thus relive or even alter events to his liking. To say the least, I was skeptical but undoubtedly enthralled at the very prospect. While in character, Parione's costume of choice consisted of a Zorro-styled half-mask tied off in back, black, three-piece tuxedo with oversized collar, tails and bolo tie and ivory-white high top Nike tennis shoes. To be kind, a rather unique combination... to be cruel, the word 'clownish' came instantly to mind. It was noted that in addition to the aforementioned powers, he also carried a lion's head 'shock'-cane with two-thousand volt capability and donned a utility belt housing mace bombs, plus a trio of palm-sized stun guns with a thousand volt capability. Having first been federally licensed to nail the bad guys in July of 2008, his suspension had become official almost three months to the day of our initial meeting, in October of 2012. The reason for the feds' actions: three separate cases of sexual harassment, all filed by current or former teammates.

During staff intros, Parione refrained from any form of verbal communication, instead preferring to casually shake hands and nod, as if sizing us up with great individual curiosity. Though initially such openly optimistic behavior seemed refreshing in the wake of Cassandra Wilkes' double-pronged barrage of personalities, it would soon prove a rather grating annoyance.

"Well, we certainly appreciate your attitude, Mister Parione," Burt replied politely enough, though I could read the skepticism in his tone. "We're definitely ahead of the game when the client displays such cooperation and willingness to meet us halfway."

"Hey, what can I say? Why pout and waste precious energy fighting the system? My goal is to leave here prepared to retake my place as a useful member of crime-fighting society. I've been granted this gift for a reason, and I'm not about to waste it."

Parione was a twenty-six-year-old Caucasian male with a head of thickly layered, pitch-black hair that seemed to flow with a life all its own from even the slightest of head movements. Listed at six-feet two and one-hundred seventy pounds, the man's thin build and hardly toned physique wasn't the least bit intimidating, nor was this lack of fearsomeness aided by his deliberate tone and sugary-polite way of speaking. Possessing a slight overbite and obscenely bushy eyebrows over deep-set eyes, one might even describe the young man as homely, yet according to the fed printout we'd all read in mild amazement, his penchant for playing ladies' man was one of the main reasons he'd been sent our way.

"First things first, Mister Parione ... " Burt began, only to halt in lieu of our client's two-handed, less-than-subtle wave off.

"Please, sir, call me Nick. In fact, I'm for discarding such formalities right from the get-go. With that in mind, *everyone* please call me Nick."

Bingo. There it was, for all of us to see. While making his impassioned plea to the entire group, the majority of Parione's focus had remained solely on

Jessica, who eventually broke eye contact by pretending to recheck her copy of the man's file.

I saw Burt roll his eyes in comic wonder before picking up where he'd left off.

"Alright then... Nick. To begin, we have a questionnaire of sorts to complete... "

During the brief session, to which it was revealed that the young man's favorite color was dark green, his favorite film (fittingly) the classic *The Time Machine* and that he had no favorite TV show to speak of, Parione displayed a wide-eyed, overwrought cheeriness that was borderline creepy. When asked to pick a favorite tune, he politely balked in stating that there were far too many to mention in a life consumed by music, which he'd used as a steady diversion since childhood.

As for the final question concerning an embarrassing episode never before revealed, Nick Parione's response was shockingly open and honest, a definite reversal from an otherwise choreographed performance.

"Oh, that's easy," he mumbled red-faced.

"I was eleven and had just discovered the wonders of masturbation in the family bathtub. Needless to say I'd heard rumors from peers equally ignorant on the subject and believed that the sensation of climax was a... (shakes head from side to side) ... a one-time deal. Thus, I... um... kind of... *rewound* the experience several times to the point of nosebleed and the edge of unconsciousness just to... well, you know, relive the thrill. Naturally it was a blessed relief the day I found out how wrong we'd been. Ah, the naivety of youth."

Following a brief pause wherein the entire

group seemed lost in separate but similar phases of embarrassment, we all shared a moment of much-needed levity fueled by Burt Hanover's usual dose of sardonic wisdom, perfectly timed and worded.

"Personally, I can't think of a better use," he'd blurted out with a cocked brow, sending the lot of us into a fit of unrestrained laughter that instantly and effectively terminated the building cloud of awkwardness present. Once the interview did resume, I felt a rush of renewed interest that appeared contagious, to include the client himself, who seemed less eager to please and increasingly sincere as time passed.

"Now, let's discuss this power to... bend or reshape time you speak of," Burt stated, completely back in character, "as I'm having a hard time with the textbook definition we were given."

"Understandable unless you're really, really into astrophysics, time-space continuums and the like, sir. May I suggest then that we skip the long-winded theories and/or scientific mumbo-jumbo and cut to the chase, so to speak?"

"What exactly are you proposing, Mister Par-um... Nick?"

"A demonstration of sorts, sir. Believe me, in the case of my... special talents, to see... or *experience* firsthand is the one and only way to begin to understand."

Obviously seeking a group opinion, Burt paused with a shrug before posing the question.

"What say you, folks?"

"I'm game," Jessica blurted out first, her cheeks practically glowing rose-red.

"What she said," Jay said excitedly. "Might be

fun at that."

"Sure, let's do it," I added with an open shudder I'd hoped wasn't as visible as it had felt.

Once Doc Gonzalez nodded a nonverbal affirmation, we were on our merry way into the bizarre world of the unknown. Speculation after the fact has never been my bag, but in retrospect I'd suspect each of us would've given an altogether different answer if not for the power of human curiosity. We'd all read what the man could supposedly do on paper. Now we'd get that rarest of opportunities to test its validity. There was no backing down once the proposition was tossed out there, as any respectable egghead worth half his or her salt would tell you. We'd all been strapped into the roller coaster and were prepping for take-off.

"Great... fantastic... super," Parione barked with an enthusiastic clapping of hands. "Fair warning, it can be a little trippy. Everyone just hang in there and don't freak out."

It was about this time that I'd barely fought off the urge to raise a hand in hesitation, and I'm fairly confident I wasn't the only one thinking along such cowardly lines. Though I considered myself as adventurous as the next paid counselor, there were limitations, guidelines to which we're normally controlled by logic and common sense. In this particular case, however, it had been preordained via group conference that such a demonstration might well be likely. Sweaty palms or no, we were bound to go through with it, if no other reason than to gain a valuable learning tool in terms of future sessions.

"First off, I'll need a volunteer from the staff."

We each shared an apprehensive glance even as Parione's own gaze once again seemed to linger exclusively Jessica's way.

"Guess I'm your man," Burt finally said with a raised hand while pushing back from the table.

"Ah, Mister Hanover, leading by example, I see. Please step my way, then."

The two met at the head of the table, shaking hands like political rivals.

"Now, what I'm going to ask you to do might sound a bit strange... just humor me, as there is a method to my apparent madness," Parione stated matter-of-factly while patting Burt lightly on one shoulder.

Talk about a first time for everything... I actually thought I had spotted an expression of mild fear in the boss' stilted reaction, that being a slight flinching back from the younger man's touch.

"This isn't going to hurt, is it? It isn't like I have a weak ticker or anything, but... " Burt grinned, playing it off beautifully. Scooting back a half-step, Parione struck a surrender pose with raised arms and exposed palms before turning away from Burt to address the group.

"Curb those concerns, folks. The most you're going to get out of this is a slight sense of disorientation. Truth is, I've even had a few people tell me it's quite the pleasant trek, a 'cool buzz' sort of feeling. As for potential dangers or hazards, the chances are slim and nil, and Slim done high-stepped from the room.

"Now, you ready, Mister Hanover, sir?" he concluded, again facing Burt, who had taken up a parade rest stance with his feet spread evenly a foot or so apart and each hand tucked snugly at the small of his back.

"As ready as I'll ever be. Beam me up, Scotty, uh, as it were."

"Relax, sir. Nothing to be nervous about. This isn't a test, just a demonstration."

"Gotcha," Burt said with a forced sigh, though he remained statue-stiff, "What next?"

"Alright, I'm going to make this easy. Please step forward and give me a light clap on the back, accompanied by the verbal greeting of your choice."

I'm fairly certain, without actual visual conformation, that each and every forehead in the room, save that of the man known as Dejà vu, creased in harmonic unison.

"Um, I'm not quite sure... clap you... on the back?" Burt queried in a barely audible mumble, another rarity.

"That's correct," Parione countered patiently, his head tilted slightly downward as if giving direction to a small child. "Just treat me as an old acquaintance you're greeting for the first time in ages at say... a company party or similar gathering. I'll do the rest... "

With a brief nod that screamed uncertainty, the boss stepped stiffly forward and spoke as if reading dialogue from a nearby teleprompter.

"Well, hello there, Nick, how's she hanging?" he barked, reaching forward a bit cautiously to tap Parione on the left shoulder.

It's truly hard to put into words what transpired next, at least without either sounding hopelessly insane or accidentally divulging the fact that in my late teens I'd indulged in my fair share of moderate to heavy pot smoking. First off, everything faded instantly to black immediately following the back slap, as if someone had reached inside my skull and literally clicked off the inner light switch. By the time said lights flickered back on, the scene on display seemed more than vaguely familiar, as Burt once again stepped forward (stiff as day-old cardboard yet again), his vocalizations unchanged and similarly mechanical.

"Well, hello there Nick, how's... she hanging?" he blurted out, reaching forward to tap Parione on the left shoulder before pausing in mid-gesture, his eyes growing as wide as saucers even as he sidestepped away in true 'hot-foot' fashion.

"What the h-hell? Didn't I... didn't we... did... didn't I...?"

Parione shook his head before facing the group to lecture, and I caught myself staring dazed at his robotic movements and continuously waving hands, my dulled senses no doubt still in red line overload mode.

"Yes, indeed you did... same movements, same words, same clap, performed exactly three point three seconds apart."

"But... how? *What* could...?" Jessica babbled, inexplicably staring at the bare palms of her hands as if expecting some sort of alien growth (probing eyeballs perhaps?) to emerge.

"I mean... we all read your file and the description of your powers, but this... this is... what *is* it exactly?"

Suddenly appearing as drained and weakened as the rest of us, Nick leaned hard against a corner table and released a laborious sigh.

"Ex-excuse me for a... a sec, people. Have to... catch my breath. I guess the trip here took more out of me than I thought. Usually such mild demos don't affect me. Just need to fight this off for a few."

Hanging his head, Nick seemed to drift away as if initiating the world's briefest power nap before arising with renewed color adorning his cheeks.

"Now then... back to the question at hand. Ah yes, the scientific definition of my gift is quite dry, I'm sure, not to mention woefully inaccurate. I'm afraid no earthly version of *Webster's* can truly capture the meaning exactly. Many theories have come my way through the years, none of which were successfully either proven or completely *miss*-proven along the way. To place it in the simplest of terms, let's just say I have the power to rewind any and all actions for a... limited timespan."

"Reply... time?" Jay inquired, his complexion ashen-colored and his usually meticulously coifed do in a comical state of Einstein-like disarray.

"You mean, you're... like a walking, talking DVD player?"

Acknowledging Jay with a cold stare and curt response, it wasn't hard to note the initial crack in Parione's ultracool armor.

"Well, in a sense, though there are no such mechanics involved."

It was then my turn to roll the dice, even as the cobwebs began to clear at least somewhat.

"How exactly does this... skill aid you in fighting crime?"

"Good question," came the cheery reply, the tenseness having instantly left his tone. Suddenly, I was reminded of an overly enthusiastic professor I'd had in college, the type who seemed to be enjoying a continuous caffeine high while discussing even the most mundane of subjects. Pulling his chair away from the conference table, Parione took a seat while propping himself against a far wall. Meanwhile, Burt walked on visually shaky limbs back to his own place and sat back down with deliberate care. I couldn't help but be relieved to find that such blatant disorientation wasn't at all isolated to me alone.

"*Damn* good question, Counselor, the answer to which isn't the least bit complicated but does require some backtracking of history on my part. I discovered what I describe as my personal '*pause and redo*' button around the age of nine in Miss Wilma Beasley's third-grade class, to be specific.

"You see, the class bully had chosen yours truly as his target for the day, shoving me into a dark hallway corner and delivering not only a combination of solid punches to the groin and ribs, but a hard uppercut that had knocked approximately three teeth loose while shattering my glasses against a far wall. Despite the extreme pain and accompanying tears, I wasn't about to allow that fat little Neanderthal jackass to just walk away, much less walk away laughing. Hey, Clark Kent goggles or no, you just don't break a kid's glasses and skip away unscathed. So, laying on that cool tile floor gargling my own blood while trying to catch a breath, I did what any abused kid might, that being wishing with every fiber in my being that the beating had never really happened. Well, before I knew it, the fat slob was standing before me once again, rearing back for that initial gut shot that would position me perfectly for the impending uppercut. Only this time, I had a few extra ticks to prepare and managed to sidestep that first haymaker while simultaneously planting the tip of my size eight Buster Browns directly into the bastard's family jewels. Needless to say, Mr. Tough Guy wasn't nearly as adapt at taking a beating as he was at dishing them out, crying and whining like a three-year old with a skinned knee in the aftermath of the pummeling I'd dished out.

"That kid never bothered me again, nor did I ever find it necessary to rewind a similar episode, as by that time my rep as a young man who spoke softly but carried a mule's kick was sealed in cement around the school grounds."

For the second time in less than a half-hour, Jay somehow misplaced the power of coherent speech.

"So, you were... you're able to actually change... to *alter* real-time events... um, real world events... just by... merely... by wishing it so?"

"World events? No, sir. Events transpiring in and around my own personal space?

"Affirmative, sir. Like I said, it's more of a... rewind effect. For this little... exercise, it was a mere three ticks, but I have been known to reset the timetable as far back as say... several hours if need be. For the record, the longer the rewind, the worse I feel afterwards. Anything over three or four hours and you're apt to find me bent down on all fours barfing up my last meal."

"But... surely there are limitations to how far back you can... rewind?"

Parione shrugged, briefly misplacing his trademark cockiness while averting his eyes to the tabletop.

"Of course... logic dictates, though I must confess the true limitations have yet to be tested."

"Reason being?" Jay replied after a short pause.

"Health mostly... purely self-preservation. I've never attempted anything over a few hours. Considering the full-blown mental and physical meltdown that ensues following such sessions, I figure any attempt to... stretch out a rewind would be... well, might possibly be fatal. There's also the matter of the countless lives I'd inadvertently affect along the way.

"It's... unexplored terrain I'd prefer to keep that way. Don't think the mere notion of... days or even weeks hasn't been a mighty temptation at certain intervals in my life. I just... can't take the chance."

As generally pat and unsatisfactory as the young man's answer had been, it still felt as if someone had just pelted my midsection with a curled fist. Following another three to five second pause, Jay managed to proceed.

"Oh, I... see. Along the same lines, if you don't... alter the events to your satisfaction, can you keep... rewinding until you do?"

Despite the awkward presentation, I couldn't help but be envious at Jay's choice of queries, as I'd been thinking along the exact same lines at the time.

"As the old saying goes," Parione responded wryly, waving a raised forefinger from side to side like a swinging pendulum, "therein lays the rub. Only one chance per incident, I'm afraid. I only get one chance, and obviously there is the matter of a dreadful time limitation, not to mention dealing with the personal aftereffects. Again, there's also the matter of the lives I'd accidentally alter by such actions."

"But... is there also a time limit for how long you might *wait* to initiate a potential... rewind?" I blurted out a bit too loudly, sounding as if I were trying desperately to beat the others to the punch, which I most certainly was. In the background, I saw Burt smile at my comical overexuberance.

"Definitely... *most* definitely... " Parione replied, flashing a warped, toothy smile my way while wiping a strand of dangling hair from his forehead.

It suddenly struck me odd how mature he sounded for a man of twenty-six; a seasoned vet in such a young buck's body. As with Cassie Wilkes, one couldn't wonder how much was sincere or what percentage was perhaps a well-staged, oft-choreographed act.

"There is indeed a deadline on being able to 'back up' time and space, as it were. Through the years I've found that to delay more than a full minute to ninety seconds is to kiss the opportunity adios for all time. You cannot know how many times through the years I've regretted... that such careless hesitations have cost not only myself but those around me. It's a burden... a pressure... that's impossible to describe. When to use it and when *not* to abuse it. Not that I haven't had my share of the latter."

Not quite satisfied, I trudged onward without hesitation.

"And what transpires before the rewind simply didn't... doesn't happen? The slate's wiped completely clean?"

"A hazy memory at best, though I've heard from a small minority that it can result in quite the hangover."

"Count me in... " I said, massaging my temples to alleviate an incessant throbbing at each. "Haven't felt this buzzed since last New Year's."

"My apologies, good sir. Now, concerning past abuses... "

Before continuing, Parione bowed his head as if to pray, "God knows I've wasted the virtues of the gift so often it's a miracle he hasn't stripped me of it by now."

"Please state some examples of said abuse, Mister Parione," Burt stated sternly, all good humor having vanished from both his tone and body language. Always the observant innkeeper of sincerity, it was apparent that the big boss man wasn't completely buying into the act, though the level of suspicion was impossible to gauge. There was little doubt Burt Hanover could spot a phony a city block away, and it seemed the jury was still out on the true character of one Nick 'Dejà vu' Parione.

"You name it, basically. There was a time, most prominently in my late teens to early twenties, that any conversation or event I deemed unsatisfactory was in for a redo of some sort."

Another short pause ensued, during which time Burt began biting his lower lip, usually an indication that a major-league grilling was imminent.

"Example please, Mister Parione. Please be specific."

"Well, I don't want to bore anyone with tales out of season, it's just tha-"

"Please, Nick... bore us. Remember, we're all here to learn. After all, with learning comes understanding."

This time, it was Nick Parione who performed a bit of lip chewing, obviously aware he was being baited, however politely.

"Understood. My apologies, I wasn't trying to sidestep the issue. As I alluded to earlier, I'd often redo simple dialogue if I thought it could benefit me in any way. I might delete ill-advised words or phrases, or even use the fresh start to correct an incorrect answer. Hard to admit, but it became common practice for me to... rephrase opening lines to girls I found... you know, attractive, figuring if one didn't work... perhaps another would.

"There is a reason, good people, that I often speak and... come off like a man ten to fifteen years my senior. Long ago I chalked up rapid maturity as a major side effect of possessing my... gift, for want of a better word."

As Parione grew silent and a tad sullen in the aftermath, the shift from lighthearted banter to a more profound dialogue came to fruition, even the air within the room seemed to grow thick with a newfound anxiety. We all knew where the questioning was headed, as all other avenues had been dully covered.

"An amazing gift, Mister Parione, I must say," Burt chimed in as Parione again wiped a gathering of disheveled bangs from his forehead while staring straight ahead as if entranced.

"Now, let's talk about the issues that have brought you to us. First off, the charges of sexual harassment from four years ago last month. Please elaborate if you will."

Parione licked his lips and released a low groan.

"Cut and dry really, at least legally. During my internship with the X-Men, Storm accused me of groping her during a training session in the Danger Room. Wolverine subsequently threatened to remove my spleen and feed it to me. Needless to say, I was permanently banished from the grounds soon thereafter. End of story. Next?"

Burt flipped through Parione's personnel file to search out a specific document.

"Federal records obtained through Xavier's school show you pleaded not guilty, Nickolaus. Do you still maintain innocence?"

"What's true is true, sir," came the chilled response. "Xavier ran a taut ship inside those hallowed walls, and the bottom line was... I just didn't fit in. Not from day one. I arrived with a rather negative rep, you see, and was unable to locate a suitable mentor who might help assist in dispelling fact from fiction to those who doubted my character."

"A... rep you say? Please explain... "

"A bit of an egomaniac... vain... arrogant... but most of all, and the most hurtful untruth of all... a selfish, unreliable teammate."

"So... you thought... think such accusations unfair... "

To this, Parione's cheeks and forehead reddened even as his voice grew shrill and his demeanor defensive.

"*Damn* right they were! They... still are. Envy can be a powerful force. From such vile jealousy can spring false accusations. Accusations made to ruin; accusations made to destroy. Accusations made not only to derail one's career endeavors, but to mark their very souls for ruination. Each and every charge attached to my name, most notably this latest case of 'she said, I say', is nothing more than a blatant attempt to run me from the business of helping mankind. I ask you, what type of so-called heroine would stoop to such methods in order to see another banned from his true calling, and for no apparent reason other than green-eyed jealousy?"

As his rant had concluded, the young man had banged his fists atop the table, lightly at first but with increased fervor until the entire room seemed to vibrate as from a mild tremor of sorts. It was readily apparent that whatever treatment lay ahead for Nickolaus Parione, he wasn't about to confess to any wrongdoing, despite the mountain of documentation at our disposal that spoke otherwise. I'd learned long ago the power of self-denial was a mighty force indeed, perhaps even surpassing that of Nick Parione's other amazing talent. Though it was far too early in the psychoanalysis game to determine, I had a less-than-pleasant feeling that the young man's problems went far beyond a simple case of self-consciousness or flagrant vanity.

"So, your claim is that each and *every* charge of sexual harassment, including this last incident in late September, are false and fall under the heading of... some sort of conspiracy?" Jay asked, breaking protocol a bit by jumping the chain of command, though Burt seemed less fazed than perhaps relieved.

For his part, Parione showed admirable restraint

when faced with such obvious sarcasm, even managing a pained smile while reaching up to massage the back of his neck.

"Conspiracy might be a tad dramatic, sir. The woman was jealous. Jealous and highly pissed off, not to mention slightly bipolar. Not a good combination that, except as fodder for folks such as yourselves. Anyway, Mindy had me dead in her crosshairs, and fired away with both barrels booming. From what I understand of her past, I was hardly the first man to fall between those lethal sites. She wants to end my career, and a First Degree SH charge was step one in that direction. You see, I'd made the mistake of confiding to her my earlier incident with Storm."

As if on cue from the female perspective, Jessica picked up the questioning in earnest, though I noticed she was being extra cautious not to lock eyes with the client.

"For the record, Nickolaus, you and... Miss Melinda Ward, AKA *The Seeker*, had been assigned as partners by the ATF, DC branch, and were working a major human trafficking case up and down the Florida, Mississippi, and Alabama coastlines."

"Correct. A real quagmire, as it turned out. Bad leads and dead ends turned a two-week assignment into a two-month ordeal. Needless to say, Mindy and I were allotted plenty of extra time to solidify our budding relationship. I won't deny a certain attraction to the girl, at least in the physical sense, despite the extreme mood swings and bouts of borderline insanity. She was a seer, after all, a four-star telepath and three-star levitator. I take it being a five-star *nut* just goes with the territory."

"Personality assassination aside, Mister Parione, you still deny the charges as they stand?"

Combing through his thick, wavy bangs with both hands, Parione's latest grin was less genial than predatory.

"Let me ask you something, Miss Lewis, not as a professional counselor, but as a woman."

Void a verbal response, Jessica merely nodded, albeit cautiously. I had a feeling Mister Dejà vu was about to tread atop painfully thin ice, credibility-wise. Handsome looks aside, Jessica Lewis was one lady not to be trifled with.

"How exactly can you charge a man with any form of sexual harassment once you've partaken in consenting sexual intercourse for an extended period of time?"

"Well, Mister Parione, I'd have to know the specifics of th-"

"I broke it off with her, Miss Lewis. If anything, she wasn't just harassing me, but stalking me. I felt her reading my thoughts... attempting to... alter my decision somehow, entrancing me into returning to the relationship. She even brainwashed my last girlfriend, for God's sake, turned her against me somehow. Of course, I have no concrete proof... but I know it. I *know* she was responsible. Now, you tell me... who's the harasser here and who's the harass-ee?"

In lieu of a response, Jessica wisely turned the proceedings back over to the top banana.

"This isn't a trial, Nickolaus," Burt said in one of his many 'kindly old Judge Hanover' incarnations, "it isn't about guilt or innocence, nor is it about perception. It's about adjustment. It's about mindset. We want to see you cleared and back out there doing what you do best. All we ask is that you give our program a fair shake. We promise to so likewise in terms of you departing this facility with a clean slate. Agreed?"

"Fair enough, sir. I... apologize for my... for the outburst. I'm afraid the mere mention of Min- of The Seeker tends to bring out the raving beast in me. Of course I'll cooperate in any way possible."

"Fine. We couldn't ask for anything more."

As Nick Parione departed, flashing a double-fisted 'peace sign' that seemed more for Jessica's sake than the rest of us, I noted with great relief the faded remnants of the migraine symptoms generated by the rewind episode. With ten full minutes having passed since the experience, and despite the irrefutable evidence that it had indeed transpired, a small part of me still doubted its validity. No denying I still had a lot to learn about hero types and their flare for the incredible, and I had a sinking feeling said lessons might well be of the *hard way* variety.

***

Personal File D-135:

Subject: Benjamin Thomason

Trade Name: (*Government copyright*): Force (previously '*Desolation Outlaw*')

Federally licensed since: March 13, 1996

License suspended since: November 26, 2013

Reason for suspension: Charged with three cases of aggravated assault on subordinates

Note: alcohol-related (has history of similar behavior).

"Are you sure you're up to this just now, Mister Thomason? I mean, we can delay if you don't feel-"

"Just a little hangover, Mac. More like the atom bomb of all hangovers, but it'll pass... eventually. Don't think a few hours is gonna help in the healin' process, though, so let's just press on."

From minute one of our initial interview, it was apparent that Benjamin Thomason, AKA 'Force', was going to be one tough nut to crack. Thomason was a gruff, foul-mouthed, twentieth-century fossil from which every spoken syllable screamed political incorrectness (possibly just an act; an elaborate cloaking device). It had already been rumored the man was bullheadedness personified in terms of making nice with the other clients, instead playing the disinterested loner part to the hilt. This of course could and more than likely *would* birth future conflict with both the clients and staff. If there was one thing we'd learned from past classes, it was that the bond created within their tight-knit unit was vital to overall program success. In other words, it mattered little how many introverts or odd couples were assigned initially, as long as the sense of camaraderie existed upon their exiting the Outpost on graduation day. In reading over Thomason's past rap sheet, it appeared it was going to take a Herculean effort from all involved to convince him of the team player philosophy.

"Hangover? Mister Thomason, you do realize that willful possession of alcoholic beverages within this compound is not only highly illegal, but also punishable by permanent banishment from further classes?" Burt replied sternly, once again utilizing his patented 'teacher politely scolds naughty student' tone.

"Don't get your panties in a wad, Mac. I've had the same skullthrobber since the assigned hover left Vegas. Sad but true. I surely ain't the highly skilled souse I used to be. Guess that's a good thing."

"Definitely, Mister Thomason, most definitely. I apologize for jumping to such a rash conclusion."

The man waved Burt off with a hand easily twice the size of my own. 'Snow-shovel-mitts', Jay had quipped upon viewing Thomason's file photo a few days earlier. With his brownish-gray locks, bushy brows and Fu Manchu-styled caterpillar-thick mustache (also streaked in gray), he resembled a character from a 19th century Western, perhaps an infamous gunslinger or high-stakes gambler/dandy. Flashing heavily tattooed biceps and forearms so chiseled and finely toned they appeared lifted from the illustrated pages of a graphic novel, Thomason's apparel of choice was simplicity in itself: light green muscle-tee (sleeveless), faded blue jeans and dark brown cowboy boots.

"No problem. It ain't as if I don't warrant such suspicion, Hoss. I noticed ya all flippin' through foot-thick file folders. Damn if *that* don't hold some seriously incriminatin' info on yours truly, I'd wager."

Despite my best efforts, I couldn't pry my focus from the man's grotesquely oversized hands, seemingly as large as regulation basketballs when fisted. One could only imagine the carnage that could be inflicted by such weapons. His federal license had been suspended the past November following thirteen years of noteworthy, if not somewhat erratic, service, for reasons similar to those of Scar Fletcher.

"Oh, and I'll try my best not to wave these around too much," Thomason said, as if reading my mind. "The old meat hooks do have a tendency to hypnotize."

"We'll... manage, Mister Thomason. Now, to begin there is the matter of a questionnaire that will immediately aid us in getting to know you better... "

Having donned a mask of indifference, Ben Thomason's lazily delivered responses revealed no real favorite color to speak of (*'got nothin' against blue, I guess, though I never really thought about it... as no real man oughta'*), while his choices for film (*'does porn count?'*) and television *('never had that much downtime-but I did catch that old serial* Heroes *a few times-what a hoot... funniest shit I ever saw... knee-slappin' hilarious*!') was similarly uninspired.

When queried concerning a possible alteration in either his appearance or personality, Thomason simply titled his head and lifted his oversized hands airborne.

"Yer jokin', right?"

Soon after, Ben announced his favorite song as *Hair of the Dog* by a 1970s hard rock band called Nazareth.

"Just listen to the lyrics, man... you'll dig 'em if you've met and mingled with half as many certified SOBs as I have."

As with the Nick Parione interview, it wasn't until Burt poised the embarrassing episode query that the big man appeared mildly piqued and things grew interesting.

"Ya mean like wettin' the bed or fartin' in church?"

"Um, if... that's something you'd like to reveal, I'd say yes," Burt replied with a barely restrained chuckle, "though we'd... prefer something a bit more... well, on an adult level, you understand."

"Oh yeah... gotcha."

Thomason paused for quite a spell, squirming in his seat like an antsy grade-schooler with a weak bladder.

"Bingo... got it!" he finally verbalized with a loud snapping of fingers. "Sorry for the rain delay... just didn't wanna shortchange ya, that's all, least not on the first day of school."

"No problem, Benjamin... please elaborate."

"Well, this was in my *Desolation Outlaw* phase, a few years before I redonned the *Force* duds and signed up for federal assignments full-time."

"Sorry to interrupt, Benjamin," Burt interceded with a raised hand, "but why exactly did you shed the *Force* persona to begin with? I'm afraid our files are a bit sketchy on details."

"Just tryin' to distance myself... for various reasons I'd prefer not to jaw about just yet. Character-wise, it kinda freed me up to let off some steam. The Outlaw was more of a rogue... a free spirit with a definite dark side. Problem was, it wasn't long before I felt the dark takin' over and decided to break out more familiar duds."

"I see. Well, we'll have plenty of time to delve into that at a later date. I apologize for the change in direction... just curious. Please continue... "

In a recharged tone that was positively chipper compared to his earlier, rather fatigued monotone, Ben Thomason's admission was equal parts comedic monologue and sports play-by-play commentary.

"I'd trailed some electrical-charged baddie named *Power-Surge* to a power plant just outside of Toledo... Toledo for cripe's sake! (shakes his head in amusement) ... anyhow, the feds wanted this hairball brought down something fierce... seems he'd been sabotagin' similar plants all over the Eastern Seaboard in a one-man protest against who the hell knows what. Hey (shrugs), it was the late '90s and power bills were up all over. Anyhow, long story short... I did find, face down and capture my quarry... but not without a totally unexpected cameo appearance to gum up the works. I'd just managed to bring Surge down by hog-tyin' his static-charged ass with a thick strand of rubber tubing when who crawls outta the woodwork but none other than Doctor David Bruce Banner, moanin', groanin, and growlin' while already in mid-transformation. In his infinite lack of wisdom, Power-Surge had kidnapped the doc and was plannin' on some kinda whacked-out gamma radiation transfer to increase his own power by about a thousandfold."

"Pardon me, Mister Thomason," I asked with the excitement of a preteen boy when speaking of a childhood idol, "you're talking about... the *Hulk*, right?"

"One and the same, Counselor." Ben nodded kindly enough, though I could read the underlying frustration in his movements from still another unprovoked query.

"Bein' that this was my first time sharin' space

with big, green and ugly, I had nothin' to go by but his rep as the strongest, meanest SOB on the planet. I'd heard there was no reasonin' with 'im, and you either stood your ground when he looked your way or hightailed it to safer climes. As it was and... I reckon still is in most cases... I never was one for backin' down from a challenge. Sure as shootin', once he'd finished up gainin' about eight or nine pant sizes, he rumbled my direction with both fists pumpin', no doubt figurin' me for Power-Surge's ally.

"Well, not bein' as old or wise in my twenties as I claim to be these days, I planted my boots firmly and braced for impact, all the while ignorin' Surge's pleadin' cries to get us both the hell outta there before a major-league squashin' commenced. Havin' grown tired of hearin' his girly beggin', I used the rubber robe to sling 'im face-first into a nearby steel girder and temporarily turn out his lights.

"But... as it turned out, Surge had a valid point. Once I'd nailed ol' jade jaws with my best right hook and got nothin' but an annoyed smirk in response, I recall this sickenin' feelin' deep down in my gut just a blink before the big guy backhanded me about sixty feet into the nearest stone wall.

"Now for the embarrassin' part (pauses, sighs) ... not that bein' swatted across the room like a common housefly wasn't degradin' enough. Once I did stumble to my feet, I... uh... well, I did somethin' I hadn't done before or since. I... ugh... kinda took the high road. Yep... ran outta there as fast as my wobbly legs could take me, leavin' my quarry to the mercy of one highly pissed off Jolly Green Giant.

By the time I did regain my senses, not to mention my balls as a whole, I reentered the facility and found Power-Surge just as I'd left 'im, bound and unconscious but without a single fresh bruise. I did notice a large, round hole in the ceilin' of the place, so I could only figure the Hulk had just stared 'im down and hopped away for greener... um... newer pastures. As it was, I hauled ol' lightning bolt outta there by his rubber binds and collected my fee without sharin' a hint about the Hulkster's presence, much less the ass kickin' I'd taken from same.

"So that's about it, gang. Up until now I'd never told anyone, not even Leah... that's the wife... about my choosin' flight over fight. Since this little session falls under the headin' of confidential, I'd surely appreciate said facts remaining filed away... as in locked and far away from the public domain, if ya grasp my hint. Tainted as it is at times, I do have a rep to consider."

"No problem, Benjamin. That goes without saying," Burt replied as the rest of us nodded in perfect synchronicity as if to punctuate his words.

"Have you... had any chance encounters with the Hulk... since that time?" Jay then blurted out, the final few words spoken in a hesitant whisper, as if perhaps fearful of the response.

I was pleasantly surprised when Thomason's reply was accompanied by a wide, toothsome grin.

"Nope, and, brother, it ain't exactly like I'm pinnin' for a rematch."

Once again, the group laughed as one, followed by a short, silent respite before a verbal shifting of gears ensued.

"Benjamin," Burt began in an obvious change

of direction, "it must be noted that a great portion of information concerning your last position for the government has been omitted or blacked out from your file for security reasons. With that in mind, we won't ask for specifics such as locations, names, and so forth. Instead we'll focus on the details of the incident itself."

Stroking the tip of his beard with a thumb and forefinger, Thomason's eyes narrowed in apparent suspicion.

"Shit, I figured you folks for the highest possible security clearance. Huh, go figure... "

"The staff does indeed hold level three clearances, Benjamin, but there still exists that rare instance when the 'need to know' factor comes into play. As for the incident, it is alleged you instigated an unprovoked attack on three co-workers, each of whom were brutally beaten and subsequently hospitalized. It was also stated you were taken into custody by a superior who was also a former teammate from the late '90s Supergroup *The Revenge Squad.*"

At this juncture, both Thomason's expression and body posture screamed disinterest-not exactly a glowing testimonial for a man so fervently confessing his guilt and was eager to make amends.

"Further, it was later confirmed via medical tests that you were well over twice the legal limit of alcohol consumption at the time of the assaults, and that this was hardly your first such incident. Currently, your former superior is being taken to task by a federal investigative board for covering up similar occurrences within the past year.

"You've been assigned to us as a code red anger

management prospect, meaning your problem has been deemed extreme and will require a unanimous vote from all staff members for reinstatement. For the record, you've pleaded guilty of instigating the brawl of November 19th of this past year. Please elaborate."

"Lord, Hoss, ain't this all covered in the manila bookends there?" Thomason replied with little zeal, pointing at the plump personnel file Burt had been using as an armrest.

"Don't wanna be a pain, but I've had to repeat this same spiel so many times it's startin' to sound more like myth than reality, even to the *author*, ya know? Cut a guy some slack. I'll be a helluva lot sharper after a warm meal... a nice, drawn-out power nap, and maybe a syringe loaded with B-12. Well, what do ya say? Just playin' truth and consequences has worn me to a frazzle."

"It's an in-processing requirement, Benjamin. The staff and I must witness your statement firsthand. Please commence... "

"Gotcha." The big man sighed, nodding solemnly. "Typical government red-tape horseshit. Ho-kay troops, here's the gist, in order of occurrence, takin' into consideration of course that I was approximately eighteen sheets in the wind at the time. An eight-pack of longneck Bud Ultras and a half-dozen shots of Gold Prime Tequila don't exactly improve long or short-term memory, ya understand. Anyhow, hold onto your privates, 'cause awwaaaaay we go... "

Approximately eighteen minutes later, Thomason's surprisingly detailed story ended, appropriately enough, with the word 'regret'.

Despite his outer gruffness and consistent, sometimes blatant use of profanity, the man had managed to come off as relatively sincere.

Leaning back with his massive hands hidden beneath the tabletop (having remained that way throughout the regaling), Thomason appeared to have grown utterly exhausted in the telling.

"So this... the warden, he immediately placed you on a probation of some sort?" Burt finally asked, having paused to give our client a much-needed sabbatical.

"Yeah, Lucas Bradley, AKA *The Guardsman*... an old teammate from the Squad. Damned good Joe, ol' Luke. Hated to put his ass in such a tight sling with the big boys."

Burt quickly flashed a raised hand in mild panic.

"Um, names are not necessary, Benjamin."

"No big deal, Hoss, it ain't like you got the resources or wherewithal to check the details, right? Luke hired me on as Chief Correctional Officer some four years back followin'... well, the prison site had kinda a... forced overhaul ya might say."

Having obviously seen Pandora's box flung wide open, Jay practically hopped out of his own flesh to spew forth the next inquiry.

"What... type of facility hires... specially endowed types such as yourself as... as common help... "

I could almost feel the searing heat shoot forth from Burt's glaring eyes, a sensation no doubt felt by my erstwhile cohort a split second later.

"That is... if you're able to... divulge such information," Jay concluded in a stilted whisper, diverting his own gaze from Burt's red-faced glare to the relative safety of the tabletop. Thomason replied blandly, all the earlier edginess having exited his tone.

"No problem, bud. Like I said, it ain't like none of this can be confirmed, least not by you folks. Anybody ya tell would just shrug it off as some kinda acid-induced fairy tale. The place was... is, in a nutshell, a federal pen built to house the baddest motherfu- um, worst supervillains the world has to offer. No run-of-the-mill murderers, rapists, or thieves need apply, no sir... *Desolation Island...* yep, that was the official name awarded to her by Uncle Sam, was built... actually *rebuilt*, to play host to killer muties, flesh-gnawin' aliens, and schemin' madmen... only those deemed a true planetary security risk. I was given the job to keep 'em locked in and away from good folks such as yourselves. It was a good ride, least for a while. But," he paused with a wry smile while staring up into the tiled ceiling, "as with everything else positive in my life, over time I eventually managed to fu- um, screw it up... in spades."

"Desolation... Island?" Jessica asked timidly while wearing a mask of skepticism.

"And where exactly is this secret facility located, Mister Thomason, the continent of *Oz*?"

For an individual infamous for his volcanic temper, Thomason did well to maintain an even keel despite Jessica's rather lame attempt at humor.

"Close enough, lady. In fact, that ain't nearly as farfetched as the truth."

"Understood," Burt wisely intervened, "it isn't important. What is, however, is that I see this latest eruption on your part was only the last in a series starting several months previous. Going by dates alone, I can only speculate that these incidents seemed to coincide with the departure of a co-worker who just happened to be your aforementioned wife, a Miss Leah Chang, also known as Marvella. Am I far off base, Benjamin?"

"Just call me Ben, Hoss," Thomason grumbled amiably enough, though there appeared to be an undercurrent of hostility present in his much-too jovial tone. "No need to be formal, right? We're gonna be sharin' a lotta face time in the next several weeks."

"Alright, Ben, then you may refer to me as Burt in lieu of Hoss or Mac."

"Agreed."

"Now, concerning my earlier theory concerning your wife... "

"Right as rain, Bart. Don't wanna sound like I'm makin' excuses for my horse's ass behavior, but... Leah's absence in my life hasn't exactly turned me into Slappy the happy clown."

"Burt."

"Sorry. Nail directly on the head, Burt. No denials there. Losin' an assistant chief and spouse in the same lump didn't do a helluva lot for my demeanor."

"You two had worked together for...?"

"About a year in the squad... that was back in the late '90s, and three and a half more on the Island. Ya might say we were hired as a team. Came aboard at the same exact time."

"And you were married soon after the dual hiring?"

"Oh, 'bout three, four months later. Could've been sooner, but we were busier than a pair of one-armed paperhangers what with an influx of CO recruit classes and the like."

"Did you generally enjoy working together?"

"It was a real hoot. Leah was a real pro. Not at all sore on the old peepers either, if I do say so myself... 'specially in those flamin' red spandex tights... "

Though his personality profile stated Thomason had a penchant for truth-stretching now and again, one peek at Leah Chang's file photo, dressed to the nines as the aforementioned heroine 'Marvella', did little to discredit his claim. *Translation*: the woman wasn't merely attractive, but what the entertainment industry used to refer to as drop-dead gorgeous, a true Asian killer in every sense of the word, though also possessing an aura of edgy intimidation equally seductive. It may sound cold, perhaps even a tad cruel, but one never thinks of such endowed types, those essentially commissioned from birth as Sentinels, as protectors, as even possessing human frailties, or moreover, requiring basic human needs such as love and companionship. Clearly, this young counselor had a lot to learn.

"Even in such a... potentially depressing atmosphere?"

"Lemme tell ya, Hos- um, Brian, it was a pleasant, lakeshore breeze compared to doin' our hero thing out on the mean streets. At least in the pen, we knew *exactly* where the bad guys were at all times."

"That's... Burt, Benjamin... Burt Hanover."

All laughed aloud at this latest faux pas save

Miss Jessica, whose bland, emotionless expression spelled out daydream in brightly lit neon, though our group giggle was quite effective in snapping her out of it.

"Sorry, pal... never was too sharp with names, least not 'til I get to know ya better."

"Accepted. So the working couple issue was never a problem between you two?"

"Not that I know of... we... I tried like hell to ensure we both worked a similar shift, if ya know what I'm sayin'."

"You never felt that perhaps you were spending too much time together?"

"Surely not from my perspective... 'course I can't speak for my better half. She probably got tired of hearin' my daily rant, and she cracked on me every now and then, but only in a jokin' manner."

"What then, caused the split, Ben?"

"Twofold, I'd wager," Ben Thomason replied, his mannerisms growing increasingly animated. It was as if as soon as the subject of Leah Chang had been breached, the weariness that had dogged him instantly dissipated. Burt had definitely struck a raw nerve, having drudged up the lone subject that even such a legendary tough guy/curmudgeon was unable to simply shrug off as inconsequential.

"First off, I'd say the first serious crack was my fallin' off the wagon after three full years of sobriety. Startin'... hangin' out with the boys. Knockin' down a few after hours, you how it is. Well, wasn't long before a few turned into a few dozen. Again, no excuses, but such a job does come with its full-tilt pressures. I mean, one of those intergalactic nutjobs escapes, the entire planet might be in for a hurtin'. It ain't... wasn't like babysittin' a passel of pickpockets, ya know? Anyhow, bottom line is this: I'm... a weak man in a lotta ways. Leah knew this when we hooked up. I guess she figured, over time, I'd cleared that particular hurdle. Guess I'd just been sidesteppin' it, is all."

"And... the second reason?"

"The job, the setting, the whole shebang grew tiresome for her. She'd been makin' a pretty fair livin' as a clothes designer in Chi-Town when the whole Desolation Island thing had blown up and she'd felt a sense of obligation to yours truly. If not for that, I don't think Leah would've ever pulled on the tights again. There were times I could read how depressed the whole hero-for-hire thing made her. Unlike me and most of my kind, she had another talent to fall back on."

Ben paused, taking in several deep breaths as if concluding a lengthy sprint. He'd sunk back into a state of apparent mental and physical fatigue, the overall hangdog look reappearing as fast as it had earlier vanished.

"So she's plying that other trade these days?"

"Yeah, got an email from her the day before my transport here. She... sounded content enough, 'course I know a part of that might be just keepin' busy at doin' something she really enjoys. Right now she's puttin' in fourteen, sixteen-hour days, no doubt just to keep my knuckleheaded high jinx off her mind."

"So she... understands your present plight?"

"Yeah, I told her what went down. She didn't sound the least bit surprised, sayin' I'd been a tickin' timebomb for the past year... year and a half. She'd even warned me of such on a regular basis. I ain't denyin' I'd only grown ornerier since Eighth Degree... uh, Jarod King's arrival as Leah's so-called replacement. Slimy jackass had been pinin' for my job since day one. Still, I could've handled it a damn sight better than gettin' loaded and wipin' up the floor with his worthless hide. Buuuttt, ya know what they say about hindsight, right?"

"So, this trial separation from your wife is of the temporary sort?"

Wiping his face and forehead with a massive palm, so large in scale it temporarily blocked out the majority of his skull, Ben regarded Burt with as grave an expression as I'd witnessed that day, though his piercing brown eyes held a small but tangible smidgen of hopefulness. Yes, the big lummox was unable to mask his true feelings concerning a certain life-partner, no matter how concerted the effort.

"Lord knows I pray so, Mister Hanover... Burt. Leah was... *is still* the only positive I've got to hang onto right about now."

"Good to hear, Ben. Tell me, do you plan on returning to this... penitentiary once you've successfully completed our course?"

"For now I'd say yeah... if they'll have me."

"Does your wife... does Leah support this decision?"

"She pretty much insisted on it, knowin' how well I did the job... once."

"Do you think she'll consider returning with you?"

"We ain't quite ironed that part of the plan out

yet. I'd like to think she would, but if not, we'll work it out somehow... someway. I'll tell ya this though... Leah's more important to me than any job. If I have to reemploy myself to catchin' the bad guys again instead of just housin' 'em, it'll be no sweat off my cowl."

Just as things seemed to be winding down to a remarkably serene conclusion, considering the present client and the history of instability he'd brought to the session, Jay had to unfurl once last, completely unnecessary query; an ill-advised, borderline unprofessional query that came off sounding more like an accusation.

"So basically, Mister Thomason, what you're indicating is this latest bout of lashing out was more about a failing marriage than potentially losing your job to a better man?"

Just that quickly, Thomason's lethargic movements and bone-weary appearance mutated into fire-breathing dragon status, his eyes spewing flames, his words shrill and confrontational.

"Yeah, Slick, I kinda figured that was self-explanatory by this point in the game, though I will state, for the record, that this 'better man' ya mentioned was long overdue for an old-fashioned ass-kickin'."

"Mister Thomason, we are here to assist you with documented anger and/or chemical dependency issues, not take sides concerning individuals we have not and will not ever meet," Jay responded, stupidly pressing the issue while inexplicably feeling the need to begin the psychoanalytical phase several sessions prematurely.

To his credit, Thomason kept relatively cool, dismissing Jay in lieu of flashing Burt a wry smile that reeked of comical bemusement.

"Slick makes a decent point, Burt. Guess this is all about the 'tough love' element rearin' its ugly mug, huh?"

"Not at all, Benjamin," Burt countered, shooting Jay an *if looks could kill you'd be cold on a concrete slab* glare, "just an overzealous counselor jumping the gun a bit, isn't that right, Mister Peterson?"

Looking as if he'd swallowed his pocket pc, charger and all, Jay gulped before responding in a subdued mumble.

"I apologize, Mister Thomason. I sincerely didn't mean to come off so... abrasive. Definitely a fault I need some work on."

Using an open hand the circumference of a partially opened umbrella, Ben Thomason waved him off.

"Awww, forget it, Ray. Vodka under the bridge, so to speak. I'm sure you and I'll be goin' face-to-face in the future, and I sure don't want ya holdin' back your professional opinion from fear of a potential butt-smackin'."

I figure Jay momentarily considered correcting the 'Ray' comment, but thought better of it and simply nodded amiably.

"We appreciate your time and honesty, Benjamin," Burt finished, having placed Thomason's file atop the other three sitting directly to his left.

"We'll continue the paperwork portion of in-processing in the morning. Until then, you'll be fed, given clothing and personal item issue before being escorted to your personal quarters. Sleep in if you'd like... phase two won't commence until ten a.m."

Thomason nodded without speaking, rising gingerly as if nursing numerous bodily injuries.

"Thanks, Burt... um, people," he said with a half-bow. "Hope ya got an extra blanket stashed away somewhere... Old Man Winter might have somethin' nasty brewin' just over the horizon. I can almost feel the chill in these creaky old bones... "

Burt tossed him a Boy Scout two-finger salute.

"Ah yes, the initial glacier-turf warning. We'll be briefing you and the others on the rather... unique weather conditions here in the valley. Take care and get some rest, Benjamin."

Thomason returned the salute weakly and slumped off like the badly hobbled victim of a recent vehicular crash.

"Not to sound overly retro, but that's one beat-down dude," I offered once a good half-minute had passed since the man's departure.

"In more ways than one, I'm afraid," Jessica countered. "I personally rank him as hands down the biggest challenge within the class."

Jay snickered while shoving his copies of the class personnel folders into a massive attache case.

"*Hands* down, Jes? As in... shovel?"

"No pun intended, of course." She grinned seductively, and I couldn't help but feel a twinge of nausea at the sickeningly sweet exchange. Their '*secret*' affair was anything but by this time, though we as a staff had continued to act as though we had no inkling.

"That's enough, you two. I would hope we're

above such juvenile ridicule concerning someone's personal looks," Burt said firmly, packing away his own collection of manila folders into a heavily taped cardboard box.

"It's now ten past four. I suggest each of you re-read the personnel folders sometime this evening. Now that we've met the people behind the paper-trail, it might just provide a keener insight to what makes them tick.

"By the way, better tuck in nice 'n warm tonight, kids. As Mister Thomason alluded to, the latest satellite reports are hinting at a bit of the nasty stuff."

We departed the conference room in single file, all going our separate ways save Jay and Jessica, who no doubt had their own brand of study time in mind.

Later that night, after a sizeable dinner and a half-hour of shooting pool in the TV/Rec room, I did indeed reinvestigate each personnel file with a fresh perspective. My conclusion in terms of ranking the clients on a scale of potentially most troubled to least varied somewhat from Miss Jessica's, as the image of one individual in particular kept shoving its way into the forefront. Despite Ben Thomason's legendary temper, Tate Fletcher's questionable devotion to our program and Nick Parione's fervent denials, it was Cassie Yates without question who poised the clearest challenge. Either that, or perhaps it was the vague yet tangible attraction I'd felt in the woman's clearly unstable presence. True, there was an obvious curiosity factor when dealing with a multiple personality, but it obviously wasn't that simple. There was also the element of danger, of helping to unlock a door to freedom from such a crippling mental state. Indeed I wanted to help the woman, first and foremost. I also wanted to know her, each *rendition* of her, while simultaneously attempting to play modern-day exorcist and allow the most dominant personality to become sole key-holder to the kingdom.

Just the thought of such a monumental challenge tripped my pulse into overdrive in a frenzied mix of exhilaration and excitement, though accompanied by an overwhelming sense of dread.

One thing appeared certain: whatever else resulted from our initial class in dealing with superhero-types, it was a safe bet the word 'boredom' would never factor into the equation.

Chapter Two

Ice World/Detoxification 101/Something Tragically Amiss

The initial whiteout of the winter season, so affectionately referred to by the locals as a 'glacier turf incident' hammered the Outpost that very first night, the eve of our first day of school, as it were. Though it wasn't of the full-blown variety, the overall effect of which would result in a post-wide HDBU (Hunker Down & Bundle Up) order, the storm still ranked as quite the chiller nonetheless, with sleet buildups measured at anywhere from two to three and a half inches within the compound perimeter. Luckily, with midday temps reaching upwards of thirty-seven balmy degrees accompanied by bright sunlight, the majority of the hockey rink effect dissipated by late evening. Obviously, this particular blower was meant as merely a sneak preview for what was to come over the next several weeks, when an entire region spanning approximately three-hundred-fifty square miles would be transformed from northwestern US climes to those more befitting of land mapped under the heading of Antarctica or Greenland.

One could logically ponder why the powers that be chose such an isolated, desolate location to construct the facility, though in truth the answer was truly a no-brainer. The lack of distraction played a major role, as did the potential healing effects of being stationed in such a spacious, picturesque setting, nestled between beauteous mountain ranges. As for the horrific winter weather that pounded the compound unmercifully during the veritable ice age months of November through early March, that had been purely accidental. Known for brutal winters even pre-BGW (Before Global Warming), the previous two seasons had seen seasonal temps drop an additional ten to twelve degrees while enduring an extra three to five feet of extra precipitation, most of it in the form of freezing rain and sleet. Concerned with the aura of forced isolation such extreme elements wrought, Burt had suggested to upper management that perhaps the facility should only remain open during spring and summer sessions, but to no avail, no doubt for political as well as financial reasons. After all, the clients in question were no longer simple working folk attempting detox in order to reestablish a sense of worth, but bona fide, federal license carrying heroes whose individual cures had been deemed priority one. *Bottom lin*e: Weather-related woes and staff concerns be damned, the program went on full steam ahead. The post had supposedly been equipped with a state-of-the-art generator and subsequent backup, not to mention three to four month stashes of food and emergency medical supplies. As a counselor, you understood and duly accepted the possibility of being away from family and friends for lengthy periods.

In all honesty, there was a sense of adventure in being assigned to Jasper Ridge that few other facilities could match, though stark (dare I say 'cold hard') reality could truly be a sharp slap in the face upon initially arriving on post. Personally, I'd craved the aforementioned excitement, choosing to apply to Jasper Ridge over several dozen potential suitors, most of which offered a safe, by-the-numbers position complete with mundane tasks and stereotypical clients. Of course, just qualifying was no given, especially in terms of obtaining such a high security clearance. I'd heard only one in ten counselors made the final grade, the last hurdle being a lie detector test that had proven to be an applicant terminator of sorts. As it was, I passed with flying colors and was accepted for the new program just months before its initiation. Weather-wise, I'd informed the hiring board that Jasper's annual tundralike conditions were of little concern. After all, this boy had been Wisconsin born and bred, so whatever brand of chill the upper Northwest could dish out was of very little concern to such a thick-skinned yank, right? Oh, so very, very wrong. Well, such is the price we pay for unchecked cockiness blended with just a touch of naivete.

Perhaps as a foreboding precursor for the plethora of ills to come, the area was drenched in a torrential downpour of freezing rain on the eve of our initial class session, followed by an eleven-inch snowfall that essentially quarantined us onto the post grounds until further notice. As a general rule, the area endured between approximately eight to ten such glacier-turf storms per season, usually starting in early December and ending in late March or early April. If the first was any indication, it was going to be a brutal stretch, being that the storms were infamous for their increased intensity as weeks passed and the warming sunlight's daily intrusion became less and less frequent.

Alas, if only bitterly cold temperatures and hockey rink ground conditions were to be the summit of our tribulations that particular season. Truly, it is to laugh, albeit sarcastically.

Following day one's in-processing and the next day's face-to-face interviews (consisting of each counselor conducting an informal chat with each client) the third day of the program had called for our initial group session. To say it didn't go as smoothly or incident free as we'd have liked is a woeful understatement. Burt had placed Jay Peterson in charge, not out of any set agenda or battlefield promotion type act, but basically because it was Jay's turn to chair an in-house training exercise; something we'd all eventually be charged with as sessions progressed. I have to confess in the aftermath of session one, a disorganized debacle from the word go, that being handed the temporary title of core counselor wasn't something I looked forward to in the least. Before that day, I never would have thought it possible to feel even a twinge of sorrow for an individual so naturally prone to arrogance as Jay. As events progressed and voices rose, however, I couldn't help but think the man wanted nothing more than to curl up in the nearest corner and suck his thumb. In truth, I might've felt a similar urge given the same scenario.

"Just calm down, Tate, I'm sure she... I'm sure Cassan- um, Cassie is regretful of her actions. Isn't that correct, Miss Wilkes? Cassie, please apologize to Tate... "

"Regret? Sorry? Wise up and stay out of this, four-eyes... and quit putting words in my mouth or I'm apt to walk over there and dropkick your testicles onto the nearest wall. Soldier boy was damned lucky he ducked in time or he'd be chomping that nasty ass tobacco with his gums."

"See there, pal? Wacky broad didn't take a poke at me by accident. I'm not one to retaliate against women, but you'd best see to it her bipolar back end keeps a safe distance from *wherever* I am from here on out."

"Or what, G.I. Joe? You thinking about taking me on? I wouldn't advise it, robocrap. Even if I can't take you, I guaran-*by god*-tee that big sis most assuredly can."

"Jesus, Ben... you wanna put a leash on your groupie chick?"

Benjamin's face crinkled in comical disgust, though it appeared he was on the very edge of bursting into hysterics.

"Whoa, Tate... leave me the hell outta this."

"Well, she's your fan club prez. Tell her to heel or toss her a rawhide chewy or something... "

With that, Benjamin nodded in apparent bewilderment, though he failed miserably in cloaking the wide grin that followed. "Aw, shit on a toasted shingle. Cas, how's about clammin' up and calmin' the hell down."

The young woman stubbornly stood her ground, growing increasingly animated. At this point, her spiked hair had begun to unfurl a bit at the tips and was beginning to resemble a bird's nest constructed of tiny lawn sprinklers.

"But, Ben, the man insulted you. You didn't deserve that crack, especially from some battlefield burnout held together by bobby pins and Super Glue."

"It wasn't an insult, lady... it was an observation. Go ahead and ask the man himself how he interpreted it. Go ahead... ask him. And for the record, it's paper clips and *Crazy* Glue."

Utilizing a particularly pathetic sense of timing, Jay picked that very moment to play *listen to the teacher*.

"Um... very good, Tate... very good suggestion. Perhaps we can clear up this misunderstanding by addressing the man in quest-"

"I told you to put a sock in it, Mister Peepers. This conversation is strictly for combat vets only... no belly button gazers allowed."

"But Miss Wilkes... Cassan- Cassie... Tate made a very good sugges-"

Benjamin smacked a flat palm hard against the slick tabletop, causing everyone present save perhaps Tate and Cassie to openly cringe in reflex.

"Pipe down, Sigmund, and let me answer the question, for cripe's sake."

"By all means... precede then, Benjamin," Jay practically whimpered.

As I previously stated, I was happily content in thinking 'better him than me'.

"That's *Force* to you, bud."

It may sound a tad cruel, but not only did I relish the harsh treatment being doled out to the staff Romeo, but figured the man had earned it to a degree with his condescending dialogue and 'I'm the counselor, you're the troubled one' attitude.

"V-very well, Force. Please continue."

"Cas, I didn't take Tate's... statement personally. Fact is, the man made a valid point, however painful it is for me to take. I do have a problem fittin' in with the group dynamic-always have. Even in my days with the Revenge Squad, I only got along with

Leah, Darkclaw and maybe Johnny Reb... squabbled like hell with everyone else, usually to the point of physical threats. Plus which, I couldn't take orders for shit, made it a point to go directly against 'em in fact. I'm just... I was just more comfortable as a solo act, that's all."

Pacing the floor like mad while filling the open air with a never-ending barrage of spastic, gyrating gestures, Cassie Wilkes appeared the quintessential bipolar stereotype.

"But... shit! It may sound the definition of cornball, but you're a legend in this business. Anyone who's walked the walk and talked the talk with such luminaries as Captain America, Iron Man, Thor and the Hulk shouldn't have *any* part of his character questioned, I say."

"Hell's *bell's,* Cas, get over it. I took a swing at roughly half the individuals you just named, and in the case of the Jolly Green Giant there, I feel damned fortunate to still be breathin' to tell the tale. It ain't like I've been bosom buddies with any of the higher echelon types-more like blind luck we stumbled onto one another while workin' the same case."

With that, Tate Fletcher reached over and lightly clapped Benjamin atop the right shoulder.

"Now that's impressive. Honest as the day is long. Sounds like you and I have a lot in common, big guy. Men like us are a lost breed. Keep it simple; tell it like it is, no matter whosoever it might royally tick off."

"No argument, man," Ben replied with a wink, landing a purposely toothless jab against the other man's upper left bicep. "Life's too short, leastways in our chosen career field, to waste time mincin' words or polishin' turds."

Cassie appeared openly sickened at the two men's obvious connection, the origin of which wasn't the least bit surprising to even the semitrained eye-after all, both were of similar age and demeanors. Old-school warriors with old-school trains of thought-dinosaurs to those too young to comprehend; idols to many within the same age bracket.

"You're a card, Thomason," Fletcher said with a nod.

"Right back atcha, Fletch," Ben shot back with a grin. "You and I definitely need to toss back a few cold ones one of these days... " he paused, the last few words trailing off as he suddenly appeared a bit embarrassed, "that is... uh... once we're cured of our ills and all. I don't mean get tanked, ya understand... just a coupla brews to... um... take the edge off."

Everyone, Cassie included, couldn't help but giggle at the big man's pathetic attempt at a verbal tap dance.

"Amazing how even a foot that colossal can still fit snugly between the teeth of its owner, isn't it?" Nick Parione quipped, pointing in the general direction of Ben's feet.

"Aw, stick it, smart ass. Just talkin' outta habit, that's all," Ben retorted coolly but without anger, no doubt directing the majority of his anger inward.

"I can take the booze or leave it... and around here there ain't no alternative but to sober up... so there's one less issue to ponder. As for temper control, I'll confess there's still a long, windin' road to cover. I'm ready to deal if these good folks are able to assist. Otherwise, I wouldn't be sittin' here jawin' like some whiny reality TV jackass lookin' for his fifteen seconds of infamy."

The orgasmic swoon that soon followed this rather crude but still strangely effective rant belonged to none other than Cassie Wilkes, whose wide, sparkling orbs fixated on her hero in a hypnotic stare I could only compare to that of someone suffering the latter stages of dementia-her glazed expression, ghostly pale complexion and shiny, spiked locks bringing to mind a Twenty-First Century version of *Bride of Frankenstein*, albeit with a killer physique. All others present, coincidentally, groaned in unison.

To backtrack a bit, as a staff we weren't at all surprised at how quickly the four had paired off into separate cliques, though the individual pairings did strike us as a bit odd.

One would have thought the generational differences would've called for a Cassandra/Cassie-Nick coupling, with the two remaining 'geezers' hanging out for no other reason than similarities in age and time in service.

As things progressed and personality issues arose, it became apparent that predictability was a mask none of our clients chose to don. While Cassandra tolerated Nick's slick rogueism's well enough, her less cerebral, hot-tempered twin did not, opting instead to set her crude yet undeniably seductive wares on none other than our resident loose cannon, Benjamin Thomason, a man she deemed a living legend whom she'd worshipped, rock-star style, as a young teen. In turn, the target of her misguided affections had seemed less than thrilled by the unexpected attention while retreating into a sullen shell. Meanwhile, Tate Fletcher, himself no stranger to the role of misunderstood introvert, played a similar card.

By day three, as the in-processing phase and individual interviews had given way to our initial group sessions, a zoolike atmosphere ruled the day, complete with varying degrees of indifference buffered by severe mood swings. It was truly a minute-to-minute proposition on what subjects to broach and which responses to take seriously, solely dependent on the client's state of mind at the time. *Translation*: a young counselor's wet dream, no doubt enhanced by the colorful pasts represented by each of our specially endowed yet emotionally fragile patients.

Tragically, I had time but for one personal, private interview with each before the program's emergency postponement, during which time I was able to sketch out brief psychological outlines that would prove to be invaluable in the coming days. Invaluable not so much in an analytical sense, but moreover, to my very own survival.

***

To wit (taken from my personal notes):

Benjamin 'Force' Thomason-Hot-headed, uncompromising, and as fossilized in his thinking as duly advertised, but also surprisingly witty and intelligent with an underlying kindness rarely displayed in mixed company. *Bottom line*: A man who is devoutly loyal to his wife and those within a small circle of friends and *extremely* wary of everyone standing outside said circle-a cynicism no doubt birthed and cultivated through years of heavy combat and inner turmoil.

Tate 'Scar' Fletcher-a gruff, uncooperative malcontent whose utilizes the 'man of few words' act as his personal body armor. Clearly a physical presence you want on your side and not as the opposition. Though an undeniably patriotic past warrants the utmost respect, I'm fairly certain he doesn't give as good as he gets. *Bottom line*: Undetermined. Instincts tell me his rage against authority goes deeper than even the recent horror story at its core. The battlefield fatigue diagnosis is far too pat. This goes deeper, I believe, than the cumulative effect of an overdose of shock and awe situations. Perhaps a dramatic new start is in order, disproving the theory that one cannot teach an aged canine fresh tricks.

Cassandra (Cassie) Wilkes (Jekyll-eye)-To paraphrase the oldest of psychological cliches, an enigma wrapped ever so tightly within the most puzzling of mysteries. Spoke exclusively to Cassandra, the dominant intellectual of the trio. Distant, guarded, introverted, yet there was a definite vibe of potential openness, as if desperate to spill secrets to clear the soul, but unable to trust any one source in order to do so. *Bottom line*: Undetermined until which time 'Cassie' can be similarly questioned. From a professional point of view, I find this woman fascinating beyond words. From a *male* point of view, I find her equally mesmerizing, a three-faced seductress whose magnetic pull is as indisputable as it is sweetly taboo.

Nick 'Dejà vu' Parione-We, that being the staff, are paid to provide professional diagnosis, not spout personal opinion based solely on the basest of emotions. As for the former, I'd venture to say Mister Parione is a strange, unfortunate bird indeed; a young man whose blatant immaturity and insincere, two-faced persona are at the core of his behavioral difficulties. As for the latter, I'd happily refer to Nick Parione as a convicted liar who dons several faces not out of some medical or mental malady, as with Miss Wilkes, but out of sheer dishonesty and an unwillingness to assume responsibility or blame for his own woefully miscalculated actions. *Bottom line*: I have witnessed the many sides of the man known as Dejà vu, and if one might pardon the pun, have no desire to repeat the experience. I simply do not believe anything the young man says can be taken as truth... period. Perhaps the future will prove otherwise.

In looking at these rather raw, curt descriptions with the convenience of hindsight as a measuring stick, the number of hits and misses seem to offset in frighteningly equal numbers. As a trained counselor of troubled individuals, there are observations that show great promise-and others which are laughably lame in their shortsightedness. *Bottom Line*: You never truly know an individual until you each share a similar crisis. In this particular case, a life-threatening nail biter that assuredly brought out the best and worst in everyone present. I can only ponder how those who bore witness to my own behavior during such trying moments saw me or rated me in terms of usefulness. One can only hope for understanding... apathy... and a heaping, healthy dose of self-deprecation from those better equipped to handle such dicey scenarios. Lord knows I tried my best, did what I could do to help, however fruitless the attempt.

In the end, whatever the outcome, that's all one can truly ask of themselves or others.

***

The latter part of day three, just as dusk fell near the hour most folks in these parts refer to as suppertime, I was exposed to a ritual of sorts. As with any newly formed group or order whose members feel the initial need to establish or prove themselves to their peers, the recently assigned clients to Jasper Outpost apparently felt the need to do just that. As a staff, we couldn't have been more unprepared for such antics, or felt more useless before, during or after the incident. Why, in the aftermath even the top dog himself, Burt *'The Alert'* Hanover had later confessed to being caught totally off-guard by the whole ordeal, not to mention blissfully ignorant of it's ancient, ritualistic slant. Supertypes, it seemed, had a lot in common with many animal species when it came to establishment of a pecking order, not to mention a chilling similarity to the forcibly incarcerated. Power was respect; respect was power. In the end, a rep in the hero business was just that. Word of mouth only went so far before the proof, as it were, would have to be placed squarely in the pudding.

It had begun with a low rumbling, not unlike the underground tremors we'd sometimes experience from being so near an active fault line.

Having lain on my cot with a warm cup of Nestle's Cocoa nearby and a newly purchased Douglas Boren seafaring murder mystery propped atop my chest, I initially ignored the distant commotion. That is, until I heard the echoes of human voices, shrill and shrieking, accompanying the thunderous wave of humanity.

By the time I'd pulled on an acceptable pair of sweatpants and matching shirt and dashed out into the hallway, it truly sounded as if a runaway freight car was bludgeoning its way through the nearest walkway and making a beeline for the living quarters.

Almost in perfect unison, both Jay and Jessica emerged from their respective quarters, each decked out in similar attire as I and displaying equally exaggerated and unintentionally comical wide-eyed expressions.

"What the hell is... is that?" Jay asked with genuine panic.

"Sounds like an earthquake," Jessica added, gripping Jay's arm and jerking him roughly toward her, a gesture that appeared to equally flatter and frighten the man.

Regardless, I couldn't argue her point, though the racket did seem to be centralized and no longer moving our way. The occasional burst of sporadic, shouted dialogue was utterly incomprehensible amid the sonic booms drowning it out.

"I... I don't know. Terrorist attack maybe? We... we have checklists to follow, don't we?"

Each regarded me with twin expressions of warped horror, to which I responded by changing the subject as quickly as humanly possible, as if the dreaded 'T' word had never been uttered aloud.

"It... it must be coming from either the mess or rec hall."

"Where's Burt?"

"Haven't seen him, Jay. I would think he's... probably up there," I replied, pointing toward the double door exit leading to the walkway.

"Should we... you know... "

"I will if you two will."

"We don't... I mean, we don't have any weapons or... anything to... to defend ourselves," Jessica pleaded, still tugging at Jay's arm as if to prevent a sudden escape attempt.

"Jessie, take a good, long listen," I said sharply, not even attempting to hide my disgust at such a lunkheaded remark. "Do you *really* think such a weapon exits within these walls to save our behinds from whatever is doing *that*?"

"Darrin's right, Jes. Let's go... somebody might need help," Jay said, nodding my way as if to congratulate me for such outright bluntness. Still, as we crept up the hall toward the glass door exit with Jessica now cradling an arm from each of us, I couldn't help but regret what Jay had considered my *words of wisdom* in regard to our prospective plight. As far as what awaited us, perhaps a locked and loaded grenade launcher or similarly armed bazooka wasn't a bad idea, after all. At that particular moment, I'd have gladly handed over the keys to my mythological kingdom for such weapons.

Even sauntering along at a snail's pace, it took us less than two minutes to cover the relatively short distance to reach the source of the ruckus. Along the way, we encountered two kitchen workers, a middle-aged Hispanic male and similarly aged black female, scampering in the opposite direction. Passing by us without so much as a nod, both appeared openly shell-shocked at whatever was transpiring in the adjoining building.

Having entered the mess hall from the dome, we'd been greeted by a trio of echoing thumps, followed by a raucous howl and what sounded like multiple cheering voices.

Marching through the recreation area toward the gym entrance, one would've thought the three of us literally joined at the hip like freaks in a sideshow carnie of old. Being that the double door entrance was wedged open on both sides, we were offered a panoramic view of the happenings without having to immediately put ourselves in harm's way.

"Holy sheeeeeeeeeet," Jay managed in a harsh, awestruck whisper, having wedged himself between myself and Jessica, whose double-clutch gasp filled my ear with her warm, peppermint-scented breath. Personally, I found the power of speech no longer a viable option. Frozen in our collective tracks a good two to three feet from the gym's hardwood flooring, we stood huddled together like shell-shocked prey and soaked in the scenario for want of having any other logical option.

Having ripped away several sizable chunks of the gym's nonpadded sections of thick stone wall, Tate Fletcher and Benjamin Thomason appeared to be engaged in an old-fashioned knock-down drag-out brawl, each man shirtless but otherwise decked out in similar workout attire-that being spandex shorts and high-top tennis shoes.

As they stood toe-to-toe at the top of the key

section of the halved basketball court, wailing away on one another with closed fists, the room's overall state of dishevelment left little to explain concerning the origin of the booming noises we'd heard.

The weight room section was a complete shambles, with various universal and free weight machines having been torn asunder and scattered about as if victimized by a category five hurricane. One particular item, a squat rack which normally held up to a thousand pounds of free weights, had literally been pulled from its base and tossed the length of the room-a span covering roughly twenty-five to thirty yards. Meanwhile, an entire wall leading into the gym's lone racquetball court had been demolished, a colossal hole driven through its center and shaped, rather conspicuously, much like the two large human bodies that had no doubt crashed through it at full bore.

"Kick the big lug's ass, Forcy! Do it for me!" a familiar female voice yelled as the combatants continued to pummel one another without pause. Tiptoeing forward as if into a live minefield, we each hugged the left entrance door and leaned in until the two figures swam clearly into view, each having plunked down on a lengthy courtside wooden bench that served as the only such place the gym offered.

"You're wearing him down, Fletcher! Once he drops those meat hooks, he's all yours for the taking, baby!" Nick Parione shouted, punctuating the words with a shrill giggle while playfully elbowing Cassie Wilkes in her side.

"Awww, kiss off, Slick," she growled, shoving

Parione roughly to the floor with a forceful, two-handed push. "My man Force don't ever 'wear down'... he just rebounds, recharges, reloads, and retaliates!"

As if to immediately justify his personal fan club's praise, Force landed a wicked uppercut that not only lifted Scar Fletcher airborne, but sent him flailing head over heels into a far wall, displacing several sizeable chunks of sheetrock upon impact.

"Hell yeah! Touchdown for the home team!" Cassie bellowed while executing a double-fist pump while Nick sidestepped away with slumped shoulders. The two were acting as if they'd placed a prefight wager.

Bouncing up quicker than humanly possible from what easily could've been a lethal blow, Scar shook off the effects with nothing more than a combination shrug and head tilt before taking off in a mad sprint back toward the man responsible.

Instead of backing away or initiating a defensive posture, Force jogged forward just as Scar closed ground to within striking distance, both men releasing similarly styled, Neanderthal-inspired warrior cries just milliseconds before colliding.

The effect was not merely a shock to the system, but akin to standing dangerously within range of a sonic boom. I felt my entire frame shake and tremble-my upper chest, rib cage and clavicle bones throbbing and aching as if I'd been physical struck. As for Jay and Jessica, there was little doubt they'd experienced a similar jolt, as the three of us seemed to melt away from one another in the aftermath to deal with our own individual ills.

As for the combatants, they seemed no worse

for wear. Once upright following the monumental crash, Tate had landed a straight kick directly onto Force's exposed midsection, followed by a solid right to the ribs and ending with a backhanded clothesline chop just below the neck. Curling his frame a la human bowling pin as he skidded across the gym floor on his bare back, Force ricocheted about like a muscle-bound pinball, effectively shredding everything in his path, his victims to include a set of ping pong tables (instantly transformed into separate piles of splintered kindling) and a regulation pool table (neatly halved as if first measured and subsequently sawed by hand).

"Don't look now, honeypot, but the fat lady's still sucking wind," Nick crowed, wildly clapping his hands and pointing at Tate Fletcher as if to say, 'you the man'.

"This here grudge match is faaaaar from over, yes sir."

Grunting in frustration, Cassie matched his smarmy grin with a rabid snarl and a two upturned middle fingers.

Having finally ended his sliding trek by slamming into the thickly padded wall beneath the basketball goal-a spot some forty to fifty feet from where his travels had begun-Ben arose with predictable shakiness, rubbing his jaw as if suffering from nothing more than a mild toothache before flashing a wide, approving, slightly bloodied grin.

"Damn good shots, Fletch. Think ya might've even loosened a fillin' or two."

Stepping ahead while winding his left arm like

a sore-armed southpaw prepping to pitch extra innings, Scar nodded appreciatively.

"Appreciate that, Benji, I surely do. Seems to me what we've got here so far is an old-fashioned draw, you think?"

Adjusting his left shoulder with a sudden jerk of his right hand as if to forcibly pop it back into place, Force pushed away from the wall and strolled briskly forward.

"Right as rain. It's been a real sister-kissin' affair alright."

I saw Ben wink before lowering his head and positioning both gargantuan fists directly beneath his own chin.

"What say we end this dance on a high note? I don't mind workin' a little OT for a good cause."

Slowing his pace as the distance between the two narrowed considerably, Scar then crossed both his arms in a 'X' shape across his massive chest.

"By all means, Brother Ben. I never could stand a tie."

As the two men closed ranks and prepped for a final round of mayhem, their respective cheerleaders filling the air with supportive, albeit mostly profane banner, the utter lunacy of the entire scenario finally hit home. These two superhuman brutes weren't actually fighting, but merely testing each other's merits in true ultramacho fashion. In truth, what we had bore witness to was more playful wrestling match than a fight to the death. True, it was professional grappling of the highest level, but nothing more.

Trading jabs while standing flat-footed amid the crushed, trampled remains of what had been a reasonably serviceable gymnasium, neither man appeared to gain a marked advantage. For every right hook that sent Force reeling back a step, Scar would soon endure similar punishment-a perfectly thrown roundhouse or forearm smash.

I can only approximate that a full two minutes of intense, unrelenting bombardment passed before each literally collapsed into the arms of the other, their chests heaving as if to implode as they crumbled to the hardwood floor.

"*No... no...* no... you can't quit now," Nick whined, departing the cheering section and making a beeline directly toward center court with Cassie hot on his heels.

By this time, both Scar and Force had collapsed in opposite directions and thus reverted back to their alter-egos with utter fatigue obviously dictating the change.

Striking a sassy, feminine pose that could easily be categorized as borderline homosexual, Nick leaned over Ben's heaving frame, ranting, raving and gesturing as if he'd just wagered and lost his life's savings in the aftermath.

"What's this horseshit, old man? I didn't think so-called living legends knew the meaning of the word quit. Now pull your tired old carcass up and finish the job... "

Between strained gasps, Ben leaned up, smiled briefly and managed a limited word response that did little to quell the younger man's temper tantrum.

"Kiss... this... tired... *old* ass, kid... show's... over... "

Mirroring her hot-headed ally, Cassie got down onto one knee and began to berate Scar Fletcher in a mean-spirited barrage that made Nick's seem lighthearted by comparison. Strange as it may sound considering the all-out battle royal I'd just witnessed, but this troubled young woman's vile-spewing tirade was easily the most cringe-inducing spectacle of the entire shebang, especially considering her target was a multidecorated war veteran.

"You got *lucky,* you mechanized asshole... and that's all. Ben... Force pulled his punches... probably scared he was gonna leave some permanent dents in that rusty chassis of yours... or maybe he realizes how tough it is to find replacement parts out here in the middle of nowhere... especially for a creaky, broken-down warhorse like you... "

"Aw, clam up already, will you?" Nick vented, his lithe frame noticeably tensing as he whipped around to better scold Cassie, whose own steely gaze remained focused on Scar throughout. "I for one am fed up to my bloodshot eyeballs with this never-ending hero worship bit. Not only is it nauseating to the extreme, but skating on the edge of perversion, dig?

"I mean, if you really want to hop in the sack with Grandpa *dozer hands* that damn bad, go ahead and make your move already."

Never breaking verbal stride, he then turned back to and readdressed Force, who was only then pushing himself upright.

"What say you, pops? Bet you're just aching for some 'bipolar queen' trim, am I right? Pack an ample supply of Viagra, did we, hummm?"

Though it was so brief as to be almost completely unnoticeable, I did see Scar and Force lock eyes and flash similar grins in the aftermath, as if they'd shared a telepathic thought.

"Ya know dipshit, I was reaaaal impressed with that classroom demo ya put on. Some seriously trippy material, yes sir. The X-Men really screwed the pooch in not addin' such a talented gem to their team arsenal, I say."

Shuffling forward while massaging his neck from the effects of the recent skirmish, Force then balled both his mammoth fists and dropped them to his sides. To his credit, Nick Parione refused to budge a single inch despite the larger man's obvious attempt at intimidation.

"Then again, I always was the 'seein' is believing' type, 'specially concernin' things I don't *quite* understand."

The two men practically bumped chests, though the dramatic difference in their respective bulks left Nick woefully overmatched.

"Question, big guy?" the man called Dejà vu inquired without a hint of outward apprehension, again to this credit, or perhaps it was more an issue of severe naivete on the young man's part.

"Just wonderin'... " Force replied with a mischievous grin. I heard Cassie Wilkes giggle, and saw her quickly clamp the palms of both hands over her mouth. Meanwhile, Scar Fletcher sidestepped over and struck a rather stiff, suspicious stand to her immediate left.

"... if it was just some fancy-pants parlor trick or a power to truly be reckoned with... "

Parione bristled a bit, but nonetheless managed to maintain his combative pose.

"I'm no David Copperfield clone, if that's what

you're shooting at, Thomason."

"So ya say, kid... so ya say. Point taken. Still, call me a born skeptic, but I can't help wondering... "

Bending his knees just slightly, Force's head shot forward in a blur, followed by a loud snapping retort not unlike that of an exploding firecracker.

"Guess there ain't but one way to find out."

Having lurched back from the force of the ferocious headbutt, Parione would've easily sailed a dozen feet or more before landing if not for Force reaching out and snagging his ankle in midflight.

As if controlling a human-sized marionette with severed strings, Force first whipped the smaller man's flaccid form back toward him, spinning him about like a human top before tossing the limp body airborne.

Nick flipped head-over-heels several times, almost scraping the twenty-foot-high ceiling before descending at a much slower rate, where Force awaited, having locked his fingers to effectively weave a wrecking ball constructed of flesh and bone.

"Oh, this is gonna be soooooooo sweet," Cassie cooed, seemingly oblivious to Scar's ominous presence mere inches to her left.

Uncoiling like a striking cobra, Force swung both arms around just as Nick was about to impact the hardwood flooring, battering the already unconscious form the length of the gymnasium. As simplistic and insensitive as it sounds, the only thing I could logically compare it to was watching someone swat a baseball during a session of batting practice. Only in this particular case, the ball in question was a one-hundred-seventy-pound man and the Louisville Slugger used to inflict the damage a pair of massively muscled arms attached to twin battering rams.

Having traveled a great distance in a line-drive altitude of approximately ten to twelve feet above the hardwood flooring, Nick Parione's eventual landing was anything but gentle, slamming into the concrete wall with enough force to jolt free a fresh slab of jagged stone. After several apprehensive ticks, there was visible movement present: a spastic twitching of the feet and hands that at least answered the question of whether the man was still alive and kicking after such a horrendous bludgeoning.

"Ohhhhh yeah! Touch 'em all, Forcy! *Touch... them... all*!" Cassie Wilkes exclaimed through cupped hands. "You got allllll of that one, baby! Grand slam in the bottom of the ninth... three on... two out... and one smart-ass punk down for the count!"

In her jubilation, she never bothered to notice that Scar had practically hitched a ride to her person, and was only then reaching over to peck her lightly on the left shoulder.

"Psssst, hey, lady... speaking of smart-ass punks... "

From a distance, the clothesline blow he'd landed across her breastbone didn't appear that forceful-a gentle tap at best. In retrospect, I'd have to say the term 'looks can be deceiving' was never more appropriate, as Cassie was tossed like windblown confetti spun from the effects of the assault, executing at least three full midair somersaults before landing face-first on a wide, padded mat normally used for aerobics sessions.

"Awww, now that ain't no way to treat a lady, Tate," Force howled, slapping a hand across his knee while keeping an eye peeled on Dejà vu's prone frame, which continued to wriggle and shake in a halfhearted attempt to rise. Stunned as I'd been at the brutality of the initial assault, it couldn't hold a candle to the second. Not only did Scar Fletcher outweigh his female victim by at least her entire body weight, the surprise aspect of the attack reeked of out-and-out cowardice, a trait I'd never have dreamt such a man possessed.

"Show me a lady and I'll treat her like one, Benjamin," came Scar's intentionally gruff reply, so casual and indifferent as to further increase the overall sense of shock.

As Cassie rolled over onto her back, moaning through a pained wince while keeping both eyes tightly clamped, Scar strode casually over as if to inflict further damage.

"Leave her alone, you... you chicken-shit *bastard*!!" a voice shrieked from my immediate left, and I turned just in time to see Jessica bolt by me in a blur. Fortunately, Jay had reached out and snagged her wrists and managed to haul her back outside the entrance.

Ignoring my cohort's venom-laced plea, Scar continued forward until he kneeled down on his haunches and leaned over Cassie's writhing form.

"I surely hope you're right about this, Ben. Otherwise, you and I have a hell of a lot to answer to."

"Hey, I just figured it was high time hotshot

here put up or shut up," Force said with a shrug, having reached his own battered quarry only to stand impatiently over him with his hands resting atop his hips.

"Jackass went too far with the Viagra remark. Battle scars and premature agin' wrinkles aside, I ain't exactly AARP material just yet. Little shit has to learn to respect his elders, right?"

Scar nodded, peering down at Cassie's body with an expression that bordered on sincere regret.

"Whatever you say, partner. So now what?"

"Give it time... his eyelids are aflutter as we speak. I'm guessin' it won't be long now."

"Better not be. Wasn't there a certain time limit involved? I mean, what if he can't... you know, do his thing? We're gonna come off as two major league assholes, and if you'll recall, I didn't think much of the idea to begin with."

Shaking his head from side to side, Force regarded the other man with a deep frown.

"Geez, Tate... damned if sometimes you don't remind me of my old lady, and I ain't talkin' about her better traits neither. Worry, worry, worry... nag, nag, nag... "

While the two men stood over their respective victims as if purposely allowing a respite before the next round of pummeling, my curiosity reached a fever pitch. Glancing over at Jay and Jessica, still locked together like the most unlikely of tag team partners, they too shared a similar look of befuddlement. It was during such times that I couldn't help but pine for Burt's rock-solid presence, and secretly wondered how he or anyone else on post could've possibly ignored or perhaps slept through such a ruckus.

"What the hell are they doing?" Jay whispered while holding Jessie in a bear hug.

"I think... they're... playing with them. Toying-some kind of sick, twisted cat-and-mouse game," Jessie growled, still struggling to break Jay's bonds, though her efforts had weakened significantly.

"No... wait a minute," I intervened, picking up a different vibe while watching Force and Scar slowly back away a step or two as both Dejà vu and Jekyll-ene appeared to be coming to.

"Something weird's going on... "

Rising shakily onto one knee, Dejà vu's head momentarily remained bowed as Force turned to address Scar a final time in a raspy whisper.

"Brace yourself, Fletch... less I miss my guess, we're in for the psychedelic ride of a lifetime."

I heard Jekyll-ene growl as she rolled onto her left side, her eyes popping open at almost the exact time that Dejà vu's head arose. Their eyes seemed to lock with their assailants in perfect synchronicity, Jekyll-ene's a glare of pure rage while her male counterpart's a more subdued, almost trancelike stare.

"Yeah, I knocked your preppy, pretty-boy block off," Force said with a smirk, his leaned-back pose a purely defensive one.

"Now what exactly are ya gonna do about it?"

As if engaged in some ancient form of martial arts and/or meditation ritual, Dejà vu's raised hands crossed in front of his face and froze there just as Cassie Wilkes' third and infinitely more dangerous personality sprang forth from the padded mat like a coiled feline and lurched directly toward Scar

Fletcher, whose own reaction was shockingly blase.

The last words I recall hearing belonged to Force, though their muffled, cloaked delivery made it a virtual impossibility to completely comprehend. I was able, however, to understand a comically drawn-out, "*Ohhhhhhhh hellllll*," amongst the barely audible mix.

Once a semblance of normalcy returned and 'real time' was reestablished, I found myself hugging one of the gym entrance doors, my entire being awash with a sluggishness I'd felt only one other time, that being immediately after Nick Parione's classroom demonstration of his Dejà vu talents during the in-processing phase.

At least there was some comfort in realizing I was hardly the only soul present awash in utter discombobulation.

"What the heeeeeeellll... " I heard Jay curse to my left as he hugged the tile flooring like a crawling toddler.

"Ohhhh my head... my-my aching... head," came a similar whine from Jessica who was inexplicably massaging her midsection despite the verbal complaint to the contrary while backed against the other double door.

Meanwhile, though still extremely woozy, I did manage to scan the gymnasium's interior while not daring to take my hands from the doorframe, and immediately noted the dramatic alteration of the players involved in what was becoming a rather bizarre, otherworldly stage play.

First off, Force and Scar stood at the basketball's foul line area, each man appearing supremely fatigued what with heavily labored breathing and their arms hanging limp at their sides, just as they'd been at the conclusion of the monumental skirmish that had started it all.

Secondly, both Dejà vu and Jekyll-ene had each resumed their prebeating positions, when they'd stood side-by-side while playing the roles of cheering, if not constantly bickering, spectators.

Stepping cautiously away from the door and placing my hands atop my knees for support, I was barely able to overhear Force and Scar's verbal exchange.

"To-to-told ya, Tate... little shit wasn't... about to take a beatin' like that and live to *bruise* over it. No tellin' how many ass-kicking's he's rewinded since... middle school. Damn... are you as... bushed as I am?"

"Benjamin," Tate huffed, "I am of the sincere belief that a cub scout could presently whip my butt like a rented mule."

"I'm right there with ya, partner. Feels like the Mount Olympics of hangovers times three."

The educator in me was tempted to scream out '*That's Olympus, Ben... you mean Mount Olympus...* ' though luckily common sense overrode the inherent need to correct a man legendary for such comical butchery of the English language.

While all present struggled mightily to regain a sense of balance in both a physical and mental sense, it was the man responsible for our collective state of bewilderment who appeared to be suffering the most. Having collapsed onto his hands and knees, Dejà vu subsequently began a series of hacking dry heaves; arching his back like a vomiting canine following the ingestion of rancid meat. Watching the usually reptilian-eyed Cassie Wilkes move to his aid was a true testament to the man's miserable state of being.

By the time Burt and Doc Gonzales joined the fray, each decked out in full winter gear as they'd been servicing the backup generator on the far eastern side of the post grounds, the lot of us had gathered in the mess hall for a pot of freshly brewed (and joyously stout) coffee.

While Burt surveyed the damage (subsequently blowing his stack, though the effort wasn't quite as volcanic as I'd anticipated), the remainder of the gathering mostly just sipped in blissful silence.

Within the next half-hour, a gradual filing out began. Interestingly, I watched both Ben Thomason and Tate Fletcher deliver similar pats on the back to one Nick Parione, who merely nodded wearily in response as the newly reemerged Cassandra Wilkes sneered sourly in the background. It was as if the two senior heroes were, in some respect, paying homage to the younger man's power and accepting him into a very select fraternity. It seemed Nick Parione had indeed passed his initiation. As for the Wilkes' sisters, such an honor had yet to be bestowed. Only future events would dictate if the newly restructured pecking order had been correctly set. Future events that would serve as the ultimate litmus test for both bravery and sacrifice.

***

The fourth day of the program was supposed to have been a relatively light one, calling for informal interviews only and an unsupervised group exercise consisting of basic teamwork drills and a follow-up grading segment. There was much emphasis on not pushing the clients too hard, thus allowing for a gradual, more natural shift of attitude. After all, adaptation to one's surroundings is a major factor in any such endeavor. In terms of the Outpost, adaptation to the unmerciful, brutish winter weather conditions was deemed enough of a strain in and of itself. The early morning hours of day four brought forth a meteorological marvel that even the most battle-tested, cold-natured veteran of tundra conditions might find intimidating. Being that day one's glacier surprise had long since melted away in the wake of almost balmy forty-degree highs and an abundance of sunlight in the previous forty-eight hour span, it served only as a mild shock to witness a second such occurrence so soon after, as such storms did sometimes strike back-to-back.

The true surprise, then, wasn't the storm itself, but the severity involved. To compare, day one's fairly thick coating had been rated a level three to three and a half by post standards, based on potential danger, i.e. frostbite and/or flesh-burn exposure, while its successor scored a four and three-quarters mark on the five scale meter. I hadn't really bothered to check a local forecast, having ignored all sources of outside communication in favor of some much-needed reading followed by that rare night's sleep that lasted longer than the usual five or six hours. Thus, one could only guess if the *Weather Channel* had doled out the familiar warnings associated with such a lethal front pushing into the area.

What we had received, mystery forecast aside,

was a foot to fourteen inches of fresh snow, accompanied by gale force winds that served to construct drifts as high as five to six feet in and around the post perimeter walls. This coming after a deluge of freezing rain had peppered the grounds with three to four inches of solid ice following a drastic drop in temperature. Making matters worse was the fact the latest snowfall didn't seem to be letting up an iota, as an updated forecast from the county seat announced an expected daytime accumulation of six to eight additional inches-in complete contrast to the glistening ivory grounds were the murky skies, which appeared dark and dusky. The relatively short trek from sleeping quarters to dining hall/recreation building was unlike anything this northern-born, northern-bred boy had ever ogled, as the glass-domed walkway resembled the freezer burned interior of a walk-in icebox. The exterior portion was coated in thick swirls of ice, the smoothed-out layers appearing almost man-made, like a meticulously formed ice sculpture, the dome's built-in heating elements hardly making a dent on the overall effect.

Eye candy aside, the reptilian shape of the dome teamed with a strangely menacing echo brought forth by several feet of extra coating created an effect less soothing than downright creepy; a *Shining* moment if I'd ever seen one, as in King's text via Kubrick's vision. Needless to say, I picked up the pace considerably just to escape its claustrophobic ensnare.

As for the post grounds and surrounding area, to take a simple stroll outdoors was to risk not only the aforementioned skin ills, but possible multiple fractures from potential falls. In vernacular terms, we were in effect under house arrest, Jasper Outpost-style. Though this was hardly an unusual situation considering the season, I did sense a rather peculiar vibe surrounding this latest weather-related quarantine.

It wasn't until I'd eaten a bite and sipped the last of my morning coffee that the origin of such foreboding surfaced as a real-world concern in the form of County Sheriff Jake Owens and the younger, brassier, and least experienced of his two assigned deputies, Randall 'RJ' Jeffries.

Approximately fifteen minutes earlier, around seven-thirty a.m., the entire staff (*save* Burt Hanover) and all assigned clients had congregated inside the mess hall, basically for want of anywhere else to go or anything to do other than nibble microwaveable muffins and slurp steaming mugs of fresh java. Despite donning an extra sweater amid the consistently regulated sixty-eight degree temps inside each post structure, I recall fighting off a constant chill.

"Jesus, did you check out that freaking popsicle tube on the way in?" I heard Cassie inquire to no one in particular, though she'd recently taken up a standing position near a table already occupied by Benjamin and Tate while Nick Parione sat alone a few booths down.

At the moment, I had secured a seat directly across from Doc Gonzales and one of that week's assigned cooks, a large, barrel-chested Hispanic male whose name escaped me. Doc had been sipping from a large, steaming mug and was in the process of staring a hole directly through Cassie

Wilkes well-defined rear end.

"Spent a few months on a training mission in Greenland a few years back," Tate replied blandly between sips. "Have to say, in all my travels, this is the only place I've seen which could give that floating iceberg a run for its money."

Ben chimed in joyously, rubbing a fresh growth of grayish stubble atop his squared chin, "A real tit stiffener, no doubt. This kinda shit is pre-cise-ly why I spend my off-time below the Mason-Dixon Line."

"Temperature gauge outside the motor pool read seven above at six a.m. sharp," the cook announced stoically, his ample midsection jiggling wildly with each spoken syllable, delivered in a thick, Spanish twang.

"High's only supposed to reach ten or eleven... low of minus eight tonight with a wind chill of almost twenty below."

"Well, thank you very much, Master Chef Sir Taco Bueno," Cassie blurted out with a sour frown, her gaze remaining steadfast in Benjamin's direction. "Anybody here order a weather report sprinkled with chili sauce? How's about a seven-day forecast wrapped in soft tortilla breading? Areeee-bah, areee-bah... an-de-lay! An-de-lay!"

With that, various winces and frowns ensued, all save Nick Parione, whose warped, wide-eyed smirk balanced a fine line between disgust and sadism. Just six and a half hours removed from gaining his cohorts' respect, the young man's attitude appeared to have reverted back to square one.

"Somebody please correct me if I'm wrong, but

such out-and-out ignorance should not be allowed a forum."

As had been the man's practice once out of Burt Hanover's personal earshot, Parione was utilizing his urban, hip-hop-styled mannerisms, the tone of which was as annoyingly shrill as the spastic thug wannabe hand gestures were comically exaggerated.

"Somebody gag that crazed, cracker chick 'fore she starts a border war. Better yet, figure out the quickest way to summon up her smarter, infinitely more pleasant sister."

Not surprisingly, Miss Wilkes' rebuttal wasn't long in coming, though her statuesque pose remained unchanged.

"Ah, clam up, rerun. Who the hell pulled your pimp boy chain anyhow? Shouldn't you go find a dark corner and toss your cookies?"

Parione continued unabated and obviously unintimidated. All the while, the subject of their barb trade-off arose and lumbered back into the kitchen, apparently uninterested in the impending outcome. Doc Gonzales shot me a bemused glance but remained characteristically mute.

"Can you say *Alamo II, The Sequel*?"

"Hey, Dick... whoops, I mean *Nick*... you bucking for mayor of Mexico City or what? Cut the sanctimonious BS, pal... and while you're at it, do us all a whale-sized favor and ditch the homeboy vibe, 'kay? If you're hardcore gangsta, buddy boy, I'm queen of the fucking Nile."

At this point, Tate stood as if to depart to safer climes just as Ben effectively cloaked his entire head inside those king-sized mitts as if to barricade himself from further exposure.

"Pathetic, isn't it?" Doc Gonzales whispered, having leaned my way until I could detect the lethal mix of stout black coffee and stale cigarettes on his breath.

"And such people are considered earth's defenders?"

Staring through the narrowest of slits provided from the colossal snowdrift engulfing a nearby window, Tate Fletcher first heard and then visualized the unexpected guests nearing the Outpost. His final few words were partially obscured by the faint echoes of what sounded at first like a car or truck horn blaring in the near distance.

"Check it out. Looks like we've got company."

Like a band of curious tourists, everyone crowded near the shoebox-sized opening to acquire a look-see even as the shrieking wail of the horn grew ever louder.

"Who the... in this weather?" Jay blurted out, having squeezed himself between Ben and Tate's mammoth (by comparison) frames for a look.

"Safe bet it ain't the pizza delivery boy," Ben cracked, receiving a sharp clap on the back from Cassie for his troubles. The young girl cackled at Force's every utterance, almost to the point where the poor man couldn't even pass gas without Cassandra's evil twin considering it the absolute 'bee's knees'. Stranger still, it was obvious that the more intellectual of the Wilkes' trio much preferred Nick Parione's company, while considering both Ben and Tate somewhat beneath her. Perhaps Cassandra was drawn to the former's faux hip-hop flavored bad-boy image, or had simply deduced him a more apt ally considering their similar ages.

"It's a snowcat alright, minus its grooming blade. Looks like somebody's out joyriding."

Tate had barely concluded such an observation when Burt came galloping in from the outer hall, the thick, ankle-length parka he wore unbuttoned and swaying about like a flowing black cape.

"It's the sheriff and one of his deputies. Devon picked up them up on the two-way a few minutes ago. Garbled but clear enough to ID 'em anyway."

Devon Levine was the post maintenance man who doubled as com officer on bad weather days. A former gang-banger from East St. Louis, he'd joined the staff as a trustee the previous spring and had quickly gained Burt's confidence-never an easy accomplishment, that.

"Weird day to be making his rounds, isn't it, boss man?" Jay inquired, having broken away from the window to retake his seat.

"Something's seriously out of alignment, alright. Dish and Internet's been down since yesterday afternoon. Couldn't even pick up K-FREEZE this morning. It appears this storm caught everybody with their pants down, so to speak."

"Kay-Freeze?" Tate asked, turning toward Burt with a cocked brow, to which the chief responded while stepping back toward the exit.

"KFRW radio out of Jasper. Local radio station we've learned to depend on when every other form of available communication takes a powder, usually from conditions just like these... well, perhaps not this severe. This particular bone chiller appears to be of the major league variety."

Despite motoring about in full code blue mode,

Burt still managed to take a moment to effectively stare down both Ben and Tate.

"Uh, about last night, Chief... I... um... that is... we both... well... " Tate began, staring down at his own colossal feet like a shy preschooler.

As if attempting a verbal rescue, Ben leapt in with both feet. Unfortunately, as the big guy was apt to do more times than not, he immediately submerged both size thirteens directly into his own mouth.

"Yeah, sorry 'bout the carnage, Hoss. Gotta say though, those gym walls were pretty damn flimsy. Any fag armed with a ball-peen hammer coulda done similar damage."

Rolling his eyes in disbelief even as his jaw literally unhinged, Burt Hanover nonetheless displayed a sense of self-control I'd never thought imaginable.

"Uh... yeah, I... guess. Anyway, the government's footing the bill, so... no harm... no foul. Then again, I did have three of the kitchen staff turn in their resignations this morning, so just watch it, okay?"

Walking over and placing a thickly-muscled arm around the smaller man's shoulder, Ben effectively killed any further discussion on the matter.

"Hoss, from what little I've tasted off the menu in these parts, ya didn't lose much."

As Ben strolled away with a freshly gnawed toothpick hanging between gnashed teeth, Burt Hanover's lips parted as to respond before clamping shut in apparent surrender. When he next spoke, it was to do what came natural: to direct a course of action and command the participants involved.

"Doc, you, Darrin and Jay grab a parka and come with me. Everyone else can relax and take five... looks like the initial session is going to be delayed a hair."

"Um, we'll be playing the role of greeting party, I assume?" Jay asked sourly just as Doc and I rose in unison.

"Affirmative, Counselor, now get a move on. It'll take me a minute to decode the main garage entrance-and possibly another five to pry the doors loose."

Snagging a pair of fur-lined jackets from a nearby supply closet (each building contained at least one such well-stocked room during the winter months), I tossed one Jay's way before pulling on my own.

"Hey... have fun, guys!" we heard Jessica roar with icy sarcasm, no pun intended, once we'd both stepped into the hallway. "Not to worry... I'll have supper on the table and frosty brews ready for you big, strong, brave male specimens when you get home!"

A loud female cackle ensued, most likely that of Cassie Wilkes. In my mind's eye, I could see Benjamin rolling his eyes in embarrassment. Despite the obvious attempt at levity, it wasn't difficult to detect a solid layer of apprehension in Jessica's tone. Along the same lines, my legs and arms felt strangely detached as Jay and I raced from the dining hall into the domed walkway and directly toward the center of the post grounds. Though perhaps not quite in full-blown premonition territory, there was a distinct vibe present-one decidedly mixed vibe that was equal parts excitement, dread and pulse-pounding fear. A small portion of my psyche, call him *Action Jackson*, welcomed it as an elixir of sorts-a caffeine and alcohol-laced kicker that provided a temporary break from the mundane, while the larger, in-charge segment, call him *Dull but Dependable Jackson*, wanted nothing more than to hide behind the nearest partition until the mystery had been safely solved and deemed nonthreatening. In any event, Jay and I trudged forward without comment or complaint, the simple act of obeying a direct order perhaps creating a protective barrier against such baseless fears.

We arrived at the main garage entrance approximately three minutes later to see Burt posed near the double doors. He was working the keypad furiously and cursing under his breath between angry huffs. It wasn't often I'd witnessed the chief so openly frustrated, and I stepped cautiously forward with Jay literally crawling up my well-insulated back. Outside the thick metal doors, an occasional horn blast could just be heard over the howling winds, the severity of which was threefold when no longer shielded by thick, concrete walls. In briefly scanning my surroundings, most of which was completely alien since I hadn't stepped foot into the garage since being in-processed as a new employee, I noted the sparse holdings contained within. Besides a lone snowplow tucked neatly away in one corner, there was a few scattered wooden chairs, a single oak desk and a few dozen mostly empty metal bins, a few of which were packed with overstuffed cardboard boxes.

"We hear you already! Hold your blasted horses!" the chief blurted out, pounding the keyboard with renewed vigor. "That Jake Owens is one annoying jackass... "

I heard Jay giggle aloud and quickly muffled the same with a gloved hand. Burt paused for a split second as if prepped to respond to such blatant disrespect before continuing his pecking assault.

"Cripes! Either of you up to date on the release code?"

Jay regarded me as if I'd sprouted a turnip from my bare forehead before nodding negatively.

"Six-three-five-eight," I spewed a bit too enthusiastically. "Um, unless it's been changed since last week's security brief." Despite a strong sense of futility, we held such meetings once a month per federal guidelines-during which times building entry and exit codes could but usually weren't tampered with, depending on current regulation instructions. Luckily, I'd served my turn as post security rep just a few short weeks prior, thus the updated entry code hadn't quite gone stale.

Burt frantically tapped in the code and we heard a familiar beeping, not unlike the ones used by backing vehicles. After a moment's pause, the double doors began a slow, deliberate ascent, accompanied by a series of sharp crunching noises.

"Better back off a step, guys," Burt warned us, stretching out each arm in spread-wing style as to prevent Jay or myself from moving forward. "It's liable to get ankle-deep any second now."

Sure enough, once the doors had creaked and groaned their way to a two to three foot height, the garage floor was soon inundated by a veritable avalanche of snow and ice, the latter in boulder-sized chunks that skidded about the concrete flooring like oversized hockey pucks.

"Should've worn our mukluks," Jay said while gracefully sidestepping the deluge.

Ducking beneath the still rising doors to catch a glimpse of our surprise guests through the blinding whiteout, Burt released a high-pitched wail before turning on his heels and leaping headfirst back into the garage.

"Get back! Incoooooommmmminnnnnng!"

As Burt whizzed by in a blur, I barely had time to snag Jay's fur-lined collar and jerk him clear of the doors just as the bottom half of each were essentially sheared off from impact.

Slipping and sliding about on the suddenly slick stone, I lurched clumsily to the left, having released Jay to his own fate. I managed to allow a stack of large supply pallets to cease my forward momentum, twisting about just in time to see the ice-entombed snowcat's jagged front-end slide to a halt less than an arm's length from the back of Burt's Hanover's booted feet.

"Wh-what in the... blue... freaking... blazes?" I heard Burt grumble angrily over the Snowcat's badly weakened horn, which was still sounding off in three to four second intervals.

"You guys... alright?"

Jay answered first, a woefully energyless mumble at best.

"Yeah... yeah, I'm fine... thanks to Big D pulling me out of harm's way."

I half-stepped over to stand between the two men, all the while keeping my eyes peeled on the idling snowcat, the glass dome of which was impossible to penetrate visually due to an overabundance of frost, ice and packed snow. For a wild moment I considered the possibility there was no driver inside at all, that perhaps the 'cat had somehow obtained the supernatural ability to steer itself from parts unknown directly into the post's lone garage.

"Still intact... upright and breathing, though a bit heavily at the moment," I finally answered while pulling the parka hood snugly over my head as temperatures began to take a massive dip.

"Hey, really appreciate the hand, dude," Jay repeated through chattering teeth, stepping over and slapping me lightly on the right shoulder.

"Not a problem."

"Seriously, that big bastard would've given me a wet, fat smooch if you hadn't acted when you did."

"Blind luck, Jay. Panic-induced instinct at best... "

"Well, whatever it was, I sure as hell owe you one. My hero... "

Smiling, I reached over and returned his slap in kind. It wasn't often one heard such tried-and-true sincerity from one Jay Peterson, at least not the unplanned/unplotted type. It was one of those rare moments I found myself actually liking the guy instead of simply tolerating him.

"Buy me a coffee when this is over... whatever *this* is."

"Done. Steaming cup of oil slick on me, and maybe a stale donut to boot."

I noticed both he and Burt were keeping similar

tabs on the vehicle, whose creaky, whining engine sounded on the verge of implosion. As for the garage doors, both were hopelessly mangled from the crash-dented in places and shredded in others, including the bottom portion rubber seals, which had been torn off to dangle free like shattered, lifeless limbs in a stiff breeze.

Following a lingering pause that might've lasted upwards of a full minute or longer, Burt stepped gingerly forward until his left boot braced against the grounded portion of the snowcat's track, from which pencil-shaped smoke tendrils arose. Despite the influx of blowing snow and frigid air, the room suddenly reeked of all manner of engine leaks, from oil to gasoline to anti-freeze. As if on cue, the 'cat's engine sputtered and died, though it was unclear if the shutdown had been machine-initiated or man-made.

As Jay and I kept a reasonable distance, shoulder to shoulder like spooked third graders, Burt reached up with a loud groan to snag the driver's side door handle, his complexion beat red. One could almost visualize puffs of white smoke spewing from the man's ears as in the classic *Looney Tunes* cartoons whenever a specific character seethed with anger.

"Blast it, Jake, I'm tempted to make a citizen's arrest. What kind of horse manure driving is that anyw-" he began, flailing back as if struck by a gale force wind as the door was shoved open from the inside, instantly filling the air with shattered shards of brownish ice and pellets of packed snow. The chief soon hugged the floor for the second time in a matter of minutes, windmilling back and sliding a good dozen feet on the ice-slick flooring before coming in for a comically clumsy head-over-heels landing. As if to add insult to potential injury, a vicious series of gusts blew through the garage opening, stabbing my eyes with icy specks while turning every freshly taken breath into a uniquely painful experience.

Rushing to our boss' aide, Jay and I each hooked a cupped hand beneath Burt's armpits and pulled him upright, temporarily oblivious to the subtle movement to our left, where someone was gradually emerging from the vehicle's chilled interior.

"Jesus... J-Jake, is... are you... is that... " I saw Burt mumble through trembling lips while raising his right hand trancelike and pointing toward the open cab.

The shambling thing that half-crawled, half-fell from the vehicle hardly resembled anything human, at least of the living and breathing variety. The thin man's upper body was chalky white, to include his head and facial hair, from which icicles hung like Christmas ornaments. It wasn't until this modern-day Jack Frost practically collapsed, tilting forward to bounce onto the snow-caked floor that the dark blue of his uniform pants swam into view-literally the only portion of the man that didn't appear freezer burned.

"S-s-sorrr-sorry... I... I... could... c-couldn't... s-s-stop... brrr-brakes... w-were ... are... .sh-shot... " the man stammered, hugging himself tightly across the chest while assuming a fetal position. His copiously layered hair was matted in snow, with his bushy eyebrows and shaggy mustache equally encrusted.

Breaking from our grip, Burt limped over and crouched down directly in front of the man, who was only then beginning to shake and tremor as if stricken with a horrid case of hypothermia.

"Jake... what happened? How... why are you... what are you doing here? Jesus, man, why aren't you wearing a parka?"

Through clattering teeth, Sheriff Jake Owens' reply was truly one for the books... that is, if the book in question specialized in nonsensical riddles.

"Didn't have... t-time... wasn't... wasn't thinking straight. H-had... had to... g-get... away. H-had to... re-regroup... th-that's a-all. H-had to... regroup... "

The three of us shared a quizzical look before Burt and Jay busied themselves with helping the sheriff up and into a nearby chair. Meanwhile, I walked over on feet of clay and took a peek into the vehicle's open cab, all the while mentally prepped to leap aside at the first hint of danger.

I spotted the still form sitting upright in the passenger's seat, its posture so stiff as to resemble a lifeless mannequin. Leaning up while balancing a bootheel on the same spot along the track Burt had utilized, I recognized the shaved head and face, despite its haggard, weather-beaten appearance as belonging to Deputy Sheriff Randall Jeffries. In time with his boss, the deputy was woefully underdressed in only his departmental uniform and long johns. For conditions calling for layer upon layer of heavy protection, both men had arrived on scene as if accidentally detoured from an outdoor barbecue.

"Deputy?" I whispered not nearly loud enough

to be heard over the howling winds. I'd met the man only briefly several months before and had exchanged amenities sparingly since, usually in passing while doing some shopping in town or while traveling in opposite directions on the narrow two-lane highway that linked Jasper Outpost to its sister cities.

"R-Randy there... he... ain't... ain't quite r-right," I heard the sheriff say, his teeth clattering like mad between words.

"He... ain't been right... since I... found 'im... found 'im like... like that."

In studying the object of the sheriff's strange comments, the 'ain't right' observation certainly had validity. Randall Jeffries stared straight ahead, his expression the very definition of deadpan. Unlike his slim, lanky supervisor, Jeffries was a large-boned African-American male of considerable girth. I couldn't help but wonder how the man had fit inside such snug quarters in the first place, much less survived such a lengthy, potentially treacherous trek. It was like viewing one of those ancient photos of early NASA astronauts being shoved into a tiny space capsule like canned sardines.

"Does he... I mean... can he move?" I asked, weirdly drawn to a frozen line of spittle that hung from the deputy's lower lip like a jagged polyp.

"He ain't even... twitched an eyebrow since... since I found 'im. Had to... carry 'im to the... cab and stick him inside. He... ain't said a word or... moved nary a muscle. I... I gotta tell you... it's scaring the living shit outta me... real... scary... shit," Owens answered weakly, sounding as though his internal battery was in desperate need of a recharge.

"Take it easy, Jake. Let's get you back inside and warm you up," Burt said as he and Jay each took an arm and helped the man to his feet. "How's a hot cup of Joe and a warm biscuit sound?"

By this time, Sheriff Owens was beyond any meaningful response, his body having slumped as his eyes lolled until only the whites were visible. I watched the trio trod slowly back toward the building entrance before retracing my attention back to Jeffries, whose glassy-eyed, droopy-jawed expression had remained fully intact, though his slick dome now glistened from partially melted precip. The flesh of his hands, each of which rested squarely atop a kneecap, appeared severely freeze-dried, as if the slightest touch might literally serve to peel them down to the bone.

"Not to worry, Deputy," I said for no apparent reason other than to keep myself company, "soon as reinforcements arrive, we'll get you out of there and right next to the nearest heating vent."

Burt and Jay were joined by Doc Gonzales upon their return, the latter toting a small brown satchel that served as his own personal little black bag.

"Has he... moved or... said anything?" Burt inquired as I backed away from the cab to allow clearance for the doc, who quickly climbed up and leaned his head and shoulders inside the truck.

"Not a single word, groan nor spastic tic of any kind, Chief."

As the doc practically vanished inside the cab, Burt began to pace the length of the vehicle while Jay and I huddled together, turning away from the influx of blustery inhumanity that continued to infiltrate the garage with increased fervor. Eventually the doc dismounted the truck wearing a befuddled expression as the chief greeted him with a shrug and upturned palms.

"So what's the diagnosis, Doc?"

"Appears to be shock of an unusually... extreme nature."

"That man's a certified genius... tops in his field," Jay whispered through a smarmy grin I didn't visualize but nonetheless knew existed.

"Prescribed treatment?" Burt asked calmly while glancing over the doc's shoulder into the cab.

"All we can do for now is warm him up. He needs warm liquids... preferably fruit juice and water. Meantime, I'll prep some B-12 injections and perhaps a saline IV."

"What about Jake? He seemed... a bit discombobulated."

"More than usual, you mean?" Doc grinned, a rarity indeed from the man known around the compound as 'Lockjaw."

"Difficult to comprehend, I know... but yeah. He was babbling a mile a minute... between all the shivering and teeth gnashing."

The doc turned to evaluate Randall Jeffries a final time before replying.

"Well, considering what they both went through to get here, it's understandable. Once their body temperatures regulate and they've had some rest, I'm sure we'll note a return to normalization in their thought process."

"Whatever you say, Professor," Burt chided playfully, turning toward Jay and I wearing a pained grimace.

"Alright, fellas... we're on. Let's get him out of that frozen tuna can and into warmer climes."

As Jay strolled slowly by the doc, he paused just long enough to nudge the man with an elbow.

"Damn it, Jim... I'm just a doctor! *Not a miracle worker*!"

In his usual stoic manner, Doc's lone reply consisted of a brief nod and weakly executed roll of the eyes.

It took the four of us a full five minutes to pry the bulky deputy free, the man's stiff, mechanical pose doing little to aid the effort. It was truly like relocating a two-hundred-and-fifty-pound mannequin. Still, I couldn't help but be grateful for the exertion in terms of the body heat it generated in light of the garage's sudden transformation into a walk-in freezer.

Utilizing a gurney Doc had retrieved from med supply, we then wheeled the deputy through the admin building and into the makeshift infirmary, where the sheriff had already taken up residence on the waiting room couch.

"Good... Jake's out like a light," Burt observed, having earlier supplied the sheriff with a wool robe and several thick blankets. I noted a soggy uniform shirt and matching pants lying nearby, along with a pair of badly scuffed steel-toed black boots from which white socks protruded like probing antennae, obviously still semifrozen.

"Help me get Randy out of those clothes," Doc instructed while pawing through the first of a trio of glass-encased medicine cabinets taking up a far corner of the room.

Tugging at Jeffries' boots while Jay began

working to unbutton the man's shirt, Burt must've noted my blank, lost look and decided I could be better utilized elsewhere.

"Darrin, run over to the com center and see if Devon's had any luck contacting anyone."

"You got it, Chief."

"Oh, and stop in the mess hall on the way and let everyone know what's happened. They all must be chomping at the bit by now."

"On my way. Back in a few," I said, feeling a definite sense of relief upon departure.

Darting through the admin wing and connecting dome at breakneck speed, at least for my decidedly nonathletic self, I reentered the mess hall/recreation building to a surprisingly banal greeting.

Other than Jessica, no one seemed the least bit interested or even faintly curious as to who our mystery guests were or why they'd chosen to brave such horrid conditions to visit in the first place. As for the rest, Tate Fletcher and Ben Thomason seemed to be swapping war stories over a fresh pot of coffee while Cassie sat quietly between them, her sole attention (and unrelenting devotion) focused solely on Ben. Meanwhile, Nick Parione continued to revel in his 'loner without a clue' role, sitting alone in a far corner with a lit cigarette parked in one hand.

It may sound childish to admit my disappointment toward the group's disinterest, but such was the case. Regardless, I tried to conceal such feelings while taking center stage, politely waving off Jessica in her attempt to gather pre-announcement information.

"Folks, if you'll just listen up for a moment. I

have some news regarding our... the visitors to the compound."

"Let me guess," Parione cracked wise between blowing smoke rings, although surprisingly void his faux street-cred voice, "hopelessly misplaced tourists in search of the *Ponderosa*?"

Inwardly disgusted, I choose to ignore the comment in lieu of acknowledging its existence.

"The county sheriff and one of his deputies have detoured our way, though exactly why is still a mystery, as both are unable to answer any questions at this time. We've taken them to the infirmary for treatment. Once they've rested a bit and... regained their senses, I'm sure we'll have more to report. As it is, today's planned sessions are going to be delayed until further notice, possibly rescheduled for tomorrow. I'll... get with Bur- the chief and let you know."

Being that reactions varied from slight disinterest (Tate, Ben) to a more extreme variation of same (Cassie) to smarmy indifference (Parione), I saw no reason to hang around for a session of Q&A that wasn't apt to materialize. Jessica followed me back toward the exit, taking my arm and surprising me with the stoutness of her grip. Sad to say, but I'd tried my best to exit without facing her. Every workplace, no matter how small in terms of number of employees, seems fated to possess in its ranks that one person who absolutely stinks in a crisis, no matter the level-that one individual whose penchant for spreading panic and/or depression in times of trouble seems to be a natural birthright. In a nutshell, the 'glass-half-empty' person. Jessica, god bless her, was our resident doomsayer slash worrywart. Veteran counselor that she was, and a tough one in regard to plying her professional craft, I'd seen a flat tire cause the poor woman to break out in hives. Strange considering her vast work experience in numerous dicey conditions, though perhaps such past overkill was the very reason for her agitated behavior.

"What's going on over there, Darrin? I mean... *really* going on," she whispered, having basically pulled me into the hallway and pinned me against the nearest stucco wall.

To my credit, I maintained a steady tone and equally casual posture despite the shooting pains being inflicted on my left forearm by her razor-sharp nails.

"Just what I said, Jes."

"Don't give me that 'everything's hunky-dory' BS, Darrin. You might fool those lunkheads," she barked harshly, pointing a thumb in the direction of the mess hall, "but I've been around you long enough to know a snow job when I hear it."

"*Snow* job?" I smiled, bending down a bit to apply a playful headbutt. "That's good, Jess, real catchy consider-"

"Cease the spiel, Jackson," she interrupted with an angry sneer, using the palms of both hands to essentially flatten me against the wall. "If something's out of kilter around here, I have the right to know. Be straight with me or I'll leave you here to baby sit the class while I walk down to the infirmary."

"Jessica, I swear I'm not intentionally keeping anything from you," I pleaded, holding up each hand in mock surrender. "Sheriff Owens and

Deputy Jeffries are a little... under the weather, that's all, and neither was up to expounding the exact reason for their visit."

"I knew it," she sighed, turning to face the mess hall entrance with her arms folded across her chest. As was the woman's habit in times of self-inflicted stress, she began a renewed, ritualistic session of nail clicking, the tick, tick, ticking of which never failed to bring to mind the ancient, fossilized typewriter once owned by my grandfather, a Selectric II model I believe they were called.

"You... knew what, Jes?" I asked, instantly regretting the act but also realizing I'd been hapless to react otherwise or the woman would've surely trailed me all the way back to the infirmary.

"I just had a feeling... that's all. My midsection's been in a twisted knot ever since those so-called heroes arrived on post. They brought something bad with them, Darrin... I just know it. Trouble follows such people, you know. It's tied to their very core."

"Let it go, Jess. We don't know a thing yet. No need to cultivate a fresh ulcer 'til there's a valid reason, yes?"

Turning on me like a wild feline with its back up, Jessica's eyes shone blood-red, her brow creased in agony. In other words, the transformation was complete from mild-mannered counselor to full-fledged paranoid schizophrenic, in many facets just as frightening a metamorphosis as anything Cassandra 'Jekyll-ene' Wilkes could cook up, if not more so. One would naturally assume an individual toting around a Master's in psychology would be beyond such malarkey. I always figured it was a good thing our Miss Lewis hadn't been born in an earlier century, lest she might well have based each and every life decision on the fictional creations of a local fortune-teller.

"Oh, wise up, Darrin. This is just the beginning, I tell you. Only... the beginning."

"Jess... listen, I need to get back to the infirmary before the chief sends out a search party."

Try as I might to flee without further lecture *slash* dressing down, I'd found through past trials that such attempts were usually fruitless.

"I hear the talk behind my back. You all think I'm overly sensitive... acutely paranoid at the first hint of trouble... "

"Jess, I don't think... I mean, I haven't heard-"

"... just another overemotional, overreactionary female with a clairvoyance complex... "

"Personally, Jess, I've never thought of you as overreac-"

"... well I'm here to tell you, Darrin... and I'll be happy to pass on this particular observation to anyone willing to listen... "

By this time, I'd stopped trying to either intervene or distract, having accepted my fate by leaning flat against the wall and staring directly up into the ivory-tiled ceiling.

"Forget my 'lunatic' premonitions for a minute and ask yourself, doesn't *everything* about the sheriff's little visit just reek of trouble?" she concluded in a low, guarded tone, having leaned in until I could detect the faint aroma of peppermint gum on her breath.

"You don't have to think about it, Darrin... no need for mental strain whatsoever... simply take a step outside and feel the burning in your lungs and watch your skin ignite as if lit ablaze. Then query this: who in their right mind would even have attempted such a hazardous, potentially fatal trek without dire cause?"

Without another word, Jessica then turned on a heel and headed back toward the dining hall, no doubt deducing she'd clearly made her point.

After a short pause to regain what little composure remained, I took off in the opposite direction with an admittedly wobbly gait, having felt as though I'd truly been through the emotional ringer, as it were.

Along the way, Jess' words rang in my ears like the piercing retort of small arms fire, more specifically the last few sentences of her 'query this' speech. Try as I might, and I certainly gave it the old college attempt, there was simply no arguing her point without tap dancing in the face of cruel, hard logic. The point perhaps being: Either Sheriff Jake Owens and his lumberjack-sized deputy were completely off their collective rockers, or both had witnessed an atrocity of some magnitude; said atrocity to remain an enigma until one or both regained his wits and/or the proper use of his vocal cords.

Either way, it seemed the residents of Jasper Outpost were in for quite the extraordinary experience, though whether or not that was a good thing remained to be seen.

***

Approaching the entrance to the infirmary, I

met the chief and Jay headed back in the other direction. While Jay's agitated, wall-eyed expression served as little shock, Burt Hanover's similar appearance most certainly did.

"What's up, Chief? Anything further to report?" I asked as both men slowed their pace in greeting.

"Nothing substantial, Darrin... actually, nothing coherent might be a better term."

"Sir?"

While Burt seemed to be avoiding eye contract, another rarity from a man legendary for his flat 'refusing to beat around the bush' ways, Jay stepped up until we practically rubbed noses.

"Trust me, bro, in this particular case, ignorance is undoubtedly bliss."

It may sound melodramatic to the extreme, but with his frazzled hair, chapped lips and puffy, bloodshot eyes complete with pronounced, dark shading beneath, I swear the man had aged a decade in the span of a half-hour.

Without speaking, I shifted my gaze from Jay to Burt several times, eventually ceasing the rubberneck tactics and focusing on the chief alone, who finally did me the courtesy of returning the favor.

"Just babbling, Darrin, frostbitten, fatigue-induced madness. The doc said Jake... Sheriff Owens was suffering from some sort of traumatic shock, probably due to the crash. Might've banged his noggin but good when they nailed those garage doors. He's got both of them under light sedation."

For a brief instant I considered arguing the point that neither man had displayed a head injury of any sort, but decided instead to bring up what I thought to be a more topical matter in terms of the staff.

"Just a head's up; Jess is playing Sally Psychic again."

Both men rolled their hang-dog eyes in perfectly timed unison.

"Don't tell me... " Jay blurted out to land the initial verbal haymaker, "she saw the post going up in flames in her morning cereal."

"Stow it, Peterson," Burt huffed, looking none too amused. "The less Jessica knows the better, then."

Suffice to say, it was my turn to roll the orbs in utter disbelief.

"Um, Chief, I surely can't divulge what I don't know, correct? Would someone please give me *something* here? I *was* present at the crash site and the removal of the bodies. I think the least one of you can do is spill a bean or two my way, for Christ's sake... "

Like the surrogate father he assuredly was to all of us, Burt placed a gentle hand atop my shoulder and spoke in an ultrasoft mode, as if consoling a badly spooked child.

"Now, settle down, son. Like Jay said, we're not keeping anything of value from you or the rest of the staff. Right now we have to focus on the task at hand, that being getting back to our clients and providing the service we're paid to provide. Sound kosher to you?"

The 'sound kosher' remark was a personal joke between the chief and I since my first week on staff, an utterance he used often if I seemed upset or particularly riled.

"Kosher as a spicy dill and a cool brew," I responded in kind, though still less than thrilled to be omitted from whatever deep, dark secret the two men shared with Doc Gonzales. To be wholly honest, I found their secretive behavior damned frightening.

"You two get back to the rec building and inform Jessica that all client sessions are back on schedule. I'll be with Devon in the com room trying to figure out a way to recontact the civilized world... and while I'm at it try to obtain an updated weather forecast.

"Here's hoping the good lord sees fit to end this blizzard soon, or they'll be digging us up around the turn of the next century as the lost colony of Jasper Ridge."

And so it went; a sincere yet ultimately wayward attempt to dive back into routine amid far-less-than-routine circumstances, an exclusively human instinctual trait. As it was, Jay and I were less than fully equipped to pull off such a blatantly phony act, at least from a mental standpoint: he with his jittery gestures and spastic eye movement, and myself so overcome by a sudden wave of dread that the act of stringing together a meaningful sentence became a Herculean chore.

Upon returning back to the mess/rec building, we found Jessica had yet to proceed without us, leaving our clients to effectively fend for themselves. While the dining hall had emptied save the two assigned kitchen workers, the rec room saw a slew of activity. In one corner, Nick Parione played a solo game of electronic darts while Tate and Ben shot a game of pool with Cassie as sole witness.

"Wonder where Jess roamed off to," I said, my words partially drowned out by Cassie's excessive cackling. Jay shook his head without responding, briefly eying his watch before clamping both hands together at his midsection as if to ward off an attack of involuntary shakes.

Benjamin was the first to notice our entry, taking a step our way with a pool cue resting behind his neck and atop his massive shoulders. Having peeled off the black leather jacket he'd donned at breakfast, he wore only a sleeveless, dark blue muscle tee and bright red bandana. From a distance, the man's chiseled torso and bulging arms appeared weirdly faux, as if he were wearing a rubber body suit made to resemble actual flesh.

"What's up, Docs? You two look like ya just took a big ol' bite outta the same turd sandwich."

With that, Cassie practically busted a gut, her shrieking howl bringing to mind every TV special I'd ever seen covering the African hyena.

"Nothing exciting to report, people. As a matter of fact, Chief Hanover has instructed us to go on with this morning's sessions."

I saw Tate put down his cue, the man's leathery, scar-riddled visage creased in a deep frown.

"So what's the deal with the two local law enforcers who crashed the party?"

"Yeah," Nick Parione suddenly chimed in full hip-hop mode, bobbing our way as the entire group slowly converged, essentially blocking off our further advance. "Talk to us, fellas. Any news is intriguing news to the involuntarily enslaved, know what I mean?"

"You tell 'em, Rap Master Snowflake," Cassie barked with a snarl I took as not containing an iota of good humor.

Clearing my throat to buy time, I wasn't able to calculate a coherent thought before Jay leapt in with both left feet, each of which belonged lodged securely between his dental work following such a pathetic attempt at diversion.

"Just Sheriff Owens and his deputy making their rounds. You know, checking on everyone's plight with the extreme conditions and all. I... think I even heard Doctor Gonzales ask them about supplies."

As if to worsen what was already a tragically off-kilter tap dance, he felt the need to add insult to injury by snapping his fingers and adding, "That's it. They were probably dropping off some extra meds in case frostbite or hypothermia becomes an issue."

Following an awkward pause wherein all save Nick traded comically strained glances, Cassie released yet another banshee howl of laughter in wake of staring at Jay as if he'd just spouted the funniest quip in comedic history.

"Saaaaay what? Dropping off meds, did you say?"

"Yeah, sounds reasonable." Tate shrugged, backstepping in the direction of the pool table. "Right, Benji?"

As if to follow the other man's lead, Ben shot me a final, disdainful glance before whipping the cue around like a ninja's blade and turning on his heels.

"Hey, I'm game 'til a better fairy tale comes along."

"Just on routine patrol, were they? Well, as Sir Charles Brown was apt to say... *good grief,*" Nick concluded, bowing his head in mock shame before exiting stage left in the direction of the dining hall.

Fighting off a stout urge to reach over and throttle my fellow counselor, I instead stuck to the B-movie script.

"Okay, folks... that's conference room one in fifteen minutes for teamwork drills."

Through the thickened stone walls, blizzard winds continued to hammer away without mercy, and I felt my head, face and neck flush with a savage inner heat.

It may sound a bit harsh, but I purposely picked up speed on the trek to the admin building, partially to work off a bit of stress, but mostly to keep my distance from Jay, whose idiotic comments continued to singe my psyche.

Approximately two hours later, just as the grading segment of our class exercise had concluded, Burt called a mandatory staff meeting in his office. Like a gargantuan jigsaw puzzle being dismantled a single piece at a time, life as we knew it within the normally tranquil borders of Jasper Ridge Outpost was on the verge of disintegration. Little did anyone know at the time just how quickly that particular house of cards was to crumble, though in hindsight it's debatable just how much a significant forewarning would've helped or altered the eventual outcome.

Still, one can't help but wonder.

Chapter Three
Campfire Tales/Power Play

"So that's pretty much the scenario in a nutshell, boss. Communication-wise, we may as well be inhabiting an igloo buried somewhere between Timbuktu and the dark side of the moon. Only option I see for the foreseeable future, that being whenever or if ever this mother of a storm finally decides to hiccup, is paper cups and twine. You remember, the grade-school equivalent of today's AT and T."

Devon Levine, bless his working-class soul, was an extremely savvy, street-smart, intelligent young man who always impressed me as an atypical underachiever. An undereducated jack-of-all-trades who had done time as a late teen for a series of identity theft related crimes, Devon's sharp wit and overly talkative ways led many to mislabel him as the local buffoon, when in reality he was a major part of the glue that held the post together. Part computer guru, part maintenance man, and full-time communications officer, the twenty-something African-American with the slick-shaved head and drink-straw build was undoubtedly the most vital member of the staff other than Burt Hanover and perhaps the doc.

"Fan-tas-tic... between landlines, six cell phones, the Internet *and* an emergency transmitter, you'd figure the odds to be favorable that at least *one* link wouldn't crap out," Burt said, standing at the head of the conference table with his hands braced on either side. Despite the record-shattering chill outside, there was little hiding the wide, circular sweat stains forming at the armpits of his turtleneck pullover.

"What about the snowcat? Didn't the sheriff or Jefferies bring a two-way or cell phone of their own?" I inquired with a raised hand, naively hopeful the subject broached was virgin territory. Sadly, I wasn't even close, as Devon soon revealed in a rather curt tone that did little to hide the fact he interpreted such simplistic thinking as a personal insult.

"Um, been there... tried that, Mister Jackson. They had a two-way hook up in the truck, but the battery is dead as a hammer, and the sheriff's cell was flashing the same 'no service' message as the rest."

"Sorry, should've known," I replied weakly, suddenly wishing I had the power of invisibility.

Hanging his head in apparent exasperation, Burt quickly shifted gears to a subject near and dear to all our hearts, specifically dealing with the 'warming cockles thereof' segment.

"What's the power situation?"

Crossing his spindly arms across an equally frail chest, Devon flashed a broad yet ultimately shaky smile that appeared fueled by a healthy dose of anxiety.

"So far, the main generator's holding up like a champ, but that old dinosaur is creaking like a professional whore on a brand-new box spring. Gotta tell you though, boss, if this shi- if this mother keeps up a similar pace for much longer, it's only a matter of time."

"Duly noted, Dev... thanks again. Keep me posted."

Sounding as optimistic as humanly possible despite the negatives piling up around us, a mandatory characteristic for good leadership in my personal book, Burt spoke with a recharged confidence.

"Alright, folks, you heard the man. Seems we have no choice but to wait this one out for the duration, whenever that may be. Luckily, we prep for such matters far ahead of time and have the necessary resources.

"Let's look at it this way; we're probably getting the worst winter has to offer out of the way right off the bat. From that perspective, it's all downhill from here."

"Don't bet on it," I heard Jessica grumble as everyone rose to signify meeting adjourned. Following the Queen of Doom and Gloom out the door, I saw Jay corner Burt beside a nearby coffee station and paused to eavesdrop.

"What about the clients, Chief? Shouldn't we play straight with them concerning the com-out problems?"

"Jay, my boy, none of them have outside com access anyway, so what's the point? Besides, they're all superhero types, right?"

Jay nodded, resting his chin on a clenched fist.

"Well then, as such I cannot see them getting overly concerned over something so routinely mundane. After all, it isn't as if the post is being purposely sabotaged by a ruthless gang of supervillains."

"Soooo, what you're saying is... continue with the status quo."

This time, it was Burt who nodded while

patting Jay gently on the shoulder.

"You got it. Let's just keep it all as nonchalant as possible."

I then waited until Jay departed before approaching the chief myself, if for no other reason than to wallow shamelessly near the man's sanguine vibe. Approaching him silently from the rear, I witnessed the man's shoulders slump dramatically as he stared out a nearby window buried in a powdery drift. He bowed his head as I drew to within a few feet and released a hoarse, pained whisper I'm sure he'd meant for no one's ears save his own.

"God help us," the chief had sighed, the overall effect more a request than a prayer.

Leaving the man to his well-deserved privacy, I managed to tiptoe away without ever revealing my presence.

Making my way casually down the hall, I tried to focus on the job at hand, which presently consisted of prepping for a one-on-one session with Nick Parione, surely to be an interesting if not infuriating half-hour. Still, as the incessant pounding from the worst glacier turf storm I'd ever witnessed continued unabated outside the post's comfortably heated interior, I couldn't help but dwell on the chief's slumping posture and the weary, biblical plea that had followed.

No matter how many times I tried to convince myself it was simply a matter of riding the storm out, there was still present a nagging ambiance that Burt Hanover was concealing something vital. In strolling through the final glass dome turned ice cavern before entering the quarters building, I felt my heart palpate from an overdose of dread. Sucking in several deep breaths before turning the doorknob to my room, I couldn't help but be sardonically amused at the thought, however depressing. Facts were indeed facts, no matter how fervent the denial: I was slowly transmutating into Jessica Lewis' male counterpart, a paranoid doomsayer with little or no justification for such behavior save a rash of bad weather (well, to be fair... *extremely* bad) and a vehicle crash. After acquiring the textbook and accompanying notepad I'd need for the Parione session, I took five to stretch out on my assigned cot and attempt to reestablish a sense of balance. Within moments, I was fast asleep, only to be awakened with a start by a loud banging at my door that practically flipped me onto the plush carpeting below. It seemed the pregame show had ended far too prematurely, having given way to the garish nightmare to come.

***

"Let me state right from the get-go that despite my outward appearance, Jake Kenneth Owens is neither doped up nor crazy, and what I'm about to tell you people is the god's honest truth as I know her to be. I need some help with... a situation I can't handle alone. First off though, you folks deserve an explanation. Might even help my present mental state to get if off my chest, since it's been weighing on me like a rockslide ever since we left Boulder Valley."

It was just past two p.m., roughly three and a half hours since our last staff powwow, the difference this time being the six extra bodies occupying the conference room's spacious yet barely lit confines. Doc Gonzales had accompanied the meeting's keynote speaker from the infirmary, while the chief had decided that excluding our four assigned clients from the plethora of recent disasters was no longer a wise or viable option.

In the hours since I'd played Rip Van Winkle atop my dorm cot, the main generator had indeed gone south, leaving the post's interior a rather dim shadow of its former brightly lit self while reducing heating levels twofold. Meanwhile, the communications problem, or complete lack thereof, had yet to see even the slightest improvement, much like the blizzard conditions themselves. The chief estimated the snowfall level at upwards of thirty-six inches, with additional layers of pure ice serving as a rock-hard foundation. In terms of further actions to take, it went without saying that we were limited to the extreme. Thus, there was ample time for Sheriff Owens to regale us with *Tales of the Tundra*, Jasper Ridge style, though the man himself did seem overtly rushed.

"Your post sawbones here tells me Randy... that's my deputy, Randy Jeffries, is under sedation for severe shock. I'd prefer to have him up and around to back up what I'm about to spew forth. But such is life. I'm on my own here, so please bear with me and try your dead letter best to suspend your disbelief 'til I've wrapped it up, that is unless the good Lord dictates I pass flat out before reaching the finish line."

In checking out my fellow audience members, I noted a great disparity in the levels of interest present. While Ben, Tate, and even Nick seemed at least vaguely intrigued, Cassie's focus seemed to be sailing about the room like windblown ash, her eyes darting wildly as the fingers of each hand pecked away at the tabletop like a concert pianist revved up on beanies. It was only then I realized it was Cassandra, not her wild-child twin, currently steering the multiple-ego-faceted ship otherwise known as Jekyll-ene, though my first hint should've been how the current incarnation seemed less interested in Ben than the color of the surrounding wallpaper.

While clients filled the table to my right, Burt, Jay, Doc and Jessica sat to my left, respectively. As if to further distance themselves from the staff, each of whom had donned either thick sweatshirts (Jay, Burt) or sweaters (Jessica, yours truly), the clients seemed perfectly content in short-sleeved (Ben, Tate) tees, parachute shorts (Nick) and flip-flops (Cassandra). Meantime, the parka-wearing sheriff had positioned a chair directly at the center of both, obviously still too weak to endure any prolonged standing. Even in the relative dimness, the poor guy appeared positively ghostly; a growth of black stubble atop his chin standing out like black licorice when compared to his otherwise deathly sallow complexion.

As story time commenced, there was a distinct sourness swirling around my gut telling me the sheriff's impending tale wasn't likely to improve post morale.

"Well, the whole mess reared its ugly head around eleven p.m. or so last night, roughly a half-hour to forty-five minutes past the time the bottom fell out weather-wise.

"I'd left the station around ten fifteen after helping ol' Chace Peters change a flat out on Harding Ridge Trail. Freezing rain had already slicked up the streets and it was snowing to beat the band, a hell of lot more than the three or four inches those boneheads in Corvallis had predicted.

"By the time I pulled up at the homestead at around eleven or just past, Marge, that's the better half, was already handing me the phone. It was Edgar Cromartie calling from his cattle ranch a few miles east of Boulder Valley yakking about some kind of fire in the sky he'd spotted off his back deck. Now, being that Edgar's well past eighty and owns the nickname 'Crazy Eddie', I figured a bottle of Jack Black might've assisted in conjuring up whatever mirage he was describing. It wasn't until I got a similar call from Betty Widham less than five minutes later that I pulled my boots back on and headed out to the Valley.

"Betty's a retired school teacher who, too many years back to properly recall, taught this future lawman a thing or two about world history. That woman had never been known to lie outright, and who was I to doubt such a stalwart reputation? She lives about a mile and a half from Eddie's place, with only a hilly pasture separating the two properties, and stated she smelled smoke and saw a bright glow coming from the West.

"I'd already hitched my mukluks back up and curled into my thickest parka when the phone rang yet again. This time it was Randy Jeffries calling on his cell from Boulder Valley. We have sort of a sheriff's office annex there, though the main station is in Jasper Ridge. Randy lives in Boulder Valley so he's viewed by many as the one and only law officer in town. Try as I might to split time between the two, the majority of my day is usually spent in Jasper."

Owens cleared his throat and took a few sips of water from a plastic cup the doc had provided. Wincing in the aftermath of few swallows, he glanced at the doc and grimaced.

"Damn, Doc, I guess anything that tastes that god-awful nasty has to be top-notch in the get-well-quick department."

The doc bristled, replying with surprising emotion considering his usual mild-mannered self.

"Sheriff, if I had it my way, you'd be in bed with a buttload of sedatives. As it is, that elixir there and those B-12 injections I administered are the only thing keeping you upright."

"I told you, Doc, I can't afford any lingering naps on duty, not when there are lives at stake," Owens snapped back tight-lipped, "so... *many* damn lives."

Burt intervened, slapping both palms sharply against the tabletop.

"Well, get on with it then, Sheriff. Exactly what lives are we talking about? I am *bound* to hear this. We all are."

Not surprisingly, when the subject of human peril arose, I noticed a tangible change in posture and expression in both Tate Fletcher and Benjamin Thomason, though the remaining two clients remained coolly remote and distant to the whole affair.

I saw Nick Parione battle to suppress a yawn,

while Cassandra Wilkes began picking at her fingernails with a small metal file.

Sheriff Owens started to reply but paused with mouth agape, executing a comical double-take in the general direction of Ben and Tate. Wearing a thin smile, he then regarded Burt while pointing toward the clients' table.

"Wow, looks like you're drawing a bulkier clientele these days, Hanover. You people counseling bodybuilders gone to seed this semester?"

Unfortunately, Burt wasn't the least bit amused, his reply as sour and indifferent as I believe the man capable of producing.

"Long story, Jake, now please cut to the chase already."

Following another brief sip and accompanying grimace, Owens sucked in a deep, labored breath and resumed.

"First off, I feel obligated to relay that Randall Jeffries is known around the Twin Cities as one cool, collected cat who isn't easily shaken or spooked, least not that I've ever witnessed. On this particular night, however, the man sounded downright petrified. I was only able to catch about half of what he was screaming into that landline, 'cause by that time the phones were already sizzling with static and his cell was fading in and out with every third syllable, but the words 'murder' and 'under attack' came through loud and clear. Needless to say, folks, those two particular nuggets we don't often hear in these here parts. We were cut off before he could even tell me his location, so I ran out to the cruiser and tried to reconnect through the two-way with no better luck. So, I had little option but to kiss Margie goodbye, check the chains on the cruiser and head west.

"To backtrack a smidgen, let me state for the record that my other deputy, Gene Wilkes, deserves some kind of premonition of the year award for choosing this particular week to take his annual vacation. I'm sure ol' Geno is having a high old time deep-sea fishing off the sunny coast of FLA while we collectively freeze our cabooses off (whispered under his breath, '*dirty rotten jackass*').

"Anyhow, it took me exactly fifty-seven agonizing minutes to cover that short thirteen-mile trek, though I appeared to be the lone traveler from either direction. This storm had swept in so quick, they didn't even have time to dispatch salt trucks out of Corvallis. It goes without saying that was one trying, drawn-out hour, what with no radio or phone contact, and forced to steer atop solid ice most of the way. Tire chains aside, anything less than a heavily armored vehicle with four-wheel drive was gonna be ditch or ravine bound, as the heavy snow had just started to layer up by the time I crossed over the Valley city limits. The power appeared to be down in the center of town, though Main Street after ten p.m. kind of naturally looks that way every blessed night. Still, the only source of light was of the occasional street variety, and I knew a few of the town merchants left emergency lighting on in their shops once closed for the day, and still didn't notice a single sign of illumination while slipping and sliding down Main toward the station."

"Hate to cut in on ya, Constable, but about what timeline are we lookin' at here?" Ben asked with a cocked brow. "Just wanna keep my facts straight unless there's a pop quiz later."

"Oh, by then it was well past midnight, closer to half-past, I'd say."

"I take it ya don't normally see this kinda late-night action in such towns."

Owens paused a few moments, shutting his eyes while reaching up weakly to scratch his chin. The poor man looked on the very verge of imminent collapse.

"Such... towns? I don't... "

"No offense, but ain't these local burgs the roll-up-the-sidewalk at nine p.m. type?"

"Oh, yeah, yeah, they most definitely are, especially in the face of an oncoming glacier-turf, but still... I could tell things were a little *too* ghostly last night, even for the Valley.

"Anyway, when I arrived at the station it was as dark as a tomb and twice as frigid, meaning the town's main power supply was fried, just as I'd suspected. I tried the main switchboard and got nothing but noise. Only thing I knew to do from there was to tool about town and try and find Randy, or anybody else for that matter. By then I'd already pushed Eddie and Betty's fire call out of my mind, otherwise I'd have considered making a run out to their respective homesteads. Good thing I didn't, in hindsight, since the secondary roads out there on those bluffs would've been too much for the cruiser. Most of 'em are a dirt/gravel mix once you get past Gil Cooper's ranch, and riddled with ruts the size of Saint Bernards.

"I'd just got back out to the cruiser when I spotted a dim set of lights moving gradually down east Main.

"Sure enough, it was Randy behind the wheel of our volunteer fire department's snowcat. I found him glassy-eyed and tongue-tied for the most part, though soon enough he was able to string together enough words to give me a notion as to what was going on. Deputy Jeffries stated he too had received several calls about a bright, glowing light a few miles east of the Valley, two of which had come from Eddie Cromartie and Betty Widham. He'd then borrowed the truck from the fire station and wheeled on out there. Bypassing the sparse ranch and farm homes out that way, Randy said he spotted the fire's glow soon enough, and by the time he reached the source, flaming debris and burned-out craters had left an easy enough trail to follow. Now, this is when things start... when things take a definite turn to the... um... weird side."

Owens hesitated as to briefly eye us all as individuals and to possibly gauge the group temperament as whether or not a green light to continue had been universally approved.

"Well, what are you waiting for, Sheriff?" Cassandra chimed in gruffly, though not yet conceding eye contact to our county-employed visitor.

"Let's wrap up this little campfire tale, shall we? I truly need to wash my hair before the *backup* generator craps out."

Naturally, Nick couldn't help but add in his obligatory two cent's worth.

"I'm with you, baby-doll. For a guy in a supposed hurry, you sure have a roundabout way to spin a yarn, Officer."

"My... my apologies to your clients, Hanover," Owens replied politely enough, temporarily lowering his head onto the table as if to nap before rising in the latter stages of a silent, drown-out yawn. "I... it's just that, I'm having a... bit of difficulty with my self-editing technique. Think my equilibrium has been kicked off-track... I surely don't mean to drag this out. It's just that... I don't want to come off like a crackpot with a fresh head wound... "

Tate Fletcher's response to this was textbook in both clarity and conciseness, a testament to the veteran soldiers' natural leadership ability. Fact is, I doubt even the chief couldn't state it better.

"Please ignore these two, Sheriff. No one here is doubting your honesty, much less your sanity. Now, hop back on that bucking steed and get to the meat of whatever it is you need from us. Like the good folks at this facility, we're here to help."

"Appreciate that, Mister... um... "

"Fletcher. Tate Fletcher. Call me Scar."

"Thanks for the confidence vote, Tate... um, Scar. Alright... here we go then... strap in tight and please try to at least... " Owens half-whispered, raising a forefinger airborne and waving it back and forth like the clicking hand of an ancient grandfather clock, "... have an open mind."

"Not to worry, Sheriff, I can almost guarantee that we as a group have heard of and seen stranger than anything you're about to reveal."

Shaking his head in mock humor, I swear Owens almost tipped onto the floor from pure fatigue.

"Remains to be seen, Mister Scar. Remains to

be seen..."

The conclusion of Sheriff Jake Owens' dismal tale lasted exactly eleven minutes according to my digital sports watch. I know because I timed the man. I timed the man because I had figured at the outset he wasn't going to last through to the conclusion before passing out cold.

In a bizarre twist for which I cannot even fathom a sensible explanation, Owens' instead seemed strangely recharged as the story pushed forward.

He stated that Randall Jeffries' swore to all that was holy that it was a military cargo plane which had crashed in the hilly pasture splitting the property of the aforementioned Eddie Cromartie and Betty Widham, and a sizeable cargo plane at that. When asked, the deputy was unable to determine what branch of the service the plane represented-be it Air Force, Navy or perhaps Army National Guard, who were known to fly periodic training missions in the area. It wasn't as if the deputy hadn't spotted an official marking amidst the burning ruins, just that the ones he was able to visualize weren't easily identified. Unable to clarify, Jeffries had discovered something infinity more sinister a few hundred feet past the final scattering of mangled, smoldering debris. He claimed to have almost driven over a man's prone body lying flat on its stomach. Upon closer inspection, Deputy Jeffries had found his initial identification to be only partially correct, as the body he had struggled so fiercely to avoid running over had already suffered a fate that no truck tire was apt to worsen. He told the sheriff the man's body appeared to have literally been split in half; ripped from groin to scalp until only the left half remained intact, propped neatly upon the ruined stump the right section had once occupied. Jeffries had stated that so neat was the carnage that even from a short distance it appeared the man's missing right half might've been buried in the building snow and thus hidden from view.

Stating he hadn't seen any other casualties, intact, dismembered or otherwise, in or around the crash site, Jeffries said he then steered the 'cat toward Eddie Cromartie's ranch, which sat approximately two-hundred yards to the east over a trio of rock-infested rolling hills. A widower for more than a decade, 'Crazy Eddie' lived alone in a two-story brick ranch he himself had built from the ground up some three decades earlier.

Upon arrival, Jeffries claimed the ranch appeared lifeless and without even lamplight present within the home's interior, despite the fact Cromartie had called the station less than a half-hour earlier. Minutes later, he'd found the local curmudgeon lying on the home's ice-crusted back deck, or at least the upper portion of him... minus a right arm and a large section of his skull. Jeffries had told the sheriff he didn't hang around to search out the mutilated old man's lower body, but instead leapt back into the truck and headed west for Betty Widham's residence. It was during this particular trek that the deputy stated to have called not only Sheriff Jake Owens via his personal cell phone, but the state police in Corvallis as well.

Approximately thirty minutes later, Jeffries had returned back into the heart of town, roughly around the same time Sheriff Owens had discovered the valley annex station deserted and without power. The sheriff stated that after all Randy Jeffries had borne witness to in the previous hour, the deputy was equal parts hysterical, terrified, and enraged; babbling a mile a minute one moment and semicatatonic the next. According to Owens, it was most likely the stop at Betty Widham's place that had sent his normally collected deputy over the edge.

Though still unsure of exactly what the man had found there, it was clear that whatever horrors Eddie Cromartie had suffered, the retired schoolteacher had apparently befallen much worse. The lone specific term Jeffries had used revolved around what a human body might resemble upon being tossed headfirst into an industrial strength woodchipper, thus the sheriff had easily surmised the elderly lady's grisly fate.

The sheriff stated that he left his cruiser parked and took the 'cat's steering wheel from Jeffries, whose behavior had begun to veer wildly from calm and rational to paranoid lunacy with each passing moment. Ambushed by a sudden wave of panic, Sheriff Owens then steered them back toward Jasper Ridge, leaving both a possible accident and double homicide scene behind. Making no apologies for his actions, Owens confessed to fearing not only for his wife's safety, but also for each and every man, woman and child residing within the Valley. But the confessional didn't quite end there. The sheriff also admitted to a possible blackout period of undetermined time, wherein he couldn't quite recall his actions.

"Never had anything like that happen to me

before... at least not when heavy doses of alcohol weren't involved, and I ain't tipped a bottle of spirits in over six years. Anyway, once I did reclaim my senses... I found myself steering us toward Jasper... it's almost like... I dunno... that whatever had happened out there in that Valley, be it terrorist or animal attack... it was too little, too late from a law enforcement standpoint," he'd croaked hoarsely, obviously exhausted from the retelling, but more so from reliving it all. "I just had to know... had to know that my side of town was still safe... that no one on that side of the Valley had befallen the same fate."

"But... didn't you ever consider the possibility that your deputy hadn't... well... gone off the deep end?" Jessica asked a bit timidly, as if ashamed to have broached the subject.

"Of course I did... of course, but the thought quickly passed. I knew... I *know* that man. I hired him... trained him... watched him gradually gain the public's trust, which around here ain't no leisurely task, especially for a man of color. I... trust Randy Jeffries is telling me the gospel truth every blamed time he opens his mouth. I wasn't about to seriously doubt his story, no matter how... unfathomable it sounded. Lord knows I still had doubts... guess it's only natural. Soon enough though... those doubts faded away... like a puff of cigar smoke in a monsoon, they faded clear away. I wish to god... wish to the good lord above they still existed... " Owens choked, his voice cracking with a sudden wave of emotion that caught us all off-guard in wake of the previous grim, by-the-numbers tone he'd exhibited.

"But... after what I... what we saw... " he pointed eastward, as if to indicate Highway 6 to the east of the post perimeter, "after what we... found just a few miles from this very spot... there ain't no further doubt in this man's mind... at least... what's left of it anyhow."

Slumping forward, the sheriff locked the fingers of both hands and promptly cupped the back of his neck, his legs splayed out in front of him like those of a discarded puppet.

The duration of his silence grew to several minutes, during which time everyone present displayed an impressive amount of patience considering the cliff's edge we'd all been placed atop.

"Sheriff... Jake... what was it you saw?" Burt finally asked, peeking over the top of his black-framed spectacles in true Rhodes scholar fashion.

It seemed to take Jake Owens an eternity to straighten his frame until he sat upright amid several deep, strenuous breaths.

"Two... two and a half miles at the most... just a few hundred yards before you get to Gilley Morton's boarded-up old Stop 'n Shop, god rest his cranky old soul. It must've been around two or three in the a.m. when we... I managed to drive the 'cat off into a soft ravine just past the old Westerley farmhouse. Place has been deserted since Pops Westerley passed last June, so with Randy in a permanent fog it was up to me to dig out by my lonesome. Took me a solid three hours with only that damn mini-shovel for company. It was close to dawn before I got us back on track.

"'Bout fifteen or twenty minutes later, give or

take a half-hour, we... I spotted a black Hummer with State Trooper insignia and matching plates. Funny thing... and I sure as hell don't mean of the 'ha ha' variety, it was just sitting there parked at the abandoned pumps as if expecting someone to run out and fill its tank. I figured it couldn't have been stationary for very long, since the hood and windshield were fairly clear, and by then the white stuff was tumbling down in buckets.

"It wasn't 'til we pulled up next to it that Randy pointed out the back glass of the Hummer was smashed clean through. Not only that, but the driver's door was dented something fierce and jarred open an inch or two. I must've hammered on that snowcat's horn a dozen times but saw nor heard any response. From that point, there wasn't much in the way of deliberation; I told Randy to stay put as I eased my .38 from her holster, rezipped my parka hood and stepped out into the blizzard with both booted feet. God knows I wish there had been some other option... any other option, 'cause I'm fairly sure that even then I realized whoever or whatever I found inside that Hummer's dark interior wasn't gonna improve on the overall situation."

The sheriff paused for several ticks, glancing toward the ceiling with a trancelike expression, his eyes glimmering wildly as if the mind behind them was experiencing a medium level of happy intoxication.

"Have to confess to not attending Sunday services the way I should, though Marge tries like the dickens to push me in that general direction once in a moon. After last night, I find myself praying a lot, either aloud or in my thoughts. Crazy how that works, ain't it? Kind of like finding religion behind bars, I reckon. Most folks don't bother 'til a troublesome incident knocks 'em to their knees. Guess I'm not any different in that regard, not after... not after poking my head inside that Hummer and getting an eyeful. The good lord knows I don't want to take that particular image to my grave... no sir. I think that's what I pray for most... to forget. Just... to forget."

Possibly in fear that the sheriff was beginning to drift away in the mental sense and that he might well suffer a complete collapse before revealing the vital punch line we'd all geared up to hear, Burt quickly intervened with expert efficiency.

"We're here to listen, not to judge. Talk to us, Jake. Don't even attempt to keep it bottled up. Take us back to that very moment and allow us to serve as buffers. You'll no longer be alone to rerun and relive such personal horror... we'll *all* be there as your personal comfort zone, from this moment on."

Rising from his chair, Burt then walked over and kneeled down in front of the sheriff, all the while maintaining eye contact, before reaching up and placing a hand on the man's right shoulder.

"Jake, trust us as you trust Randall... "

The sheriff stood, so gingerly that from a distance he might've appeared a crippled, arthritis-ravaged old man, and shuffled over to the room's lone window, the glass of which appeared on the verge of implosion from a generous build-up of impacted snow and ice.

"Not sure exactly why, but I didn't pull that Hummer's driver door open a bit at a time, but instead jerked it open like I was half-expecting an armed suspect to be sitting behind her wheel. Instead... what I found was... well, it was one of those scenes that, for several heartbeats, the eye and mind are unable to agree on a proper description. In hindsight, the only thing I can compare it to is the money-shot in a horror flick, you know... the grisliest of gore scenes that as younger folks we all dared each other to watch when the time came. In this particular case, the difference is... *was* that it wasn't any fancy computer-generated effect or anything of the like. Swear it appeared someone had drenched the interior with the reddest shade of paint you could imagine. Red streams hung from the ceiling in fully formed icicles. Took these tired-old orbs of mine a few seconds to adjust from such a... shocking kaleidoscope... and gradually visualize the body propped no more than a foot from the face-lining of my city-issued parka.

"The trooper was dead for real... dead and... spread out all over the interior of that Hummer like a slaughterhouse bovine."

At this point, staring into that frost-infested window, Jake Owens truly appeared to be reliving the horrific imagery as if peeking into a one-sided mirror. His hands, hanging limp by his sides, began to visibly tremor; his knees similarly shaking as if on the very edge of collapse. Just watching a twenty-year law enforcement veteran, one who had patrolled the mean streets of Houston, Texas for more than a decade before traveling and settled into more peaceful climes, reduced to such a sorry state was easily as frightening as the story at the core of such fears.

"I never... saw... found the man's head. It was

just gone... like it'd been plucked from his body like overripe fruit. Might've been lying in the passenger's floorboard with the other... assorted scraps... I thought I caught a glimpse of a severed arm curled mostly beneath the seat, right next to a displaced leg, polished boot and all, but I wasn't about to... hang around to take inventory.

"Still, what little upper torso remained was sitting upright, his right hand still locked on that wheel in a... (laughed weakly) ... well, I guess you could truly call it a 'death grip', no... pun intended.

"Anyways, that was all I needed to see... and more. In the end, I was damned grateful for the frigid conditions, otherwise the smell of punctured gut and a few gallons of spilt blood surely would've resulted in a certain country sheriff losing his lunch, something this boy hasn't done since his first on-scene auto pile-up 'bout twenty-one years back. I recall turning about in such a lurch that I almost tripped and flew headfirst into the 'cat's grille. I put the pedal to the metal and skidded back onto Highway 6, no doubt babbling to Randy a mile a minute as to the horrors I'd found. Have to confess I felt a twinge of jealousy, 'cause by that time my deputy was way beyond caring. His eyes had grown all wide and teary but the man never blinked or hardly twitched, no matter how deep the pothole or dramatic the slide. It was like he was... entranced by the storm, like a little kid watching his first snowfall. Guess I realized even then he was in shock, but it isn't as if I could've done or said anything to reverse the effect. Besides, I was too busy making damned sure we got some distance between ourselves and Boulder Valley, specifically that beat-down old service station. It wasn't 'til we passed Elmer Massey's farm that I heard the gears begin to grind and whine like howling banshees, and knew the 'cat was nearing lock-down mode. I pulled in here with two things in mind, folks... a respite from the madness I'd... we'd witnessed and to hopefully find some form of communication to the outside world.

"I ain't about to openly fib," he concluded, turning about to display a complexion as pale as the window's chilling reflection at his back, "not at this juncture. It wasn't solely the mutilation of one Wyoming State Trooper that fueled our lightning-quick departure from that ramshackle old gas station, no sir. I had what you might call... extra special motivation to keep my bootheel pressed tightly against that truck's accelerator 'til we arrived here as your uninvited guests; that being the thought that whoever or *whatever* was tearing the locals apart like Christmas geese was nearby and stalking about. Whatever you may be thinking, I'm not yellow by nature, folks... never even knew I *possessed* that particularly shaded gene, in fact. Guess it's true what they say. One never fully knows oneself... up until the day they place you in a pine box and toss on the dirt. You just... never really know.

"There's one thing I *do* know, however. I just experienced the longest night in all my years, hands down. Here's hoping the one to come is a tad bit shorter, say by... oh, a year or two."

***

While Doc Gonzales tended to the sheriff with yet another series of inoculations he stoically referred to as 'knee unbucklers', the rest of our ragtag group converged in the dimly lit mess hall over several pots of freshly brewed java. As to Jake Owens' tale of mass murder with a distinctive creature-feature vibe, opinions were many and varied as to such points as validity and probability. As far as particular points of view, verbal outbursts included, but were not limited to, the following gems of wisdom of the knee-jerk variety:

Jessica (sporting wide, unblinking, panic-filled eyes and a comically warped, static cling hairdo straight from the B-52s in their pop culture heyday): "It'll come here... eventually. Whatever it is... there won't be any hiding from it... (singing in a harsh, gravelly whisper) *... nowhere to run, baby... nowhere to hide...* "

Nick 'Dejà vu' Parione (his trademark smirk set firmly in place): "Well, wasn't that one freaky-deeky, goose pimply ride into the sad, tragic realm of mental illness? What's next, body of Big Foot found trapped in massive snowdrift while wearing ladies undies? (feigning a horrid Southern accent) The Loch Ness Monster spotted on ice skates down at Grover's Pond? Cut me some slack, pleeeeasssse... "

Tate 'Scar' Fletcher (speaking exclusively to Benjamin Thomason): "Man sounded stable enough to me. Just might be something to it. Face it, we've both heard... and seen, stranger."

Benjamin 'Force' Thomason (replying exclusively to Fletcher while using a gaint-sized forefinger to stroke each side of his bushy Fu

Manchu): "Damned tootin' we have at that, Sarge. Still, I've watched more than one man go off the deep end from cabin fever-type weather conditions such as these. Story would hold a lot more water if that deputy could back up some of the facts."

Cassandra 'Jekyll-ene' Wilkes (with a level of indifference that could only be described as 'off the charts'): "Crock of nonsensical bull. Spook stories for the mentally challenged and woefully gullible, from which this room seems very well-stocked indeed."

Burt 'The Chief' Hanover (addressing myself and Jay between noisy slurps of steaming coffee): "I think both of them require psychological care we simply can't provide here. Damn it, if we could only contact someone... anyone on the outside."

Jay Peterson (frantically sucking on at least his third cigarette since the sheriff's monologue had ceased): "We might as well be stranded on Mars (suddenly introspective, as if talking quietly to himself) ... shit, what if even half of what he said was true? What if... Jessica is right? What then?"

Mentally prepping for a general comment never fated to be verbalized, my lips briefly parted but quickly clamped upon noticing everyone glaring toward the dining hall's entrance, where the doc walked side by side with a still very shaky looking County Sheriff Jake Owens.

"Sorry about that, folks. Lost my oats there for a sec, but thanks to good old Doc Syringe over here, I'm slowly recouping."

He'd been wrapped in one of the post's 'exclusive for federally placed clients' bulky, puke-green parkas, though his body was still openly wracked with the occasional shiver.

"Between needle jabs, I've been speaking to the doc here, kind of... proposing what I think is the only logical plan of action... considering the circumstances as I see... as I've seen them."

To his left, Doc Gonzales merely shook his head in response.

"What might that be, Sheriff?" Burt asked, temporarily shoving his coffee mug aside.

The sheriff shrugged, hugging himself tightly through the coat's thick fur-lining.

"Pretty simple, really.

"Search and... possible rescue. We... I need... *have* to find out if the good folks in Jasper are better off than those I've heard about... and seen on the Boulder Valley side. Needless to say, I'm gonna need some help carrying out this little mission."

Following several seconds of a silence so absolute I actually heard Jay's strained swallow several feet to my right, the air was pierced by a shrieking yowl I could only compare to that of the localized coyotes during mating season. Cassandra Wilkes, having taken up residence in the hall's northernmost booth and essentially turning her back on the proceedings, was nonetheless the very first to object to the initial idea suggested.

"Well then, Marshall Dillon, I suggest you send out an immediate SOS for *Frosty the Snowman* or his close-knit cousin *Abominable*, 'cause they'd be the only ones noodleheaded enough to accept said mission."

Still another bout of fleeting silence ensued, interrupted only by Nick Parione's muffled giggles.

"So does everyone concur with such an opinion

or do I have a second motion?" Jake Owens asked sternly, his roving eyes eventually settling on everyone present while awaiting a response. After a bit, his focused appeared to settle exclusively on Ben and Tate, who stood shoulder to shoulder like massive bookends.

"Doc here told me that four of you are superhero types. If that's so... I could sure use some of the *hero* part to live up to its rep. In truth, the whole community would sure be obliged. Me... I'd take it as a personal favor. One I might not ever be able to repay, mind you, but it wouldn't be from a lack of effort."

"Now, hold on here a minute, Jake," Burt objected, though a more timid effort I'd rarely seen from the man. "There are legal ramifications to discuss. These people are federally assigned to my care. Damn it, voluntary endangerment isn't part of the planned curriculum. I... we could lose our license to practice if... if something goes haywire out there."

Not surprisingly, the first to intervene was Ben, the lone client whose file claimed had served in any long-term supervisor capacity.

"Cool your jets, boss man. Think of it as a... field trip. Yeah, just what the doctor ordered, ya might say, for both education and therapeutic purposes. Besides, what better way than to clear the mind than gettin' back to nature, right?"

As if on cue, Tate Fletcher chimed in next.

"Yeah, picturesque mountain ranges, clean, crisp air, wide open spaces... "

"... Blizzard conditions that make the Antarctic look like Waikiki beach in July," Burt finished in a mocking huff.

Not to be denied, Fletcher quickly discarded any attempt at levity, stepping forward with his arms crossed defiantly and his head slightly cocked to the left.

"Believe me, Chief Hanover, I've been exposed to worse, and with far less clothing covering this leathery old hide."

"Ditto, Chief," Ben added, his demeanor similarly grim. "As for legalities, we'll each take personal responsibility for placin' our own asses on the line. From what the marshall and his gun hand there are implyin', it seems to me like the locals ain't just dealin' with some random slasher on the loose. Much as I hate to come off like a walkin', talkin' cliche, this here mission calls for your regulation spandex types... meanin' us of course."

Before Burt could even properly reply, Sheriff Owens practically leapt forward and positioned himself directly between the bantering trio as if to cut off any further dialogue. The man had made quite the rapid recovery; his cheeks regaining a semblance of color even as his movements grew less robotic and gained animation.

"Sounds like I have two willing and definitely able volunteers. Of course I'll need to swear you both in as temporary deputies... just to keep things kosher from a city government standpoint, you understand."

Even as Tate and Ben exchanged a look of utter perplexity, I saw Burt fidgeting in the background, his upper body beginning to shake and convulse as if undergoing the final stages of a severe epileptic fit. I'd seen the man this upset, borderline volatile, on very few occasions in the past year, usually with government bureaucracy as the target. Obviously having picked up on the same vibe, Jay lightly nudged my side with an elbow just as Burt rediscovered his authoritative tone and subsequently fired away with vocal cords smokin'. Meanwhile, both Nick Parione and Cassandra Wilkes had exited stage left, slinking from the room with not so much as a disapproving grunt. In turn, neither Burt nor the sheriff gave either a second look as they'd departed, probably having already deduced the pair's disinterest and/or utter uselessness.

"You people don't seem to understand the seriousness of such a rash proposal. Not only is it potentially a legal snake pit, but in terms of common sense, it's about as sensible as riding an inner tube down the Colorado rapids."

With his back still turned, Sheriff Owens' rebuttal was made while casually zipping his parka to the neck. Meanwhile, the two soon-to-be sworn-in deputies of Jasper County, Wyoming stood silently as if awaiting the echoing of a ringside bell to determine the final outcome.

"Burt, I have a sneaking feeling that as a rule, logic has taken the high road out of Boulder Valley. Happened about the same time the weather turned to absolute shit and local citizens began to die unnatural deaths."

Unabated, Burt picked up the dialogue as if the sheriff's comments had never been spoken aloud, although our erstwhile post general began pacing at the other man's back with both hands gesturing wildly.

"The people assigned to this facility are my

responsibility and mine alone, Sheriff. If there is an immediate danger located outside these grounds, it is my duty to make sure they are not exposed to said dan-"

It wasn't so much the content of the rebuttal that initiated a group wince, but rather the delivery itself. Sheriff Jake Owens had spun around on his heels with such unexpected speed and grace that even Burt had executed an involuntary flinch.

"No, Burt, it seems you're the one having the comprehension problems. I've got people being murdered out there in the towns I'm responsible to protect-people with families that I'm paid to oversee when they're not able to do so. This is about saving human lives I'm talking about, Hanover... not dealing with government regulated, red-tape bullshit! If the blood of innocents is being spilled out there, it's my job to find out why and put a stop to it by any means necessary, and if at a later date I have to take a shot on the shins from some bored-to-tears fed with a bug up his ass about rules and regulations, so be it."

"Damn it, Jake, if they go out and get themselves killed, it's on my head!"

"You've got what... fifteen, twenty folks assigned here, Burt?"

Burt shrugged, a good portion of his vent and vigor having already vanished in wake of Jake Owens' sudden outburst.

"Y-yes, about that... presently."

"Well, I'm talking more along the lines of twelve hundred, not counting the dozen or so homesteads residing smack dab between the city limits of either town. You start spouting numbers to impress, Hanover, you'd damned well better be able to outstat the other fella."

"Alright then, understood. But it's past three already and fast growing dark as a coal mine out there. Can't this fool's escapade wait 'til morning?"

"Can't take that chance, Burt. Folks might be screaming out for help as we speak."

"But the conditions might actually improve overni-"

"Slick roads and snowdrifts be damned. We have to hit the trail now while it's still somewhat passable."

Backing up several steps until he stood directly between the hulking figures of Tate and Ben, the sheriff raised a hand on either side and placed them on the men's shoulders.

"Now, these two brave, heroic clients of yours have volunteered to assist me in my quest. First off though, I need to ask two additional favors of you."

Burt nodded, his shoulders having already slumped in apparent defeat.

"We'll need a few supplies and... I'll need to commandeer that snowplow you have tucked away so neatly in the back of the garage. I wouldn't ask, but you've seen the snowcat. Ain't no mechanic alive going to get that baby up and running again before spring, leastways no one around these parts."

"Alright, you've got it," Burt conceded with a sigh before sidestepping over to effectively block the exit.

"Someone from the staff has to ride along. We're all licensed to drive that beast... " he said, rotating a forefinger until he'd pointed at Tate, Ben and the sheriff individually, "you guys aren't."

The sheriff started to open his mouth, no doubt in protest, but was quickly cut off as Burt turned away with his hands balanced on his sides.

"Hey, it's a standard part of our initial in-processing to work here. We have bimonthly recert classes on that ton and a half.

"After all, I have to keep something legal about this mess... in case something does... in case there is trouble."

At the mere prospect of playing chauffeur for such a potentially exciting outing, I felt my heart skip a beat and I was wracked by an inner shudder of equal parts fear and exhilaration. Moments later, such exasperations were relegated to woefully premature as Burt spat out a list of probable drivers.

"Whatever you say, Burt, but make it quick. We need to hit the road before another foot of the white stuff falls and we're stranded here for the duration. Worse yet, dusk is only a few hours off, and the temps are surely gonna dip below the zilch line soon thereafter," the sheriff bristled.

"Yeah, we're wastin' precious time and daylight here, Chief," Ben added, taking a seat to refit the calf-high mukluks both he and Tate had been provided from post supply. "Why bother anyhow? There ain't a vehicle been bolted together this man can't operate. Safe bet the Sarge here is just as capable, if not more so."

"Right as rain... just hand over the keys and watch me," Tate confirmed with a stiff, emotionless nod, "and the only license I ever *legally* held was Class B. Some rust-bucket ton and a half doesn't exactly fall under the heading of a bona fide challenge."

At this juncture, I swear the chief was on the edge of hysterics, his midsection all atremor as if a raucous, uncontrollable laughing jag was mere moments away. Sad to speculate, but I couldn't help but ponder if the 'licensed' snowplow driver bit was just a ploy to either delay the mission or worse, simply meant to infuriate Sheriff Jake Owens, whose rank-pulling power play had no doubt gotten under Burt's normally ultrathick skin.

"Regardless, men, I'm assigning a driver... case closed, and for the record, Mister Fletcher, a 2010 model GMC with five-hundred plus horses and less than six thousand miles beneath her saddle can hardly be referred to as a rust-bucket."

"Sorry, Teach," Tate replied, covering his mouth as to conceal the grin beneath. "Nothing personal."

Without warning, Jay leapt into the banter-laced fray with both casual dress shoe-covered feet, his motive for doing so becoming crystal clear almost immediately.

"So who's the unlucky duck then, Burt? You have a maintenance man assigned to this burg... a janitor maybe?"

"Hang on, Jay... I'm thinking... "

"Um, Burt?"

"Not now, Jay... "

"How about Chuck? He seems a logical choice."

"Chuck isn't on post, Jay. He left yesterday before the fallout and isn't due back 'til tomorrow."

Chuck James was indeed the post's hired handyman slash Mister Fix-it, a sixtyish pit bull of man whose shaggy gray hair, short, stocky build and snappish attitude had earned him the nickname 'Chopper." Chuck had, for whatever reason, considered the snowplow his personal playtoy, going so far as arranging prewinter refresher driving courses for all staff members and keeping the plow's keys tucked away in the maintenance safe. Jay's little reminder to Burt was based solely on the hope that Chuck was indeed present somewhere on post, thereby eliminating the possibility of anyone else, specifically his own cowardly hide, getting nailed with the assignment.

"How about Devon, then? He's always struck me as the daredevil type."

"Negative. I need him to stick near home base to keep that backup generator operational."

"I hear Jose once drove semis for a living south of the border... "

I heard Ben snicker, and have to admit to feeling a bit embarrassed for the man myself once the attempt was made to sacrifice the post cook to the snowplow gods. Besides, the fact Jose Garcia weighed upwards of four-hundred pounds and most likely couldn't fit into the truck's interior without assistance from multiple crowbars made the suggestion even more pathetic.

"For cripe's sake, Jay," Burt finally blurted out, waving both arms in mock surrender, "try to refrain from hyperventilating. I'm not going to ask *you*, alright?"

"I'll go, Chief," I heard myself say just as Jay had backed away clearing his throat. In truth, I wasn't even positive I'd spoken aloud until all heads twisted in my direction.

"Appreciate the bravery, Darrin, but I'd rather

bypass my counselors if at all possi-"

"But I'm due the hours," I countered with as much grit and backbone as was humanly possible considering the way my knees shook and convulsed at the time, still locked in self-awe mode that I'd even offered.

"You mean the mandatory off-post counseling thing? Darrin, that's... I mean, I'm not sure something like this would even count in terms of official therapy. I'd have to check the books to see if such a precedent exits."

"Well, I would be in the company of two clients," I continued, the confidence in my voice belying the barrage of static-charged spasms racking every nerve ending I possessed.

"The trek itself will most likely be time-consuming, as will the subsequent investigation. This will leave a wide window open in terms of counseling opportunities, correct?"

"Yes, I... it might... it probably... but I'm... not sure... maybe I should just... waive the license thing after all."

I had him over a barrel and he knew it. Besides, other than Jessica, Jay or himself, the remaining choices consisted of two elderly kitchen workers and Devon, whom Burt had already deemed mission essential to remaining on post.

"Chief... Burt, it's okay really. I want to go."

Sidestepping over, Burt placed an arm around my shoulders and led me into the nearest hallway, shifting his weight to turn us both away from all prying eyes and ears.

"Jesus, Darrin, this isn't necessary. I was just trying to... well, get back at Owens for playing

General Patton on my turf. The man pissed on my Wheaties for certain, but to allow you to go through with this is more than imbecilic, it's downright deranged. I don't want anyone, leastways a highly trained, skilled counselor being placed in harm's way."

Staring my supervisor squarely in the eye, I struggled to maintain orb contact but ultimately succeeded, more than likely due to the fact I wasn't just spouting meaningless dribble, but truly meant every word. "Chief, let me repeat... I want to go. I've been on post for three straight months now and have discovered something vital."

"That being?"

"Cabin fever isn't just a mindset. It's a tangible condition. I need an outing. I need the adventure. Plus which, I'm the only counselor who hasn't put in his time off-post. Jay worked the drunk tank at county lockup just last month, remember? Jessica went to Jasper High and played guidance counselor. I'm due, Burt. I'm due, and more importantly, I'm chomping at the bit."

"Chomping at the bit to play amateur detective alongside a pair of muscle-bound malcontents and a sheriff who just might possibly be delusional in the extreme?"

"Yes, sir. Sounds like a... now what's that expression I've heard that's so popular around there... sounds like a real *hoot*."

"Traipsing around in conditions a polar bear would shy away from sounds like a hoot to you, son?"

Clicking my heels together to come to full attention, I smiled broadly and raised two fingers in the age-old 'scouts honor' salute.

"I'll dress warm, Mother... I promise."

Burt seemed to drag the contemplation phase into a half-hour of frantic pacing, head rubs and hand wringing, when in reality it probably lasted no more than three full minutes.

"Go then, get your jollies, but don't come crying to me if you come back with frosty balls in the literal sense."

Moments later, Burt informed Sheriff Owens of said decision, but not without first proclaiming that the snowplow would not depart the premises until assured of two-way radio contact between Devon in the com center and the truck's inhabitants.

Exactly one hour and five minutes later, the four of us loaded into the snowplow's cramped interior armed with a hand-held walkie-talkie seemingly teleported from another era, its bulky design and excess weight bringing to mind similar devices utilized decades earlier, when such oversized, limited-use devices were deemed state-of-the-art. Devon had indeed pulled them from his personal collection of such ancient gadgets and deemed them operational for a maximum range of not over five to seven miles.

"Damned thing looks like a stadium speaker with grips," Ben had quipped, ducking his head to one side as to avoid the radio's lengthy antennae, "but hey... retro's cool... long as it works."

The post's skeletal crew had gathered in the chilling confines of the wrecked garage to see us off at a quarter past four. Though Devon had done an admirable job of hanging plastic sheeting over the open dock door, the temperature had nonetheless dropped near the zero mark in the time since the crash. Both Tate and Benjamin had wisely foregone the beach bum look for long johns, mukluks and thick wool jackets, bypassing the standard issue parkas only because none could be found large enough to accommodate their respective builds. As a substitute for ear, neck and head protection, each had been afforded polypro balaclavas and also given ultrathick Dachstein wool mittens, though Ben was later forced to toss his aside for obvious size-discrepancy reasons.

"Dude," he'd scolded Devon playfully while tossing the mittens aside, "I can do without the *thumb* warmers if it's all the same to ya."

While the staff stood in and around the sufficiently heated truck, Nick and Cassandra posed near the building entrance like wary sentries, their collective expressions as nonpartisan as ever. We were just getting set to mount up when Devon dashed back over to supply us with a large thermos of fresh coffee and accompanying mugs. Meanwhile, Doc Gonazles had brought along a surprise guest to the exit party; one Deputy Randall Jeffries, who had just moments earlier pleaded (albeit weakly considering his battered condition) with his boss to be allowed a space inside the vehicle, to which he was sternly denied.

"You're not up to it, Randy. Stay here and rest... recoup. Lord knows you look as though you need about a month's worth. If necessary, aid these good folks in case of... well, in case there's any kind of trouble here," I'd heard Jake Owens shout over the vehicle's roaring engine, "and if by some miracle communication to the outside world is restored, call the state boys back and let 'em know we got serious problems."

In the end, the four of us departed at a snail's pace with yours truly behind the wheel of a barely used GMC ton and a half equipped with a heavy-duty straight blade and extended moldboard, the massive adrenaline rush flowing through my veins as powerful as any I'd ever experienced. Actually, to leave the relative safety of the post grounds behind didn't seem that big of a deal at the moment.

Little did I or anyone else present know at the time that no such safe haven existed within the desolate locales surrounding all of Boulder Valley.

Nor were any of us privy to the information that the initial glacier storm of the winter season, and the worst in recorded history, had brought something extra along with it-a mysterious, scientifically inexplicable, ultimately deadly *something* that ensured the word 'safe' be stricken from our collective vocabularies.

Chapter Four

Crash and Burn/Missing Link

Despite the ten-plus extra miles it added to the trip, Sheriff Owens insisted we check out the plane crash site first. Thus, I steered the truck westward toward the land shared by alleged homicide victims Edward Cromartie and Betty Widham. Not surprisingly, road conditions were horrific, limiting our top speed to just over twenty miles per hour while basically carving out a fresh trail along the snow and ice-encrusted pavement. Fortunately once the sky grew beyond merely murky to pitch-black status, a bright moon shone above, allowing for a fair amount of illumination along the narrow two-way, otherwise I'd have likely driven us off the nearest embankment before we'd traveled two miles from the post grounds. As it was, I felt fresh sweat stains coat my well-insulated underarms. In terms of piloting the plow in extreme weather conditions, the worst I'd experienced was a four to five inch snow at the tail end of the previous winter. Thus, playing the dual roles of navigator and pilot while careening through at least three times that amount was no easy chore from a mental breakdown standpoint, though on the bright side the heavy downpour had dwindled to a faint flurry by the time we'd covered half the distance to Boulder Valley.

Although kept extremely occupied with the double duty of not only maintaining a safe traveling speed but also ensuring the vehicle continued to travel atop paved road as opposed to loose dirt and/or gravel shoulder, I was able to sit back and enjoy the lively banter of my three comrades.

Crammed together as we were, a fact hardly improved on by our two ride-along heroes' natural bulkiness, there was little choice but to accept a forced dose of camaraderie. Ben sat to my immediate right, with the sheriff packed between him and Tate in a less-than-spacious interior constructed to house a maximum of four *average*-sized adults.

Less than two minutes in, just as we'd departed the post's steel gate entrance for the mostly buried lanes of Highway 6, a fascinating dialogue ensued, or at least one in my chosen profession would deem as such. During these sometimes morose, ofttimes priceless exchanges, I was rarely offered the opportunity to divert my eyes from the treacherous roads in order to view the facial expressions matching the spoken words. Of the few times I did chance a brief glance, said expressions could only be described as ad lib masterpieces of comic genius, the majority of said gems belonging to none other than Benjamin Thomason. Who knew a man whose personnel file described as possessing a temper of legendary proportions and a penchant for uncontrollable bouts of rage also had the power to summon his inner comedian at will? Then again, there couldn't have been a more effective straight man for either superhero type than the good Sheriff Jake Owens, never a man to mince words.

Sheriff Owens: "So you're both on the fed payroll as hired muscle?"

Tate Fletcher: "Yeah, you might say that."

Sheriff Owens: "So how come you both look so... so plain? Hell, at first I thought Burt and his crew had taken on a couple of retired pro ballplayers gone to seed... (*cleared throat*) ... no offense intended, but you both appear a bit long in the choppers."

Ben Thomason (*laughed*): "Ya ain't one to withhold an opinion, are ya, Marshall?"

Sheriff Owens: "Never been accused, no."

Tate Fletcher: "What do you mean by *plain*?"

Sheriff Owens: "Oh, I don't know. It's just that, when I think superhero I expect to see fancy costumes and... well, you know... accessories."

Ben Thomason: "Accessories? Ya mean like jewelry or-"

Sheriff Owens: "No, no, you know, Thor's got his sledgehammer... Captain America lugs that shield around like a security blanket... even that Silver Samurai dude skis around on that surfboard like Peter Pan on crack... those kinds of things."

Ben Thomason (*laughed*): "I think ya mean the Silver Surfer."

Sheriff Owens: "Whatever. That one always looked a bit too slick for me, if you get my drift, as in 'queer eye for the shiny guy' (paused as the other two men laughed aloud).

"So neither of you carry any kind of special cargo along in case the combat gets a little too hot and heavy for just plain old fisticuffs?"

Tate Fletcher: "Nothing permanent, though I once did own a nine-inch bladed Bowie I grew quite fond of. Called her 'Sally Slice 'n Dice' after a chick I'd been shacking up with in Cambodia. Yeah, I held onto that gorgeous hunk of steel for almost five years before she got seared in half by a broadsword off the coast of Thailand. I guess that's the closest I ever had to hauling around a symbol of my chosen profession. How about you, Benji?"

Ben Thomason: "Yer kiddin', right (*held up both his massive hands and playfully wriggled them*)? Check out these two heavy duty dough-kneaders and tell me what could possibly match 'em for intimidation *slash* symbolism purposes?"

Sheriff Owens (*laughed*): "Good point, my man. You could hide a freaking bowling ball in each palm."

Ben Thomason: "That I could, Marshall. They don't call me shovel-mitts, among other things, for nothin'."

Tate Fletcher (*pointed toward the hood of the truck*): "Better yet, Benji, if those plow blades happen to snap off, we can always bind your ass to the hood and let you whack away."

Ben Thomason (*Executes several abbreviated 'karate chop' blows*): "See there, Marshall? Who needs man-made accessories when naturally cultivated mutations like these will do?"

Sheriff Owens: "Speaking of which, what's the story with those other two sourpusses back there? Your fellow inmates, I mean. Appeared to me neither of them seemed too damn heroic-cowering in the corner like they were afraid someone might ask 'em for a favor."

Tate Fletcher: "In Nick Parione's case, I think the guy's a Grade-A asshole... period, end of sentence. Cassie Wilkes on the other hand (shrugged)... only her shrink knows for sure."

Ben Thomason: "Ya nailed Parione like a twenty-penny nail, Fletch. 21st century superpunk: arrogant; conceited; self-centered. As for 'Sybil' Wilkes, she's as nutty as a freshly baked fruitcake, no matter the incarnation. Poor girl's misplaced the majority of her face cards."

Sheriff Owens (*laughed*): "What makes either of them special? I mean, they must have a power, right?"

Ben Thomason (*sipping coffee from a dark red Denver Broncos mug*): "Parione goes by the name Dejà vu. Little Jackass is a walkin', talkin' time machine... with limitations. Gotta admit though, it was a real headtripper. Wilkes goes by 'Jekyll-ene'... a multiple personality type who grows stronger, meaner, and increasingly moronic with each subsequent change. That whacky chick is a goony bird; several *dozen* bricks shy of a load."

Tate Fletcher: "Still, if push comes to shove and something does go down at the post while we're gone, I don't think either will hesitate to flex a little muscle to protect the others."

Sheriff Owens (*paused, leaned forward and peeked upward as to check the blackened skies*): "Figures not a blamed one of you has the power of flight. We could've hitched up a saddle and flown over the storm clouds-bet that Shining Surfer dude could've got me to the Cromartie place in two winks and a shake of his girly hips."

Ben Thomason (*shaking his head in obvious bemusement*): "That's Silver Sur- ah, forget it already. Ya ain't much for names, are ya, Marshall?"

Sheriff Owens (*pulling back his parka hood and wiping a hand through his disheveled, grayish locks*): "Nope, not 'til we've become acquainted on at least a semiregular basis. I could, however, name off just about every man, woman, and child residing in and around the Twin Cities.

(*The sheriff's expression turned abruptly grim, his voice instantly dropping several octaves)*

"I hope like hell I don't end up reciting the majority of them at a mass funeral."

Tate Fletcher: "No need to coat your ulcers with hot sauce, Sheriff, at least not yet."

Ben Thomason: "Tate's right. For now ya got two dead locals confirmed, along with a plane crash victim and one state trooper. Take it from a man who knows, Constable Owens, playin' doomsayer is a damn waste of time and peace of mind 'til the worst *does* happen."

Sheriff Owens (*repositioned his parka hood before taking a long sip of steaming java*): "You don't know how much I pray you're both right, but this constant gnawing at my gut tells an altogether different story."

Each man grew deathly silent in the aftermath of the rather grim musings of Jake Owens, a man I'd grown to respect since his unexpected arrival into our midst. Despite the welcome respite the trio's (mostly) witty banter had provided, I still couldn't quite shake the man's horror tale involving the state trooper. As perilous as it was, treading icy, snow-coated roads couldn't hold a candle to such a grisly discovery. I could only hope to be spared any similar scenes as the trek proceeded.

Roughly forty minutes since our departure from the outpost, I steered the truck over the last of a trio of winding, steep hills whose true height was impossible to gauge due to the massive snowdrifts dotting the landscape. Amazingly, the midnight sky had arrived at just past eighteen-thirty, in great part due to a buildup of massive storm clouds that had so effectively doused the aforementioned moonshine.

Upon starting a purposely sluggish descent down the final slope, there appeared a dim glow to the east, like the fading embers from a distant campfire. For at least the twentieth time since leaving the post grounds, the sheriff tried to utilize the Jurassic era walkie-talkie, but to no avail as waves of blistering static once again ruled the day.

"Might as well be using Dixie cups with strings attached to 'em, Hoss," Ben quipped as the sheriff tossed the oversized relic beneath the seat in frustration.

"Jesus, back to the Dark Ages. It's like somebody unplugged the entire region. It isn't like we haven't been through storms around here before."

The fire glow grew brighter as I navigated through still another winding curve, momentarily losing track of where the road was supposed to be.

"There ya go, Slick," Ben barked, nudging my left shoulder with one of his king-sized digits.

"Yep, I see her," I replied, my voice a sullen croak born from both a build-up of stress and such a lengthy period of silence.

"I won't have to take any unexpected detours to reach that spot, will I, Sheriff?"

"Nope. Just stay on the road for the next mile or so. We'll dismount just east of Crazy Eddie's and hoof it from there... probably no more than a hundred yards or so."

The light grew brighter as we neared, fading a bit each time the road dipped, until we crested the steepest of hills and were finally able to identify the source in full view.

"Well, I guess this takes that theory about my deputy being delusional and flushes it straight down the nearest crapper," the sheriff said, pointing to my immediate left to indicate a suitable parking space. Cutting sharp, I soon spotted the top line of a barbwire fence as I'd braked, the left corner of the plow blade faintly tapping a wooden post that had been completely submerged in a three to four foot drift. The sheriff leaned over and looked past me to the top portion of the post, which shook and gyrated from impact, instantly clearing itself from an icy camouflage.

"Close shave there, Mister Chauffeur. The shoulder here is five, six feet from the pavement, but just past that flimsy barricade is a ten, twelve-foot drop. Another foot or so and we'd all be playing polar bear."

Despite the chill, I feel a sudden rush of heat flush my neck, face and head. If not for the parka hood's effective concealment, I'm quite certain the hair atop my scalp would've stood stiffly at attention as if from a sudden burst of electrical static.

"Sorry about that. I must've skipped the class on parking in blizzard conditions."

"Touche, counselor. Fact is, you did a fine job in getting us this far," he replied blandly as all present stared out the driver's window at the scattered spattering of dwindling flames that cut a lengthy trail through the nearby pastureland. Separate tree lines lined the highway on either side, as winter-ravaged oaks, pines and elms stood as gnarled, grotesque symbols of foreboding to our very presence. As if to sever the hypnotic effect and thereby snap the group trance we'd unwittingly fallen into, Tate Fletcher slapped his gloved palms briskly together and spoke at a much higher volume than was necessary in such close-knit quarters.

"Well, what say we blow this popsickle stand and warm our mitts by the fire, so to speak?"

"I'm with you, pal," Ben replied, blinking madly as if to fully evaporate the effects of a particularly stout daze. "Looks like somebody held a major league weenie roast and didn't invite us."

As those two prepped to evacuate by zipping their parkas to the full tunnel-vision effect, Sheriff Owens reached into his own coat and retrieved not one but two marble-handled revolvers, one a snub nose and the other of the long-barrel variety.

"You know how to handle one of these, Mister Jackson?" he asked, reaching past Ben and offering up the snub nose.

"Well, I've... to tell the truth, I've never actually fired one, no."

"It's not brain surgery by any stretch. Safety's on. If you feel the need, release it... just point and fire. Got it? Now, you stay put and keep the engine warm while we check out the crash site."

My mouth went instantly dry even as my palms grew moist. It wasn't as if I were a pacifist or a conscientious objector, it was simply that since a very early age firearms had scared the living bejebbers out of me.

"I don't think... I mean, it's just that... I'm not too... comfortable lugging that thing around, much less attempting to use it."

Utilizing a borderline patronizing tone, the sheriff seemed on the verge of laying the revolver in my lap.

"Think of it as an insurance policy, Darrin. Think of it as... peace of mind."

"Sheriff, I... I'm not much for... that is, I'd rather take my chances unarmed."

"Just take the damn peashooter already... " Ben barked impatiently before softening his stance with a dose of dry humor. "Hey, don't sweat it, Counselor. Nobody's askin' ya to be Dirty Harry. It's just a precaution, right, Marshal? Nothin' to milk your drawers over. Besides, Tate and me are takin' point, so you got no worries."

Realizing it was neither the time nor place for a debate on gun control, I reached over and took the weapon from the sheriff's open palm, never even bothering to inquire of its loaded status. From my personal point of view, such a trivial detail seemed quite irrelevant, figuring that if it came down to my possession of a firearm to save our ragtag group, all might as well save time and bother by voluntarily hopping into the nearest open grave.

"There ya go," Ben spat out jovially just as Tate cracked the passenger's door and the temperature inside the cab seemed to instantly plummet fifty degrees. "Back in two winks, Teach. You just keep the motor hummin' and that heater cranked."

"Um, don't... be too long, you hear?" I replied, instantly regretting the spooked nerd stereotype for which I continued, however unintentionally, to give credence.

The sheriff followed Tate's lead, leaping from the cab and instantly vanishing from my line of sight, as if he'd dived from an airline hatch at three-thousand feet instead of a four-foot drop from a truck cab. Ben was the last to depart, uncoiling like a striking reptile and bounding into the unknown with a rebel yell of admittedly minor substance, the gist of his warrior's shriek swallowed unmercifully by the howling winds. The slamming of the vehicle's passenger door was as strangely comforting as it was terrifying. In terms of the former, there was a sense, however temporary, of relief in simply being alone. As for the latter, there was an equally powerful and, unfortunately, more viable feeling of dread for the same exact reason.

***

Once isolated with only the rhythmic clicking of the vehicle's wiper blades and the loud thumping of the pulse at my temples as companions, I was astonished at how spacious the vehicle's interior truly was minus all the beef that had just exited.

Scooting over the slick vinyl seat, I used the parka's fur-lined left sleeve to wipe away the buildup of condensation from the passenger window and could just make out the outline of the trio of men cutting a trail up an oval-shaped hillside riddled with snowdrifts of various heights and widths. Bringing up the rear, I watched Ben soon vanish from sight amid a spattering of dwindling flames dancing atop the opposite hill. In studying the surrounding woods a bit more intently, it became apparent all the trappings of a stereotypical plane crash were indeed present, from a lengthy, mostly burnt-out slug trail consisting of mangled trees and singed, blackened shrubs to a smoke-tinged sky from which equal amounts of charred ash and icy precipitation rained down. Moving back over to the driver's side, I initiated the wipers for several reps and watched the blackened remnants of nearby vegetation riddle the glass in dark, soggy smears.

Hunting desperately for distraction as tension-filled moments ticked by at a snail's pace, I fumbled about with the truck's radio and was greeted with intermediate waves of blaring static. Checking my watch once futility set in, I saw it had been just over sixteen minutes since the search party had exited. Scanning the truck's panel readings, I noted we had just over three-fourth's of a tank of fuel remaining, though running short on petrol wasn't a serious concern being that the behemoth had a spare tank which held an additional forty gallons. Meanwhile, the oil and water temperatures appeared normal despite the engine's drawn-out idling.

I had been peering blankly out the driver's window at a ponderously moving, oval-shaped cloud of blackish smoke floating just above the tree line to the west when the passenger door flew open with a loud creak. It wasn't until the door slammed shut and Tate Fletcher's considerable bulk filled the open space, removing his parka hood and sitting down with a loud grunt that I realized I'd trained the barrel end of the revolver directly at his bared forehead.

"Whoaaaa there, Wild Bill... it's only me... " he said with both palms raised, "you can lower the peashooter."

Practically tossing the weapon onto the seat between us, I felt my face grow hot despite the sudden influx of frigid air.

"Sorry... sorry, Tate. I didn't... I mean, d-damn... it happened so fast. You... you scared the crap out of... "

"Forget it, Darrin. My fault for not providing a courtesy knock, it's just that... well, circumstances dictate my thought process might be a bit off-kilter at the moment."

In the sparse light provided by the distant, dimming flames, I could see solid ice formations had formed on both the man's eyebrows and beard stubble.

"What... circumstances? What did you guys find out at the-"

Cut off abruptly as the door opened yet again, I was unable to refrain from executing my second involuntary wince in a matter of minutes.

The sheriff climbed in with a pained groan muffled somewhat by the parka's snug cloaking, followed closely by Ben, who had apparently remained hoodless on the trip back and had received a thoroughly frosted hairdo and mustache for his troubles. I had only begun to reform the words for a suitable query when Sheriff Owens peeled off his hood and fired the first grumble.

"I still say the post makes more sense. For one thing, it's a damn sight closer and for another... well, there's always the possibility they've regained communications, since it seems obvious all cell phones have so rudely taken the night off."

"We need to check your town first, Sheriff. You saw the direction of that... slug trail leading out of the cargo hold," Tate insisted between blowing into his bare hands, his ice-crusted gloves now lying crumbled in the seat between us. Owens started to argue, raising a finger in opposition just as Ben chimed in.

"I'm with Fletch on this one, Marshall. Whatever the hell that thing is, it's already acquired a healthy appetite for the locals, kinda like a hungry griz after his first taste of man-meat. Might not be too late to save some of 'em... leastways we gotta give it a shot."

Hugging his midsection as if concealing something within the parka's interior, the sheriff released a trio of pained, laborious sighs, leaving me hesitant to break in to inquire about whatever mystery subject they spoke of. After all, in terms of what I brought to the table in such a situation, there was little doubt of my standing in the present pecking order. In military terminology, I was a lowly buck private at best, education level notwithstanding. I truly had no problem accepting this, though being so utterly ignored and thus blatantly disrespected was beginning to take its toll on my otherwise easygoing demeanor.

"You're right, of course. I can't... I didn't mean to sound... to come off like some selfish jackass trying to save his own hide. It's just the opposite, believe it or not. In case no one recalls, I *do* have a wife and twelve-year-old son residing on the far western side of Jasper. *Damn it*, of course my gut is telling me to say the hell with the town's problems... just get to them and... and protect them.

"I just thought... figured if communications *were* back up, we could get some more help out here to... well, fight this thing off."

After a moment's pause and out of sheer frustration, I decided to chance breaking their reverie, protocol be damned. Unfortunately, Tate picked that exact moment to resume the dialogue even as the sheriff continued to fiddle about with some as-of-yet unseen object he'd pulled from his parka.

"Forget it, Sheriff. We understand and appreciate your sacrifice. What we... what Ben and I do is also all about protecting the innocent... including your loved ones."

"Yeah, don't sweat it, Marshall. It's just that, me and Tate here are kinda... used to this kinda shit," Ben concluded, giving the hillside they'd just trekked across a final look just as the frequency of the snowfall seemed to pick back up to miniblizzard level.

"As for needin' more soldiers, and I apologize in advance for soundin' overly cocky, but I can't agree on the bringin' in reinforcements idea just yet."

Almost losing his grip on the object tucked between his gloved hands, the sheriff slowly twisted his head about and regarded Ben Thomason with an expression of equal parts disbelief and disgust, as if the larger man had just spoken in tongue.

"What? Correct me if I'm wrong, but didn't you and I just witness the same carnage back there in that burning wreckage, Mister Thompson?"

"*Thomason*, Marshall, Ben Thomason." Ben grinned, briefly looking past the sheriff and flashing Tate Fletcher a 'here we go' glance that spoke volumes in terms of his and Fletcher's natural connection as hero types forced to mingle with us normal folk. I wouldn't go so far as to label it arrogance, though perhaps highly overconfident is a bit too tame a definition.

"Hell, just call me *Force*."

The sheriff practically bristled, and I could almost *hear* Tate Fletcher roll his eyes in exasperation. For several moments, the two men's fascinating exchange made me forget that I had no earthly idea what they were arguing about.

"Alright then,... *Force*. You're honestly saying that what you saw out there... just minutes ago... doesn't concern you in the least for your own safety or the safety of others?"

"What I'm tellin' ya, Sheriff Owens, is that I've seen worse and on a damned sight bigger scale. What I'm also sayin' is... you bring out the state boys on this one and there's a strong possibility of more fatalities, either from the weather or the mystery trespasser. Last thing we need is more folks to protect. For example, think about that trooper ya found.

"'Sides, I feel pretty damn secure with Tate backin' me up on this particular shindig into the unknown."

Without further comment, Sheriff Owens turned about to gauge Tate Fletcher's immediate reaction.

"What *he* said, Sheriff," Tate said, pointing a thumb Ben's way. "We can handle it without more bodies and possible victims being tossed into the mix, innocent or job-related. Right now it isn't about strength in numbers, but perhaps weakness instead. Let's gauge it a bit more before shooting off flares."

Tossing his hands up in apparent surrender, the sheriff huffed loudly and turned his attention back to the square, black metallic object resting in his lap.

It was around this specific juncture, as the three men grew temporarily silent for the first time since entering the vehicle, that I essentially, pardon the ancient term borrowed from my very own father, *blew my stack.*

"If it's not too much trouble... would anyone *mind* letting the chauffeur in on exactly what the hell this little bull session is all about?"

Once the bulk brothers had exchanged yet another wry glance at my expense, Tate gladly handed the verbal reins to Benjamin while Sheriff Tate appeared indifferent as he continued to dicker with the square object in his lap.

"Sorry for the omit, Counselor. It ain't... wasn't intentional."

"Accepted," I said, though with a tint of gruffness just for good measure. "So what was out there? What's this... thing you keep referring to that's on some kind of murder spree?"

Before Ben could respond to my tirade, I pointed to the object that apparently had the county sheriff thoroughly hypnotized.

"And what is *that* damned thing anyhow?"

"Cool your jets, Counselor. I'll tell ya if you'll just hit the brakes for a damn sec-"

"It's Darrin, by the way, since everyone else is on a first-name basis, and we all seem to be sharing the same nightmare."

"Gotcha, Derrick. Now, one question at a time... "

"Darrin, not Derrick," I scolded harshly, Ben's goggle-eyed reaction causing the three of us, Tate included, to simultaneously burst out into uncontrollable laughter.

Moments later, while wiping warm tears from the sides of my eyes, I noticed Sheriff Owens had yet to rejoin the group from his trance, his bare fingers still busy prying about the mysterious metallic box.

"My fault, Benjamin... please continue back with question one," I managed with a dry croak.

"You got it, Tea- um, Darrin, but like the man said, it ain't a story for the weak at heart, not to mention midsection."

For the next five-plus minutes, Benjamin told of their trek up the hill and down into that singed valley, leading to the grave discovery previously covered by Randall Jeffries.

There had indeed been a crashed plane, what Tate Fletcher called a 'medium-sized cargo stump-jumper' in military jargon, not unlike an aircraft he referred to as a smaller version of the Japanese Army's legendary Kawasaki C-1. It had, as previously reported, been found laying all about the valley, though the cargo hold and fuselage had remained mostly intact.

Several bodies, or at least various portions torn from multiple victims, had been scattered about, including a single gnarled fist protruding from a freshly formed snowdrift that, upon closer inspection, had most likely been the 'halved' corpse Deputy Jeffries had so dramatically described in his own witness testimony. *A personal note here*: having never viewed a deceased human form save that of my elderly grandfather the day of his open casket funeral when I was not yet ten years of age, I couldn't at all identify with the casual tones utilized by both Ben and Tate when speaking of the grisly horrors they'd just witnessed firsthand. Perhaps, once again, it is simply a matter of experience in such matters, a *thickening of the emotional hide* so to speak. Regardless, as chilling as the descriptions were, there were times I found their laid-back attitudes imminently more disturbing.

"Poor asshole looked like some lunatic magician had buzzsawed 'im in half," Ben had spewed forth almost humorously, as if waxing poetically with tongue planted firmly in cheek. Again, as hard as this was to listen to, the commentaries were infinitely more painful to take. To be fair, there is little doubt a lifetime of witnessing such visceral carnage could and mostly likely would transform at least a portion of a man's soul artic-cold. Sad to say, but in time I would grow jealous of said trait, praying that someday I too would be less affected by the evil deeds I'd seen.

Ben approximated, and Tate silently nodded in agreement, that the sum of discovered body parts might easily have equaled up to five potential victims. Both also agreed, and this time with Sheriff Owens' nonverbal blessing (a stiff nod) that the majority had not perished as a result of the crash, but soon *after* the fragmented aircraft had slid to its final resting stop, slamming nose-first into a pair of ancient, thickly based elm trees.

Sidestepping both the human and material carnage, they then searched the gutted cargo hold and fuselage. What they discovered only added to the growing mystery, though the most popular theory born from said discoveries sounded logical enough from a novice's standpoint. First off, Tate

Fletcher retrieved the cockpit voice recorder from its CSMU (Crash-Survivable Memory Unit) from its metal housing, thus at least solving the enigma of the 'toy' Sheriff Owens seemed to cherish so. Also found amid the rubble was what appeared to an ordinary, unmarked compact disc stored in a silver, metallic case.

Whether or not the CD or more importantly the black box in question would lead to similar answers was anybody's guess. As far as the memory unit, retrieving said information was a tedious affair involving sophisticated lab and technical equipment far beyond the capabilities of such isolated, small-town burgs as Jasper and Boulder Valley.

Thus, it was the third discovery that carried the most weight in terms of determining why specifically the plane had went down, who exactly was aboard at the time, and how it seemed more than just a simple coincidence that some of the locals began to die soon thereafter.

Ben had been the first to check the cargo hold, the narrow beam of his flashlight almost immediately zoning in on the severed skull of what he referred to as a 'Towel Head', later defined by the man himself as meaning a male of Middle East descent. The walls, he said, practically gleamed with an infinite amount of icy blood spatters, the coppery scent of which was almost overwhelming despite the source's mostly frozen state.

Foraging through the hold, which Ben approximated to be fifteen to twenty feet in length and at least double that in width, he first circled and then halted at the base of what he described as a square, giant-sized strongbox constructed of a clear, ultrathick glass compound. Despite having been overturned and obviously kicked around a bit in the crash, he stated the box had remained undamaged save a single golf-ball sized hole at the tip of its metal housing.

"Damned thing looked like a reinforced fish tank," Ben had said thoughtfully, "like it was used to house toxic waste. Had a pair of built-in pinholes drilled into the top... more than likely for siphoning purposes."

He then stated that several prewrapped and unused syringes had been seen scattered about the debris, a few of which he accidentally shattered beneath his boots.

"What about... the content? I mean, did you take a sample?" I asked, instantly regretting the words as I feared Ben might misconstrue the inquiry as somehow doubting his intelligence. Luckily, he understood my question as being born of simple curiosity and not laced with malice of any kind. I would learn over time that the big fella was a good-natured, fun-loving lug the majority of the time; it was that small minority one had to fear.

"Sorry, Counselor... didn't have a Q-tip handy, and I wasn't about to risk exposin' bare flesh. Besides, the tank appeared pretty well bone-dry, and whatever had seeped out had either soaked through or vaporized... maybe from the heat of the flames." He paused, raising a finger airborne as to emphasize. "Tell ya what though... it's a safe bet they weren't sippin' Gatorade from that bad boy. I ain't exactly goin' out on a limb in thinkin' the source of all our misery drained from that tank... either purposely or accidentallike. For one, it stank like a sow's asshole... almost like freshly sliced gut but without the mess. Secondly, the walls were coated in some kinda blackish goo bubblin' and hissin' like a witch's brew despite the subzero temps inside. Reekin' shit looked like recently poured tar with a Texas Tea chaser."

"You... you didn't... touch it, did you?"

"Well, I thought about droppin' trow and takin' a sample with the head of my Johnson... " Ben replied sourly before pausing for dramatic effect as Tate giggled in the background.

"Of course I didn't touch it! Damn, Teach! I may be butt ugly but I ain't a moron!"

I had, of course, deserved such ridicule, having actually cringed back from the man as if he were the superhero version of Typhoid Mary.

"Sorry. Stupid question. So, you think the tar was some sort of residue from what had spilt from the tank?"

"Could be. I doubt it's the original brew. Besides, if it's a chemical weapon of some sort, it's a slow workin'' one, since I ain't showin' no symptoms despite invadin' its space."

Tate picked up the story from there, Ben having turned his attention to the sheriff and his never-ending obsession with the little black box, which was beginning to reach Rubik's Cube proportions.

"Well, since what little of the flight plan we found unburned appears written in Arabic and the majority of the crew... at least the ones still identifiable, don't exactly resemble any of the locals, I'd wager a hefty sum we're talking a terrorism plot gone to pot, big time."

"Gone to complete shit's more like it," Ben

barked as the effect of the truck's heater blasting away on its highest setting slowly returned the normal brown-grayish tint to his mustache and eyebrows.

"Those camel-humpers were armed for bear to boot. The perimeter of the crash site is littered with small arms munitions, and you can bet your sweet ass they weren't flyin' down to some local gun and knife show to set up a display."

As my mind boggled over this new, fantastic revelation, Sheriff Owens finally chimed in, though his voice sounded strangely distant and detached. I had a sinking feeling he was on the verge of cracking, the monumental type of mental meltdown fueled by the worse kind of worry; that being the safety and welfare to those closest to you. Owens' wife and child were listed among the very vulnerable, as were all residing within the valley, and it was becoming apparent in the good sheriff's behavior that no one realized that particular fact more than he.

"Probably headed for Vegas. The President was scheduled to fly in late last night to survey the damage from that six-point quake last week."

The snapping of Ben's gargantuan fingers was akin to the piercing echo of a pistol shot.

"Bingo. Probably flew in from the West Coast. Since the bird shows signs of military nomenclature, they probably lifted it from some National Guard base."

Both Tate and Owens nodded silently in response.

"Ya gotta figure Omar and his all-Taliban crew had hoped to time their arrival to Sin City just in time for the big cheese's visit (laughed). Well, they sure as hell couldn't have picked a worse time *or* location for an engine FUBAR."

Feeling downright flushed from the glut of information weighing down my battered senses, it took me several deep breaths and a hard swallow or two in order to verbally rejoin the fray.

"So... back to the mysterious box... "

"Flight voice recorder... have to be taken to Corvallis, maybe even Cheyenne to be properly dissect-"

"No, no," I ranted, waving my hands wildly to cut off the sheriff's robotic monotone, which was serving not only to grate on my last nerve, but royally creep me out. It was almost as if cradling that square box had transformed the good sheriff into a replicated 'pod person' of body-snatching fame.

"I meant the fish tank box inside the cargo hold... "

As if waiting for Sheriff Owens to reply, both Tate and Ben hesitated for several ticks as we all temporarily fell under the hypnotic spell of the truck's wiper blades' relentless devotion in keeping the windshield flake and ice-speck free. Ultimately, it was Tate who welcomed the challenge of fielding twenty questions from the local counselor, whose own morbid curiosity had not even begun to be properly quenched.

"May not be chemical... but that sure doesn't mean it's harmless by any stretch. Maybe once the plane went down, somebody went out of their way to free... or take the contents in lieu of someone else finding and procuring it."

"Could it be... biological in nature?"

"Possibly, though I've never heard of a viral strain tearing a man in half, have you?"

"I... well, no... I guess not. But... what proof do you have that such an enemy even exists? I mean, besides wild speculation. There's still a good chance the crash itself might've had the same ef-"

It was Ben who interrupted in an uncharacteristically sarcasm-free tone that had the desired effect: I instantly clammed up as if backhanded across the lips.

"There was a slug trail leadin' outta that cargo hold, Counselor. A slick, wide smear the same color and texture of what was runnin' down the inside walls of that bird. We followed it a good two-dozen feet or more, least 'til scorched earth gave way to fresh snow. No two ways about it; somethin' deboarded that bird, and it ain't likely lookin' to make peace with the locals."

"So, you... think someone... one of the crewmembers... might've purposely ingested the mystery liquid and... changed into some kind of killing machine?"

"I'd say yeah, be it purposely or by accident. One thing's for sure... who or whatever this thing is," Tate then continued with similar grimness, "its creators must've underestimated its appetite for destruction. We may never know what happened inside that cargo hold to cause that bird to nosedive into peaceful valley here, but it's safe to say our mystery fugitive isn't done wreaking havoc just yet, what with all the bodies piling up around us."

"Yeah, we're talkin' one highly pissed off stowaway that probably ain't nearly done checkin' out the local cuisine, if ya get my drift," Ben added while, *unbelievably*, stifling a yawn. "It's for damn certain we ain't talkin' about some run-of-the-mill lunatic with an axe blade here. Something's turnin' folks into sausage links and seems to be enjoyin' the process to boot.

"We'd better cruise on into Jasper and see if we can track this certain sombitch down."

"But... how do we find it?" I asked, already shifting gears while prepping to make an ultracautious U-turn.

"Shouldn't be too hard with the mess it's leavin' behind. Talk about conspicuous, damn thing oughta be holdin' up a neon sign that reads *will kill and/or maim for food*."

With that, silence reigned supreme for the next ten to twelve minutes as we made our way ever so painstakingly toward Jasper, only to be broken by a predictable source once the ice-coated 'city limits' sign swam into view just two and a half miles from what served as Main Street.

"Tate, have ya ever wondered why folks in our line of work seem to step directly into the eye of such shitstorms no matter how hard we try to avoid 'em?" came the question.

"Comes with the territory, I guess," came the answer after the briefest of pauses. "Sanity's a brittle thing in the so-called hero fraternity. Too much introspection on matters of fate can crack that particular Pandora's box wide-ass open, you know? Might leave a man slumped in a corner playing with his own toes."

In a textbook example of perfect comic timing, Ben Thomason waited until the pale, dim lights of

Jasper, Wyoming filled our collective pupils to utter a response.

"Knew a chick named Pandora once... sassy little stripper from Birmingham," he said dryly. "Cracked her box wipe open, as a matter of fact."

Despite the coiled tension in my gut, I laughed long and hearty.

If I recall correctly, it would be the last such incident of jocularity on what was to become the longest twenty-four hours of my young life.

***

As it was the initial residence heading toward Main Street, I was told to brake in front of a rather drab-looking manufactured home the sheriff identified as being owned by Cyril James Jacoby, well-known alcoholic and long-time mechanic at the local Jasper *Auto Doctor* garage. Following a winding trek through three-foot snowdrifts and a lengthy knock at the mobile home's lone entrance/exit, the sheriff allowed Ben to shoulder his way inside, where the domicile was officially declared deserted with no signs of foul play. Once back inside the truck, Owens stated that both power and phone lines were still officially out of commission. Though his dialogue had remained spookily mechanical, at least his expression and hand gestures appeared to be regaining a sense of normalcy. I couldn't help but wonder how tempted the man was to leap from that truck screaming, braving both the elements and an unknown killer just to check the welfare of his wife and child. He was, after all, a husband and father first and a law enforcement officer second. Personally, I cannot even imagine the torment Jake Owens must've been experiencing, and felt a slight twinge of guilt at my earlier grading of his behavior.

The second homestead checked, roughly a mile and a half further down Highway 6, was that of William and Jacqueline Bartlett, a senior couple Sheriff Owens said had moved into the community some six months earlier from Chicago. Fulfilling a lifelong dream of living out their golden years in the wide-open spaces, both had been career defense lawyers in Chitown's Upper East Side, the ranch-style, three-thousand-plus square foot log home encased by a five-foot-high stone wall a testament to their retirement planning skills, not to mention the newer model twin Escalades parked out front.

"Nice digs," Ben remarked while scanning the perimeter as I succeeded in effectively clearing the Bartlett's drive before coming in for a smooth landing directly behind both SUVs.

"Somebody oughta be home with all this shiny new hardware parked out front."

"No lights apparent," Tate replied, already pulling the passenger door ajar, "not even candlelight. Looks like another dead end... "

Unfortunately, Scar Fletcher's off-the-cuff remark would soon prove to be sadly prophetic.

They'd found the twin oak door front entrance slightly ajar, and entered the darkened interior with great caution. Upon further inspection, the rear of the home had been utterly demolished, and with it, God help them... so had the inhabitants.

"Well, judging by that tarry substance on the back deck, it definitely entered the house through the sliding glass door," the sheriff deduced as I steered the plow back over the cleared off drive leading away from the Bartletts. The cool, emotionless tone and stiff posture were back at full strength, as if the man were discussing a particularly gruesome scene from a recently viewed Sci-Fi flick in lieu of a real-life slaughter. I'd been spared the grisly particulars, at least until we'd reentered the highway and veered slightly to the left onto Main Street Jasper, the town's lone pair of lifeless red lights barely visible from a distance; both frozen solid and swinging about like twin pendulums in the gusty winds.

"Entire rear of the house was gutted but good, most of it solid brick," Tate finally muttered, shaking his head in apparent awe.

"Looked like a bulldozer ran through her... several times."

"Yeah, a bulldozer with teeth the size of a Mack truck grille... " Ben added solemnly. "I've seen some bloodbaths in my time, Fletch, but none much messier than that."

"Ditto."

"Wasn't enough left of the old man to smear on a Ritz."

"Looked like the family dog tried to play protector... poor old mutt."

"Shit, Tate, how could ya really tell? We had retriever parts mixed with the old lady's... look like somethin' cooked up by Doctor Monroe."

"Doctor Moreau," Tate corrected politely.

"Say what?"

"Doctor Moreau, as in... Island of?"

"Yeah, that's the one. Anyhow, it sure makes ya

wonder what this thing is usin' for weapons to turn flesh, muscle and bone into blood 'n gut gumbo."

With that, I felt my stomach actually churn, and not just in the literal sense, thankful once again to my maker that I'd been spared the matching visuals. As if sensing my discomfort, the two fell mercifully silent as what served as Jasper's main drag loomed.

Digging a path down the center of Main at just less than ten miles per hour, we passed a series of small shops, among them *Massey's Hardware & Dollar Store*, *Farm Supply Depot*, and *The Burnt-Lip Cafe*, the latter of which I couldn't help but admire in terms of small-town originality. Previously known as simply as *Charlie's Coffee Shop*, I'd spent many a chilly morning sipping away at a tall mug of Columbian Supreme that first winter in Wyoming. I had to admit that the name change was a real hoot, even though the interior of the place hadn't been altered one iota, at least from what I'd seen the last time I'd frequented it.

The tiny burg's twin banks sit directly across from one another, as did the only pair of gas stations, the latter of which could be politely described as ramshackle and possessed but a single pump. Along the mile-long strip sat a half-dozen abandoned vehicles, all shoved up against the curve and virtually impossible to ID by make or model beneath mounds of snow. As for the aforementioned shops, all had been predictably life and lightless.

"Talk about your ancient myths comin' to life... what we have here is an au-then-tic western ghost town in the frigid flesh," Ben whispered softly as if thinking aloud.

"Yep, probably the spitting image of its sister

city right about now," Tate replied just as quietly. Glancing over, I noticed Sheriff Owens staring blankly ahead, his badly chapped lips curled into a pained grimace. Astonishingly, the man's complexion appeared paler than even the surrounding landscape. He seemed on the very edge of self-implosion. Despite all my years of training, I'd never felt more utterly useless.

It wasn't until we'd passed beneath the back-to-back red lights that he openly broached the subject I'd personally been obsessed with since our departure from the post.

"Take a left at that four-way," he said calmly, pointing ahead to a snow-crusted stop sign.

"Where we headed, Sheriff?" Tate inquired with a puzzled glance.

Owens didn't blink as his hand slowly descended back into his lap, where he continued to cradle the black box.

"I... have to know. As hard as it is to admit... I've... I dread it like nothing else in my life to this point, but... I... just have to know if... they're okay."

"You got it, Sheriff," I heard myself say with a renewed surge of exuberance. "Just point the way and we're there."

"They're safe and sound, Sheriff," Tate concluded before a lengthy period of uneasy silence. "My gut instinct tells me so, and it isn't wrong very often."

Probably feeling pressure to play joiner in our little gang cheer-up effort, Ben's attempt at reassurance didn't quite come out the way he'd intended.

"I got the same vibe as Fletch, Marshall.

Besides, the ravenous bastard oughta be ready to pop like a ripe tick by now, what with all the shredded partials we've already run across."

In recalling the personnel file of one Ben Thomason, one particular item under personality quirks had read 'master of the malaprop', meaning the man possessed a rather comically warped way with words and how he expressed himself verbally, most notably while engaged in lethal combat. I hadn't thought much of it at the time, but was beginning to understand why this particular text had been bolded and placed in upper caps.

Suffice it to say, the next several minutes were dominated solely by the hum of the truck's heater and the sound of several thousand pounds of snow and ice being shoved aside.

"How much farther, Sheriff?" I finally inquired, feeling strangely chipper if for no other reason than the cursed snowfall had temporarily ceased.

"Two, two and a half miles tops. We... purposely picked a place as far out in the sticks as possible. Margie wanted lots of elbow room after all those years in the city, space to breathe, plant a garden, you know, all that jazz."

I *did* understand. The truth was, I'd become so acclimated with the wide-open spaces of Boulder Valley, Wyoming that it was going to be a difficult transition back to city living once my assignment was up. Not just acclimated, mind you, but grown very fond of as well. I'd gone so far as thinking of applying for a permanent position on Burt's staff, though I'd yet to broach the subject with the head honcho himself, more than likely in fear of being rejected flat-out. Still, it was an option that never failed to stimulate a deep-seeded twinge of excitement.

The Owens' residence was located a fair distance from the connecting highway (listed as RR14 on local maps), a one-story abode whose present appearance was hard to properly gauge underneath a virtual avalanche's worth of fallen snow that had engulfed her from front to back, including a sizeable connecting garage whose doors were currently blocked by a nearly ceiling-high drift. A line of equally tall shrubbery appeared to circle the perimeter of the home, though the rear of both the residence and garage remained out of sight as we neared the front drive.

Taking a slight right onto what the sheriff had indicated was a paved drive, I steered the truck along a flat, narrow path that soon transformed into a fairly steep upgrade before resettling once again as I pulled into the driveway. I braked to the left of what appeared to be an older model Buick, perhaps a Le Sabre of the mid-nineties variety. As with every structure we'd come across since departing the post, Jake Owens' residence appeared dark and desolate. In terms of positive omens, I hadn't spotted a single track or tar-baby slug trail leading up the drive or the snow-packed walkway toward the front door.

"Ya want some company in there, Marshall?" Ben asked with a shrug. "Me and Tate can check her out first if you'd like... kinda police up the area... I mean, in case somethin' ain't... well... you know."

The sheriff shoved the passenger door open and took a step out before replying, his voice every bit as detached as earlier, despite what had to be a firestorm of emotion swirling about his subconscious.

"Thanks... I got it. Give me five minutes to... explain things to them. If you don't hear from me in that time, by all means don't wait for a written invite."

The three of us watched with great trepidation as the sheriff waddled through thigh-deep snow to reach the front door, the deep, tunnellike tracks he left in his wake reminding me of animated moon craters, as if they'd been drawn on with a child's black crayon.

"Soooo, if they are home, what then? They going to hitch a ride back to the post with us or stay here?" Tate queried, scanning the surrounding grounds with fierce intenseness, as if expecting an impending ambush at any moment.

"I wouldn't think he'd want them to stay... alone I mean. I know they're pretty isolated out here, but that doesn't mean that thing can't or *won't* find them."

"Damn right. No way he's leavin' 'em behind to fend for themselves," Ben agreed, and I felt a burst of self-pride. "We'll fit 'em inside this tank somehow."

Standing in the gleam of the truck's blaring headlights, we watched the sheriff carefully key the front door with his right hand, his left curled over the holstered .38 hanging from his gun belt. With two quick steps he vanished into the house, the burnt stain oak door shutting gradually behind him.

"Probably shut away in a back bedroom with a few candles lit," I heard Tate say, feeling a fresh wave of icy chills douse my backbone.

"Yeah, or maybe takin' a nap... snorin' the curtains off the walls," Ben added, twisting his head about to give the driveway and distant highway a brief inspection. In terms of security, I realized how lucky I was to be in such regal company, and didn't feel even a flicker of embarrassment at understanding and accepting the level of my own fear. Though I would've never summoned the courage to ask, I secretly wondered if either of the battle-tested and similarly scarred individuals sharing the inside of that snowplow would dare admit to experiencing a comparable emotion. If based solely on appearance and/or demeanor, one would have to state an irrefutable no in bold lettering, followed by a half-dozen exclamation points. Bottom line-of course I felt a strong sense of security by the mere presence of these superbeings. Did this completely quell my reservations that an abrupt, horrible death might be imminent? *Not... even... close.*

Approximately thirty seconds before the aforementioned five-minute limit expired, Sheriff Owens emerged from the house, followed closely by two cloaked figures decked out in what appeared to be several dozen layers of protective clothing.

Introductions were brief and predictably awkward as Marge Owens and the couple's only child, Lawrence, piled into the cab. Though largely concealed by a fur-lined hoodie, Marge looked to be in her late thirties to early forties; a big-boned, authoritative woman whose stilted tone and equally wooden posture seemed to indicate a 'take charge and don't take no bull' type personality.

As for young Lawrence Owens, having just

turned twelve a month previous according to his dad, mum was definitely the word, his saucer-wide eyes and flaring nostrils a walking advertisement for stark fear at its basest level. In light of the newsflash passed on by his father mere moments earlier, such a reaction wouldn't have been surprising coming from a battle-hardened soldier, much less a preteen child.

Sitting in her husband's lap, I heard Marge grunt as I navigated a wide right turn in order to exit back toward the highway. Meantime, Lawrence sat propped quietly atop Tate Fletcher's knees, the young man's eyes spinning about like rolled marbles. Once Highway 6 loomed, I posed a question whose answer seemed obvious. Still, there was the matter of protocol.

"Back to the post, I take it?"

I saw Tate and Ben exchange a look before both turned silently toward the sheriff.

"Yeah, just backtrack and take a right at the stop sign leading onto Main. With the path you've already cleared and the blade raised, we should be able to make it back there in half the time."

"Check," I replied, whipping the wheel hard to the right and feeling the packed snow crunch beneath our tires.

Once securely fitted into the eight-foot wide groove I'd dug out on the way out of town, I raised the plow and gradually sped up to a comfortably safe speed of just under twenty-five. Not exactly breaking the sound barrier, I know, but such a mark was at least twice that of shoveling speed.

"Sure hope the back-up power is holdin' up," Ben remarked, stifling yet another yawn. "I could use a hot cup of Joe."

"Or maybe a *hot toddy*, right, Benji?"

"Ohhhh no ya don't, Fletch. Booze is what got me sent here in the first place, remember? This boy's a card-carryin' wagon rider 'til further notice, or at least 'til I can park my happy ass in a warmer clime."

As the two veteran warriors continued their light banter and a fresh coating of falling snow began to coat the windshield, I caught a revealing glimpse of Marge Owens in the rearview. She'd pulled her parka hood free, revealing thick, brownish hair streaked with random steaks of blondish/gray. She'd been staring downward, directly into her husband's face. Strange as it is to describe without actually knowing what the woman was thinking at that very moment, I can only define her expression as extremely puzzled. Averting my eyes back to the road, I returned to Mrs. Owens' reflection several times as the trek commenced, only to be greeted by the same perplexed look. Only once, after I'd pulled back onto Main Street Jasper, did the two of us accidentally lock eyes.

Though she'd looked quickly away upon discovering my visual intrusion, I was nonetheless able to read the silent cry reflected in Marge Owens' squirming, bloodshot eyes.

It was a look of pure desperation.

It was a look that cried out for help.

It was a look that defined the word *haunted.*

Tate Fletcher's booming vocals snapped me from the self-induced trance.

"A light! Over there! I see a light flashing on and off... see it?" he bellowed, and I had to fight to keep the truck from sliding sideways as I practically shoved the brake pedal flush to the carpeted floor.

"That's... city hall," Sheriff Owens croaked, pointing a gloved hand toward a dim yet tangible light source that appeared to be flashing on and off in timed intervals in true lighthouse beacon fashion.

"It's coming from the basement window."

"Looks like that warm cup o' Joe is gonna have to be put on the back-burner for now," Ben said, though sounding anything but disappointed. "We might just have some asses to pull from the proverbial sling after all."

***

"How much farther, Mister Jackson?" came the familiar query, though worded a bit differently as to cloak its redundancy. Sporting chubby cheeks which glowed apple-red and a balding plate now moistened with melted snow, Mayor Doug Boren whipped his head about like a bobblehead doll with a busted spring.

"I'd say we're about fifteen, twenty minutes out, Mayor, which is roughly four or five less than the last time you inquired."

I heard Wanda Jelks grunt, though it was unclear whether its origin had been birthed from her boss' question or my openly annoyed response. Having served as the mayor's personal secretary for the majority of his three full terms, you'd have thought she'd be used to hearing similar barbs tossed the man's way.

"This is no time for such unwarranted sarcasm, Mister Jackson," the mayor rebuked hatefully, as if

I'd slapped him across the jaw with a loose glove. "We... these fine people need shelter... a safe haven as soon as possible."

Somewhat reluctantly, I apologized if for no other reason than to end the discussion. Though the snow had ceased, the matted down precip had transformed the asphalt underneath our wheels into a paved hockey rink, and I was still struggling at times to keep us from fishtailing onto the shoulder while also keeping a close watch on the Dodge Ram four-wheeler trailing closely behind.

"Sorry, Mister Mayor... no disrespect intended. I'm just... a bit edgy is all."

"Accepted and understood, son. I'd say we've all bore witness to things this night that we'd rather forget," he'd said sincerely enough before botching the epilogue with predictable arrogance, pointing at the road as if I'd been purposely napping behind the wheel. "Just try to maintain your focus and get us there in one piece, will you?"

Seemingly as annoying as he was grating, Jasper's head official didn't exactly command respect, having earned the nickname *Windmill Dougy* for his riding the fence approach to all matters governmental. Political shortcomings aside, the man had somehow gained the people's confidence, having been elected by large margins in three straight elections. Perhaps it had simply been a woeful lack of competition, for in my few dealings with the honorable Douglas Boren, the only apt description I could drudge up was one my grandfather had used often when defining the majority of politicians, that being 'insufferable windbag'.

"And who says it's any more *safe* out there anyway, Douglas?" Jelks blurted out, the first actual words I'd heard her utter since our hurried departure from the city hall's rear, employees only parking lot.

"Miss Jelks, if you'd please jus-"

"All I do know is that it's a hell of a lot more isolated, and that nothing or *nobody* had tried to get to us back at the building... at least not *inside* the building."

"But, Wanda, we *weren't* safe in that basement. You saw Cyril Jacoby's bod-"

"For all we know, whoever or whatever is behind this... this murder spree is waiting for us there... "

"It was a false sense of security, Wanda. We had no way to defend ourselves if... well, you saw what they... what it did to poor Cyril... may God rest his pitiful old soul... "

"... when we were sitting snug as a bug in a rug with the state police on their way 'til you got the bright idea to start waving a flashlight around... "

"... not to mention what it probably did to Mason. I couldn't risk hiding out... cowering like some scared rabbit... we had to seek help immediately... "

"... like some almighty hero to the rescue when we all know you're nothing but... "

"... right away since it might take the state authorities another half-day to reach us in this damnable storm... "

"... an egotistical, do-nothing, mealy-mouthed *asshole*!!"

During the lingering silence that ensued in the aftermath of Wanda Jelks' rather jarring pronouncement, my thoughts rewound to the moment we'd entered the city hall basement, courtesy of Tate Fletcher's effortless splintering of a locked, solid oak door with a single jerk of its iced-over knob. Though the basement's interior had been relatively dim and I'd been bringing up the rear behind Tate and Ben, the sheriff having remained in the truck with his family, I was still able to see a heavy-set black female emerge from between two head-high metal cabinets, waving an aluminum baseball bat while screeching at the top of her lungs.

Tate had endured a series of metal-on-metal blows to his left forearm before gently disarming Miss Wanda Jelks and assuring all other hidden inhabitants that we were indeed there to help.

Besides the mayor and Miss Jelks, we were soon introduced to a skinny young man with shaggy hair and dark-rimmed glasses named Paul Redrick, a stocker at the local Circle G Food Mart and his kid sister, a rather chubby thirteen-year-old named Marie.

"Hey... *hey*! You... you're that guy... that superhero guy... " Paul Redrick blurted out, lifting a badly shaking right arm and pointing directly at Ben. The poor young man was as pale as any snowdrift I'd seen that evening, his eyes positively boggling behind the ultrathick lenses of the glasses parked at the edge of his pointed nose. Not to be cruel, but the word 'homely' wasn't nearly a strong enough term to adequately describe the boy's physical appearance.

"M-my dad had your trading card... yeah, that's it. I remember he had a whole shoebox full he'd pulled from cereal boxes. Brute Force, right? Your professional name is Brute Force."

"Force, kid. Just plain *Force*. Nice to greet ya," Ben replied as politely as humanly possible while doing his best to sidestep by the young man in order to better greet the oldest adult present. Instead, the kid continued to block his path by hopping around like a line-dancer with a belly full of barbiturates.

"Yeah, it is you! Called yourself Desecration Outlaw for a spell, right?"

"Ugh, *Desolation* Outlaw, yeah. Listen, kid... "

"My dad had cards with both your IDs... I always thought the Outlaw costume made you look a little pussy... but *Force*, man! What a bad ass! You're... s-still a bad ass, right? Still kicking bad guy rear end like there's no tomorrow, r-right?"

"Yeah, kid... still kickin' ass and scribblin' down names. Now, just gimme a sec and I promise I'll come back and autograph whatever ya want with a Sharpie... uh, anything *but* genitalia that is."

Just as Ben had gripped Redrick by the shoulders and gently pushed him aside, the young man's tone switched from gleeful adoration to panic-stricken desperation.

"You can kill this... that thing out th-there... right, Force? I m-mean, you and that... " he paused while giving Tate a quick once-over, "other big dude over there ain't going to let... let it get to m-me... or my kid sister, right? *Tell me you can kill the goddamn thing!*"

"It's okay, kid... chill out... everything's gonna be alright," Ben consoled softly, though it was obvious by both his expression and body language it was a role he was hardly comfortable playing. The big guy might as well have been attempting to change the dirty diaper on a screeching toddler.

"Of course I can waste it. Hell, the baddie ain't been bred that me and Scar over there can't dropkick. Once we find it, it's dead meat... plain and simple, okay?"

Fortunately for Ben, who for once actually appeared lost for further words, Wanda Jelks stepped forward and led the sniveling teen away.

Once the other, rather terse amenities had commenced, Tate and Ben pulled Mayor Bowen aside and the trio swapped whispers while the rest of us shuffled aimlessly about the chilled, gloomy room, lit by sparse candlelight only. Not soon after, the mayor led myself, Tate and Ben up a flight of narrow, creaky wooden stairs and through a double-padlocked door leading into the lobby. Blazing the darkened trail with the same narrow flashlight beam that had beckoned us from Main Street, the mayor's voice cracked with emotion while describing the horrors witnessed earlier that evening as he and the hall's sparse patrons had prepped to close up for the night. Struggling to focus the shaking light, he nonetheless managed to pinpoint a wide, frozen smear coating the glass windows to the left of the building's double-door entrance. Despite the hard frost setting, the smear's reddish origins were still clearly intact.

"We were all... rushing around to close up. I'd sent most of the staff home early, just before the storm hit full force. Wanda and I were... we stuck around to finish up a budget report. Sounds stupid I know, but... I mean, we didn't have a clue how nasty conditions were apt to get. Well, once the power went, all bets were off. The Redrick boy and his sister had come down a few hours earlier to visit their uncle... Cyril... in the drunk tank... um... holding cell. By then the phones were down and our cells were pretty much useless, so I wasn't able to track down Jake. Instead, I instructed Mason Drury, that's the building's maintenance man and janitor, to go ahead and release Cyril so I could send everyone home. A few minutes later, as Wanda and I were prepping to lock up my office, we heard a loud commotion coming from the lobby... followed by the sound of a young child screaming. By the time Wanda and I dashed downstairs, I was... I'm still not sure exactly what... I saw... though I... we certainly got an eyeful of the human carnage it left behind."

With our collective noses practically pressed against the freezing glass, we all followed the wavering light's slim trail as it hovered about an unidentifiable mass laying atop the sidewalk and into the nearby street.

"The screaming had been courtesy of Marie Redrick. We'd found the child curled underneath a counter, weeping and wailing like a busted siren. It took a hard, firm slap, followed by an equally forceful hug from Wanda... Miss Jelks to cease the girl's cries. As for Paul, well, he told us what he'd seen, and regardless of how farfetched or stone-cold crazy it sounds, I don't doubt the kid for a minute. Not after... well, you can see for yourself.

"The Redrick kid was adamant he saw some sort of shadowy giant; a scaly-skinned version of Big Foot that shredded his uncle and then dragged poor old Mason Drury down the street like windblown trash. Said Mason had practically tossed him and his sister back inside the building just before the... the thing scooped him up and vanished around the next street corner.

"At first I just chalked up his description to overexposure to video games and late-night cable horror flicks... that is, until I laid my eyes on that mutilated mess that... had been one of the best damn auto mechanics this town ever employed."

"Identical MO alright," I heard Ben say as he and Tate gradually backed away from the glass, leaving only myself and the mayor to resume a rather grisly game of 'CSI, Jasper'. While I struggled to gain a sense of logic from the gruesome reality staring me directly in the face, a midroom discussion ensued that I caught only vague fragments of.

Ben: "... cuts down on prime suspects, don't it?"

Tate: "... that right, partner. I have to say, this shit is getting downright spooky."

Ben: "... ain't seen much worse. What say... load up... haul ass to the post. I've got a sneakin' suspicion... "

Tate: "... riders. Need another form of transport... "

Ben: "... one of those big four-wheel drive jobs... thinkin' it was a Dodge... hot wire that bad boy if ya have to."

Once the bizarre, fragmented images I'd been so utterly unable to piece together did start to make sense, everything else around me, including outside dialogue, faded away as if suddenly transported to a far distance. Though all three separate components were frozen solid and coated in several layers of ice, it became possible to not only identify them, but piece them together as being connected to the same big picture. In part, it was like looking at a shattered statue whose parts had been dismantled upon impact with a hard surface.

The top half of Cyril Jacoby, aforementioned local mechanic and amiable town drunk, laid face down on the ice-packed sidewalk less than two feet from the entrance. He'd obviously been wearing his work duds, as even frosted over like freezer-burned meat, the bluish tint of his coveralls were clearly visible. Initially, I'd made the honest mistake of thinking he was laying face up, considering what little remained of the man's badly crushed skull and shredded facial features pointed upward to the tiled overhang that ran the length of the hall's front side. That was, of course, before I noted the outline of his bony shoulder blades and the fact his hands lay palms down in a thick, frozen pool of his own seepage.

As for piece two, that being a pair of detached legs, the work boot adorning the left foot had been partially dragged onto Main Street while the right had managed to hold position on the nearby sidewalk, its knee bent and bootless, the sock-covered foot seemingly gripping the edge as if to avoid a similar fate as its dislodged twin.

Between was puzzle piece number three-easily the most distracting and downright surreal of the trio. Thinking back, I have little doubt this particular tidbit of visual horror was the one thing which kept me from instantly recognizing the big picture. More than likely a case of my subconscious attempting to place a barrier of sorts-a mental roadblock or psychological force-field if you will-in order to protect my already battered senses from further shock. Alas, a noble stand in the 'you can't be scared of what you can't identify' mode which was doomed to eventual failure once cold hard reality reared its ugly head. Unfortunately enough, given time I was able to break through the subliminal blockade and recognize that the only thing still holding both sections of Cyril Jacoby together were several bloated, blackened strands of intestine that the subzero temperatures had made resemble a haphazardly piled stack of PVC pipe. The man had literally been torn in half-ripped into equal shares-segmented like a farm animal at a slaughterhouse-as if he'd fallen asleep on a train track or fallen beneath the whirring blades of a threshing machine...

... or been yanked into separate sections via the ancient torture device known as the 'rack'...

... or been tied with chains between two dueling semis heading in opposite directions...

... or been gutted by a giant, swinging pendulum blade or been...

It had been a combination of Ben's gruff voice and steely grip that broke me from a self-imposed daze the likes of which I'd never before experienced. If I'd thought the big man wouldn't have slugged me, I'd have surely kissed him squarely on the jaw in appreciation.

"Get a move on, Counselor. We're haulin' ass outta here pronto."

Less than ten minutes later, we'd been split into two factions sharing an equal amount of vehicles. Scar Fletcher would pilot Cyril Jacoby's four-wheel drive Dodge Ram, having first been tasked to retrieve the keys from the dead man's pants pocket (and thus from the garments adorning a pair of severed legs), his passenger list made up of Paul and Marie Redrick and the Owens clan: Sheriff Jake, Marge and young Lawrence. Meanwhile, I would continue on point, steering the snowplow in the company of Mayor Boren, Wanda Jelks and the man called Force. In the case of the latter, he and Tate had mutually decided that it would be best if they split up in order to better play security escort for the rest. As we'd departed the building a two-vehicle, ten-person convoy enroute to the Jasper Ridge Outpost, a fresh round of heavy snowfall began to fall.

"Oh wonderful," the mayor had griped upon noticing the thick flakes pelt the windshield, "just what the doctor ordered... those state boys are never gonna get here."

"Uh, Mayor?" I inquired hesitantly, in some ways not really wanting to hear the forthcoming answer.

"Yes, Mister Jackson?"

"When exactly did you contact the state authorities?"

"Right before our cell phones conked out... Wanda's was still functional... "

As if on cue, Wanda Jelks gave a curt nod while continuing to stare straight ahead.

"... wasn't more than five minutes after the assault on Cyril. Why do you ask?"

"Oh, no reason. Just trying to set a timetable in my mind," I lied with brutal images of Jake Owens' tale of the headless state trooper filling my thoughts.

"Not to worry, Mister Jackson. After the story I told that lieutenant, they're likely to send a dozen cars *and* a fleet of rubber trucks to boot."

Not exactly sure why I'd decided to delay passing on the sad, cruel truth to the man, though it probably had more to do with sparing Wanda Jelks the bad news than the mayor. Regardless, it took Force exactly five seconds to blow my cover.

"Sorry to pop your bubble, Mayor, but the calvary's done been here."

"Wha-? The state police have... "

"Sheriff Jake found one of 'em at some abandoned gas 'n go... "

"And?"

"Uh, let's just say the dude was plenty messed up. It's doubtful we'll see any more outside aid 'til this storm breaks, anyhow. I'd say whatever happens in the next twelve to twenty-four is all on us."

Tossing her meaty arms into the air in comical frustration, Wanda Jelks' reaction to Force's blunt honestly was one that ordinarily would've sent me into a fit of out-and-out hysterics. As it was, her words fit the moment as perfectly fitting.

"Ohhhh, rat turds on rye toast... "

I'd been checking the rearview to ensure the Dodge's presence, at least a once every ten second habit since our departing Main Street Jasper, when a loud, abrupt burst of static ensued, causing all present save perhaps Force to flinch involuntarily as if physically goosed.

Chapter Five
Distress Call/Cornered

"I tell you, it was Burt's voice... and he was yelling 'May Day'," I insisted, my face flushed with fever despite the subzero temps.

"He repeated it twice and started a third rendition when the static drowned him out. I've had several instances of speaking with Burt Hanover via two-way, and I'll telling you, that was *him*."

By the time Ben had managed to pull the radio free from beneath the seat, no further messages, be they real or imaginary would be forthcoming. Still, upon his order I'd slowed and parked onto the wide shoulder and allowed Tate to pull alongside, the sheriff's frowning mug greeting us from the Dodge's passenger side. Once I'd relayed what I was sure I'd heard, it was as if I was then charged with proving such a seemingly wild statement in the face of great skepticism, some of which had originated from inside the same vehicle I'd been piloting.

"Why exactly are we arguing about this? We're less than five miles out. I say we just... speed up the process a bit without driving overly reckless."

"We're not arguing with you, Darrin," Tate replied, leaning over the truck's steering wheel to be clearly seen from the driver's seat.

"It's just that, if they are under attack, we have to consider an alternative approach to the post grounds."

"Damn straight," Ben agreed. "I never minded bein' ambushed... that is, not when I *knew* it was comin', if ya get my drift."

Tate laughed aloud, causing Sheriff Jake

Owens and his wife to openly cringe.

"Precisely what I was getting to. Darrin, put pedal to medal 'til we clear that sharp curve just outside the post main gate, then slow up and park it wherever... in the middle of the road if you have to."

"Understood. You still bringing up the rear?" I asked with no small measure of trepidation, my facial skin under constant bombardment from tiny specks of ice that might as well have been poison-tipped spears from the stinging effect.

"I've got your back. Remember to douse your lights once we clear that curve."

Less than ten minutes later, the post's outside emergency beacon lights loomed over a far hill.

As directed, I waited until the snowplow had successfully cleared a severe left curve past a series of snow-heightened hills before braking for good. A steep downgrade loomed just ahead, perhaps fifty yards or so, the descent of which would lead directly onto the post grounds.

Once Tate had parked the Dodge a few dozen feet behind us, Ben quickly zipped up his parka hood and got out of the vehicle, the slamming of the passenger side door so forceful I was amazed the window hadn't shattered or at least suffered a hairline crack.

Peeking in the rearview, I watched him and Tate's brief exchange outside the Dodge, then saw Tate hop back into the truck as Ben jogged our way. All the while, neither the mayor nor Wanda Jelks had uttered so much as a grunt.

Accompanied by a gusting wind and fresh layer of snow sticking to the fur lining of his jacket, Ben hopped back into the vehicle with an audible shiver.

"Okay, folks... here's the deal. Me and Tate are gonna hoof it into camp and give it a good policin' up. Everybody else stays put 'til one or both of us reappears. Darrin, you got a watch?"

"Yeah, right here," I croaked, holding up my right arm and forcing multiple sleeves down to reveal a cheap but reliable sports watch I'd owned for the better part of two years.

"Give us twenty minutes from the time I jump outta this heap, then turn this bad boy around and drive the hell away from here, you got it?"

"Drive? And where exactly do you expect us to *drive* to?" the mayor barked, essentially beating me to the punch, though admittedly in a more direct, sardonic tone.

Once again to his credit, Ben maintained a level of cool far beyond that for which his legendary reputation as a hothead should've allowed.

"Well, lemme tell ya, Mister Mayor... if there is someone or something toolin' about those grounds that can take out the likes of Scar Fletcher and myself, I'd say drive as far away from Boulder Valley as available gas fumes will take ya."

Turning his steely glare my way, Ben and I shared a brief nod of complete comprehension.

"Sound about right to you, Darrin?"

"Affirmative. I'm showing a full tank and a quarter counting the backup tank. With that, I can clear a path more than halfway to Corvallis."

"That a boy," he replied, reaching over both the mayor and Miss Jelks to deliver a solid pat to my left shoulder with that enormous mitt of his.

"Keep the engine fired, the doors locked and that heater cranked.

"Oh yeah, when ya do find some help of the official kind, make damn sure you explain the seriousness of the situation. The cops are gonna think you're nuts, of course, but if enough of ya stick to the same story, it might just save some lives when they come back to check on us."

Pausing to readjust his parka hood, Ben must've noted the doomsday vibe he'd just helped cultivate, and thus tried to quickly quell the tide as best he could.

"'Course, I'm talkin' speculative... just preppin' for a worst-case scenario. Occupational habit, ya might say. More than likely you'll be seein' my ugly mug back here before you could hop outside and build a snowman."

Wanda Jelks then openly sobbed, burying her face in her gloved hands as the mayor reached over to console her with a gentle hug.

"Ya might wanna save the tears for the enemy, lady," Ben concluded through gnashing teeth just seconds before departing the vehicle yet again. "I got a stout hunch he, she or *it* is gonna need an assload of sympathy 'fore this night is done."

Moments later, we all watched with the highest imaginable level of apprehension as the two warriors of our personal apocalypse trudged through knee-deep snow onto the marginally packed down roadway, melting into the landscape as they descended the hill and ultimately vanished from sight.

"What... do you think they're going to find in there?" Wanda asked sternly while wiping tears from the corners of both eyes.

Checking my watch for proper synchronization,

my response was as straightforward and honest as any I'd ever uttered in a lifetime of similar mutterings.

"I hope... nothing. I pray they find nothing at all."

For the next sixteen minutes and twenty-eight seconds, time literally seemed to stand still. During that span, a moderately heavy snowfall transformed into a major-league whiteout, meaning visibility in and around both idling vehicles was practically nil. To state the obvious, this hardly served to soothe the frazzled nerves of all present, including myself. As a result, dialogue during this painful session of 'hurry up and wait' was severely limited.

"Are they... is he really... some kind of... superhero as Paul said?" the mayor had inquired early on in the proceedings, to which I'd replied with as little explanation as was necessary to avoid delving into details of a more confidential nature, outpost regulation-wise.

"They both make a living as such, yes."

"What's their... what do they call themselves again? Demolition Force? Brute Desolation?"

In response, I found myself fighting the urge to both groan and roll my eyes in disbelief. It seemed nobody listened anymore.

"The man riding with us is Force. The other is known as Scar. Both are veterans in their respective fields."

"It shows," Wanda Jelks remarked, using her coat sleeve to clear the passenger's window of building condensation.

"Regular folks would never have the courage to walk out in *this*... much less traipse off into the unknown, especially with what might be waiting for them."

I managed a stiff nod, hoping the slight disinterest in my tone would close the subject from further discussion.

"It's what they do. It's what they... know. I never was much on fate, but I find it damned hard to believe these people were assigned to the post by mere chance. This... " I paused, raising a forefinger into the air for proper effect, "is a good sign, folks. A very good sign."

Not an additional word was uttered in the ten-plus minutes that followed; not until Wanda Jelks' sudden, shrieking yelp caused me to jump high enough from the driver's seat to actually bang my skull against the interior's frigid roof.

Not being able to visualize his arrival through the falling torrent, Ben had banged on the locked passenger door forcefully enough to bring to mind a series of explosions detonating just outside the truck.

I instructed Miss Jelks to allow entry only after he'd essentially pasted his frozen mug against the window and mumbled various yet mercifully inaudible obscenities.

Lurching into the vehicle as if literally tossed inside by some unseen force, I could actually hear the man's teeth chattering from inside the parka hood as massive chunks of accumulated snow and sleet fell from his person.

"S-s-sorry, l-la-lady," he muttered, visibly shivering as he peeled off the hood and inadvertently coated Wanda Jelks in the bone-chilling fallout. In lighter times, it might've been viewed as a scene played strictly for laughs, perhaps even taken from an old Warner Brother's cartoon, as in Wylie Coyote trapped inside a packed snowman and forced to dig his way out (utilizing various *Acme* brand tools, no less). As it was, there was nary an ounce of humor to be found, only deep concern and no small amount of sympathy for the man's frigid state.

"You... are you alright, Mister? Was everything... did you find-" the mayor croaked, all wide-eyed and swallowing nervously between every other word.

Leaning his head against the back glass and releasing a labored sigh, Ben paused to remove his ice-crusted gloves.

"Oh, we... f-found plenty, Hoss. I-items of interest... a-abound, ya might say. I'll give ya the free tour once we get back there."

"Soooo, no mysterious enemy in sight then?"

"Not that we came across, no, though there's ample evidence the bloodthirsty bastard did pay 'em a visit in our absence. Drive the hell on, Darrin," he groaned, pointing with a gnarled, slightly purple-colored forefinger in the general direction of the outpost grounds.

"I've gotta get my toes warmed up 'fore the damn things snap off."

"How exactly did you get volunteered to make the trek back?" I asked off-handedly while gearing down to steer us back onto the roadway, though its exact location was anybody's guess following the latest deluge.

Smiling despite obvious agony, Ben gestured in the classic 'paper, rock, scissors' tradition.

"Damned if I don't *always* forget that paper covers rock."

As the whiteout had mercifully eased up a bit by the time we'd half-rolled, half-slid down the hill, the post's outdoor emergency lights were dim but visible, as were the Dodge's headlights reflecting off the rearview mirror. Pulling onto the grounds at less than five miles per hour, I could just make out the faint outline of a large, RV-like vehicle in the distance, parked at a decidedly warped angle near a grouping of snow-covered construction equipment. Earlier that fall, a local crew had been hired to build a small addition to the quarters building, a plan that had been nixed less than two full days into the actual execution due to a sudden slashing of government funds. Thus, in the wake of their abrupt exodus from the grounds, the crew had left behind a pale remnant of what was to be, to include a complete fifteen-by-twenty-by-eighteen cement foundation, several piles of stacked eight-by-ten planks, a half-dozen concrete-based metal poles apparently to be used as girders, and a trio of metal Porta Potties. Burt had planned on having said items removed before the winter season was upon us, but had put it off until it was too late to act until the following spring. Fittingly for the scenario at hand, the skeletal remains now stood out like the ancient, abandoned ruins of some lost civilization.

"What in the world is that?"

"County school bus," Ben answered flatly, "what's left of it anyhow."

Essentially stealing my thunder yet again, the mayor quickly intervened with a burst of renewed energy.

"But who... what's it doing here?"

"Seems one of your locals drivers took it upon himself to collect and transport as many neighbors as possible. They were tryin' to get outta town when the storm diverted 'em here."

Feeling a renewed sense of dread, I was extra careful to keep a relatively safe distance from the hulking vehicle, putting at least two car lengths between us while pulling past it to eventually settle on a parking spot on its loading/unloading side.

Once we'd pulled even with the bus, I was somewhat relieved when the mayor and Wanda Jelks' twin gasps managed to drown out my own.

"What... happened to it? Jesus, did they crash?"

"Long story for another time *and* warmer climate, Mayor... let's get inside by the fire and I'll make sure to give ya the full scoop."

Clearing his throat, Ben concluded on a rather ominous note: an unapologetic forewarning targeted mostly at people just like myself who simply cannot stomach surprises of the grisly kind.

"Fair warnin', folks. Ya might see a few scattered remains on the walk in. From what I've been told, it was the bus driver. Do yourself a favor and try like hell to overlook it. Your nightmares will thank ya for it later."

I waited for everyone else to exit before shutting off the plow's engine, and soon discovered that stepping from the truck's toasty confines into knee-deep snow wasn't nearly as uncomfortable or shocking as viewing firsthand the condition of that county school bus.

While the snow-coated hood looked mostly unscathed and the windshield remained (miraculously) intact, the entire left side appeared to have been caved in by a great weight, as if a house-sized boulder had slammed into its side and rolled over a large portion of its roof. Also, a set of rear tires had apparently blown and the bus lurched hard to the right from a woeful lack of stability.

"Come on, Counselor, unless ya wanna stay out here and roast some weenies the hard way," Ben yelled into the wind, gesturing me forward.

Turning briefly, I peeked through the candlelight shaped tunnel in my parka's hood to watch the others pile from the Dodge with Sheriff Owens playing the role of shepherd. Ben soon joined him at the rear of the single-formed line, directing them toward the center of the compound. Initially, I thought this strange or perhaps just a tactical error, as the most logical place to enter from our current location would've been the shipping/receiving dock we'd departed from.

As promised, I did spot what appeared to be a freeze-dried human appendage sticking from the snow a few dozen feet from our trampled path. Though mostly submerged, it appeared to be a brown work boot and attached ankle. Up the trail a bit lay what might've been shredded viscera, perhaps several loops of large intestine judging by the wide circle of melted snow surrounding the remains, logical considering the natural warmth of said entrails once extracted.

Doing my best to maintain an even keel, I was nonetheless forced to swallow a mouthful of my own bile. Similarly, I saw both Wanda Jelks and Marge Owens turn away from the butchery as if warding off the evil responsible simply by refusing to acknowledge its handiwork.

Once we neared the post's middle domed walkway, it became all too apparent why Ben had chosen it as the most convenient for group entry.

A gaping hole had been smashed in the foot-thick, supposed shatterproof glass large enough to drive a team of Clydesdales through.

While passing through the jagged chasm, careful to sidestep as many scattered shards of glass as possible, I noted a coal-black, tarry substance lining the edges of the shattered barricade. Having heard Ben, Tate and the sheriff speak of a similar residue being present at several of the local murder scenes, it didn't take a nuclear physicist to deduce this latest discovery was more than likely of similar origin.

Once everyone had cleared the walkway and entered the dimly lit personal quarters building, Ben peeled away his parka and addressed the ragtag formation.

"In case your all wonderin', our current destination is the generator room-just a few hundred feet ahead and down a single flight of stairs. Keep it as close-knit as possible without steppin' on each other's feet. Marshall, I'll need ya to bring up the rear while I take point. Everybody else just stay together and keep the dialogue to a bare minimum."

Walking past Sheriff Owens, who'd nodded amiably enough following Ben's suggestion, I heard the man curse under his breath as if perturbed at the very notion. At the time, I figured it a natural response at being ordered to distance himself from his immediate family. Still, I couldn't help but think such a reaction mildly peculiar. Stranger still, the vibe I received from Marge Owens in being temporarily separated from her husband's protective custody was not the least bit negative-instead I watched her release a heavy, long-winded sigh of what sounded like unbridled relief, dragging her young son away as if escaping the ruthless clutches of a tyrannical despot.

As for the generator room being hand-picked as the post's chosen safe haven, I wasn't quite seeing the logic. True, it was the single underground space and was at least marginally spacious, but also contained no exit save the single-door entrance, and thus could be easily transformed into an isolated deathtrap once penetrated.

Strolling through the hazily lit corridors, I felt a sudden urge to dash into my private quarters and lock myself in, perhaps to bury my head into my pillow and pray for a respite from the surrealistic nightmare currently underway. Instead, I kept my eyes focused on the backs of the mayor's leather Buster Browns and the slight hitch in the man's giddy-up. The pudgy little politician walked as though he had sewing needles embedded into each heel, and I couldn't help but think his dark brown socks must've been soaking wet from the snow melting at the shoe's top edges.

In testament to the subzero temperatures outdoors, it had taken less than four hours without heat for the interior readings to reach the freezing mark, proof being that I could clearly view the frosty vapor trail of my own breath with each new exhale.

"Damn... backup generator must be crappin' out... what the hell good is emergency lightin' with no heat?," I heard Ben grumble to a chorus of impending groans.

We reached the generator room a few minutes later, with Ben keying the thick metal door from a string of keys I instantly recognized as being masters, no doubt given to him by Burt on his initial trek inside.

Backing away once the lock was engaged, the large man with the even larger mitts played the role of sentinel while allowing us to file inside one-by-one.

After descending a short, railed stairway, we passed through yet another barrier, this one being held open by Tate Fletcher, who greeted each new visitor with a solemn nod.

Illuminated by a half-dozen battery-operated strobes, the room's damp, musky-scented interior was nearly blinding by comparison to the outer hall, and it took me several moments to adjust. Though occupied by several fuse boxes of various sizes, it was the main generator that easily took up the majority of square footage. Surrounded by a wire fence that stretched all the way to the ceiling, it resembled some ancient metallic monstrosity from another era-an oversized relic without a valid purpose or use within modern times. I recall Devon telling me (during a mandatory intro training session on how to operate the beast), that the powers that be had purchased it at a bargain-basement price in an attempt to keep expenses low upon the post's inaugural session. According to the resident communications guru and part-time janitor/maintenance man, it had been built in the late '80s and had spent the previous umpteen years stored away in some long-ago shut-down Denver warehouse. Though it had somewhat managed to pass annual inspections, it had obviously failed miserably during a true time of need. The backup generator had also been a Salvation Army cast-off of some type, and supplied just enough juice to keep the emergency lights flickering, albeit dimly.

Once my orbs had sufficiently adjusted to the strobes, I noted not only a handful of new faces having joined the ranks, but at least one mysterious omission that I couldn't yet put my finger on. It was the sound of Ben's pounding footsteps coming down the steps that distracted my thoughts just enough to temporarily put off identifying whoever was among the missing. Bringing up the rear was Sheriff Owens, the man's appearance and movements the very definition of extreme fatigue. With a heavy, pained sigh, he literally collapsed outside the entrance to take a hard seat on the top step, using the railing there as a physical crutch. His face appeared slick with sweat, despite the less-than-tropical climate. All dramatics aside, it seemed to me the poor man had aged a full decade since we'd departed the post together. Peeking around Wanda Jelks, who had practically sewn her left shoulder to my right since we'd departed the hallway, I caught a glimpse of Devon tinkering with the backup generator, aiming a penlight into the monstrosity's guts from between clenched teeth as both his hands vanished deeper into same. Burt stood just to Devon's right, monitoring prospective progress. He turned and shot me a quick nod, to which I smiled and raised a hand in reply. It was truly a relief to see the big boss man again, and I instantly felt a deeper sense of security, however false.

The mayor, possibly feeling an obligation to do so, spoke first once we'd all began to congregate near the open entrance to the generator cage.

"Kurt... Jerry... Melissa... glad to... see you here... and safe."

The two men, one a middle-aged, big-boned type wearing a rather shabby Colorado Rockies cap and the other a rail-thin young man of perhaps thirty, stepped forward and shook the mayor's hand briefly without verbal response. As for the heavy-set woman he'd referred to as Melissa, she merely nodded without expression and increased the grip on the two youngsters pressed firmly against her. The boy, perhaps five or six at the outset, was shaking as if he'd contracted yellow fever, while a girl of no more than eight or nine stood crookedly with her mouth agape as thin tendrils of mucus drained from each nostril onto her upper lip. The woman appeared too old to be the children's mother-more than likely an aunt or perhaps even their grandmother. Sitting on the floor just to her right were Jay and Jessica, who were huddled together like conjoined twins. Once the three of us locked eyes we managed to trade smiles, though on their part the effort appeared strained and woefully insincere.

It wasn't until I'd twisted around to give Burt and Devon another glance that I noticed the last of the stranded bus party leaning against a stack of empty pallets, his clothing hanging loose as if several sizes too large. Tall, gaunt, and sporting grayish/silver hair and a matching goatee, the man was frighteningly pale, his age virtually impossible to gauge behind dull, unblinking eyes which stared straight ahead without a hint of emotion. Slack-jawed and eerily motionless, my initial diagnosis of the man, even from afar, would've obviously been mild to medium shock. Not exactly earthshaking considering the situation, as I secretly wondered how the entire lot of us weren't already raving like overmedicated lunatics.

"Guy's name is Bill Casey," Tate whispered near my left ear, having obviously noticed my interest. "Dental techie from Washington State. Came in on the bus, though he's not a local like the rest. Said he was on his way to Seattle when the storm hit, so he rented a room at the Jasper motel. Only guest booked, he claimed. Once the power went out at the inn, he decided to hoof it down to the nearest eatery for a bite, figuring a little snow and ice couldn't hurt. Wasn't long after he got caught in a whiteout and couldn't make heads from tails. Bus driver spotted 'im and picked 'im up a mile and a half from the motel, wandering blind down a side street. Lucky he isn't dead already. I think... whatever they went through here hit that dude the hardest."

"Looks like. Jesus, Tate... what did happen here anyway?"

"Not real sure about all the specifics. I believe your boss is planning a powwow as we speak."

As Tate and Ben simultaneously stepped to the center of the gathering, I glanced to my left as a slight movement caught my eye. There, crouched in the shadows near a shoulder-high stack of cardboard boxes, lay Nick Parione, his shoulders badly slumped and his booted feet sprawled in opposite directions. Leaning over him as if to administer first aid was Cassie or perhaps Cassandra Wilkes, as it was impossible to correctly decipher which personality was in charge until the woman spoke or began to gesture. I saw Ben saunter over to check on their welfare, only to be politely rebuffed as Wilkes raised her right hand palms out and nodded as if to cut off any potential dialogue before it started. Ben quickly honored this gesture by returning the nod and backing away.

"As you could tell on your way in, this place wasn't exactly incident-free in our absence," Tate began, having turned to brief our little clan as we were clearly the new arrivals on scene.

"Is... is Deja... is Nickolaus alright?" I whispered as not to be overheard in the deafening silence.

"Yeah, he'll make it. He's just... recovering from his own special brand of medicine, you might say. He says it drains him something fierce, especially when the rewind in question goes a bit longer than planned."

"Would someone mind telling me what the hell is going on here?" Doug Boren spewed angrily, waving his arms about like twin windmills. "I mean, that damaged bus... the... remains we saw on the way in. Does it have something to do with *why* we're being relegated to behaving like cornered rats? I for one am fed up with hiding from some... unseen, unsubstantiated menace. This kind of... fearmongering is exactly why we left that damned basement in city hall! Aren't you... *some* of you people supposed to possess superpowers... save the world and all that jazz? Well? Are the good citizens of Boulder Valley beyond such heroics?"

In the aftermath of the mayor's temper tantrum-fueled rant, I saw little Marie Redrick hug her older brother ever closer just as the as-of-yet unidentified toddlers acquired similarly snug grips on the woman charged with their care.

Clearing his throat, Ben took a single, lengthy stride forward and planted a hand firmly atop the mayor's shoulder, a hand possessing cigar-sized fingers that seemed to engulf roughly half the smaller man's upper arm. In turn, Mayor Boren winced as if preparing to be jowl-slapped.

"With all due respect, Mayor, you mind zippin' it 'til we have a chance to explain? Now, if ya find our cowardly company too much to bear and ya feel a real strong urge to go solo, then by all means plop your happy ass outside and take your chances. Meanwhile, the rest of us have crucial matters to discuss, savvy?"

"I... yes, yes, please continue then."

Backing away, the honorable mayor truly resembled a scolded child on the brink of sobbing.

"Appreciate that," Tate spat out sarcastically as Burt emerged from the generator cage with a huff. My God, and I'd thought Sheriff Owens the textbook poster child for haggardness. By comparison with my boss and mentor, Owens appeared positively daisy fresh. What with his ruffled hair, pale features and tattered clothing (to include a ripped sleeve on his parka jacket and a torn collar on the shirt beneath, among other assorted damage), Burt Hanover resembled some battered, homeless alter-ego of the man I'd seen less than three hours ago.

"Main generator appears a wash, folks. Damn clunker went down not twenty minutes after you guys drove away. Devon's doing all he can with the backup, but it appears hopeless.

"As such, now going on four hours without heat, the temperature is only gonna dip further to the south, I'm afraid. We do have extra blankets and such in the supply room. Just a matter of someone making the trip, though I still say we ought to at least try putting together a rolling convoy and get the hell off these grounds."

Tate rolled his eyes in obvious disagreement.

"Chief Hanover, we've been over this alrea-"

"We have the snowplow, the Dodge, and a handful of staff vehicles to choose from... I'd bet we could cram at least five bodies in my Forerunner. With the plow leading the way, we could put some serious distance between ourselves and... that thing lurking about outside."

"You happen to get an eyeful of that bus, Hoss?" Ben broke in with a scowl. "Ain't no guarantee we're any safer out there. Fact is, you'd be fightin' two enemies... the mystery assassin and the conditions. Besides, your staff vehicles are on the other side of the compound, right?"

"Yeah, but what's that got to do wit-"

"So if this walkin' shredder is half as badass as I'm hearin', just makin' that trek is takin' one hell of a chance with these people's lives."

"But what if... it comes back? It wasn't killed you know. It just appeared to be... staggered. What happens when it comes back to finish the job?"

"Let the four of us worry about that, Burt," Tate answered, pointing in the general direction of Nick and Cassie. "Our main focus is to keep you folks out of the line of fire... at all costs."

Ben nodded, forcefully pounding his upper chest with a clenched fist.

"Yeah, we're back at full fightin' strength now, Chief. There won't be no more separatin' us from here on in, that's a promise. Got another for ya while I'm dolin' 'em out... the bad guy's goin' down... and goin' down hard."

With that, Burt backed away with a shrug, though both his movements and expression did appear less animated, less desperate, as if the sincere confidence that Ben Thomason exuded with every word and gesture had indeed rubbed off, at least somewhat.

As the room grew silent, I found myself unable to refrain from retraining my focus elsewhere. With great curiosity, I watched as Cassandra Wilkes (simple logic, figuring that Cassie wouldn't dare appear so concerned or helpful to anyone) as she held a rag of some sort flush against Nick Parione's bare forehead. Sidestepping over until I was practically rubbing shoulders with Burt, I had again meant to keep my voice down but had underestimated the level of silence.

"Burt, what happened? Where's... where's the doc?" I heard myself ask, having abruptly figured out who amongst the staff was missing from our little hideaway roundtable.

"Yeah, and while we're on the subject of missing persons... " Sheriff Jake Owens snarled, "where's my deputy?"

Inhaling deeply as if prepping to dive underwater, the tale Burt regaled us with was a harrowing one indeed, making our little road trip excursion seem like a virtual joyride by comparison.

***

As Burt told it, we'd only been away from the post grounds for a little less than a half-hour when the mayhem ensued. First off, the generator had croaked as if on cue from some hidden disciple of Murphy's Law.

Doc Gonzales had gone to stay with his patient, Deputy Jeffries, who had experienced a sudden, mysterious setback almost immediately after we'd piled into the snowplow and departed the grounds. Complaining of severe stomach cramps and an extreme migraine, Doc had literally helped carry the man back down to sickbay, stating 'it was probably just the effects of the medication' he'd prescribed.

While Burt and Devon stayed busy attempting to regain power and contact authorities via the two-way, Jay and Jessica had been tasked to pull extra blankets, batteries and other essentials from the supply room.

Burt stated that he was just leaving the com room to meet Chuck James, the post's head maintenance man, when Devon was able to initiate contact with trooper headquarters in Corvallis. Incredibly, James had arrived on time for his schedule workday despite the horrid conditions via a comically dented late '90s four-wheel drive Jeep he had nicknamed *Brute*, supposedly after an ex-wife.

Moments later, after being reassured the state police were already en-route from several previous reports of trouble in the area, a series of thundering crashes reverberated through the halls. Burt claimed the accompanying vibrations were so intense they caused a hefty metal filing cabinet to crash over and also jarred several paintings from the walls. Making a beeline toward sickbay, which was a relatively short trek since both offices were contained in the same building, Burt swore he thought he heard several muffled cries of anguish in a voice most likely belonging to Doc Gonzales, as several of the barely audible words had been spoken in a shrieking Spanish dialect.

"It took us less than forty-five seconds to reach sickbay, tops... a fact that made what we found there even more mind-blowing.

"A large section of wall... I'm not talking stucco but solid brick... eight-feet high and at least that wide was... well, it was just... gone, blasted into gravel bits as if dynamited. Doc's main medicine cabinet had been toppled, along with several cots, including the one previously occupied by Deputy Jeffries.

"More... there was a... several black smears and spatters all about the room. It was like someone had blasted the place with one of those paintball guns. Wasn't any sign of the doc or Deputy Jeffries outside either... just a tar trail that ended after a few dozen feet or so. I... followed the markings in the snow 'til it just... petered out completely, swallowed up by fresh snowfall."

Strictly adhering to set government regulation, Burt had immediately ordered the room quarantined and closed off that entire section of the building pending a full CDC investigation of the unidentified substance, and declared Doctor Gonzales and Deputy Jeffries as officially MIA.

"Of course, Dejà vu and Jeyl- Nick and Cassie volunteered to go out and search the grounds, but I couldn't approve of such potential endangerment. Besides, I figured we'd surely need their... special skills if our mystery guest returned for more... specimens.

"Well, as things turned out, it was certainly the right call."

"Devon and Chunk James had been the first to verify the arrival of the bus, having spotted the vehicle's headlights while standing inside the domed walkway between buildings. At the time, they'd been returning from the supply room with heavy duty caulking and masking tape in order to seal off the sickbay door.

"That damned hole was turning the entire building into a walk-in freezer, so I told them to seal the room off as tight as possible. I'd been in the mess hall attempting to ingest the last of the lukewarm coffee when Devon came sprinting in yelping about new arrivals. I swear, this was less than ten blessed minutes after the sickbay incident.

"There'd hardly been time to catch a decent breath before matters went from bad to extremely worse."

By this time, Dejà vu and Cassie had joined them as they made their way back to the admin building and all four witnessed the approaching vehicle lights from the glassed dome.

"It wasn't until it made a hard left for no apparent reason, almost tipping itself over on its side in the process, that we knew something wasn't at all normal about its approach... much less it's landing."

Burt said it had slid front to rear, performing the kind of textbook three-sixty spin you'd usually only see successfully executed by professional stunt drivers.

"It was like something out of *Smokey and the Bandit*," Burt had remarked with barely restrained enthusiasm, clearly showing both his age and cinematic tastes.

"Big yellow bastard skidded to a stop, barely missing a tall stack of wooden planks those blasted freelance builders left behind, and that's when the real weirdness commenced... "

According to Burt, the four of them spotted Chunk James exit a side door from the mess hall to greet the mystery guests, and they hardly had time to contemplate a similar path when the bus began to shake and convulse as if being brutally impacted from the opposite side by a similarly bulky object.

"No shit... looked like another bus had T-boned it... several times... either that or it had parked smack dab atop an active fault line... " Devon injected between curses while still piddling with the generator.

Burt resumed in a bone-weary tone, having kneeled down and run a hand through his disheveled coif. I'd never seen the man in such a state. It was downright depressing to witness.

"The unexpected movement of the bus more or less... froze us into place for a few seconds-long enough to see Chuck walk cautiously forward and then vanish while headed to the loading side. Can't say exactly why... but for... just an instant I felt like screaming out a warning to him to back off and... to get away from that damn bus, but then I figured it was a case of creeping paranoia fueled by everything else that had gone wrong.

"Well, like they say," he sighed, "always stick with your initial instinct... "

Just as Devon exited the cage and joined our little campfire gathering, Burt stood and began to pace the limited space between the entranceway and the cage's chain-link perimeter, both the story he told and the ultragrim tone he used to do so equally mesmerizing. That is, to all but those who had witnessed the terror close up, as I watched Jay and Jessica lower their heads as if utterly disinterested while the two men and the woman safeguarding the small children all averted their eyes elsewhere, as if searching for some viable distraction. By this time, the Redrick kid and his little sister had taken up residence next to the older lady, who had somehow became the house mother by proxy for all underage types. Meanwhile, Cassandra Wilkes continued to administer a wet rag to Nick Parione's forehead while the latter appeared to have dozed off.

As for me and the rest of the new arrivals, the natural human trait of curiosity had definitely kicked into overdrive. It was a case of not really wanting to know, but having no conscious choice but to listen-akin to hearing the grisly details of a horrific crime scene or automobile crash.

"While Cassie took off in a sprint for the mess hall entrance, the rest of us stood there and just... gaped as the bus finally ceased its pronounced rocking movements. Problem was, the hard snow was making it damn near impossible to get a clear visual. I heard Deja- I heard Nick say something like 'you two stay put... we've got trouble' and take off in a jog just as an unidentified object went sailing over the top of the bus. At first I thought it was... I know it sounds crazy... but I thought it was somebody's hat... that somebody's headgear had been blown off by the gale winds. But... then we saw something else take flight, a... larger object. And we... we heard... screams... mixed... garbled, almost drowned out by the wind and some kind of loud metal against metal screeching sound. After a few seconds, there was no mistaking what they were... human screams."

Following a lengthy pause, during which time Burt appeared on the brink of actually tipping over from a heavy dose of weariness, he happily turned the floor over to Devon.

"That... larger object boss man spoke about turned out to be what was left of the bus driver... some dude named Walker or Walters or something... "

"Eugene Walker... " the middle-aged man earlier referred to as Kurt injected softly, reaching up to adjust his baseball cap every few seconds. "He lives just down the block from me on Vesper Drive. Came around last night pounding on doors, warning of some kind of danger in the locality-we all thought he was talking about a chemical spill or something... not... well, whatever *this* is. Anyhow, he was driving around the neighborhood in the bus trying to convince folks of the coming danger. Said he'd heard... then seen something... well, unnatural out by his shed that had... slaughtered several of his cattle. He was offering to get us out of town, least 'til the storm died down.

"Me... I... I live alone since my wife passed. Figured Gene might need some... my help. God rest his kind, gentle soul."

The man had welled up at the end, finally turning to face the opposite direction while wiping vigorously across both eyes with a shirt sleeve.

"A good man, Gene Walker... a brave man," the individual named Jerry added, reaching over to console Kurt with a gentle tap of the shoulder. "He didn't deserve to die... like that. *Nobody* deserves... to go like... that."

"He surely saved a lot of lives this night," Bill Casey added from a dozen feet away while tugging at the waistline of his comically baggy jeans, possibly to prevent them from falling down around his ankles, "saved at least... for now."

Everyone seemed to ponder this last, rather grim statement for one moment before resuming the discussion. Meanwhile, Bill Casey silently turned and strolled to a far corner of the room as if to escape further scrutiny, stepping gingerly as if scared he might literally walk out of his shoes.

"Well, all I know is... I wouldn't wish what happened to that poor dude on my worst enemy," Devon remarked, becoming increasingly animated as he picked up the narrative from there.

"Me and Burt... um, boss man, just stood there, staring through that glass like trapped lab rats while all hell broke loose outside. All of the sudden that bus' rear end whipped around like some invisible Mack truck had barreled into her, spinning like a top and blowing a rear tire in the process. It was about then that Cass- Jekyll-eye and Rewi- Dejà vu made an appearance, both of 'em sprinting out the side door and headed straight into the eye of the storm, yes sir.

"'Course, what with the whiteout blowin' at full steam teamed with the crappy angle we had of the action, visibility was pretty much for shit. We could see movement from underneath the bus, but couldn't really get a useable grip on what was happening. Can't really speak for boss man, but I was weak-kneed and damn near hysterical at that particular juncture, and watching Chuck James' severed head smack that glass dome like a ripe melon thumpin' concrete a second later didn't exactly do much for my frazzled nerves, if you know what I'm saying.

"Worse yet, Chuck's mashed noggin squirmed down that glass real gradual like, leaving a wide, thick maroon smear behind that froze up almost instantly. Man, you talk about gut-churning; watching that jagged ass neck stub slide down the dome like a chilled slug trying to find a place to hide was downright c-r-e-e-p-y with a capitol C.

"Can't really say what happened to the rest of his corpse... probably won't really know 'til all this shit thaws... mid-April at the latest, right, boss?"

Staring downward at the toe portion of his mukluks, Burt nodded weakly.

"Sure, sure... just get me *to* April first, then we'll worry about gathering bones... and, Devon?"

"Yeah, boss?"

"You mind being a little... less graphic? I mean, there are kids present... "

Devon shrugged good-naturedly, seemingly oblivious to whatever form of etiquette he'd breached.

"Gotcha, boss... anyhow, we didn't see much more, least not 'til Dejà vu and Miss Jekyll hopped back inside the corridor and the real roller-coaster ride began. One thing's for damn sure... the *mess* hall is aptly named right about now. Looks like a train derailed in there."

As Tate and Ben sidestepped away, thus concluding the mini-conference, I attempted to stick close without seeming obvious.

Half-whispering, Ben spoke with his head bowed as to further muffle the volume.

"Well, whatever went down, Nick must've been forced to do some serious rewindin'. Kid looks like he just swallowed a rat turd with a horse piss chaser."

"Looks like he blew a fuse alright," Tate mumbled beneath a cupped palm. "Don't think he's gonna be of much use to us if there is a round two anytime soon."

"Nope. Down for the count for sure. Right now he ain't nothin' but another body to protect."

Though not intentionally executed, we all seemed to pick that very moment to gradually twist about and look Nick's way, only to be greeted by Cassie Wilkes' stern stare and equally unyielding pose.

"What Nick Parione *is*, Ben Thomason, is a genuine hero, and not just in the 'for hire' mode, either."

From there, the second and easily strongest willed of the Jekyll-ene trio most assuredly preached on it.

***

"While Nick helped pull the folks off the bus and get 'em inside, I managed to keep the ugly bastard occupied. Have to confess, it didn't take very long to realize that this girl was waaaay over her head in the physical match up department."

Shuffling about like a small child desperate to find a bathroom, I was surprised Ben didn't actually raise a hand for permission before speaking.

"So what kinda beastie we talkin' about here, Cas? Mutie? Bone-cruncher from another galaxy... what?"

Relaxing her stiffened posture a bit, Cassie paused and stared blankly ahead as if trying to successfully plunder a long-faded memory. Meanwhile, I couldn't help but wonder why Ben or Tate wasn't sharing the information we'd stumbled across at the crash site, that being the speculation that the aforementioned threat was terrorism related.

"It was mutated for sure... though from *what* is anybody's guess. Its whole body was smooth and black as tar, but shiny... and moist... oozing some kind of fluid from head to toe.

"Otherwise, it possessed atypical human features... arms, legs, torso, head... even a set of eyes. Nose was more like a beak... and that mouth... *holy shit*... like a goddamned threshing machine. It had a frothy maw that seemed to reach from ear to ear, and choppers like rail spikes.

"Size-wise it was one cloud-scraping SOB... big and wiry... seven and a half feet at least, skinny as shit except for its arms and legs, which were... muscled but not overly so... just finely cut and chiseled, like it was wearing one of those

Hollywood bulk suits cut off at the shoulders. Stout as a runaway freight, of that I can personally testify."

"What else... any weapons to speak of?"

"Oh yeah, besides the aforementioned teeth, it owned a set of claws that would make a full-grown grizzly green with envy. Hooked and at least as long as the fingers housing 'em-just made for shredding. "

"Oh, for cripe's sake... that's *it*?" Ben growled, tossing his arms airborne as he began to pace a small semicircle. "Not one but *two* towns cower in the dark like whipped pups and we all sit around with our thumbs planted firmly up our whazoos over some overgrown teddy bear that leaks pudding from its pores? Pardon my butchered French, but fuck me to tears... "

Despite an atmosphere ripe with doom and gloom, Tate and I couldn't help but share a smile over Ben's maniacal rant, a brief moment of levity that evaporated soon enough once Cassie leapt forward and practically sent the big man reeling with a solid body block. All at once, everyone froze and the term 'you could've heard a pin drop' was never more apt. I even thought I heard several gasps executed simultaneously.

"You always this cocksure about shit you know *nothing* about, Thomason?" she spat out angrily, leaning on her tiptoes with balled fists to stare directly into the big man's eyes, suddenly pulled saucer-wide.

"Maybe I had you pegged wrong after all. Maybe you are just a porn 'stashe wearing, loudmouth, blowhard jackass with a penchant for the bottle and little regard for anything or anyone else... "

"Listen, Cas, I didn't mean... "

"Maybe that skinny little *kid* as you call him really is twice the man you'll ever be... "

"Cassie... *shit*... sheath the claws already... I was just... talkin' out my ass... bad habit I can't seem to shake... "

Backing away a step, Cassie Wilkes paused for a moment before sighing wearily. Meantime, the wide smile spreading across Ben's haggard face appeared fueled by equal parts relief and newfound respect.

"Yeah, it is... and yes, you were. Now do us *all* a favor and give that constantly wagging tongue of yours a rest, alright? I wasn't finished yet... "

Ben bowed as gracefully as his immense bulk would allow.

"Yes, ma'am. By all means, continue... "

"The thing's main weapon was brute strength, plain and simple. Damn thing was like a giant tar baby *Hulk* come to life. While Nick herded the folks off the bus and into the building, I did my best live bait imitation, a role I'm not exactly familiar or comfortable with."

Squatting onto one knee, Cassie ran a hand through her bangs, her trademark spiked do mostly matted as a result of both the elements and the recent scuffle she continued to describe.

"Believe me, I'd only had one thing in mind once outside... and ashamed as I am to confess it, it wasn't saving those people. Man, I just wanted blood to flow, plain and simple. The enemy's blood by *my* hands. It wasn't 'til I saw what this enemy was made of... more importantly, *capable* of... that the secondary plan of flight over fight came into play."

"So what exactly *are* we talking about here?" Tate asked, as squinty-eyed and square-jawed as I'd ever seen him.

"Well... it had its back turned, still bashing the hell out of that bus, when I delivered my best flying double-heel kick to the back of its slick, cone-shaped noggin. By the time I'd executed a full midair somersault and just managed to land upright on the packed snow, I was a good dozen to fifteen feet away."

Pausing for dramatic effect, Cassie then arched her left brow and snapped the sharp-tipped fingers of her right hand.

"Damn golem didn't even blink... far as I could tell, it hadn't even felt the blow at all. When it finally did turn around, that only after I'd belted out a rebel yell or two, I watched it take those lobster claws and rip a three-foot section from the hood of the bus and toss it aside like so much shredded confetti. Impressive as that was, it wasn't 'til it sidekicked the back end of the bus three or four feet just to move it out of the way that I started feeling a little squirrelly about my chances.

"Once it did charge, I backstepped in high gear and struck a defensive pose. I'd meant to let it bull forward and do a leap over at the last second. Only thing was, I sorely miscalculated both the iced asphalt and that thing's reach *and* quickness. It clipped my ankles about midway and I must've completed four or five full flips before landing on my back about twenty yards from where I'd timed my jump.

"Now, what happened next made me begin to understand and... accept how overmatched I was... and even *big bad sis* would be once she made the scene, which wasn't long in the making the way my scalp was tingling.

"To my left I caught a hint of movement, and suddenly this dude comes running outta nowhere directly at the thing, screaming his lungs out and waving a meat clever over his head. Hanover later told me the guy's name was Jerold Garcia, one of the post's kitchen workers and a former marine. I can't for the life of me figure out what the guy was thinking... not that I don't appreciate and respect the gesture, but he had to know it wasn't gonna turn out good once he made that charge... "

Cassie then lowered her voice to a raspy whisper, no doubt to shield the grislier details from youthful ears.

"One swipe... I'm talking one half-hearted, lazy ass *wave* of that thing's left hand ripped that poor dude into two neatly sliced sections... from groin to scalp... a neater segmentation I've never witnessed... and I've seen several. Once I saw the thing start to casually lick the gore from its nailtips, eyeing me like a slab of cherry cobbler, I knew it was time to make tracks for safer climes... or at least call in for reinforcements. Figuring Nick and the others had at least cleared the mess hall, I hightailed it for the entrance."

Peeking over yet again as Cassie paused to stand and work out the kinks, I noticed Nick had at least brought his knees to his chest and his head was no longer hanging but staring straight ahead at our little impromptu group session.

"I never looked back to see if the ugly shit was tailing me and I'd cleared roughly half the dome when the enclosure exploded just over my left shoulder, showering me in glass. To my credit, I didn't lose a step... just kept on picking 'em up and laying 'em down 'til I entered the mess hall. It must be noted, by this time big sis was just aching to get in on the action. I mean, my head was thumping like a jackhammer while every nerve ending I own was lit up like Thomason on New Year's Eve... " she paused to shoot Ben a playful wink, to which he simply nodded without reply. "I was nearing the gym entrance when the door flew inward. Let me tell you, if my progress had been even a couple of feet further ahead, me and ol' Nicky boy over there wouldn't have shared one painful-ass kiss. He was yelling for me to follow him and take cover, but by then big sis had other plans and I wasn't in any position to argue. I told him to get back to the civilians and play sentinel while I stood my ground. We were standing there arguing back and forth when big, black and gruesome blasted through the mess hall door, shattering that thick oak sucker into kindling.

"I recall shoving Nick back and reaching for that paneled soda cooler... you remember the one," she paused, looking to myself, Ben and Tate as we all nodded knowingly. It had been a fairly large metallic cooler with a sliding glass top where various brands of soda and bottled water were kept stocked for both staff and guests. What with its steel outer shell and the fact that on any given day it held up to eighty cans and/or bottles, I would've approximated its weight to be upwards of three-hundred pounds easy, perhaps even as high as five.

"Well, I heaved that sucker overhead, did a quick spin for momentum's sake, and heaved it for all I was worth. To be completely honest, I should say we heaved it, 'cause it was about that time that big sis was in full takeover mode. Don't recall much more, but right before everything faded to black, I did see that thing swat the cooler out of midair with practically no effort. I mean, shit... it could've easily sidestepped it altogether, but nooo... it chose to play batting practice instead. As it was, he nailed it hard enough to turn it into a shrapnel piñata. It was like dodging live fire.

"Hard as this is to admit, fellas," Cassie concluded gravely, "my last conscious thought was... well, that I probably wouldn't be waking up. Big sis is one strong, vicious mother, as you've all heard. Girl went toe-to-toe with Iron Man once... beat the living crap out of the Sub-Mariner a few years back. Psychotic bitch doesn't know the meaning of the word quit. But from what I gather, Nick's the only reason I'm still standing here conversing. He's yet to give me the details... and it's a toss-up whether or not I really wanna know. Like a wise man once said, or maybe it was a wise*ass*... this girl's just happy to be here."

Looking a bit piqued, Cassie suddenly staggered forward and was quickly braced by Tate, who gripped her by the shoulders before walking her over to an empty crate propped near the Owens' family. Speaking of which, I'd found it both odd and strangely intriguing that neither wife nor son had seen fit to join the sheriff near the entrance steps, where he sat slumped and horribly pale-faced.

"Now that's some weird shit, ain't it?" Ben whispered next to me, having obviously picked up the vibe in following my path of vision.

"What's that?" I asked ignorantly, switching focus back to Cassie, who sat gingerly atop the wooden crate while Tate stood nearby like some gargantuan nursemaid.

"How the constable's lovin' wife and kid are treatin' 'im like he's a bubonic plague carrier pigeon, that's what. They ain't as much as locked eyes since we got here. Kid looks petrified, and I beginnin' to think it ain't the mystery monster at the core of his fears."

"Marital spat maybe," I said inanely, instantly regretting offering up such a ludicrous opinion.

"Sure, Counselor, sure. Marshall probably left the toilet seat up one too many times. Talk about holdin' a grudge... what with possible death starin' her in the face and all... damn, that woman surely puts the 'S' in stubborn."

My face grew hot with embarrassment despite the frigid conditions.

"It is strange behavior, Ben, but we can't even begin to speculate on things we know nothing about."

"I reckon," Ben replied while taking an initial step in the general direction of Nick Parione, "but my gut is tellin' me the situation bears watchin' just the same."

"Benjamin?"

He paused mid-step, though maintaining eye contact with Nick, who had managed to stand upright with Herculean effort.

"Yeah?"

"Why aren't you... why aren't we telling them about... what we found at the crash site? You know... the possible link to terrorism."

I saw the big man visibly stiffen. He turned to me, the left side of his bushy, Fu Manchu mustache comically warped.

"Oh, I meant to tell ya earlier, Darrin. We're... keepin' that on the QT for now. Let's just say... for security reasons. Besides, a bloodthirsty mutant is a bloodthirsty mutant, no matter its birthin' origin, right?"

"I... yeah, I guess."

"We'll weed out the details in time. Right now we don't wanna add to the overload of paranoia already present, dig?"

Warped as his logic was, it did make a certain amount of sense.

Moments later, after shooting a final glance Cassie Wilkes' way, I joined him in greeting Nick. While Cassie had buried her head in her hands to apparently attempt a brief power nap, I saw Marge Owens leaning in close and whispering something to Tate Fletcher, who in turn eyed Jake Owens with an arched brow.

"Hiya, Rerun. Long time, no see. So how ya doin', kid?" I heard Ben ask, breaking my own semidaze. In regarding us through baggy, bloodshot eyes, it was obvious Nick had been through a major ringer that had fatigued him both in a physical and mental sense.

"I've... felt better, smart guy. Have to say... you're looking chipper, though. How'd the sightseeing venture make out?"

"Apparently, a regular sun-soaked picnic compared to what ya ran into here. Cassie was just tellin' us how you pulled her bacon outta the fire."

"I... it was no big deal. I came... I saw... I kicked *mutated-freak-from-hell* rear end... as usual," he quipped, though having to pause every few words to take in additional lung filler.

"She don't remember shit. Said Jekyll-ene had run her into la la land just after you arrived on scene. I get the feelin' Cas has a new boyfriend, kid," Ben said with a gentle nudge. "I oughta kick your skinny rear for stealin' my girl, but in light of your present condition, I'll let it pass."

"You're... all heart, dozer-mitts."

Feeling a small measure of guilt in breaking the unique moment of playful banter between two men who had so naturally played the role of adversaries, I nonetheless pressed onward.

"What happened in there, Nick? How'd you do it?"

"How... did I do what, Counselor?"

"Drive the thing off... defeat it... "

"Brother, the way I'm feeling right now, I'm in no position to boast about getting lucky."

"Lucky? But... how? I mean, after what Cassie said about how strong... how ferocious that thing was, it must've taken a great effort to get rid-"

With a wry, rather pathetic smile, Nick lowered his head while raising a shaky hand airborne. He then leaned between myself and Ben and purposely whispered his response.

"Mister Jackson, preceding my... magnificent triumph over the forces of evil, I alone was privy to watching Cas-awwww shit, *Jekyll-ene* being gutted not once but twice. Hey, in her defense... she gave the enemy hell that first round, pummeling the crap out of 'im with left hooks, right jabs, and combinations of punches that would've even rocked Thor's boat but good. For a few seconds there, I really thought... she had a fighting chance. Of course, that was before I saw her body slammed, flung airborne, bounced off the ceiling like a... a... ricocheting pinball, and then gutted from belly button to chin upon descent."

As he paused for air, I couldn't help but refocus on Cassie, still inhabiting that rickety crate while wearing a mask of fatigue to match Nick's own. Meantime, Tate had broken away from Marge Owens and was headed back our way. In the background, I noticed Bill Casey regarding our little group with the fisheye, having kneeled down like a praying monk and propped his chin atop a clenched fist. Every few seconds, he'd affix his steely glare upon Sheriff Jake Owens before refocusing our way. It seemed rather peculiar that the man wasn't at all influenced by my returning his stare, as if he were either completely oblivious or simply didn't care. Either way, the vibe was of the vaguely creepy variety. It wasn't until Nick resumed his monologue that I was able to shake the feeling that something wasn't quite kosher with the lone soul in the room labeled a 'stranger in town', though at the time it was easily dismissed as simple paranoia.

"After he... *it* had flung her corpse halfway across the room to splatter against a far wall like a bloody rag, the thing then turned... his attention to... guess who? Sooooo, not one to wait around to be shredded like a cornhusk, I powered up the old wayback machine and set it for a full one-minute duration. When... things resumed, it was just after Jekyll-ene had tossed that drink cooler and he was in the process of swatting it away like an empty tin can. The enemy did seem a bit perplexed at the time warp, but not nearly enough as... much as I'd hoped for."

Tate joined our close-knit trio as Nick paused yet again, obviously still struggling to maintain focus as well as the required lung intake.

"I... I figured... *prayed*... that given a second chance to do her thing, Jekyll-ene might just find a way to off the thing, especially since the usual side effects of the time-transformation might not affect her as much as say... a more stable being.

"Anyway... turned out to be a pipe dream. While she did land a few more haymakers, it didn't alter the outcome a damn bit. This time he... this time that damn *Grendel*-looking freakoid practically snapped her in half... *shit*, there just isn't any mistaking the retort of a cracked spine."

Predictably lost having joined in on the story at the midway point, I could tell Tate wanted desperately to interrupt but refrained.

"I was still so shaken from the first rewind that I barely had the fuel to crank out another. Luckily, big, spindly and gruesome wasn't exactly sharp as a tack itself, and didn't move to put out my lights right away. Otherwise... well... I'd rather not think about it.

"Even moving like it was treading in knee-deep quicksand, the thing was crowding my personal space something fierce by the time I *was* able to engage the second rewind. I had to try to back it up at least another thirty to forty-five seconds, and the strain of back-to-backs was frying my brainpan as it was.

"Have to confess I was pleasantly surprised at the outcome; a ninety-second alteration and I still maintained consciousness, jogging up the hallway toward the mess hall with a headache that would've paralyzed a bull elephant.

"Suffice to say, the third trip through that swinging door was the charm. Even as dazed as she was from the twin time warps, Cassie still managed to heave that cooler overhead and wing it fastball style just as black beastie made its preordained appearance at the opposite entranceway. Funny, boy couldn't quite muster the strength to bash the door in this time... just kind of... pushed it open just enough to walk through and stepped on in. Just before that cooler bashed it 'bout chest high, I noticed those coal-black eyes were spinning like pinwheels. Yep, the second rewind had taken its toll for damn certain. At impact, it cartwheeled back and took at least a ten-by-ten section of concrete wall with it. Me and Jekyll-ene paused a good fifteen, twenty seconds to see if it was bucking for a rematch but never saw hide nor tar-coated hair or heard a single moan or groan over the gale force winds whistling through that hole in the dome. With no further fisticuffs required, Jekyll-ene had reverted back to Cassie and we proceeded to hide out here and wait for help."

"Ya did good, kid," Ben exclaimed after a rather strained moment of silence. "Dug down deep and found a gear ya didn't even know ya owned. Producin' under pressure is what this line of work's all about."

"Yeah, well, thanks, coach... what else was I going to do? Stand there like lunchmeat on legs? Not that much bravery involved in saving one's own butt cheeks.

"I... can't help but ponder though, you know?" he concluded, reaching back to wipe a bare palm across the nape of his neck, which I'd noticed was coated in fresh sweat beneath the collar of his field jacket. All previous fits of self-bravado aside, Nick Pacione appeared permanently haunted by what he'd witnessed inside that mess hall.

"What's that, kid?"

"What if... the second alteration hadn't worked any better than the first? I mean, there wasn't a chance in hell I could've attempted... another. Cas would've been toast... again, and I'd have surely followed. It isn't like I could've fought that damn monster off with a few well-placed punches or kicks. My hocus-pocus act might not seem like much to guys like you, but it's all this boy's got. Hey, it's no coincidence I'm always applying for team status instead of going solo. I'm a straight man all the way, baby. Set 'em up for the fall, then let somebody else come in and close the deal. If only I could learn to keep my priorities straight and these wandering hands tucked away instead of reaching out to pinch some cute female caboose. Well, such is life, right? We all have our weaknesses or we wouldn't even be standing here."

"Take a rest, Nick," Tate said while gently nudging Ben to join him in putting some distance between themselves and everyone else.

"You've earned it."

Reading the nonverbal hint, Ben slowly followed Tate's path to the far west corner of the room.

"Just recharge those batteries, Nick. We might need ya to apply those special skills of yours again later on."

"I'll, um, have Burt bring you some more water from one of the canteens," I added shamelessly, once again careful not to allow Ben and Tate to stray too far from hearing distance.

"Got the skinny on the sheriff's wife and kid," I heard Tate mumble as both men turned to face the wall. Though I'd taken up position less than four feet away, I'd decided to back toward them, thus creating a facade of disinterest.

"Yeah?"

"She leaned in, right out of the blue, and get this: she asked me if something had happened to him."

"Happened to 'im? Meanin' what?"

"I guess she meant some kind of physical injury... a bump on the head... something along those lines."

"She have some reason to believe it had?"

"According to her, he was not only acting strange, but downright scary... scary and... ill. She even said she's keeping her distance because she's afraid for the kid."

"No *shit*. Did he threaten 'em on the ride in?"

"Jake Owens didn't utter one word the whole way back, Ben. Just kinda stared straight and never moved, like he was sleeping with his eyes open. I just figured it was due to bone-weariness... mental fatigue. She's acting like he's contagious."

"Ya know, I did notice he was lookin' mighty sickly on the walk in. Kinda just chalked it up to stress. Hey, check it out... "

Figuring they'd turned about to check out the sheriff, I knelt down and pretended to retie my bootlaces.

"Looks like he's on the verge of passing out alright."

"Yeah, well... that's probably a helluva long line at this point, Fletch."

"I agree, but he looks more than tired. Look at his hands shaking... man looks like he's contracted a viral infection."

"Dude's been through the ringer. Guess losin' his deputy was the last straw."

"All I know is, the woman said he isn't the same man who left their house late last night. Said he wasn't acting right, wasn't moving right, and weirdest of all, didn't even *smell* right, and she wasn't talking about your everyday, regulation BO either."

"Weird. Hey, button it for a sec... looks like Hanover's headin' our way."

"Oh, by the way," I heard Tate say in a noticeably louder voice, "you can cease and desist with the espionage tactics, Darrin... we know you're there."

Standing with a loud pop from both knees, I couldn't help but smile and started to turn just as each man gently jostled me from either side.

"Don't blame ya for bein' curious, Counselor, but like I said before, keep it all on the down low for now. These folks are paranoid enough as it is. We sure as hell don't need to be tossin' more fuel onto the flames."

"Understood," was all I could sneak in just as Burt and Devon walked up to join the mix.

"So what's the plan, Thomason... Fletcher?" Burt asked curtly, having placed his hands atop his hips.

"Plan? Well, if there's any way we can procure some chow, I'd sure appreci-"

"I'm talking about a plan of *action*, Fletcher. That is, unless cowering inside this damn room for the duration sums up the gist."

"Reel in the fangs, Hoss. That ain't the gist," Ben shot back, though careful to maintain a relatively low volume.

"Good to hear, since that *Godzilla versus Mothra* castoff might just come a knocking any minute now, and the entire lot of us are cornered, sitting ducks. I still say we should make a run for the vehicles and hightail it off these grounds... away from the Twin Cities *period*."

"We've already been over that, Hanover. It's too risky for the civilians, especially with both Nick and Cassie both temporarily out of commission. Ben and I can't protect everyone once the whole group's exposed out in the open."

"Yes, but-"

"Besides, there might be more than one of those things roaming about... what then?"

"I still say it's better than squatting in a corner waiting to be jumped."

"Just cool your jets a second," Ben blurted out a bit louder than he'd intended, instantly toning it back down as a few heads had twisted about in reaction, all that is, save Sheriff Jake Owens, who continued to nod away on the stairwell while being studied with great interest by one Bill Casey, mysterious dental technician at large.

"Here's the deal... while I go scout out the grounds, Tate's gonna stick with the group for bodyguard purposes. Just knowin' the coast is clear is sure to help blow away the cloud of dread currently floatin' about."

"But, Benjamin... "

"Yeah, Hoss?"

"What if the enemy finds you?"

Ben grinned mischievously.

"I'll beat down that bridge when I come to it, Mister Hanover."

"But... " Burt stewed, waving his arms about in frustration, "I still say the best thing we can do is distance ourselves from the potential dang-"

It took me a moment to realize that the remainder of Burt's impassioned plea was being systematically drowned out by a building racket somewhere inside the room.

It took me an additional moment, before which both Ben and Tate had taken off in a mad sprint toward the room entrance, to correctly identify both the source of said racket and the specific noise the question.

Less than fifty feet from where I'd stood frozen into place, Sheriff Jakes Owens was literally screaming his lungs out.

Chapter Six

A Last, Futile Stand at 'Alamo' Ridge/Enemy Within

Once my initial daze had passed and I joined the sudden gathering around the person of Sheriff Owens, it became apparent that his wasn't the only set of lungs on display within the room's cramped confines. For one, there was Marge Owens' banshee shrieks from my right, bookended by Wanda Jelks' ear-splitting concerto perhaps a dozen feet to my left, though not to be outdone by the much-too-feminine wails of one Mayor Doug Boren. In stark contrast, I did note Bill Casey backing ever so casually from the scene like a tiptoeing burglar.

As my momentum carried me past the retreating minimob, I wasn't yet able to visualize the source of all the mayhem due to Ben and Tate standing directly in my line of vision, their collective bulks blocking all but the sheriff's booted feet, each of which squirmed about like freshly placed worms on a hook.

"What the hell's the matter with 'im?" I heard Ben ask with a shrug of his massive shoulders.

"Look at the eyes, Ben... check out the man's eyes!" came Tate's booming, ultraexcited response as I saw him lift his right arm and point directly at the sheriff.

His entire frame tensing as if bracing for impact, Ben moved back and over a half-step, allowing me my first unobstructed view.

"Yeah, I see it... color-scheme looks damned familiar, don't it?"

Laying back on the steps as if being forced

down and held into place by some invisible entity, Jake Owens was barely recognizable as the same man who'd arrived in our midst mere hours earlier. In fact, at that moment he was barely recognizable as a *man*, period. So grotesquely bloated to the point of actually popping the buttons from his uniform shirt, the sheriff's sweat-drenched face appeared to literally be melting away. Worse yet, steady streams of a glutinous blackish fluid leaked from the left corner of his mouth, his right nostril, and both eyes. Before my focus was distracted elsewhere, I thought I even saw the same dark, gooey discharge begin to ooze from the man's fingertips.

"We gotta get 'im outta here, Fletch... whatever the hell it is, it might be contagious," I heard Ben bark just before Owens' horrified wife let loose with the granddaddy of all screams, rushing forward in a lurch before being tackled to the floor and restrained by Cassie, who practically sat on the hysterical woman's back.

"Stay here and guard the rest, Ben... I'm taking him out."

With that, Tate Fletcher jogged forward and in one swift, fluid movement hauled the spasm-racked body of Jake Owens up and over his left shoulder before sprinting up the short stairwell and through the open door with a level of agility and grace that belied his considerable bulk.

Turning toward us wearing a scowl of untold fury, Ben's authoritative roar dwarfed all that came before it.

"Get back, damn it! Everybody haul ass into the generator cage... *now*!"

A few desperate heartbeats later, well over a

dozen people had crammed into a space that might've comfortably held perhaps five while Ben, Nick and Cassie stood posed just outside the cage's opening like a trio of stalwart, dedicated border guards, which they most certainly were.

For several heart-stopping, terror-filled moments, no one dared speak nor even breathe heavily. The deafening, hysterical outbursts of Marge Owens were no more, replaced by a barely audible whine as she clung to her young son like a protective lioness. I thought I heard Jay wording a silent prayer just to my left even as Jessica reached over and gripped my right hand in her own, squeezing so tightly my fingers quickly went numb.

Outside the generator room, the very walls of the personnel barracks building sounded as if they were being bludgeoned and battered into obscurity.

"What the hell?" I heard both Burt and Nick inquire at precisely the same time, though Burt's sounded less driven by curiosity than primal fear.

"You two up to playin' bodyguard?" Ben asked standing between Nick and Cassie with his gargantuan fists balled at his sides. The tone of his voice had dropped several octaves even as his every movement appeared overexaggerated... even borderline jittery. To use layman, Force was primed for battle and thus chomping at the bit to aid his teammate with whatever threat lay beyond our pathetic basement safe haven.

While Nick merely nodded, Cassie responded both verbally and with a forceful slap across the big man's shoulders.

"We've got it under control, big guy. Go do your thing. We'll be waiting."

Bounding away in three quick strides, Ben leapt up the steps and vanished in the time it took me to reach over and stroke Jessica's free hand, which was cold and clammy to the touch.

In the immediate moments following Ben's retreat, the sounds of a major league ruckus had continued unabated, fueling Mayor Boren to repeat the phrase '*gotta get outta here... gotta get out... gotta get out...* ' in a continuous, frighteningly robotic monotone from directly behind me. Barely able to crane my neck due to severe space limitations, I was able to spot Bill Casey bringing up the rear of the anchovy brigade, an expression of pure smugness plastered across his deathly pale, gaunt face. Perhaps it was merely a case of a person who refused to believe what was transpiring around him, but that had been at least the third time I'd noticed such an out-of-place reaction. Paranoia aside, Bill Casey was the sole stranger among us, and I was beginning to have some serious reservations about sharing such limited space with the man.

Soon enough however, two or three of the longest minutes I'd ever known, it grew eerily quiet. This, I realized, was most likely due to two separate and distinct scenarios having been played out. *One*: either our unknown enemy had been successfully vanquished or, god help us all, our first line of defense had been similarly eliminated.

Two: it was merely, despisers of well-worn cliches forgive me, the calm before the storm.

I saw Nick and Cassie exchange a worrisome look, Cassie quickly squatting down and executing what appeared to be a rapid set of calf, thigh and upper body stretches as if prepping for impending combat. Not exactly a comforting thought that, and hardly a vote of confidence for her fellow supertypes.

"Do you... do you think they... won?" Jay asked timidly, dark bags having settled beneath each eye as he reached up to ruffle his sweat-greased hair. I never would've thought it possible for so many people to sweat so freely in temperatures well below the freezing mark.

"We'll know soon enough, Jay, but my money's on the big guys. Just... just try to relax, okay?" I managed, holding out supreme confidence (at least on the outside) that the baddie had yet to be born who could lick two men referred to in such macho, tough-as-nails terms as *Scar* and *Force*. I mean, Scar had survived how many wars? And Force had gone, however unsuccessfully, toe-to-toe with the Incredible Hulk, for Christ's sake.

"I... I think we... we really ought to... I believe we... I think I... w-we really need t-to... l-leave now," the mayor babbled.

To which Wanda Jelks so comically replied, "Oh, would you please just put a sock in it? Act like you've still *own* a pair, will you?"

I heard several muffled, borderline maniacal giggles, one of which just might've been my own.

It is truly otherworldly, not to mention downright horrifying how situations can be so drastically altered within the matter of a few scant human heartbeats. Crammed inside that chain-linked fence, huddled together like potential lambs to the slaughter, we'd all shared a moment of tranquil levity that had been, in reality, nothing more than a cruel illusion. First off, the thundering sounds of battle returned twofold, though it was readily apparent they were originating from a farther distance, perhaps northward in the vicinity of the admin building. Secondly, the inherent build-up of tension among those around me had led to a predictable group meltdown upon the brutal realization that all was indeed not well, birthing a sudden epidemic of extreme panic.

The first to give in to the basest of human instincts was none other than Marge Owens, who took off in a wild, arm-waving, leg-pumping sprint, having shoved aside both the mayor and the young man named Kurt in her mad dash from the cage.

"Shit, grab her!" Cassie blurted out once Marge had so effectively split the defense, ducking beneath Nick's rather lackluster attempt at stopping her with a single outstretched arm. Marge hadn't quite reached the bottom step of the stairwell when Cassie took off after her, only to spin about on one heel as the real stampede began.

Sometime during the mass exodus, I was tripped to the concrete flooring and subsequently stomped on the left upper thigh and ankle, then rolled over and trampled just beneath the ribcage on my right side. During the melee, I'd heard fragments of panic-laced dialogue, most notably Mayor Doug Boren screaming, "*Get out of my goddamned way*!" at the top of his pudgy lungs. Ultimately it was Jessica and Jay who pulled me up from the cool hardness of the cage floor as Nick and Cassie struggled to maintain control of the situation by literally blocking the stairwell with their bodies.

"Calm down, damn it! You're safer in here!"

Nick proclaimed, holding the mayor in a firm but nonlethal sleeper hold.

"He's right, people. You... we don't know what's out there, don't you understand? We can protect you in here... I... we can't make the same promise if you leave this room," Cassie followed-up, holding the dental technician airborne by the collar of his oversized jacket while using the other arm to literally stiff-arm a trio of others into submission.

I can't honestly say what drove me to chase off after Marge Owens like some overaged Boy Scout. It's not like I'd ever been branded the hero type, and for good reason. Perhaps it was the hangover effect of watching people like Nick, Cassie, Ben and Tate in action, and the reckless abandon with which they plied their trade. Perhaps it was pure stupidity. I'd like to think more of the former than the latter, but even as I'd ascended the short stairwell and burst through the generator room door into the murky hallway, there still existed a stout, resounding urge to immediately turn back and resume cowering.

Jogging up the center of the hall, I saw Marge nearing the bombed-out, rubble-strewn exit into the connecting glass dome, roughly two-hundred feet ahead. Even amid the booming echoes of a nearby battle royal, I could hear her shrill wailings, which seemed to continue unabated as if regulated breathing wasn't an issue.

I'd cleared roughly half the same distance, attempting to maintain a stern focus while surveying all manner of carnage. Despite a woeful lack of lighting, I'd managed to dodge or sidestep large chunks of wood and stone that had apparently been dislodged in a ferocious melee. In the numerous spots where the rock walls had actually been indented, there had been left behind a blackish smear almost identical to that I'd seen dripping from the damaged dome glass. It was when I'd temporarily slowed my momentum in order to better study one of the splattered indentations that I spotted the sheriff's badly shredded blue parka jacket lying over the outer edges of what had been his gun belt. A bit farther down I noticed a lone discarded and horribly torn mukluk and pieces of an equally mutilated blue uniform shirt with a barely attached, soot-covered silver badge. I recall briefly pondering the sheriff's fate, holding out faint hope that Tate had been able to fight off whatever monster was responsible for such vile carnage subjected to a man I'd quickly grown to admire and respect.

Kneeling down, I scooped up a shard of splintered wood and used it to slide the tattered jacket to one side, thus revealing the gun belt and accompanying holster in their entirety.

As for why acquiring Sheriff Owens' holstered .38 was suddenly akin to discovering the Golden Fleece, I'm afraid the answer is just as inanely inexplicable as my very presence in that darkened hallway. It wasn't as if I'd ever been a 'gun person', per se. Just the opposite in fact, as I'd never actually held or fired a weapon of any sort, unless owning a pellet gun around age eleven or twelve counted.

Still, as I unlatched the holster strap and pulled that blue steel baby free, I can't deny the sense of instant empowerment it provided, especially as the surrounding commotion suddenly escalated to near earthquake levels. With shaking hands, I fumbled and groped in utter futility but eventually managed to pop free and check the cylinder for available ammo, where I discovered but one bullet housed inside alongside five hollow slots.

Laughing aloud and no doubt resembling a man having misplaced his final mental marble, I could only figure Sheriff Jake Owens to be a lost-long relative of that legendary sitcom lawman, Barney Fife.

Crazily, I lingered about, retrieving the wooden shard in order to root about within the sheriff's torn jacket pockets for additional bullets. I'd been scoping about in the right shirt pocket when a trio of items popped free, all of which landed near my right bootheel, causing me to dance an impromptu jig and almost roll over onto my back.

Still weary of touching anything despite gloved hands, I used the trusty shard to flip said objects about until I could properly separate and study them. They appeared to be laminated IDs of some sort, possibly the type used by the military and government authorities to enter restricted areas. I'd briefly scanned the first two of these without fanfare but stopped cold on the third, no doubt executing a classic 'double-take' once the face on display came clearly into focus. Discombobulated and disjointed thoughts aside, and at the time my brain was practically overloaded with such, it took but mere seconds for me to place a name with a face. Unsure of the significance of such a finding, I quickly secured all three IDs inside my parka's left front pocket and hightailed it down the hall, resigned to the fact that one shot was all I was going to be allowed as far as self-protection was concerned. I could only pray it wouldn't come to that, as such an occurrence would most assuredly spell my doom.

What transpired in the next few moments, perhaps even a full minute or two, are a bit unclear; a blurred tapestry of images, smells and sounds that combined to batter my senses into a temporary haze for which only Marge Owens' ear-splitting screams could effectively penetrate. After briefly looking back and feeling a wave of relief that no one else had yet escaped from the generator room, I'd darted through an impossibly wide gap where the entrance to the dome had once been, though the door in question was mysteriously MIA, having apparently been torn away like soggy cardboard along with roughly eight to ten square feet of surrounding wall. Unlike the interior hallway, the dome was fairly well lit, what with two operational emergency lights originating from near the connecting entrance to the mess hall.

"*Where's my husband? What have you done with my Jake!*" Marge bellowed, standing at the dome's shattered opening located about midway up the walkway. Like a stuck CD or ancient LP hung in a deep groove, she continued to repeat the same refrain every two to three seconds while cupping a crumpled, tar-coated mukluk to her chest.

"Miss Owens!" I yelled, feeling the frigid air rake the exposed flesh on my face and neck like the edge of a dull razor. "Get away from the opening! Marge!"

Approaching her with great caution, as was natural when dealing with individuals whose rational side had temporarily taken a hike to parts unknown, I nonetheless kept the .38's sights trained straight ahead into the gloominess which permeated the dome's inner housing. As for the condition of the dome itself, the tar-smeared hole from earlier had been widened quite dramatically, now sporting a twenty to twenty-five foot chasm that ran from just outside the stone floor to directly overhead, where a metal ceiling brace hung at a warped angle void any connecting glass whatsoever.

"Marge... it's Darrin... Darrin Jack-"

"*Bring Jakey back to me! He didn't do anything to you!*"

"You need to come back to the generator room with m-"

"*He's a good man, my Jake! A good father! His son... needs him...* lord help me... his son needs him so bad... "

"It's gonna be okay, Miss Owens. We'll... we'll find Jake. I'm sure he's... o-okay."

"No... no... he's... he's not... something... something... wasn't right back there. Jakey... wasn't... Jakey no more... he just... *wasn't...* "

The woman had practically collapsed into my arms, and I was almost taken to my knees upon being forced to accommodate her bulk, accidentally pressing the gun barrel into the small of her back while backing us both into the opposite end of the hall, as far away from the gaping hole as possible.

It was only then, a full minute to ninety seconds since entering the ultrafrigid walkway, that I first dared peek out into the nearby courtyard to catch a glimpse of what could only fairly be described as a full-scale war.

I recall croaking aloud, something along the

lines of 'my god' or perhaps 'oh lord'... something biblical and spoken with the awestruck wonder of a man witnessing a scene his mind cannot quite comprehend.

Hugging Marge Owens close as she continued to blubber and moan while pressing her face flush against my chest, I did not, as would have been advisable, immediately lead us to safer climes. Instead, I found myself entranced... literally frozen into place as the battle raged not thirty yards from where we stood posed like some abstract sculpture; the sheriff's wife whose brittle mind had snapped in wake of her husband's apparent demise and the shaky yet undeniably stalwart counselor who'd risked his own hide to see her safely returned to the care of her young son. Such dramatic bunk aside, the truth of the matter wasn't nearly as tragic or heroic. *Bottom line*: I wanted to witness this phenomenal battle of the titans unfold firsthand. Shamelessly reverting to the basest juvenile desires, I simply wanted to see the fight to its conclusion. Potential dangers aside, and they were surely of the tangible sort, I wasn't going to allow my fears to rob me of such a rare opportunity. Marge Owens' safety be damned, we were going to suck it up and stick it out 'til the end, regardless of whether or not the *end* in question might well be our very own. Later, in calmer, more retrospective moments, I'd surely question my own behavior. At the time, I was beyond caring.

As for the battle itself, while there are specific actions and movements that are virtually impossible to mentally retrace verbatim, the majority of what I saw transpire on that hard winter's night within that rectangular-shaped courtyard will never, ever be forgotten, no matter the level of desire to do so. I would compare it to anyone privy to a particularly horrific automobile accident. There is simply no wiping the images from one's subconscious, not even as the ravages of old age take hold and certain memory cells begin to flicker and fade. To use the vernacular, it was that amazing... that incredibly awesome a spectacle, equally horrifying and enticing, that the eyes simply refused to avert.

***

First off, allow me to state that Cassie Wilkes' rather unintentionally humorous description of the beast, that being a giant tar Hulk, turned out to be dead-letter perfection. With its lanky yet sleekly muscled frame, alienesque facial features and flesh the color of burnt ash, it appeared a walking oil slick come to mutated life, albeit an oil slick fueled by some immensely powerful growth hormone. To further elaborate on the mutated segment of the equation, I had noted three distinct physical characteristics that bore out such a conclusion: the thing's hands resembled the clawlike pinchers of a giant crustacean, possessing a thumb and two overly thick, severely gnarled digits. Secondly, its similarly developed cloven feet which brought to mind the centaur, a mythical beast of half-man, half-horse origin. It must be noted that both the beast's feet and hands were armed with lengthy hooked nails that explained a lot in terms of the many mutilations and dismemberments discovered around the Twin Cities that evening. Lastly, its cone-shaped head, spearlike snout and grotesquely oversized mouth (complete with spear-tipped 'piranha' teeth) were sure signs the thing's DNA sample wasn't likely to be on file at any state or federal lab. I recalled Nick's 'Grendel' reference and was again shaken by the accuracy of such a description, as the legendary beast of *Beowulf* fame could've easily been conceived from the otherworldly monstrosity standing before us.

My initial glimpse of the beast came as it spun Scar Fletcher about by the right ankle, the big bionic GI slung airborne some thirty to forty feet to slam headfirst against a row of three Porta Potty units subsequently mowed down like bowling pins. Whether it had been the beast or our two heroes who had chosen that particular spot as a potentially comforting battlefield was up in the air, but I'd have surely guessed the latter, considering the plethora of abandoned construction equipment lying nearby. Ben and Tate had probably figured some of the larger objects might come in handy as weapons and/or personal blockades as the skirmish progressed.

As the ebony beast howled an apparent victory wail (I half-expected it to pound its chest *King Kong* style), I saw Ben leap into the fray from behind one of several large metal dumpsters normally used by the kitchen staff. Much like Tate, it appeared as though the majority of Ben's parka had been ripped away and was hanging about his upper body in tatters. As for the beast, it was nude save a pair of horribly ripped, blackish pants strangling its broad waist, though in truth the dark aura of its skin made it difficult to determine a particular shade of fabric.

True to his name, Ben used those

sledgehammer fists to great advantage, landing a flurry of bone-crunching blows to the beasts' spindly neck and upper chest (the enemy's face seemingly out of his reach due to a height differential of at least a foot and a half) before thumping it across the abdomen with a vicious backhand that sent it skidding back on its heels. Not allowing the creature to regain its wits, he followed that up with a lightning-quick combo of kicks, front, side and finally of the reverse heel-to-the-groin variety, the impact of which sent the beast sailing into and practically through one of the aforementioned metal dumpsters. I recall swallowing a lump roughly the size of North Dakota, naively thinking Ben's ferocious barrage had pretty much wrapped up the party, but far too quickly felt the lump reform as the beast emerged from the mangled metal with a primal scream of its own before tossing the remnants of the truck-sized dumpster aside like a wad of mangled tinfoil.

Winding its arms like twin circular saws, the beast charged Ben's way with a full head of steam, each step more akin to a twenty-foot leap. Backtracking at warp speed, Ben retreated a half-dozen steps and proceeded to yank a pair of iced-over iron girders from their concrete base, spinning them about like boat oars as the beast neared. I now realized for certain why Ben and Tate had chosen the incomplete building site as their arena of choice, as it was becoming painfully obvious that taking on the giant beast with just bare knuckles wasn't going to suffice.

Displaying a feline agility, the beast hopped over the first of the girders, only to be nailed chest-high by the second and sent sailing head over hooves into a shoulder-high stack of wooden pallets lying at least a dozen yards away, most of which instantly scattered like snow-encrusted bowling pins upon impact.

Before stomping purposely ahead toward the spot where the beast had landed, slow going considering the two to three feet of snow present, I saw Ben toss the badly warped girder aside like a broken matchstick. As Marge continued to blabber incoherently into my chest cavity, I craned my neck in order to better scan the landscape, particularly the area where I'd last seen Tate Fletcher. Though I did manage to spot the tops of the toppled Porta Potty units, nothing in the way of movement transpired. In trying desperately to remain upbeat, I couldn't help but ponder the big man's fate, since his initial battle with the beast was such a mystery, as was the fate of Sheriff Jake Owens.

By the time I turned my focus back to Ben, he'd covered roughly two-thirds of the distance toward the beast's landing zone. He was yelling something, though the gist was lost amid both the gusting winds and Marge's nonsensical blathering. Cold as it may sound, the woman was grating on my last nerve. I know I should've been more sympathetic considering her apparent loss, but all I could think about at the time was how much easier it would've been if she were to simply faint away from exhaustion or shock instead of clinging to me like some parasitic slug.

I'm fairly sure Ben was calling out for Tate, perhaps attempting to find out if his tag team partner was still conscious and if so, his exact location and the extent of any possible injuries.

Sadly, Ben wasn't able to conclude whatever request he'd initiated, because just as he came within reaching distance of where the wooden pallets had originally lain before being so dramatically relocated, the beast sprang forth from the splintered pile and ensnared him in a grisly lover's embrace.

"Ahhhh, shiiiittttt!" I heard Ben curse as the thing's impossibly long, lithe arms wrapped around his upper chest like constricting tentacles.

Twisted about until his back now faced me, I saw Ben's head shoot forward several times, a delayed cracking noise following each blurred thrust. By the fourth or fifth blow, the vicious series of headbutts apparently garnered the desired effect, as the beast's grip loosened just enough for Ben to squirm free and begin battering away with a fresh flurry of lefts, rights and uppercuts that mostly found their mark despite the dramatic height difference between the two. Even from such a distance, I could see streams of blackish fluid flow freely from the thing's upturned, v-shaped nostrils, as well as the corners of its ghoulish mouth. Still, despite the barrage of blows, a few of which I can safely assume would've easily killed a normal man, the beast seemed to shriek more out of frustration than actual pain. Most frightening of all, the backhand that lifted Ben airborne appeared to be delivered almost casually, as if the thing had been shooing away a pesky fly. Regardless of the half-hearted effort on the beast's part, Ben shot toward us like a streaking missile, covering a distance of at least twenty yards before slamming into an as of yet untouched section of the dome glass and shattering it with jackhammer force.

Sometime between Ben's crash landing through one side of the dome and having his momentum broken by the opposite wall, I'd practically fallen onto Marge Owens' trembling body to protect us both from the onslaught of flying glass and metal slivers. Positioned on all fours with Marge's upper body cradled beneath my midsection, I peeked over to see that Ben had indeed smashed into the opposite wall and was leaning against the cracked glass that had so rudely halted his forward progress. Amazingly, the man was not only conscious but already struggling to stand.

"Daaaammmnn... " I heard him mumble while picking bloody shards from his exposed right bicep and forearm, the parka jacket hopelessly tattered in a half-dozen spots. "Why is it I can never... I mean fucking ever... land in a soft pile of hay?"

"B-Ben... you... you okay?" I asked, slowly crawling away from Marge, who had apparently assumed a permanent fetal position.

Twisting about to face me and almost tipping over backward in the process, the big man's eyes grew wide once we locked onto one another.

"Wha-what the hell are you doin' out here, Jackson?"

Suddenly aware of Marge's curled frame a few feet to my rear, Ben cocked an eyebrow in apparent disbelief.

"Jesus crow, man... ain't that the constable's wife?"

"Ye-yeah, she made a run for it and I... I ran out to get her."

"Is that right? Well, now that you've caught her, how's about haulin' both your asses outta here pronto before that flesh-grindin' son of a bitch catches a whiff of fresh mea-" Ben halted in mid-scold, his focus abruptly averted back toward the jagged hole he'd carved out into the dome on his way inside.

"Get out now, Darrin... grab the dame and... make tracks... while I play the role of highly pissed off... and slightly bruised... diversion... "

By the time I'd stood in a slight crouch and began to back step in the general vicinity of Marge's prone frame, I caught a glimpse of the looming shadow standing just outside the dome's newest accidental entryway. As the thing stuck its medicine-ball sized head inside the hole and began gradually scanning the interior through freakishly oversized bug eyes whose pits shone a bright red hue, there was little doubting the origin of a warm wetness threatening to stream down my left thigh.

"Ben... wh-what should... sh-should I move?"

"Make tracks... post haste... " Ben replied sternly as the thing seemed to purposely pause to take in our dialogue.

"And don't stop runnin' no matter what you hear. When ya get back to the generator room, tell Nick and Cas to prep for the worst. Now go... "

Crazily, I found myself pulling the revolver from my front pocket with my right hand while attempting to haul a mostly unresponsive Marge Owens to her feet with my left.

What transpired next I can only recall in fragmented segments, much like a badly edited dream, or perhaps nightmare is the more apt term.

Just as I'd managed to wrestle Marge Owens from the floor, wrapping her left arm around my shoulders in order to obtain a measured order of stability, we were yet again showered in glass fragments from the explosion at our backs. Toppling forward in the aftermath, I did my best to buffer the impact of the fall by pulling Marge over onto me as my right shoulder took the brunt. Continuing to display the telltale personality traits of the chronically shell-shocked, Jake Owens' better half merely moaned in response to our abrupt descent and landing, her eyes noticeably glazed and her mouth hanging partially agape. Gently rolling her dead weight off of me, I turned back toward the source of the commotion, pleasantly surprised to find the pistol still gripped tightly in my right hand.

The beast had apparently torn through a previously undamaged portion of the dome, ripping a fresh ten to twelve foot section free and essentially initiated a complete collapse of the wall's left side. Still backed against the same wall that had buffered his descent just moments earlier, Ben waited until the lumbering giant was basically lying on top of him before crouching down and delivering a lightning-fast sweep kick that worked to perfection. Clipped at its knobby ankles, the beast performed an impromptu break dance in an attempt to regain its balance but instead landed headfirst on the hard stone less than a dozen feet from where I stood.

"Damn it... thought I told ya to beat it, Counselor!" Ben growled before leaping forward and driving the thing's head into the granite with both feet. Jumping off the shrieking, squirming creature, Ben's landing was surprisingly graceful as he shot me yet another fearsome scowl.

"You need a permission slip, son? Now pull your thumb outta your ass and get that woman outta here!"

Seemingly bleeding from every orifice it possessed, the beast had just managed to pull itself upright when Ben looped a sledgehammer right that caught it flush on the right side of the face. The sharp crunching sound that ensued left little doubt that bones had been severely shattered in the aftermath, the only question being the victim of the breakage.

In wake of the colossal blow, a punch that might've possibly decapitated a lesser opponent, the beast pinwheeled back through the same exact space in the dome it had previously torn asunder. Having stumbled back from the impact of his own mammoth blow, Ben's chest heaved from exertion as he leaned against the dome wall and massaged his bloodied knuckles. Haplessly gullible as I was concerning matters of combat, I actually recall a sensation of unbridled relief showering my senses. So foolish, as I'd actually thought the worst was over, that there was simply no way on god's green earth any entity could survive such a monumental show of superhuman strength.

Turning about for a brief moment, I saw Marge had budged nary an inch. By the time I retrained my focus Ben's way, the beast had apparently reentered the dome with the stealth of a prowling feline and was holding the big man airborne with one clawed hand curled around Ben's throat and the other gripping the same bloodied fist he'd been favoring.

It's hard... so very, very difficult to see such a

hero humbled. It's especially gut-wrenching when you've been afforded that rare opportunity to bypass the mythical status tied to those in the superhero trade via establishment of a personal relationship. In a relatively short span, I'd learned to respect, admire, and yes, fear to some degree, the man known in the trades by the name Force. I'd learned he, Tate Fletcher, Nick Parione and Cassie Wilkes were much more than their print clippings advertised. They were the real deal.

This, of course, made it all the more painful to personally witness such a man suffer mortal injury. More pitiful still, I was quickly reminded of my own mortal limitations, forced to stand by helplessly and watch it transpire while powerless to do anything about it.

Unable to break the beast's double grip despite landing a half-dozen or more solid left hooks to its shoulder, neck and skull, Ben began swinging his body back and forth until he worked up momentum to kick out with both feet. Though the creature was obviously shaken by the impact, its only reaction was a mild moan followed by an enraged growl, the latter of which no doubt fueled the pervasive actions that followed. First, it temporarily released Ben's right arm in order to curl the same claw beneath his armpit as to gain further leverage. Just as Ben cocked the freed appendage to attempt yet another bone-jarring combination, the beast shoved him straight up and head first into the top of a previously unshattered portion of the dome. With a thundering crash, Ben's skull penetrated the glass like a ricocheting bullet before being forced back down through the same jagged space. Hanging from the beast's grip in a limp, rag doll pose, Ben's face was bleeding profusely from several deep gashes on both cheeks.

I recall screaming something at the beast, perhaps even cursing it at the top of my lungs. A sad attempt at diversion, but it was all I knew to do at the time, especially since my lower extremities steadfastly refused to take any sort of physical action.

Utterly ignoring my cries, probably due to the fact it felt no inkling of a threat, the beast then unclenched his claws and allowed Ben's slumped form to fall to the floor. Naively, I had thought this action was due to the fact that it no longer considered Force a viable opponent and had simply discarded him like a broken toy. In truth, it was merely toying with the big man like a housecat might a mortally wounded mouse. You see, this thing somehow understood the demeanor of its opposition. It had accurately, perhaps through a telepathic vibe of sorts, pinned down the character of Ben Thomason as your basic 'never say die' sort. Thus, the evil son of a bitch wasn't about to allow the element of mercy to intervene. At this point, it actually stood back in a deliberate pause, folding its taut, tentaclelike arms across its chest to wait for Ben to make the next move. As I watched Ben's eyes flutter and finally reopen, and saw him struggle and strain with Herculean effort merely to prop himself up on all fours, I finally rediscovered the power of movement. I vividly recall the enormous weight of the revolver as I raised it with both hands and attempted to focus on the twin sights, all the while half-stepping forward on feet literally constructed of the heaviest of clay.

I watched Ben weave and bob from side to side like a punch drunk pugilist before finally stabilizing in a wide-open stance with both his mighty fists raised. The beast took a stride forward, its spindly arms spread wide as if in greeting. I took another half-step forward, narrowing the distance between myself and the creature to less than a dozen feet.

I heard Ben Thomason curse, blood pouring from his left nostril to mix with the steady streams already leaking from the deep grooves about his face. Utilizing the 'bird' finger of his right hand, he then gestured a rather unconventional come hither gesture toward the beast while cocking back his left like a spring-loaded catapult. I took another half-step forward, unable to steady the sights as my hands began to tremor uncontrollably, as if they belonged to a man suffering the latter stages of Parkinson's.

"One last... dance, Hoss. I'm... savin' it just for... you.

"Come... an' get me... then, ya ugly... fuck."

I watched the man called Force amble forward with surprising quickness, the rebel yell he'd bellowed equally impressive if not downright awe-inspiring. Unfortunately, it soon became agonizingly obvious that such a blatantly offensive stance was merely falling into the set trap of an entity that had expected and no doubt, hoped for such a brazen yet ill-advised attack.

After enduring several well-aimed but mostly ineffective blows to its chest and midsection, the beast first shoved Ben back a few steps as to properly pose him before imposing a grisly mix of bludgeoning and butchery. Meanwhile, I had shuffled forth another half-step and was so close I could actually smell the reek of the beast as well as the coppery scent of Force's extensive blood loss. Still, I could not effectively aim the revolver, despite the close proximity and immense size of my target. In truth, with every passing moment, my legs and arms grew increasingly leaden even as the flesh of my face grew numb and my scalp tingled as if set ablaze.

Despite the ultrafrigid temperatures inside that mangled dome, I personally felt as if I were standing atop lit coals with yellow-tinted flames bathing my clammy flesh.

As far as the scenario at hand, two things seemed a dead certainty, pardon the rather tasteless pun. Firstly, Ben Thomason's checkered career as a supposed second-rate, second-team superhero was about to come to a rather gruesome, unceremonious end. Secondly, a second-rate assistant counselor was sure to follow suit soon thereafter.

So the million dollar question was, where the hell was Scar? Despite possibly being mere moments from a death that was apt to be anything but painless, I couldn't help but pose the question. Had Tate Fletcher already joined the growing ranks of the deceased in and around the post grounds? Logically speaking, it was more than possible. After all, I'd seen him thrown across the compound to land headfirst into a trio of metal Porta Potties like a human cannonball. Incredible war record, tough-as-nails demeanor and bionic capabilities aside, Scar Fletcher was merely flesh and bone after all, much like Ben and myself. There were no immortals present in that particular brawl for the ages... no sons of Odin or daughters of Iris. We were all potential victims, regardless of sex, gender, age or occupation. This thing showed no quarter for any particular clique: the elderly; the very young; even state and local law enforcement. It mattered not... if you had the potential to bleed and die, the attraction... the draw... the attractiveness... seemed the same. Some were easier prey, for certain... yours truly being no exception within that particular clique.

In retrospect, I'd have to speculate that all thoughts of Tate Fletcher and his potential whereabouts had subconsciously been tied to a faint hope of rescue; that he would suddenly gallop into view riding a white horse to slay the fearsome giant.

In reality, such hopes were minimal at best and soon dashed in the wake of the savagery bestowed upon Ben Thomason. All the while, in the thirty to forty-five second span it took for the tragic events to unfold, I found myself still frozen into place with a loaded revolver clasped within my sweaty right palm, my arms and hands flapping about as if struck by hurricane winds. As for what remained of the clash itself, there would be three significant blows struck.

The first tore across Ben's upper chest like an axe blade, essentially tearing away what little had remained of his parka and clothing underneath and transforming his upper torso into a dark maroon canvas.

The second opened a deep gash along his upper left shoulder near the neck, releasing a veritable gusher that I could only pray wasn't tied to his carotid artery.

Incredibly, despite suffering such horrendous wounds and losing an inordinate amount of blood, Ben simply refused to fall. Even as his left arm hung loose as if severely dislocated, he managed to attempt an overhand right but was cut off in mid-swing by the same pincher-claw that had previously opened his chest like some colossal straight razor.

As the beast once again pulled Ben airborne by the wrist and slowly raised his free claw to strike, I finally, miraculously, rediscovered the power to control my own appendages. Trudging forth another half-step, I was able to point the weapon out and up in the general vicinity of the thing's massive, misshapen cranium and line the sights directly at the left side of its skull.

"D-drop him, you ugly bastard!" I pleaded more than commanded, feeling the trigger give way just an iota beneath the strain. True, it was like the old fable of a man attempting to fell a bull elephant with a peashooter, but it was all I had.

For once, the creature actually took a moment to acknowledge my presence, twisting its slim, tubular neck and peering down at me as if I were a particularly amusing zoo exhibit.

"I s-said... drop him!"

I know it sounds haplessly melodramatic in the face of what had come before, but I can honestly state that in that moment I truly believed the thing understood my request and might've even felt a twinge of bewilderment and perhaps even fear. In the next moment, I saw the thing's mouth stretch apart like a feeding great white and grin. In that moment, it was I who understood. I understood the face of true evil: merciless; remorseless; and utterly without conscience.

The message was clear. Playtime was over. It meant to get down to the business of mass killing... of hero slaughter. Oh, it was going to comply with my order alright, but not without an unthinkable price to pay.

Quickly retraining its focus and shunning me as the pathetic nonthreat I most assuredly was, its expanded claw then descended in a blackened blur.

Though I saw Ben's body collapse onto the floor in a bloodied heap, it wasn't until I glanced back up to see a still-quivering, severed arm hanging from the creature's gnarled pincher that the totality of what had just transpired completely sank in.

"Hey! Over here!" I screamed until my throat burned, "Over here, you... you sadistic piece of *shit*!"

Discarding Ben's arm with a quick flick over its left shoulder, it whipped its head around and growled-no doubt regarding me as a pesky fly long overdue for a fatal swat. To backtrack, I'd seen the tossed appendage clear the shattered dome top and spin into the darkness beyond, no doubt to land in a pile of soft, virgin snow and subsequently redden the area like a bucket of spilt paint. A grisly thought, I know, but a petrified, partially fractured mind does tend to think along such lines.

I'm fairly certain the retort of the .38 took me more by surprise than my intended target. The beast had yet to turn its perpetually bent, spindly body my way when I saw the slug dig a quarter-sized hole into a large, scaly polyp overlapping its left breast.

I'd felt my right wrist grow instantly numb, the blast itself serving to deafen the proceedings considerably.

Confidentially, I wondered how many men are afforded a few precious moments to ponder the inhumanity of it all when knowing they are about to die. Having taken classes and made a hobby on studying past wars and the soldiers fated to fight them, I'd often wondered how such men had represented themselves when they knew the time was near to leave this world for whatever lay beyond.

I recall backing away ever so cautious, continuing to squeeze the trigger out of pure reflex and hearing a resounding click with each passing of an empty cylinder. I then became acutely aware of the bone-chilling conditions, my temporary fever having so abruptly broken in the wake of a reality equally frigid. Meantime, the beast had turned away from Ben's frighteningly still body toward me, having shrugged off the open slug wound like your basic mosquito bite. Strange, but even as I saw its legs tense as if prepping to spring forward, my most vivid memory of the moment just before my mortal soul was to be so viciously taken way was the freshly falling snow filtering in from the dome's open roof. Caught in the dim but still tangible illumination provided by a nearby bulb, it appeared as if tiny, miniature stars were levitating down to see what all the fuss was about. As I alluded to earlier, I guess it only natural a man's mind tends to drift during such stressful times.

Inane as it may sound, I'd actually reared back to hurl the revolver at the approaching monster when an object substantially larger, not to mention weightier, sailed overhead in a grayish blur and nailed the beast at chest level, sending it rolling halfway down the curved hall.

Before I was even able to execute a full turn, I heard Jekyll-ene's animalistic growls and then caught a hasty glimpse of her lithe form sprinting by at full bore. The desk she'd thrown had appeared to be one of the heavy oak variety, though exactly what room she'd lifted it from would forever remain a mystery. Regardless, at that moment I was beyond any rational thought other than that of being supremely grateful to still be upright and possessing all of my appendages.

Down and crawling on all fours toward Ben, I saw the beast batter the desk into several dozen splinter fragments and arise with a baying howl that seemed to originate from the center of its devilish soul, only to be hoisted airborne by its neck and groin and tossed out into the compound yard. We'd all been told, albeit warned, about Jekyll-ene's fighting prowess and/or the brute strength she possessed when compared to her smarter yet infinitely weaker twins. Seeing her bound through the dome's shattered roof and into that snowy compound in three short leaps, it was still another case of reality overtaking legend. There was little doubt this woman, however deranged, however uncontrollable, could put a serious hurt on whatever target she so rightly chose to dismantle. Then again, I'd seen this... thing... rip Ben Thomason apart in a matter of minutes, so I wasn't about to allow yet another wave of overconfidence dent my already severely weakened mental armor. The important thing at the time was to see about Ben. That was priority one, though I cannot deny that priority two, that being saving one's own precious hide, had been gaining mass levels of momentum as seconds passed.

To paraphrase a rural term from decades gone by, Ben had been bleeding like a stuck pig by the time I'd crawled over to him. His breathing was shallow, his complexion as pale as the whitish landscape beyond. Lying on his left side, the jagged stump that had been his right arm appeared to be spewing forth blood by the quart. From what little remained of his upper bicep protruded a sharp-edged bone that actual resembled a burst pipe leaking its content in thick, blackish-red streams.

"Hiya, C-Counselor," the big man mumbled, having reopened his eyes upon my intrusion.

"Wouldn't... h-happen to have a... a band aid on ya, by chance... "

"Don't talk, Ben... just lay there quietly. I'm... I'm going to tie off the wound as best I can."

"D-damn, son, if you ain't the king of s-stubborn. H-how... many times I... gotta tell you to m-make t-t-tracks? 'Fraid... I'm y-your basic... lost cause at... this... juncture."

Busying myself tearing loose several long, tight strips from the tattered remains of Ben's parka as well as the sweatshirt beneath, I fought to ignore both my patient's delirious dialogue and the rumble of combat originating from the compound yard.

"G-get l-lost, D-Darrin. I ain't worth... wastin' time over. F-find... Tate... or that... psycho chick... Cassie's lun-lunatic older s-siblin'... she's... th-they gotta... gotta pro-protect the women... and... ankle...

ankle-biters... "

"Clam up, damn it," I scolded, trying desperately to tie off the first of a trio of tightly twisted strips despite having precious little room to work. "Cassie's already on the scene... big sis is taking care of business as we speak."

While the upper portion of his bicep was still intact, there remained only a two to three inch area beneath the shoulder, making it extremely difficult to both place and subsequently tighten a tourniquet. I'd only begun to wrap the second of the three strips when I became aware of a new presence at my back. Since the sounds of mortal combat still echoed from the compound grounds and Marge Owens lay like an overgrown fetus a dozen feet to my left, I was clueless of the new arrival's identity before spinning about on my left heel to face whoever or whatever had crashed the party.

"Shiiitttt!" I yelped, cringing back and almost sitting atop Ben's slumped frame.

"Back away, Darrin... I've got him," Tate groaned wearily, stepping forward with an as of yet unidentified metallic cylinder tucked beneath his right arm-an arm completely stripped of its faux flesh, unveiling bolted segments of steel plating and the multicolored wiring beneath. Only the tips of his fingers still possessed any hint of the scientifically manufactured skin, frayed wires protruding from between each knuckle like probing antennae. As he brushed by with a noticeable limp, I caught a whiff of burning metal, and saw tiny plumes of smoke rising from his exposed forearm, where a deep, horizontal gash had been inflicted. Much like Ben, most of Tate's parka had been torn away, as had selected sections of the clothing underneath. Besides the missing flesh from his bionic right arm, he sported large splotches of caked blood beneath each nostril and a horribly split, mangled bottom lip that caused many of his words to slur. Additionally, his left eye was swollen shut and he seemed to be favoring his right (nonbionic) leg.

"But... I didn't finish tying off his... the wound."

"Looks like the bleeding's slowed. Gotta cauterize it ASAP."

"Cauterize? But wh- how?" I babbled, peeking out from the dome's wide chasm and trying to catch a peek at the combatants who at the time I could only hear but not at all visualize.

"Found this in the supply shack," he replied, nodding toward the pill-shaped cylinder, which I now recognized as the type used in acetylene welding.

Leaning down, Tate placed a hand behind Ben's head and carefully helped him sit up a bit straighter, then began slowly unscrewing a circular handle at the cylinder's tip, which soon resulted in a faint hissing sound.

"Figured to try and use it on big, bad and ugly out there... looks like the good lord had a totally different use in mind after all."

Hey, Benji... it's Tate. You with me, partner?"

I saw Ben's eyes flutter several times before remaining open in a tight squint.

"Well, s-shit, Fletch. I... figured your worn-out... old ass for worm dirt long... ago. Good to... see ya, pal. I'd... shake hands, but well, ya know... "

With a grim nod, Tate positioned the tip of the cylinder a mere six to eight inches from the bloody stump.

"I'm gonna have to seal that wound, Ben."

"G-gotcha, Hoss. Do me a... favor though and... cook 'er good but... fast."

"You got it, bud. You need something to gnaw on?"

I saw Ben shake his head weakly, flashing a wide, blood-filled grin despite it all. I could only imagine the big man's level of tolerance for physical pain. The term 'off the charts' wouldn't begin to cover it-yet another dramatic example of the difference between their kind and us mortals.

"Nah. I'll just... find a happy... place. Go ahead... t-torch me, big guy."

Pulling a small Bic lighter from his front pants pocket, Tate leaned back and calmly ignited the fire, the sudden flash of blue and yellowish flames temporarily bathing the murky dome in a colorful explosion of light. I won't lie and claim I watched the procedure in its entirety. In fact, I had turned away long before the sound of sizzling flesh and Ben's muted moans of agony, focusing instead on the compound grounds, which were both mysteriously desolate and tranquil, with nary a combatant in sight.

It had taken Tate less than thirty seconds to complete the process, his heavy sighs spelling the conclusion of what had to have been a hellish task. Standing up rather stiffly, he tucked the cylinder back underneath his arm and tightened the valve until the flames vanished and the accompanying hissing sounds abated.

With great dread, I shot a brief glimpse at Ben and saw he'd passed out against the dome glass, the outer edges of the circular nub burnt to a blackish/blue turn but no longer displaying even the most minute leakage.

"Is he... going to be... I mean, that is... wi-will he sur-"

Mercifully, my stuttering babble session was cut off as Tate stepped by me and gave Marge Owen's prone frame a solemn once-over.

"He's breathing. Man's got a strong heart and an even stronger will. He'll make it, but we've got to get him some serious medical attention pretty damn quick.

"What's her story?"

"That's Marge Owens, Tate, remember? Jake Owens' wife... "

Tate frowned, casually flipping the cylinder over his shoulder and propping it there like an oversized water bottle.

"No shit... that's the sheriff's wife? I didn't even recognize her. She conscious?"

"Just in... shock, I guess. She came unglued once you carried Jake out of the generator room... "

I paused for a moment, stealing another glance at Ben to ensure his chest was indeed still rising and falling in some sort of natural rhythm.

"I... take it he didn't make it."

"Who's that?" Tate queried wearily, using his free hand to wipe a patch of semidried blood from his forehead.

"Jake... I mean, did that... did the beast get... to him?"

Dropping the cylinder to his side, Tate walked forward and placed a hand atop my shoulder before giving it a firm squeeze. He wore the haggard, worn expression of a man literally at the end of his rope. When he smiled, it was hardly a gesture of humor, but instead a grin constructed of the purest form of irony.

"Darrin, that thing out there... that beast... is Jake Owens."

For a moment, my lungs no longer functioned. My chapped and freeze dried lips might have quivered if not for the extreme cold which relegated them motionless. My mouth as a whole went bone dry. A series of spastic palpitations abducted my heart muscle and assaulted its surrounding arteries with very little quarter. After all I'd seen and heard in the previous eight hours, Tate Fletcher's words had essentially paralyzed my every function like the stoutest of narcotics. I experienced a sudden surge of visual flashbacks: Jake Owens' bloated, blue-tinted face just before Tate had extracted him from our midst... the sheriff's shredded uniform left discarded in the hallway and coated in the same slick, black substance the beast appeared to use for bodily fluids. It all made sense... sure, while simultaneously making no damn sense whatsoever, at least in the logical sense.

"But... how? What happened to... turn him... change him into... something so... well, shit... like that thing out there?"

"Hard to say... I've got a theory, but it'll have to wait."

We fell silent for a short spell, during which time it hit me like a lead pipe to the skull that something dramatic had transpired while Tate had been playing roadside doctor.

"Tate... you notice something?" I practically

whispered, suddenly aware of the eerie silence.

As we both shuffled toward the wide, v-shaped chasm where once a six-inch thick wall of reinforced glass had stood, I found myself purposely positioned a step or two behind the larger man, forced to stand on tiptoes in order to peek over his left shoulder out into the compound.

"Quite as a church organ on Saturday night alright," he replied while slowly scanning the grounds.

"Looks like Cass- Jekyll-ene must've put up one whale of a scrap. Check out the bus."

"Good lord," I croaked once the object came fully into focus. "It's... totaled."

"I'd say yeah. Guess we can permanently chuck the idea of loading up as a group and making tracks out of here in that thing."

The school bus, while not nearly in tiptop shape upon our arrival, now lay in two separate sections, the largest of which being the engine, hood and roughly a third of the seating portion. The back end, to include the final dozen or so seats, six flattened tires and badly dented rims, had been torn free and flipped at least twenty yards to the east.

As for the remainder of the snow-crusted compound grounds, it was a maze of deeply grooved footprints and haphazardly dug out trail markings, a few of which actually held the shape of human appendages. The construction zone had been completely demolished, littering the grounds with splintered planks. In terms of movement and the sounds accompanying such, there was nil, a truly frightening concept from what had come before.

"Don't you think if Cassie... if Jekyll-ene had...

you know, been able to kill it, I mean, wouldn't she... where is she then? Shouldn't we have heard from her by now?"

"Not necessarily. She might just be sprawled out there in the snow somewhere... injured, unconscious or probably both."

"But what if... the... that creature... you know... "

I was babbling like a spooked fifth grader, but totally helpless to do otherwise. I recall watching my frosty breath coat the back of Tate's bare neck. A neck outlined in dried, semifrozen blood and shaped, I swear, like some grisly, homemade skull and crossbones tattoo.

"Tuck in those nerves, Counselor. I think the stillness is a good sign. If that thing had killed Cas, more than likely it wouldn't have hesitated to hop right back over here and finish the job on us."

"What... what now?"

He turned gracefully on one heel, once again balancing the cylinder on his broad shoulder like a rifle barrel. Kneeling down to equal our heights a bit, Scar Fletcher and I locked eyes. His steely gaze had a message to relay, regardless of the words that would soon accompany them. It was simple really; there would be no giving up... no waving of a white flag, either physically or emotionally, on this veteran trooper's watch. Much like earlier in the evening, just when hopes had begun to darken and bleakness seemed to be the order of the day, I recall feeling a sudden rush of confidence... and, as reckless as it sounded, of hope as well.

"Well, it's a given I need to check on Cassie, but first off, help me get Marge Owens and Ben to the generator room. You take her... I've got the big guy.

"Once they're tucked away safe and sound... " he continued, reaching up with his free hand to pat the cylinder as if it were a loyal pet, "me and a few of my newest pals are off on a little scavenger hunt. Got a half-dozen more of these bad boys loaded onto a gurney outside supply. If I can't bludgeon the son of a bitch into submission, and it sure didn't work out the first time... we're gonna have us one hell of a barbecue.

"Hopefully, Cassie's considerably meaner older sis has already done the work for me."

Forcing a smile, I nodded and moved back toward Marge Owens, who had rolled onto her stomach and splayed out so it appeared she was attempting to make a snow angel in reverse.

Hooking my arms beneath her own, I managed to haul her to her feet, though it was apparent I would have to drag and/or carry her dead weight for the majority of the trek.

Meanwhile, Tate had secured Ben's massive frame over his right shoulder while using the cylinder as a counterbalance atop the other.

"Forward march then," Tate said with a slight nod, and I graciously allowed him to take point.

We hadn't yet covered half the dome's curved walkway, surely no more than twelve or fifteen yards, when the distant sounds of smashed glass followed by a low, thundering rumble froze us in our collective tracks.

Chapter Seven
Slaughter of the Masses/Flashback

"Sounds like a wall just gave way," Tate said, having paused once we'd neared the jagged chasm that had previously served as the entranceway to the quarters building. Dropping to one knee, he carefully laid Ben's limp frame atop one of the few sections of tile flooring left uncluttered by splintered wood, shattered glass fragments or metallic shards.

"It probably crashed... through one of the barrack's room... windows," I chimed in with a labored huff, sucking wind like a Hoover Deluxe from the effects of having to drag, push and pull Marge Owens down the hall. Just as I'd freed myself of the excess weight by leaning her against the last surviving intact strip of dome glass, we heard the initial series of screams.

Dropping the gas cylinder to one side, I saw Tate flash Ben a quick, forlorn glance, as if painfully torn about executing a plan of action without being able to simultaneously safeguard his fallen comrade, before leaping through the darkened chasm in two lightning-quick bounds.

"Tate... what... what about... us?"

Embarrassing as it is to confess, I'd instantly reverted back to the approximate age of five: a scared, hapless child searching desperately for comfort in any form available. Sad to say, as the screams of the dying or soon-to-be dying echoed down that murky hallway like some hellish choir of the damned, there was simply no such salvation to be had. It was dreadfully obvious that despite a valiant effort, Jekyll-ene too had failed to stop the beast, and thus it had somehow sniffed out the group of survivors inside the generator room and created its own shortcut to order to reach them.

"Guard 'em as best you can, Darrin. I'll be back!" Tate yelled back in response to my childish, selfish plea, and I felt an instantaneous shrinkage of both my pride and self-dignity. Falling to one knee, I sucked in a double lung full of frigid winter air and exhaled in purposely gradual segments, even as the collective wails of agony grew louder, crisper, and ever nearer.

Rising with a newfound determination, or at least a facimile of sorts, I had come to a rather cliched but unreservedly bold conclusion: that being if a man was surely going to perish and perhaps perish badly, the least he could do was go out with a measure of dignity and not as a sniveling, shivering coward. Most assuredly, I'd witnessed what Ben Thomason would've refered to as a 'buttload' of bravery in the previous eight to ten hours. I'd decided not to disservice such displays and instead add my name to the list of those who'd decided to fight the good fight in lieu of running away and hiding like some cowering prey animal and nonetheless suffer the same fate when all was said and done.

With that in mind, I'd searched out and scooped up a shard of bent metal roughly the size and shape of a meat clever from the scattered debris and lunged forward to enter the building only to be sent reeling back on my heels.

"Get outta my way, damn it... he's... it's coming... lord god it's coming for us *all*!"

Having been shoved back into the dome walkway, I barely recognized Mayor Boren as he'd lumbered by like a charging bull. What little hair the man possessed stuck out like live electrical wire, his nostrils flared wildly and his eyes bugged as to literally pop from their sockets. I'd barely regained my balance before another body stumbled by in a clumsly lurch, accompanied by windmilling arms and a low-pitched, never-ending screech that brought to mind a household smoke alarm that refused to be deactivated.

"What's... what are you running from? What's down there?" I asked repeatedly, even as Boren and the woman I now recoginzed as one of my own collegues, none other than the perpually paranoid Jessica Lewis, had both slid to an abrupt halt just as the hallway had neared the sharpest point of its curved shape, whereas I was unable to visualize whatever it was they were seeing. As it was, I must've completely ignored their suddenly slack-jawed appearance as they both began to slowly backtrack.

"What is... it? Well? What now?"

Hard as it was to believe, a sudden rush of extreme anger had overshadowed any and all fear I'd previously felt. I found myself royally pissed off, both at their blatant cowardice and selfishness. Here they'd scrambled past two fallen bodies, one of which sported potentially fatal wounds, and practically trampled me in their mad dash to survive at any costs. In truth, my rage might well have been directed inward, as a large part of my pysche wanted nothing more than to join them in finding a warm, safe place to hide out.

"Well?" I spewed, jogging toward them while waving the metal cleaver about like some sort of medieval battle axe.

"Speak up, damn you! Why don't you just keep running? What's stopping you? Worthless... fucking... cowards... "

Jes turned to face me, perhaps really seeing me for the first time, and literally fainted into my arms, her eyes rolled into her head 'til only the whites of each was visable. Meanwhile, the honorable Mayor Douglas Boren leapt behind me as to utilize both Jess and I as human shields of a sort from whatever had spooked them into such hysterical behavior.

"There's... it's... ano-another one... b-bigger... bigger than the last... " he panted, and I felt his bare, ice-cold palms grip my left forearm in a vice.

"What're you mumbling about, Mayor?" I asked angrily, though in truth I didn't want to know...not in the least. Sadly, I had no choice but to investiate, even as several other potential escapees huddled in behind us like herded sheep to the slaughter. Despite gargantuan reservations, I quickly recalled my recent quest for inner bravery and moved forward, shaking off the mayor's steely grip and wielding the metal shard like a protective shield.

"No, don't go... don't go... we have to t-turn around... find another way out," Boren pleaded.

I heard someone else, perhaps the teenaged kid named Redrick, shout for everyone to, "Cool it!" in a high-pitched shriek even as several more random screams could be heard ringing out in the distance.

Tiptoeing forward as if I were treading atop a live minefield, I'd reached the steepest bend in the curve and paused to crane my neck just enough to view what lay beyond.

I guess I'd figured at this point in the game I was somehow immune to further shocks to the system. As Burt had been so fond of spouting, this of course is why you cannot spell the word assume without an *'ass'* riding shotgun.

"Dear god... " I'd whispered with a stout lean toward actual prayer, the shard trickling from my fingers in realization of how pathetically useless it would be in terms of self-protection.

"This just keep getting better and better... "

The beast stood defiant with its spindly legs spread wide and its arms crossed at its chest as it appeared to relish the role of hallway sentinel; readily prepared to eliminate any and all who dared to attempt safe passage.

In terms of striking stark fear, it wasn't merely the thing's daunting, rather myterious presence (after all, shouldn't it have been pursuing its hapless prey from the *other* end of the hall?) that had caused me to once again temporarily misplace my manhood for infancy, but the particular choice of ornaments it had chosen to display as some sort of ritualistic symbol of terror. No shame in confesssing that I was not only duly terrified, but equally sickened and forced to swallow the hot bile that had snaked up my throat. It wasn't so much what was suddenly so plainly revealed of the creature's facial features in the dome lighting, which was indeed a shocking enough revelation, but the makeshift work of abstract art it so boldly displayed for all who dared to see.

Perhaps, like Tate had said, Cassie Wilkes had put up the good fight, for whatever good it had done the poor woman. Her upper torso, severed cleanly just below the rib cage, impaled upon one of the same iron girders I'd seen Ben rip from the compound grounds a half-hour earlier. Mercifully, her head hung limp from what appeared to be a severely fractured neck, sparing me the horror of looking at the final expression she'd ever wear, no doubt one of indescribable pain and suffering. As for the whereabouts of her missing lower half, it would have to remain as mysteriously enigmatic as the twin disapperances of both Doc Gonzales and Deputy Jeffries.

"Everybody stay back... just... stay back... " I said, reaching back with both hands in a blocking stance.

"Get back into the building... we can't reach the opening from here."

This suggestion was met, predicably, with a wave of negativity, ranging from Mayor Boren's panic-laden, "*Oh noooo... hell no, I ain't walking back into that slaugtherhouse! I'd rather take my chances with this one*!"

To an unidenfied female (possibly that of the unofficial foster mother of earlier) screeching, "*I'd rather just die out here if that's what's meant to happen*,"in a comically downtrodden tone that was creeping defeatism at its most blatant.

Meanwhile, I'd noted a lack of additional cries emanating from inside the barracks building, meaning the threat had either been eliminated or... heaven forbid... there were simply no more screams to be heard due to a sudden lack of potential victims of the living, breathing variety. Shoving away such thoughts with great effort, I tried to remember that

Scar Fletcher, multiwar veteran and a man of superhuman strength, immeasurable bravery and undying will had entered that building to thwart said threat with extreme prejuduce. I had to believe he'd succeeded in doing so, as the alternatives were far too horrific to contemplate. Plus which, Nick Parione wasn't liable to go down without a fight as well. With that, I decided to hasten my own retreat, regardless of what was being bantered about by the surrounding horde.

"It's up to you, Mayor, but out here we've got no protection against that thing, not to mention the elements. In there... " I pointed back toward the tattered entrance, "Scar Fletcher and Nick Parione might possibly save our collective hides."

"Nick Par- you mean that so-called *hero* you left us as a bodyguard? Haaaaaaaaaaaaa!" I heard Boren howl in sarcastic glee as I pushed past both Jessica and one of the two local men we'd been introduced to earlier. "Yeah, that's it, Jackson. Go take a look at your precious protector. Take a *good* look. You'll see why we scampered out of there like goosed jackrabbits!"

Taking off in a shaky jog, I entered the barracks and was instantly taken aback by the lack of lighting. If the dome had been correctly deemed murky, the narrow corridors of the quarters building was an unlit mineshaft by comparison. Oh, if only the human eye didn't so miraculously adhere to such conditions, as in retrospect I'd have happily remained as blind as an albino mole staring straight into the noonday sun. As for Mayor Boren and his tiny cast of followers, it had taken less than thirty seconds after I'd departed the dome before their collective cries reached a throat-scorching cresendo, only to be just as abruptly cut off as if the beast had bore into them with buzz saw efficency. I'd felt a double-barrelled twinge of regret for not only leaving a semicomatose Marge Owens at the mercy of her former husband and current mutated monstrosity, but also for not at least trying to persuade poor Jessica to follow my lead, though in truth with fear and panic as my guide, the path to clear, logical thought had been hopelessly misplaced.

Remarkable how I'd managed to ignore the mass carnage that lay afoot, never even breaking stride while making an empassioned effort to reach the generator room for whatever reason. It would have been so easy to slide to the floor, curl into a trembling ball and await certain death amongst the many scattered corpses that lay strewn about like gutted cattle. For one, I guess there was a part of me that just had to see what the commotion was about. I mean, how could any potential threat be worse than that walking meat grinder inhabiting the glass dome? Secondly, the now late and surely not so great Mayor Douglas Boren's comments concerning Nick Parione had touched off an even deeper level of curiosity. These were questions I found as alluring and seductive as they were weirdly addictive. As for the aforementioned carnage, I'd obviously developed a thick skin concerning such matters in a frighteningly short time, as even the overwhelming stench of spilt blood and punctured gut did little to slow the quest for potential answers.

I found it bizarre yet somewhat fitting that the only victim I'd recognized while sprinting by in a blur had been that of Burt Hanover, his haunted eyes still open and seemingly aware despite the lower part of his jaw having been removed and a good portion of his skull peeled away like a melon rind. Damn if I hadn't liked and respected that man, and it hit me how utterly wrong it was for someone of his ilk to die in such a prehistoric way. If allowed ample time to mull it over, I'd have surely broken down at the mere thought.

Winding my way around and over still more fallen bodies, one of which appeared to be the horribly mutilated corpse of the young Pendrick girl, I'd weaved and dodged my way to within ten yards or so from the generator room door when I came upon Tate Fletcher lying from one side of the hall to the other like some human barricade.

"D-Darrin... don't... don't go any further... st-stay out of... th-there... " he gasped, almost choking between words from the cascade of blood bubbling forth with each spoken syllable.

Try as I might, it was virtually impossible not to make note of the damage bestowed upon the man, perhaps the worst being a foot-long slash across his bare chest from which could be viewed a glimpse of blood-smeared white breastbone. Just as shocking was the fact Fletcher was practically lying atop his own shattered left arm, which had been fractured so horribly it appeared to be a single tendon tearing away from being totally severed. As for his left, the bionic of the two appendages, it lay across his abdomen in a mess of twisted, smoldering wires, the hand itself turned palm up despite the opposite positioning of the connected forearm. I'm sure there were other significant injuries that held a smilarly grisly theme, and found myself again appreciative for the lack of lighting available.

"That... thing is... in there. Couldn't... c-couldn't stop... it... or even... sl-slow it down r-really... don't think... it can b-be... stopped."

"I... but... where's Nick?" I blurted out, averting my eyes to a wide, blackish smear coating the generator door, which hung crookedly from a shattered top hinge.

"N-not s-sure. I... never made it... inside... but I s-saw the crea-creature... go in... I guess to f-finish off who-whoever was left... "

Coughing weakly, I heard Tate begin to gurgle on his own blood. Reaching down, I cupped the back of his head, already coated in copper-scented stickiness and attempted to pull him upright to ease the hacking.

"G-go... get out... t-take as many as... you can... st-stay on the m-main road. Some-someone will... find y-you at... fi-first light... somebody will... come... "

"Tate... I don't think there *is* anyone else," I replied, warm tears burning the corners of my eyes. "The... that beast inside the generator room is a... different one. The sheriff... the Jake Owens' version is at the other end of the hall. It... it already... they were trying to escape through the dome when it... there's more than one of those damn things! How in god's name am I supposed to deal with *that* without your... without *someone's* help?"

During a break in my blubbering rant, I heard a soft gasp, and looked down to see Scar Fletcher staring back up at me with a single open eye, his crimson-caked mouth hanging partially agape but no longer serving as an active passage for air intake.

I can't say for sure how long I remained on my knees with the man's head tucked tightly against my ribcage. Nor can I accurately gauge how many times I repeated the same silent prayer or the exact contents of said verbal meditation. What I do recall with crystal clarity is what caused me to snap out of that self-imposed daze and get on with whatever fruitless plan of action was to commence. The zone breaker in question had consisted of twin growls which had overlapped each other only slightly, almost as if choroegraphed telepathically from each source. The first, I believe, had originated from the generator room-a rage-filled cry of apparent frustration, while the second had come from up the hall, this one infinitely more subdued but somehow doubly threatening. I didn't even bother to turn around to visualize the walking horror headed my way. It wasn't necessary. The unstoppable killing machine formerly known as County Sheriff Jake Owens had surely grown impatient with no further victims to dispatch, and so had sought out the one man who'd thus far escaped the fury of its retracted claws and razor-edged teeth. It wasn't a difficult decision really, much easier than I would've ever thought, to decide upon a method of one's own demise. Upon gently placing Tate's head back atop the blood-drenched hall carpeting, I'd already come to the conclusion that I wasn't about to give the ugly bastard the satisfaction.

"Well, you can just eat shit and die, Sheriff," I mumbled, or perhaps just thought aloud before taking off in a clumsy sprint toward the generator room. "Think I'd rather take my chances with your evil twin."

Upon hopping down the stairs two at a time, my forward momentum carried me almost to the center of the room (perhaps a shade lighter than the adjoining hallway, but only just), eventually sliding to a lurching halt with my boot tips mere inches from the stilled form of Wanda Jelks lying atop a steaming pile of her own viscera. Just to her left, sitting upright like some grisly abstract carving was the severed head of Jay Peterson, whom it had taken me several seconds to properly identify as my eyes hadn't quite adjusted. Standing so evenly erect was the man's dislodged noggin that it truly appeared like some magically rendered special effect, or perhaps that his body was somehow submerged into the cemet flooring with only the head protruding above the ground. Regardless, I took note of the crooked sitting of the man's spectacles and was briefly tempted to reach down and straighten them, thus recalling Jay's rather annoying, reoccuring habit of doing so. In fairness to how unbelieveably cold or wildly off-kilter that sounds, one must consider how emotionally disconnected I was at this particular juncture due to a rather extreme level of shock. Honestly, it was hard to feel anything other than jumbled discombobulation, otherwise, why in god's name had I entered that damned room to begin with?

Other than a few other sordid piles of splattered, torn or otherwise mutilated human remains, there seemed to be only two other living, breathing entities occupying the same space as I (*I would later find out how pathetically wrong such an assumption had been*), neither coming as much of a surprise considering the addition by subtraction rule.

While the beast (*this one appeared a bit shorter, stouter and a noticeably darker shade of pitch-black, if that was indeed possible*) stood before the generator's mesh cage entrace with its arms and spearlike fingers spread wide (*the fingers curling and uncurling every few seconds*) as to possibly ensnare whoever might attempt to elude its reach, I could just make out Nick Parione's bowed form by peeking through the beast's splayed legs. Down on his knees with his arms stretched similarly wide and his chin pointed upward, Nick had his back to the beast and appeared to be literally praying to the main generator unit.

Utterly lost in what specific action to take next, I basically did nothing but stand there ogling the beast and what was to be his final conquest, at least as far as the *more than merely mortal* crowd was concerned. In trying to recall exactly why I'd been so adamant to enter the room in the first place, I drew a total blank. Then again, it wasn't as if turning about and retracing my steps would do much good, not with mutated lawman number one roaming the hall in search of fresh victims to skewer. Worse yet, what with Ben (*it hurt beyond words to think I'd been forced to leave him behind with such potentially fatal injuries*), Tate, and Cassie all permanently down for the count and a bowing Nick Parione apparently praying for mercy, the supertypes who had once been our only hope had each been duly faced down and exterminated.

I must've released a heavy, saddened sigh, as the creature's slimy, slick, warped noggin abruptly twisted my way, looking me up and down with a rumbling growl as if deciding whether or not I was even worth the bother.

It was then I was able to officially ID beastie number two, a surreal unmasking that might've caused quite the jolt to my already deep-fried senses if not for a similar occurrence just minutes earlier within the glass dome leading into the building.

As with his slightly taller, equally grostesque twin whom Tate had earlier revealed to me as the one-time county sheriff, a similar transformation had begun to take place in the shorter, bulkier built of the twin monstrosities.

To backtrack a shade, when I'd once again come face to face with the sheriff/beast mutation as it had positioned itself as a walking blockade or sorts, complete with Cassie Wilkes' impaled upper body dangling from a metal pole like a human popsicle stick, I'd first thought the changes in its facial features to be some sort of hallucination; a cruel joke set up by a battered subconscious and triggered by the fact Tate Fletcher had just told me the thing had indeed emerged from Jake Owens. Unlike the right, which appeared wholly unchanged, the left side of its face had seen dramatic alterations in both bone structure and overall shape, to include the eye (complete with one bushy eyebrow), nose (the wide nostril flaring wildly), and the ear (same slightly outwardly positioned *Dumbo* look as the former sheriff). The thing had even utilized the eye to shoot me a quick wink of sorts, though whether or not this was purposeful or just a random twitch is impossible to know.

As for the sheriff's bile-spewing, black-eraser

shaded twin, who better to logically fill the bill-with his close-set eyes, prominent overbite, and Jay Leno-sized chin-it wasn't at all difficult to connect said features to former Deputy Sheriff Randall Jeffries. As with his former boss, the partial transformation was eerily similar to the old Batman villian of DC comics fame, *Two-Face*, wherein only one side of the face seemed to have reverted back to human form. Of course, there was no way to even speculate if the two *were* perhaps gradually changing back to human form, or if this was merely part of the overall mutation process. Regardless, the effect was bone-chilling to state the very least, and I couldn't help but attempt some type of civilized communication in hopes that a tiny bit of Randall Jeffries was still present inside that massive alien shell. In truth, it was more probable I was within mere moments of being gutted like a range elk, but what exacty did I have to lose?

"Randall? Randall... it's Darrin. Darrin Jackson... remem-remember me?" I asked softly, shuffling forward with my hands raised like a surrending soldier standing at the center of a bloody battlefield massacre, which in retrospect I certainly was.

The Jeffries thing repeated a more gutteral recreation of its earlier growl, nodding slightly and shrugging its spiny shoulders as if becoming increasingly annoyed by my presence.

"Randy... do you... understand? I'm... we're not your enemy. You don't... need to do this. I... I'll do my best to get you help... you and Sheriff Owens. This... this whole mess... isn't your fault. I can make them understand that. Neither you nor Jake will be blamed for what's happened... for what was... done to you. Everything... everything is going to work out... "

Ridiculous isn't nearly a strong enough word to define how I'd felt at that moment-marching about like some mobile shrink attempting to reach, console, and to some degree, con a creature whose use for humanity and penchant for compassion was obviously sorely lacking.

Yet again, I digress. The bottom line was clear and bold: I was trying to save Nick Parione's, and more importantly, my own hide. As for how confident I'd felt in the final outcome of that little battlefield counseling session, let's just say I'd already managed to complete a silent prayer for both our souls.

A split second later, before I could even begin to put together an additional string of useless, cliche-ridden blather, the beast gave its answer in most resounding terms, leaping over in one fluid movement and lifting me airborne by my parka's collar with one extended claw. As it toyed with me, at once swinging me from the left to the right like some human pendulum, I caught a substantial whiff of the thing's indescribably rancid breath, a cool, putrifying mix that made the most rotten of raw sewage smell practically rosy by comparison.

In the few moments before what I was certain to be my own rather painful demise, I just happened to peek over and around the thing's pointed left ear to see a completely nude Nick Parione standing just outside the generator cage with his arms crossed tightly over his bare chest, a pile of haphazardly tossed clothing lying just to his right.

Oh, I get it, I recall deducing crazily, *he's trying the old 'human sacrifice bit', to ward off any future killings by offering himself up like a pork chop on a platter.*

Nice try but no cigar, Nick old boy... afraid it's faaaarrrrr too late in the game for such noble, however archaic, gestures, I'd thought crazily just as the beast slung back its free arm and its bony fingers curled into a makeshift hook... all the better to fillet its hapless prey. Surprisingly, my first reaction wasn't to close my eyes and await the killing blow, but to continue focusing on Nick, whose bizarre behavior apparently served as a perfect distraction-even to one surely about to die.

"Hang on, Darrin!" he screamed, having unfolded his arms while crouching on one knee and using his hands for balance on either side of the floor. As if in deep meditation, Nick then bowed his head and I saw his entire body begin to shake and tremble.

"Hang on... and... don't fight it! Go with... the flow and... just... don't... fight it!"

With an angry growl, my ertswhile assassin turned its attention back toward Nick just as the young man's head arose and he let forth with an anguish-racked cry of mutiple fire alarm proportions. Again, whether or not what followed was linked to hallucination was still to be determined, but at the time I couldn't help but laugh aloud at the sheer preposterousness of it all, even as I was being unceremoniously dumped to the stone floor. Nick Parione's eyes had shown like twin diamonds glistening in a noonday sun, his forehead, cheeks and neck riddled with purplish veins the size of cable cords.

It was while curling into a ball and screaming like mad as sharp pains raced up my right leg, that I first caught a glimpse of still another cellar dweller, one I'd somehow missed upon initially entering the room.

The thing emerged from the shadows of the back wall like a slumbering black widow uncoiling from its web. Though the darkness and my sudden bout of physical agony didn't allow for more than a few seconds of concentration, it was obvious that this particular beast was cut from the same mutated cloth as the other two, but with a sizeable difference. It appeared at least eight to eight and a half feet tall, its sinewy arms noticably longer, while its freakishly elongated legs actually bent inward at the knee. Granddaddy longlegs, indeed. Sad to say, it never emerged into the faint light to allow a glimpse at its facial region. I heard a thundering growl, and quickly rolled over onto my right side following the less-than-graceful landing wherein I'm fairly certain my right ankle was severely fractured.

I watched the Jeffries thing lunge toward Nick and freeze in midair, temporarily resembling some sort of sculptured gargoyle instead of a live being. From that exact moment, things didn't exactly follow a conhesive script. What I do recall, though not in any particular order, might well read like the lunatic rantings of a hopeless schizophrenic. At the time, I wouldn't have even bothered to argue. Case, or cases, in point:

... the deputy beast whirls back around, and I am magically (perhaps tragically?) transported back into his steely, slimy grip, my ankle and leg no longer aching like a busted tooth... that is, until...

... I rapidly back up the generator steps and into the hall as if being forced by some giant, unseen magnetic device that has somehow locked onto my very flesh... the frenzied rewind continues unabated, until...

... I again lean over the brutalized body of Scar Fletcher... until...

... I am back inside the glass dome walkway, arguing with Mayor Bowen, whose hyperquick movements seem mechanical, robotic... until...

... I see Scar Fletcher leaning over to whisper to Ben Thomason... I smell the stench of cooked flesh... then watch Scar back quickly away in a bizarre 'moon walk' before vanishing from the dome altogether, leaving me alone to deal with Ben, who is speaking to me through lips that appear stuck in fast motion... from there...

... things begin to happen... images appear and disappear at warp speed, allowing for just the briefest of glances into incidents and situations already experienced...

... I stand inside the generator room and carefully eavesdrop on Ben and Tate as they discuss a potential plan of action...

... I'm back inside the snowplow, conversing with the mayor and Wanda Jelks while battling to keep us from sliding off into the nearest gully...

... I'm still navigating the snowplow, this time with Ben, Tate, and Sheriff Owens riding shotgun...

... I'm inside the receiving warehouse, assisting Owens and his comatose deputy exit their battered vehicle as Burt Hanover circles us like a predatory vulture, ranting and raving about the demolished dock door (as with all participants in this surreal little dance, Burt's incessant pacing is being accomplished completely in reverse... just as the words he speaks sound more like the inane chants of a devout devil worshipper than everyday English) ...

... I'm sitting in conference room one, exchanging pleasantries with the Cassie Wilkes personality that makes up one-third of the heroine Jekyll-ene and failing miserably to fight off urges of arousal while in her enigmatic presence...

... I'm inside Burt Hanover's well-heated office, discussing the individual case studies of four newly assigned but yet to arrive superhero types we'll soon be tasked to counsel in a recently inked government contracted deal...

From there, I recall only blackness, but not of the fearful, foreboding type... more like being wrapped in the toasty confines of a thick, wool blanket and taking a lengthy, much-needed power nap... that is, until it all rushed back in tidal wave proportions...

***

"Time?" I inquired while scanning the darkened skies like an overzealous UFO hunter, biting my left thumbnail to the quick.

I heard several pained groans before anyone bothered to verbally reply.

"Damn, ain't you the anal one? For the record and I reckon your own personal piece of mind, it is now eight minutes past eleven in the p.m., local time."

"And what was the approximate landing time again?"

"Hell's bell's, Hoss... I never thought any manner of rerun could possibly give me a nastier head-thumper than that last whopper... but you're gettin' close. Anybody got a Tylenol? Advil Extra Strength? Quart of vodka maybe?"

"Roughly four to six minutes from right now," another, infinitely calmer and much less sarcastic voice interrupted. "'Course, that's based on when old man Cromartie spoke to Marge, so it could easily be off a minute or more either way."

"Not to sound paranoid here," still another chimed in, standing out simply because it was the lone female representative, "but are we sure of the landing spot? After all, the white stuff's been coming down in buckets... "

A response came only after a resounding sigh.

"*Damned* sure, yes, ma'am. See that bent oak over there?"

"Yeah, so?"

"Well, first go-round, Benji over there carved his initials into the trunk."

"Sure 'nuff did, agin' prostate or no, I can still piss laser beams after a half-pot of coffee's poured down the old gizzard."

With that, even the normally stoic deputy sheriff joined in on a group snicker.

"Hey, I just don't want that damned fireball using me as a landing strip, okay?"

"Acquire a grip, Cas. We're a good seventy-five yards from where its journey *ends*."

Leaning against the cruiser's relatively warm, snow-free engine, which purred to a soothing rhythm while parked atop the road's wide shoulder, I couldn't help but study the behavior and body language of all present, while simultaneously mourning for the one conspicuously absent from the ranks; the one solely responsible for our being there and thus being allowed a second chance to make things right.

Decked out in shiny silver fireproof suits sans the attached hoods, Ben and Tate both kneeled a half-dozen feet away to my right, the two of them practically joined at the hip since being reunited.

Standing a few feet further to the right stood Cassie Wilkes, the whole of her curvaceous body successfully camouflaged by an oversized parka. Though her outward persona remained ultrasassy, as was the middle sister's trademark, it was obvious just a smidgen of levity had been added since the unexpected reunion. I could only speculate why it was Cas who had emerged as the dominant personality once the stage had been so magically reset. Regardless, I have to admit to always fancying Cassie over the more serious, rather snooty Cassandra. Hopefully, we'd seen the last of sis number three, though it was always a relief knowing Jekyll-ene could always make a showing if combat situations dictated.

As for Sheriff Jake Owens and his stone-faced deputy, Randall Jeffries, it was more difficult to gauge. Both seemed a bit distracted at times... even a shade distant. Perhaps it had something to do with the dramatic transformations each had undergone still having some kind of inward scarring effect despite the reversal process. Hard to say for one so unfamiliar with such subjects as astrophysics or time travel. I guess some things truly aren't meant to be understood by the human mind. You just have to go with the flow. Having seen fate turned on its collective ear, a person finds he really has no choice in the matter.

Physically, I felt fine... top-notch in fact, as if awakened from a long, restful slumber. Mentally, that was a whole 'nother ballgame. The majority of the fog had lifted, the first five or ten minutes being the haziest, leaving behind a layer of grogginess I can only compare to the morning after following a triple-shot of Nyquil. As for what Ben described as the 'WTF' aspect (use your imagination-or if you must, a copy of the *Modern Dictionary of Profanity*) of the whole ordeal, I was still struggling with that one. Indeed, I'd been an active player in a miraculous, mind-blowing, brain-numbing, scientifically improbable spectacle. Something right out of an old H.G. Wells novel, only infinitely more remarkable in scope. I'd always heard, and often repeated the phrase *seeing is believing*. Well, I saw... yes indeed I had seen... I was standing and breathing with an active pulse as living proof... but I was still having a hell of a difficult time with the *believing* part. Like I said, sometimes a person has no choice but to go with flow and see where the river goes. Regardless, the overall vibe was of the 'happy to be here' variety, though accompanied by a hefty serving of cautious optimism. There was, after all, the matter of making sure the previous chain of events were snapped in their entirely and without a single loose end dangling about.

"I think I see her lights," Sheriff Owens proclaimed, quickly handing his binoculars to

Jeffries, who whipped off a fresh build-up of snow from the lenses before concentrating on the same chunk of pitch-black sky.

"Yep. Has to be it. Looks like she might be burning already. That's way too much light."

Tate jogged over and took a quick peek as both Owens and Jeffries headed for the cruiser's open trunk.

"Sure looks that way, all right. Right wing is flaming like a lit torch. She's bobbing and weaving just as predicted."

"Ya mean *ordained*, don't ya, Fletch?" Ben said with a shrug, wiping a good half-inch of the white stuff from each of the firesuit's shoulders. "This is truly some weird, wild shit, ain't it? Like watchin' a rerun on TV, only in truth it's a show ya ain't never really seen."

I heard Cas snicker, and knew she wouldn't be able to resist such an opening.

"Oh, that's deep, Benjamin... reaaaaal deep. Like a foot of dirty bathtub water deep."

Standing with a loud grunt, Ben glanced over at Cas and frowned.

"Ya know, I think I liked you better as a groupie after all. Amble on over here and give Papa Thomason a big hug... "

"Dream on, pops."

Handing the binoculars to Ben, who'd joined him at the front of the cruiser, Tate then strolled past me toward the trunk, where Jake and Randall were busy arming themselves to the teeth.

"We've got three minutes to impact, tops."

"Jackson, get over here and load up!" I heard Tate roar, as if yelling at me from a hundred yards away instead of a distance of less than a dozen feet. Still, I wasn't about to complain or dare procrastinate in the face of such gruff authority, especially one I so largely respected. After all, the man had managed to piece together a pretty impressive plan in severely limited time. Strategically, it was sound. Logically, there wasn't an alternative. It simply *had* to work, or else one man's ultimate sacrifice would've been completely in vain, and a slew of innocents would be fated to perish... yet again.

"Hey, Counselor, don't forget to toss *Sergeant Rock* there a salute or he's liable to have ya peelin' taters by nightfall," Ben cracked, lumbering over like some bulky reject from a Hollywood backlot.

As Randall Jeffries commandeered the binoculars and continued to scan the skies, Tate and Ben each reached back to pull the flame-retardant hoods over their faces.

"You about ready, smart ass?" Tate inquired just as the glass shield slid over and was snapped into place at the neckline.

"By all means, G.I Shmoe, let's go play French fry."

Meantime, Jake Owens tossed me the rifle, which he described as a .30 gauge, before pulling me to the side for a quick training session.

The thick gloves I'd donned made the barrel feel overly slick, and I had a sudden fear of it sailing out of my hands upon my firing the first shot. I could only hope that the very act of pulling the trigger would never become necessary.

I was still fiddling with the safety mechanism when Cassie strolled up and nudged me with a shoulder.

"Don't sweat it, Darrin. If one of 'em does happen to breach that invisible perimeter, I'll be here to dole out some much-needed discipline."

"That's certainly reassuring, Cassie, because if it comes down to yours truly as the last line of defense, we are most certainly screwed."

"Yeah... she's coming down all right... post haste," Randall Jeffries proclaimed blandly, as if announcing the late arrival of a city bus instead of a streaking ball of flame falling from the sky and headed directly our way.

For those next thirty to forty-five seconds, we all stood silently and watched the swiveling, smoldering aircraft descend closer and closer to ground level until it began to sever the tops off several oak and elm trees capping a nearby mountain range.

After tapping Ben lightly on one shoulder, Tate half-sprinted, half-skated down the hill toward the spot he earlier labeled as ground zero. Before departing in three lengthy strides, Ben turned to specifically address Jake and Randall.

"Later, gators... and don't even think about mowin' anybody or anything down with those peashooters 'til you're damn sure we ain't standin' in the line of fire. Me and Fletch are a lotta things, but bulletproof ain't one of 'em."

The scorched aircraft's initial touchdown atop the rocky, uneven terrain almost instantly shredded the landing gear and left its considerable bulk to slide down the rolling hills like a greased sled. Before lurching dramatically onto its left side and severing a wing, it had managed to chop down a handful of trees to their respective roots while digging a wide groove through what had been virgin snow.

By the time it ground to a halt in almost the precise spot predicted, it was literally nothing more than a smoking husk, having left behind a slug trail of burnt or burning parts in its wake, the majority of which hissed like boiling water on a kettle from contact with the icy surface. With its crumpled tail section cocked toward the sky and its crushed nose rooted at the edge of a V-shaped gully, the craft still sat a good fifty to sixty yards away as Jake, Randall, Cassie and I spread out to form a partial perimeter.

"Look alive, folks, and shoot anything that darts out of that bird that ain't wearing fireproof suits," Jake Owens said before executing a double-take Cassie's way. "That is... uh... those of us who *are* carrying."

I didn't have to see Cassie's face to see the smirk I knew she'd donned. The sassy tone of that silken voice was all I needed to hear.

"Not to worry, Sheriff. I can run 'em down and put out their lights as fast and effectively as any bullet. Fact is, I'm kind of hoping Ben and Tate let at least one slip through the cracks... one rat bastard in *particular*, if you catch my drift."

"Let's just hope that don't happen, Missy. I just ain't into taking such chances at this late stage... or is it... early stage? Aw hell... let's move out."

With that, we all trudged off into high ankle-deep snow quickly rising to knee level.

By the time I'd reached my assigned space, some fifteen to twenty yards from Cassie on my left and Deputy Jeffries on the right, Ben had already ripped away the fuselage door before he and Tate entered the burning aircraft.

Despite the occasional ice shard bouncing off my face like a tiny speck of sharpened gravel, I found it impossible to drown out or successfully distract the incessant pounding of the pulse at my temples. I was finding it increasingly hard to breathe normally, and if not for the thick sweats and long johns covering my knees, they'd have most assuredly been knocking together for all to hear.

It wasn't as if my confidence in Ben and Tate had totally abated, but after all, I had seen both of them perish by the hands, or claws if one prefers, of the beast. The hope was such an imminent assault on the downed craft would result in an interception of sorts. That is, we could only pray to catch the main source before transformation, or at least in mid-change, before its power was at its monstrous peak.

Glancing over to my left through the blinding snow, I saw Cassie crouch down in a parody of the classic three-prong football stance. Even from such a distance and with limited visibility, I could see the angry sneer creasing her face. Further down, Sheriff Jake Owens had assumed a similarly well-known shooter's pose: down on one knee and staring directly through his rifle sights.

I was just about to turn to check Deputy Jeffries' status when a series of somewhat muffled retorts filled the air, followed by a trio of loud thumps as the craft shook and shimmied as if sitting atop a live fault line.

Falling to one knee, I'd been attempting to acquire a serviceable shooting stance when the first body sailed from the open fuselage like a spinning top, followed by a second, and finally a third, all landing twenty to twenty-five feet from the craft in various stages of unconsciousness.

While Cassie streaked toward the fallen men to ensure their inability to retaliate, the rest of us stood our ground. Moments later, about the time we heard what sounded like something vital give way near the rear of the plane, two additional men exited the aircraft, each with their hands atop their respective heads as if forced at gunpoint. Much like the trio who had been so roughly ejected from the craft moments earlier, the two uniformed men shared similar physical characteristics, to include close-shaved buzz cut hairdos and the deep, dark complexions normally associated with those of Middle Eastern descent. As I heard the men curse the fates in whatever native tongue was their own, I couldn't help but feel a bit bemused as well as dumfounded at the lack of conspicuity involved. It was as if they'd never bothered with a plan B in case A was to fail as miserably as it apparently had, sauntering from that burning fuselage resembling stereotypical terrorists straight from a Hollywood B movie casting call. No matter really, as those men were mere fodder compared to the individual we'd all come to think of as 'Mister Big'. As Tate was the next to deplane, I felt a major surge of fear unsuccessfully masquerading as mere apprehension as to who might or might not exit next. Being as I'd been the one to first suspect and subsequently ID the supposed head honcho of the entire sordid mess, it would truly have been a colossal egg to the face if said hunch turned out to be nothing more than fictional speculation.

Less than five seconds later, during which time I truly thought my heart was going to exit my chest via my throat, such fears were mercifully banished.

Though Ben had the suspect in question tossed over his left shoulder like so much bagged laundry, I caught several clear, unobstructed glimpses of the man's face as he'd leaned up to fire off various profanities. His hands had been secured behind his back via a pair of plastic cuffs borrowed from Jake Owens' cruiser.

"Is it... is it him?" I heard Sheriff Owens bellow, having shouldered his weapon and stepped slowly ahead as to meet the approaching group halfway. Meantime, Cassie had busied herself dragging the trio of fallen terrorists along by the ankles, effectively digging out a three-pronged pathway through the rapidly thickening snow.

"Oh yeah, it's him alright," Tate replied with a self-assured nod, having peeled off his hood and peeked back briefly as to ensure Ben's escape as the craft began to visibly implode from the effects of the unrelenting flames.

"Notice how his present wardrobe rates compared to what we saw hanging off him back in the generator room. Guess he found an empty phone booth along the way and pulled a quick Houdini, hmm?"

Sardonic humor aside, Tate's point was a valid one. The man's present ensemble, that of light blue jean jacket with white button-up dress shirt beneath, Dickies work pants and brown hiking boots was far removed from the baggy get up we'd witnessed during that earlier meeting. Obviously somewhere along the winding trail of mass destruction, he'd obtained *slash* stolen a serviceable yet comically oversized replacement.

Hoisting his quarry airborne with the casual flip of a wrist, Ben began to playfully twirl the man in a counterclockwise motion, all the while cackling like a hyena on laughing gas.

"Re-release... p-put... put me... p-put me d-down you... y-you... m-maniac... y-you basssssttttttaaaarrdddd!" the man protested between spins, his image growing increasingly blurred with each complete revolution.

"Ah, quit horsing around, Benji... " Tate said with a barely concealed grin. "They'll be plenty of time for torture during the interrogation phase."

Removing his own fireproof hood with a snap of the wrist, Ben flashed a comic pout while allowing his prisoner's limp noodle form to drop back onto his husky shoulder.

"Sorry, Dad. I wasn't tryin' to hurt the bad man... leastways... not yet."

All good feelings and potential vindication aside, I'd literally felt a truckload of bricks slide from my shoulders. Within minutes, we'd all congregated back near the cruiser and snowplow, just as a final, violent explosion racked the downed aircraft and the murky, smoke-filled sky temporarily gained daylight status.

It was at this point that the head bad guy himself officially blew a gasket, shrieking like a banshee once Ben had shoved him roughly against the snowplow's rear bumper. Meanwhile, Cassie had piled the fallen prisoners next to the cruiser's left rear passenger door. All three appeared to be breathing, though at least two sported caked blood beneath their nostrils. Tate had already placed the two 'live' ones into the backseat and locked them in.

"You'll... you brutish cretins will pay for this... oh, *how* you'll pay. You have no idea what you've just destroyed!"

Backing off to remove the rest of his suit, Ben grunted sarcastically while shooting the man a playful wink.

"Actually, we've got a pretty good notion at that, ya eggheaded nutsack. Fact is, you'd best be considerin' yourself ex-treme-ly *fortunate* you ain't fryin' right alongside it."

Shuffling over, I stood next to Ben and whispered behind a cupped palm.

"So it was... still intact? Undamaged?"

"Yep, not a scratch on 'er!" he practically screamed in reply, causing me to flinch back involuntarily and almost slip in the tightly packed snow. "And why exactly are we whisperin', Darrin? I don't give two hoots in hell if Doctor *Frankenstein* over there hears what I've got to say."

Stomping past me like an angry bull while donned in only a painfully thin long john top and blue jeans, Ben grabbed the object of his rage by the collar and jerked him airborne before lowering him just enough so the two were posed eye to eye.

"Face it, pal... ballgame's over. Your master plan is for shit. 'Sides, you're pretty much neutered without the magic elixir doin' your dirty work, right? Just like an unarmed sniper... gutless... ballless... clueless."

"Perhaps you have... gravely underestimated my capabilities," came an equally intense, predatory reply. "A tragic mistake, that. Tragic but not unexpected from such lowbrow brutes with miniscule IQs to match."

"Lowbrow brutes?" Ben howled, releasing the man with a stout shove. "Ya hear that, Fletch? I do believe ol' Doc Mengele here just called us stupid. Now, if such is the case, why do you suppose he's the captive and we're the captors?"

Bouncing from the passenger door of the cruiser like a ricocheting pinball, the man slid face first into a fresh mound of virgin snow. Once his head arose from the fluffy pile, he choked and spat as if drowning in a shallow stream.

Groaning in what sounded like mild disgust, Jake Owens lumbered over and helped the man to his feet, leaning him against the hood and even reaching up to wipe some of the caked snow from his eyes.

"That's enough playing judge and jury, Thomason. We are still tramping about on U.S. soil, right? They'll be no unauthorized beat downs in this man's jurisdiction."

With that, our main captive seemed to perk right up, even sticking out his bony chest in defiance.

"Th-thank you, Officer. It's good to see there's at least one civilized party within such hooligan ranks."

Owens stomped off without giving the man a second look.

"Save the thanks for the day they sentence your sadistic ass, buddy boy. I'll be the one sitting in the front row holding the noose."

Not surprisingly, the man hardly blinked in

response, though I did notice a slight upturn of his left eyebrow.

Following a brief group snicker wherein all but a tight-lipped Deputy Randall Jeffries participated, I heard a muffled moan and looked over to see that one of the fallen soldiers appeared to be waking.

"We got room in the cruiser for the three stooges here, Sheriff?" Cassie inquired, leaning over the man just as his eyes began to flicker open.

Owens shrugged wearily, waving at the falling snow as if it were a swarm of pesky flies.

"Gonna have to make some, I reckon. Sure can't fit 'em into the plow."

"Why not avoid the dilemma altogether and just hook 'em to the bumper?" Ben said, reaching up to scratch a thick growth of grayish stubble atop his squared chin.

A loud sneeze ensued, triggering Randall Jeffries' first verbal folly since our *arrival* on scene.

"Whatever we're going to do, let's just *do* it already," he blurted out crankily while wiping his nose with a white hanky retrieved from the back pocket of his dark blue uniform pants. "It ain't getting any warmer out here, Jake." Truly, a man of few words but deep wisdom, our man Randall.

Jake Owens sidestepped his stoic deputy and posed in front of the cruiser's passenger door, reaching for the handle while wearing the perpetual scowl of a chronic pain sufferer.

"Can't argue with you there, RJ. Blizzard conditions ain't exactly doing wonders for this damn headache either. Alright, folks, let's load 'em up and head 'em out. I'll call the state boys from HQ to come pick up the rat pack here after buzzing the fire department out of Corvallis."

Once the trio of still mostly incoherent mercenary types were packed into the backseat with their two buddies, Owens walked over and started to guide our main prisoner into the front.

"Hang on, Jake. That one stays here," a voice stated sternly but without malice.

"What? Stays here? You mean... leave him? What're you tal-"

"No, I just mean he won't be accompanying his merry band of terrorists back to HQ."

Removing his hand from the passenger's side door handle, Jake then shared a quizzical glance with Randall before releasing the prisoner and stepping forward with his hands propped atop his hips.

"Speak to me then, Mister Fletcher. What, pray tell, are you proposing we do with him? Give him a running start and then set out on the hunt?"

Taking two long strides forward, Tate Fletcher uncapped his left fist as to display the slim object lying atop his open palm. Meanwhile, I saw Ben stroll around to the front of the snowplow and eventually vanish behind its bulk while Cassie circled around to the front of the cruiser and positioned herself like an assigned sentry. Since I'd only been privy to a small portion of their plan, this sudden plethora of subversive movement was as much a mystery to me as everyone else.

"I found this on the floor of the fuselage. Came close to stomping on it, in fact. Take a good, hard look at the contents. Note the color scheme."

From my vantage point, I could make out the syringe with its tar-black contents; a shade that had become sickeningly familiar of late.

Jake leaned over and studied the object cautiously, as if it were a deadly contaminant of some sort, which of course was a strong possibility.

"I don't... what does it mean?"

"Well, there is the possibility it's been used, though it's damn hard to prove just by looking."

"So you're saying that... maybe he... " Jake began, gesturing toward our captive with a slight nod, the man in question now leaning against the passenger door with his head bowed, as if meditating. I noticed the bald spot at the top of the man's scalp had filled with falling flakes, giving the illusion he might've dyed that portion of his hair ivory white.

"I'm just saying... it's possible."

"And that... the crap coming from that needle is what caused... you know... "

"Very likely."

"Sooooo, the plan is to... what again?"

"Simplicity itself, Sheriff."

With that, Tate Fletcher surged ahead and past Jake Owens in three quick steps, pulling the prisoner airborne and tossing him into the wide clearing to our left just as Ben emerged from the shadow of the snowplow carrying an industrial-sized flamethrower of the homemade variety, its coil wire barrel leading the way like a probing insect feeler.

"Hey now... wait just a damn minute here... " the sheriff protested, slip-sliding ahead with his right hand resting on the holster of his .38, a weapon I suddenly recalled sharing a brief affair with in some warped alternative universe.

"What's the homemade rocket launcher for?"

Acting with the speed and reflexes of a jungle cat, Cassie Wilkes leapt out of nowhere to subdue the man with a forearm wedged tightly across the chest of his parka.

"Save it, Owens. This is the only option."

Not nearly as quick but equally effective, I still managed to play my role efficiently enough, leveling the sights of the shotgun chest level at Deputy Randall Jeffries, whose eyes instantly grew saucer-sized. Whether or not I could've backed up such a threat will, thankfully, never be known.

"What the hell?"

"No interference, Randy. That's all. You'll... you'll both understand once it's over."

Ben and Tate formed a semicircle around the fallen man, who lay silent and unmoving on his belly after digging a wide, lengthy trench through the snow with his head and upper body.

"He's right, Jake. When it comes to the big picture, you and your hired gun there are still pretty much wandering around in the dark. We're not sure why, but figure it has something to do with the trauma you both suffered by being... altered the way you were. You must've... carried some of it back with you, I... we don't know. Regardless, you have to believe us when we tell you this isn't what it appears to be."

"And what's that exactly, Fletcher? A gangland murder? An assassination? Gotta say, that's the *big picture* that's forming in this man's mind. Tell you what... while you're at it, why not just fry 'em all?" he continued, pointing at the prisoners already tucked away inside the cruiser.

"He wouldn't inject them, Jake. Oh, I'm sure he thought of them as expendable enough, but not as test subjects. Let's just say on our first go-round, we discovered the soldier boys there in various states of dismemberment, and not just from the plane crash. Logic dictates nothing's changed this time around... they're clean."

"I'm supposed to buy that crock of mule manure as gospel? Jesus, listen to yourse-"

"Trust me, Sheriff, this is for the best, not only for the Twin Cities, but for the whole blessed world in general... "

Reaching down, Tate hauled Konrad up by the back of his collar and stood him up.

"Tell you what... let's just see what the doc has to say then. Go ahead then, plead your case. Explain to the good sheriff here why what we're about to do is so damn wrong."

Keeping his head bowed, the man remained stubbornly silent.

"Fine and dandy then... if that's the way it's gonna be. You gave 'im a fair shot. Let's get on with this... " Ben remarked, stepping forward and leading with the metallic contraption pointed forward like twin cannons.

"But... what if you're wrong?" the individual once introduced to us as Bill Casey, friendly out-of-town dental technician, suddenly whispered. As when he and I had been first acquainted in that cramped generator room, every little nuance the man possessed screamed distrust. Despite my initial gut instinct concerning Casey panning out, albeit in such a mind-numbing fashion, I felt very little in the way of satisfaction, a la clapping myself on the back with a hardy *told ya so*. On the contrary, it left nothing but the sourest of aftertastes.

"What was that, Billy boy?" Tate inquired, leaning toward the man with a palm planted behind his ear.

"Or should I refer to you by your actual name, Doctor William Jared Konrad? Better yet, maybe you'd prefer one of your other alias... Kirk Derek Waters or the ever-popular Lee Carlton Dean? Spent ample time with your finger planted randomly in a phone book, have we?"

"I said... " Konrad replied, lifting his head up ever so gradually to reveal a wicked smirk and slit-narrow eyes in true Jack Nicholson style from Kubrick's classic horror film *The Shining*.

'... what if you are... wrong... about me?"

This time it was Ben who intervened, temporarily slinging the double-barreled flamethrower to one side, the acetylene cylinders slapping together nosily. I had a brief image of the haphazardly taped/tacked/stapled-together contraption exploding in our collective faces, but then recalled the precision and expertise with which Tate had assembled it. A true master of improvisation, that Tate Fletcher, at least where weaponry was concerned-we'd all stood back in awe as the man had played *MacGuyver*-though in truth I'd never been told its intended use.

"Don't think so, sunshine... ya see, we had just enough time back at the post to get in a little background check, courtesy of the FBI's official website and more specific the America's Most Wanted page... "

"Fine," Konrad conceded with a nod, though

still looking a bit too smug for the position he found himself in.

"Do past transgressions usually result in instantaneous corporate punishment such as a premeditated public hanging?"

"Why not at all, Doc. Folks can be forgiven for their pasts. It's human nature," Cassie injected from my right, standing with her rear end shoved against the cruiser's passenger door, where the men inside sat slumped in unison.

"What we can't forgive you for is... well, that humdinger of a *future* transgression you planned on releasing onto the whole of society, beginning with sleepy little Boulder Valley."

"Excuse me, Miss? Perhaps I still have some frozen precipitation packed into my ears, but did you really just say... *future* transgression? My god, how is it all you people talk as if you know me?"

"Forget it, Konrad," Cassie replied, wagging a forefinger back and forth in windshield wiper style. In retrospect, the lady infamous for flying off the handle had thus far remained the epitome of cool-headed behavior.

"Despite all your supposed scientific genius, you'd never buy into the truth behind the theory... much less comprehend it. Just take our word for it, bright eyes. Let's just say you've just been busted by a roving gang of future cops and leave it lay."

"And this... future crime I'm supposed to have committed is enough justification in you people's minds to... allow me to revert to a crude vernacular... snuff me out, as it were?"

"Damn straight, *as it were...* " Ben scowled, reshouldering the thrower. I could tell the big guy's trigger finger was itching to fire it up and let loose with that man-made incinerator, and from a moral standpoint I should've felt at least a twinge of guilt. After all, despite the atrocities Konrad was predestined to oversee, there was no proof he'd contaminated himself with the syringe. Still, much like the others, I felt a need to watch his sentence carried out right then and there, minus the months and possibly even years a court trial would take. A court trial that, at worst, would convict the man of terroristic acts, but not the countless slaughter of innocents perpetrated in a future now never to be. Only we as a group knew what he was capable of, and would do, if he somehow escaped our grasp.

"Ya see, we also had just enough time to study over that madman's manifesto ya left behind. Kind of a *mad scientist's greatest hits package*, ya might say. Didn't exactly leave much to the imagination, did ya, bucket mouth?"

"Manifesto?" Konrad croaked, twisting about to study the smoking ruins of the crash site.

"But... I don't... the... that package should still be aboard... how did you... that is, when could you have... "

Cassie's high-pitched, cackling laugh was borderline demented.

"Don't ask us, smart guy. Again, falls under the heading of strange but true phenomenon. You'd think a test tube hugger like yourself would have an open mind to the bizarre, especially with that mutant brew you concocted."

Mumbling incoherently, Konrad then lowered his head once again, shaking it gently from side to side as if to possibly awaken himself from a particularly troublesome nightmare. Even Ben's growling rhetoric induced nary a flinch.

"Enough with this horseshit dialogue already! My ears are startin' to bleed. This asshole don't deserve no explanation. I don't give a rat's rancid ass if he understands how it is we know what he was plannin'. Sad truth is, I ain't sure *I* get it completely. Let's just end this so I can find an open bar somewhere. Fletch? If ya please, big guy... "

"Oh yeah, by all means, Ben, it'll be my pleasure... "

With a single, forceful shove to the chest, Tate sent the good doctor sprawling back a good dozen or so feet to land on his backside. I couldn't help but think Konrad had been fortunate Fletcher had chosen to use his nonbionic arm. In retrospect, this had been no accident, but strategic. Tate and Ben had wanted the man completely conscious and aware for what transpired next. Conscious, and very, very agitated.

"That's what I'm talkin' about," Ben said, stomping forward with the thrower's coil barrel tip tilted slightly downward.

"Goddamn murder is what it is... first degree homicide! Killing a man over some... science fiction bullshit I can't even make heads or tails about anyhow!" Jake Owens protested, backed by a decisive *damn straight* chorus provided by his usually stiff-lipped deputy.

"Don't think I'm gonna forget this, Fletcher... any of you... the county don't pay us to forget... it don't matter if this man is the bastard child of Adolf Hitler, he still deserves a fair shake in a court of law."

Scrambling to his knees, Konrad's tone was no longer cocky or smug, but layered in panic in the form of the desperate pleas of the soon-to-be executed. If I hadn't already seen what the man was capable of and heard his rhetoric of hate-filled death mongering, I might have actually felt pity.

"I... don't do this! Whatever you... think I've done or... will do. I... you've already st-stopped it... there's no reason to... go through with this. I'll tell... I'll confess to everything... but this... this isn't... this isn't necessary... "

For a tense few seconds, Ben held his ground without evidence of wavering. All was deadly silent and eerily still. Even the heavy snowfall appeared to have briefly subsided as if to provide all with a better view of the proceedings. I could hear the gas hissing from the tips of each cylinder as Ben's thumb and forefinger sat curled around a built-in lighter guard with which the flames would soon erupt. In response, an openly whimpering William Konrad dived stomach-first onto the packed ice, twisting his head to the far left to provide as small a target as possible.

Finally, Ben lifted the thrower's barrel airborne, twisting his head to regard Tate with a creased brow.

"Well... shit. Guess he didn't plug a vein after all."

Tate walked over and studied the cowering man, balancing his chin atop a clenched fist in true *Thinker* mode.

"Apparently not. If the little weasel was ever going to mutate for motives of self-preservation, that definitely would've been the time for it. You agree, Cas?"

Without hesitation, Cassie flashed a double thumbs up.

"One hundred ten percent. I'd say he's safe to transport."

Nodding my head in a mix of disbelief, comical awe, and not a small portion of relief, I couldn't help but laugh aloud, more so once Konrad had rolled over onto his belly wearing an open-mouthed expression of utter dismay right out of an old Looney Tunes cartoon. Similarly, Jake Owens and Randall Jeffries briefly resembled a bemused pair of Bobbsey Twins, with matching arched brows and grim, twisted smiles.

"Did I miss... what the hell was that?" Owens finally spat out, the tension leaving his slumped shoulders like a punctured balloon. "You mean to tell me... you mean it... a *bluff*... it was all nothing but a cotton-pickin' bluff... "

"That it was, Constable," Ben replied, shouldering the thrower and walking casually back toward the snowplow.

"But only if *Herr* Konrad over there didn't sprout symptoms of turnin' tall, black and ugly. Otherwise, I wouldn't have thought twice about crispy fryin' 'im into charred gristle."

Meanwhile, Tate had already retrieved Konrad and was pulling him roughly toward the cruiser.

"We had to know, Sheriff. Plain and simple. Now we can turn that loaded syringe over to the CDC or whoever is deemed worthy of studying a sample. See what makes it tick, so to speak, 'cause I have a sneaky suspicion big Bill here ain't gonna *volunteer* squat, right, Doc?"

Predictably, Konrad refused to even acknowledge the query, choosing instead to stare down at his own dirt, ice, and snow-coated work boots while being steered toward the waiting vehicle, where Sheriff Owens was already holding the passenger door ajar.

Tate quickly waved this notion off and gestured toward the truck, where Ben had already cranked the engine and engaged both the headlamps and windshield wipers.

"Afraid he'll need to ride with us in the plow, Sheriff. Just in case... well, something out of the ordinary does happen. Cas, climb on in. Darrin, you'll be riding with Jake and Randall. Jake, keep a safe distance in case there are issues... at least five or six car lengths."

"Sure you got the cell space, Sheriff?" I asked, peeking inside the cruiser and through the wire mesh that would separate us from Konrad's partners in past and future crimes.

Jakes Owens gave me a soft pat on the shoulder and I barely refrained from shrieking aloud.

"We'll make do 'til the state and fed boys arrive, I reckon. 'Sides, I get the feeling these guys are accustomed to close quarters."

Leaning back out, I watched Tate and finally Cassie climb into the snowplow behind William Konrad as Ben took the wheel. I then looked up into the flake-filled sky as Deputy Jeffries stepped in behind me wearing a worrisome look.

"We'd better vamoose, Sheriff. Storm's picking up but good."

"Yep. If it keeps up this pace for much longer, the roads past Mills Gap are gonna be impassable within the hour."

"Take my word for it, Sheriff, the um... *pace* does pick up, and then some."

"Well then, Mister Jackson, we'd damn well better step on it."

As instructed, Jakes Owens was careful to stay at least four or five car lengths behind the plow as road conditions became increasingly precarious.

Five to ten minutes removed from the crash site, I actually felt a rush of sweet relief in thinking the worst was finally behind us. My God, was I *ever* going to learn my lesson?

Chapter Eight

Final Meltdown/Scars from Futures Past

As the rear bumper of the snowplow had vanished from sight approximately five seconds earlier, we'd just begun to descend what the locals referred to as Thrill Hill, a steep, curving patch of narrow two-lane. Like the veteran Valley resident he was, Sheriff Owens had been extra careful not to ride the brake to prevent us from winding up buried in a nearby ditch. Other than the occasional mumble of Middle Eastern dialect originating from the backseat (cursing of some sort, I'd venture), we rode in silence save for the synchronized clicking of the wipers and the heater's steady hum.

"Dear god, what now?" I heard Randall Jeffries mutter.

This was followed by Jake Owens yelling, "Shit a brick!" in a much clearer, louder tone.

My own self-imposed daze so very rudely snapped by the rather bizarre vision of the snowplow sliding across the flat, icy grade on its left side, creating a mobile wall of metallic sparks, ice chunks and sheared asphalt in its grinding wake.

"They must've tipped over coming out of that last curve," Owens growled, whipping the wheel to the left to avoid Tate's handmade flamethrower, which had apparently been thrown from the back of the truck and was lying at the center of the roadway. Mercifully, the snowplow's progress eventually slowed as we approached to within two car lengths of its mangled rear bumper.

By the time it did grind to a full stop, the badly bent plow portion of the front end hung off the edge of a steep grade, it became painfully obvious the crash had been anything but accidental.

I pointed at the vehicle's roof, which appeared to be denting outward as if someone were attempting to beat out an escape hatch with their bare fists.

"What's... what's going on inside the cab?"

Without reply or hesitation, Jake Owens immediately shifted the cruiser into reverse and backed away, the sudden jerking motion causing myself and Randall Jeffries to forcefully bump heads.

We slid to a halt a good thirty to forty feet back from where we'd originally stopped; from what Jake must've thought was at least a marginally safe vantage point as he and Randall pulled their respective revolvers. From there, we watched as the driver's side door of the snowplow tore away and spun into the pitch-black night like a tossed Frisbee.

"Awwww shiiiiitttt," the sheriff groaned, and I felt a sudden, sharp ache at my bladder.

"That *can't* be good."

Cassie bailed first, leaping from the cab as if sprung by a trampoline (it would later be divulged that the leap was in reality a forceful shove from Tate Fletcher) and landing catlike on her feet on the opposite shoulder of the road.

Tate was next to emerge from the chasm, scrambling from the cab and performing a combat roll on the ice-packed roadway until he was at least a dozen feet from the overturned vehicle.

After a three-to-five second pause that seemed to last an eternity, Ben could be seen backing from the cab while tossing looping haymakers with both of those bowling-ball sized fists. For a brief moment, I swore I saw what appeared to be a blackish tentacle or similar appendage briefly snag his right ankle before being shaken off with a few stout kicks.

Cursing in what sounded like at least two separate languages, one of which I'm faintly sure was Korean, Ben then clung to the outer edges of the cab while administering several dozen such kicks with the bootheels of both feet before hopping away as if to avoid the impending explosion of a ticking time bomb. In turn, the roof of the cab suddenly stretched dramatically outward, resembling an overinflated balloon. At this point, it didn't exactly take a nuclear physicist to deduce what might be causing such a wild commotion. It mattered little in turns of priority. What was most vital was to eliminate the source as soon as physically possible. With this in mind, I actually had my hand wrapped tightly around the passenger side door handle, though in all honestly I had no clue as far as a plan of action was concerned. Luckily, my pathetic version of winging it as part-time counselor, part-time action hero was never to see fruition. As the old saying goes, 'leave professional matters to the professionals'.

"Bring the heat, Fletch! Fry that ugly fucker!" Ben exclaimed while frantically crawling away from the overturned truck on this hands and knees.

Having focused the whole of my concentration on Ben's frenzied antics, I had totally missed the fact that Tate had sprinted over and retrieved the flamethrower. Meantime, Cassie had jogged *slash* slid over the icy pavement and helped Ben to his feet, as the big guy appeared a tad unsteady.

"What Fletcher doing?" I heard the sheriff inquire in a low, barely audible murmur.

"Looks like he's trying to light up... " Deputy Jeffries added in a deep baritone that reeked of a deep-seated fear I could truly identify with, especially at that particular moment as my ears rang and my fingers tingled with a light yet palpable numbness.

Tate was being forced to click the built-on striker over and over to no avail as he neared the overturned snowplow, which was beginning to shake, rattle and tremor as if it possessed a life of its very own.

"Flame on, you piece of *shit*!" he cursed, halting in his tracks less than five feet from the same exact spot he'd landed just moments before after rolling from the cab.

I felt myself wanting to yell out for Tate to get out of there, or at least back away until he could get the 'thrower lit, but I found the power of human speech had long since abated. Fortunately, Cassie Wilkes *was* able to voice a similar concern, and in no uncertain terms.

"Back off! You're too close!"

Ben chimed in next, standing to Cassie's left and barely a dozen feet from the cruiser's snow-splattered hood.

"Cas is right, Hoss... you're gonna roast your own weenie at that distance... "

The roof of the cab then split open like a ripe banana peel just as a surge of billowing yellow flames illuminated the surrounding landscape like a lingering lightning strike, temporarily blinding me in the process.

Seconds later, both Jake Owens and Randall Jeffries exited the cruiser with weapons suitably drawn.

"Park your rear ends back in that vehicle... *now*!" Cassie barked, and both men instantly froze.

"I mean it, Sheriff... we appreciate the thought, but those peashooters are about as useful as a flicked booger right about now. Just stay back and prep to kick it into gear in case that thing does manage to get past us."

"Trigger that son of a bitch, Fletch!" Ben shrieked, slipsliding toward Tate with Cassie hot on his heels.

"Roast its ass!"

My pupils having adjusted to the sudden brightness, I caught an ever so brief but full-on glimpse of the half-man, half-monstrosity as it spilled from the shredded roof like a predatory insect from its nest. Thus far, only his hands, arms and a portion of his neck and chest cavity had completed the change; the head, face and lower torso appearing all-too human and thus, equally vulnerable.

That said, it had taken nothing more than those pincher-claw hands to peel away the hard metal of the snowplow's roof like the thinnest layer of tinfoil, so taking the creature wasn't a wise option.

As Konrad lumbered forward on stick-thin, sickly pale legs that hardly matched the taut muscularity of his arms, Tate took an additional step forward with Ben and Cas backing him on either side.

Just as Tate fired up the 'thrower and let loose

with an arrow-straight shot of thick flames, the creature lunged hard to one side and rolled away with surprising dexterity.

Quickly adjusting both his stance and the height of the flamethrower, Tate attempted to place the creature back in his sights for a second attempt. Unfortunately, the Konrad creature must've somehow anticipated the move and dived in the opposite direction, thereby avoiding a fatal torching yet again. At once, the creature turned and began to lumber away in the direction of the opposite shoulder as if to jump into a nearby ditch to reach the wide pastureland and tree line beyond. Its logic was clear: find a nice, quiet spot to complete the transformation.

"Shit! It's making a run for it!"

"Not on my watch, by god... " Ben shouted, racing past Tate and diving headfirst onto the icy road, his forward momentum shooting him forward like a human bobsled. He rammed the Konrad creature ankle high, flipping it into the air and onto its back with a resounding thud. The creature shrieked as it arose, a loud, ear-piercing howl that sounded less human in origin than like a coyote.

By the time the beast appeared to have regained the majority of its balance, Ben stepped up and delivered several forceful body shots and a wicked front kick to its upper chest, sending it skidding back toward the downed truck.

"Double-time that 'thrower over here, Fletch... ugly bastard is growin' stouter by the second!"

As Tate did just that, jogging over with Cassie only a few short steps behind, the beast howled yet again, this time in apparent frustration. It wasn't until Tate fired a short burst of flame overhead that the reason for the creature's agony-filled cries swam clearly into view. Konrad's neck, face and skull had bloated to twice their normal size, swelling and throbbing to grotesque proportions as skin peeled and flaked away like floating ash.

I heard Cassie spit out a resounding, "Ewwwww," before she managed to tack on a few actual words to such a comically disgusted reaction.

"Blast it, Tate... before it has a chance to complete the cycle!"

The creature had locked onto the snowplow's damaged bumper with both claws, as if using the vehicle's weight for support. At least, that's what I figured before seeing the entire truck swing around in a tight circle, the back end nailing Ben full-force and swatting him airborne. Using the two-ton vehicle like a makeshift club, the beast then spun it around in the opposite direction as sparks and smoke filled the air in a vaporish funnel cloud. I heard both Tate and Cassie curse in almost perfect unison while splitting off in opposite directions to avoid impact. The next voice I heard was that of Deputy Jeffries, his tone simultaneously solemn and awestuck.

"Looks like... that thing's unstoppable, boss. What... should we... shouldn't we make tracks, like Fletcher said? I mean, what if they... they can't stop it?"

Jake Owens' reply was equally morose, but also sternly defiant. I recall being both impressed and a bit concerned about such a high level of bravery.

"We're not budging from this spot, Randy. If it... if it *does* manage to get by them, we gotta go after it ourselves. I ain't leaving the townsfolk at its mercy... no way."

Swallowing hard, I felt my palms grow slick with sweat while gripping the rifle's stock. With the 'thrower's flame all but extinguished, Tate, Ben and Cas had temporarily vanished into the darkness as the beast finally released the truck's bumper and allowed it to topple over into a nearby ravine, leaving only the severed blade resting in the middle of the roadway. As for the creature itself, I could only make out its looming shadow teetering over the ditch as if admiring its handiwork. In the meantime, it was obvious the change was still ongoing, as its overall frame had gained several inches in height since escaping the truck, not to mention a dramatic difference in the shape and circumference of both its torso and head. It was only a matter of minutes before the alteration would be complete, and the giant killing machine I'd so briefly visualized back at the post would live again... to kill again... and again... without provocation and for the sheer enjoyment of it.

Reaching up to grip the gear shift with great care, Jake Owens addressed me without diverting his eyes from the mutating specter standing less than thirty yards from our position.

"You've got a vote here, Jackson... what say you?"

Owens' inquiry had caught me off-guard, to say the very least. My reply was delayed several seconds due to the boulder-sized lump taking up residence at the center of my throat. For some inexplicable reason, my response emerged as a hoarse whisper, as if keeping the volume down might actually prevent the creature from targeting our exact whereabouts. Hard trick that, considering the hum of the cruiser's engine and the fact that ours was the lone vehicle left standing upright.

"I... guess you're right. We have to at least try to stop it. We've... *I've* seen the potential for carnage if it's allowed to roam free. Waste of time or not... we have to tr-"

The low-pitched, feline whine that cut short my rather pathetic 'doomed if we do, doomed if we don't' speech had originated from the throat of Randall Jeffries.

"Ohhh lord... "

To accurately describe how the three of us had departed that cruiser once we'd seen the streaking abomination headed our way is difficult without leading off with the word 'panic'.

Both Jake and Randall had briefly attempted to pull the screaming, cursing terrorists from the backseat, but had been stubbornly rebuffed at every turn.

As weird as it sounds, it's as if the soldiers had decided to play the part of martyr, preferring to perish at the hands of their monstrous superior than to be charged and tried in court in enemy terrain. As it was, I'd actually jerked Jake from the vehicle by his jacket collar. From a distance, it might have mistakenly appeared as though bravery might have played a part in such rash actions, but the bottom line was that we all understood what our fates might've been if the beast had reached *us* while still trapped inside the vehicle. Sad to say, but those men had made their choice, and nothing we could've done in such a limited timespan was going to save them.

The beast began its frenzied siege by crushing the hood before proceeding to shatter the windshield with a single blow, then peeling the rooftop like a rusty tin can.

It is indeed amazing how fast one can move in such a situation, almost as if an internal gear kicks in that most never realized they possessed, nor ever had the opportunity to utilize.

As the creature continued to hack and pound away at the cruiser, tearing away chunks of metal, fiberglass, and the occasional severed body part from the suddenly quieted soldiers, a peculiar thing happened (yes, even more peculiar than how rawhide thick my hide had grown in the face of such visceral horrors). Instead of running helter-skelter from the scene like petrified rabbits, the three of us stood our ground from roughly the same distance but distinctly different angles and began to fire away at our erstwhile pursuer.

Being that my eyes had at least somewhat readjusted to the darkness, helped a great deal by the ivory landscape provided by Mother Nature, I was able to draw a decent bead on the thing's spindly torso, though I cannot by any means claim a single legitimate hit in the handful of shots I'd managed to pull off. Regardless, I guess something positive can be said of the effort. Once again, I saw it purely as a case of survival... kill or be killed, and despite our best attempt at a successful last stand, the beast appeared less than impressed, much less wounded in any way. The sad fact was, once the bullets had been completely exhausted, leaving the three of us clicking away at triggers and firing mechanisms that no longer possessed the required ammo to complete the cycle, I'm fairly certain we all understood certain death was eminent. Personally, as this had been at least the third time in a matter of hours, a great portion of the expected fear and dread had vanished, replaced by a rather grim yet not all together unpleasant acceptance.

"Make tracks, Jackson... " I heard the sheriff say from what sounded like a great distance, my hearing obviously numbed by the barrage of pistol and rifle retorts. He was standing a good twenty feet to my left, just to the edge of a steep, tree-lined hill leading into a blackened forest.

"Try to get back to the post... get some help out here."

To my right approximately ten yards away was his deputy, crouched on one knee and digging frantically into his parka's side pockets for additional ammo.

"Y-yeah... take off, man. We'll... try to distract it... k-keep it occupied," Jackson proclaimed, his voice cracking as if on the verge of tears.

For possibly the first time that entire hellish evening, my reply to the two stalwart lawmen's sincere yet ludicrous suggestion came straight from the gut; void of all psychological conjecture and similar meanderings often used to soften the cold, hard truth of a situation.

"Forget it, guys. Afraid the old gas tank's bone dry. Besides, I'm through running from the son of a bitch. He wants me... he can come get me."

Just then, as if to underscore the naivete of such brass machismo on my part, the beast lunged forward and literally cut Randall Jeffries in half at the waist with a single swooping strike, tossing his upper half into a nearby snowbank and subsequently kicking aside the quivering legs like discarded bowling pins.

"Oh J-Jesus... " I heard Jakes Owens cry as my knees buckled and I found myself inadvertently in praying mode as the Konrad thing bayed triumphantly before lumbering over my way.

"Get... get outta there, Jackson!" Owens pleaded just before I saw him take off up the hill, slipping and sliding like a man attempting to climb a glacier while wearing slick-bottomed flip-flops.

Unable to locate the aforementioned internal gear necessary to follow his lead, I was only able to lift my head upright with great effort.

Why I felt it necessary to stare into the mutated, inhuman eyes of my assassin is unknown. Call it a matter of pride. Call it a matter of dignity. Call it a pathetic attempt to obtain a higher sense of being in death that can never quite be achieved in life.

I recall the beast leaning down and studying me for a split second through those shiny, slimy, yellow-tinted orbs, as if it indeed did recognize me from the moment we'd shared in the generator room... or *not yet* shared, depending on one's belief in time travel. As it cocked its massive head to the left and began flaring its nostrils like an enraged bull, I noted that any resemblance to Doctor William Konrad would've been purely accidental. I could even make out a series of muted snapping sounds, as if bones and cartilage were being broken and reset almost in unison beneath that slick, scaly flesh.

As it straightened up and reared back the same

claw that had so effortlessly segmented Deputy Jeffries into two distinct portions just moments before, I closed my eyes and tried desperately to put together a final prayer in introduction to whatever afterlife lay ahead.

For a moment, I was certain the lashing, hard, thumping blow I'd heard was my head being viciously torn from my body. I then realized, with the kind assistance of my very own groping hands, I was indeed still intact, and peeked cautiously through splayed fingers to see Ben and Cassie standing shoulder-to-shoulder at the center of the road less than two-dozen feet away. Shifting my line of sight with a quick roll over, I saw the beast's trembling form laid out on the far left shoulder a good fifty feet away, the badly warped snowplow blade practically embedded in its breastbone.

"Nice toss, sweets," I heard Ben declare, clapping Cas on the right shoulder.

"Guess there's nothin' like gettin' a half-ton facial from a spinnin' metal slab to make one lose their mutated boner, so to speak."

"Couldn't have done it without you, old timer. Hey, you okay, Counselor?" Cas then inquired, jogging over and helping me up.

"Y-yeah, I guess... long as I still own the deed for all my arms and legs."

"Appreciate the diversion you three provided. Gave us time to catch our breath and hatch a counterattack."

I peeked over her left shoulder and saw Ben leaning over the lower remains of Randall Jeffries.

"What... happened in there?" I croaked as pointed shards of sleet pelted my exposed cheekbones like miniature spears. Ben walked over and placed one of his oversized mitts on my shoulder and goosed it playfully.

"Well, first off, ol' psycho sawbones started gigglin' like he'd just inhaled some of Columbia's finest wacky weed, then Cas noticed his fingers had turned a dark shade of blue. It was right around then his eyes started spewin' blue Kool-Aid, and he reached over and jerked the wheel right outta Fletch's grip. Next thing ya know, a friggin' hockey game broke out."

I forced a smile as Ben lumbered away, taking a quick peek at the bottom half of Randall Jeffries as it lay in a wide pool of semifrozen blood.

"Jesus... poor Randy," I offered as much to myself as anyone else. "Looks like the rewind didn't do much to alter his fate after all."

Awkwardly out of her league in such matters, Cassie nonetheless did her best to console.

"Wasn't meant to be is all. Nobody's fault. We'll see to it he gets a proper burial."

Out of the left corner of my eye, I saw Jake Owens slide down the same steep hill he'd recently attempted to scale. For obvious reasons, the sheriff did his best to avoid eye contact with his former deputy and friend's mutilated remains.

"He... Randy served himself up for me. Both of them did. Stood smack dab in the line of fire."

Jake soon joined us, greeting me with a solemn nod. I returned the gesture and even managed a pained smile.

Tate soon emerged from the shadows as well, hardly missing a step as he scooped up the flamethrower from the pavement and made his way quickly toward the Konrad thing.

As if in the latter stages of complete physical fatigue, Ben fell to one knee between myself and Cassie and slapped the frigid asphalt with the palms of both gargantuan hands.

"Stage is all yours, Fletch. What say let's lower the curtain on this nasty fucker for good... "

Following a faint click, the flame relit with a whooshing sound.

"Say no more, Benjamin. I'm on it... "

As if sensing its own impending demise, the beast attempted to rise with one final flurry of energy, tossing the massive blade aside and rolling onto its belly. Pumping its badly shattered legs like a drowning man swimming against the incoming tide, it indeed appeared to be trying to crawl away to safer climes.

Literally standing directly over the squirming giant, Tate let loose with both barrels, bathing its back and lower torso in a sea of bluish flame.

All told, it took mere minutes to transform the scaly horror once known as Doctor William Konrad into a quivering mass of melted scales, sheared tendon and crackling bone. At the very end, when what little remains hadn't been scorched to blackened ash, I could've sworn I heard a final cry that held at least a hint of humanity, as if the good doctor hadn't quite escaped his own demise completely unscathed. If so, he'd have been hard-pressed to find even a smidgen of pity among the witnesses present. As it was, I believe a full-blown square dance might've ensued if any of us had possessed the energy.

For good measure, Tate continued to bathe the

charred remains in constant flame until both cylinders ran dry. Working in relative silence, he and Ben then retrieved a shovel and several large trash bags from the cruiser's smashed trunk and strolled back over to the burn area.

In the meantime, Cassie Wilkes, Jakes Owens and myself walked north a bit to distance ourselves from the smell of death littering that icy stretch of highway, the sheriff in particular appearing the poster child for haggardness. He'd lost both a loyal employee and a close friend, and it wasn't at all difficult to read the deeply grooved measures of misery painted across his rugged features.

"What about the crash site? Thinks it safe to just... leave behind to burn?" he finally asked Cassie, who had lowered her head to attempt a quick power nap even as we trudged slowly onward.

"Who cares? Long as the damn thing burns."

"But what if a citizen happens to stumble onto it? I mean, what if there's some sort of contaminant present? We might have to quarantine both cities if the-"

"Jake... " I intervened, feeling the need to inject some logic while watching Ben and Tate take turns shoveling piles of ash, gristle and bone into three separate clear-colored trash bags. More than once they'd been forced to pause in order to snap the larger bones into suitably sized pieces for bagging. Some thirty-six hours later, those same sample bags would be turned over to CDC officials for study.

"Look up... look around. Storm's coming in fast. There won't be any citizens out and about to stumble upon the site. You already called and warned old man Cromartie and old lady Widham to steer clear of the area due to some kind of chemical spill and subsequent fire, remember? No one else is going to brave the area, and even if they do... " I paused, shifting my position slightly to avoid a chunk of brownish ice that looked to have possibly wedged free from the undercarriage of a passing semitruck.

"... There won't be anything to recover but smoldering ashes and molten metal... " Cas finished, her eyes still closed tight. "The potion is toast, Sheriff. Relax. You've... we've done all we can do for now, except maybe figure out how to get back to the post without freezing solid on the side of the road."

"Good point," Jake replied as we all watched a passel of larger flakes begin to fall. "But what about... them?"

The sheriff had gestured toward the mashed cruiser, which was literally awash in the blood of the slaughtered terrorists.

Ben stepped forward and studied the mangled stew of metal, fiberglass, bone and blood with his squared chin propped atop a massive, clenched fist.

"Far as the state authorities are concerned, it's gonna look like one gangbuster of an auto crash... snowplow and country police cruiser smackin' heads with several fatalities. Afraid your deputy is gonna be listed among the casualties, Constable."

"He's right," Tate added. "Besides, it'll be buried under two feet of snow by the time they discover it. Fed boys are liable to dig a bit deeper for answers, but we'll worry about that when the time comes."

With a slight shrug, Jake seemed satisfied with

the answers provided, or perhaps he was simply too exhausted to push the subject.

"It's coming down like gangbusters now, for sure, and we're SOL in terms of working transportation. Hell, it's just like I told those guys earlier tonight... or was that yesterday... or maybe tomorrow... "

I couldn't help but grin despite it all as Jake looked me squarely in the eyes.

"What's that, Sheriff?"

"If you people was gonna counsel a group of superhero types, why not include at least *one* who could fly?"

As Tate and Ben finished collecting samples, Sheriff Owens walked over to the battered cruiser and attempted without success to reach someone through crackling waves of static. He soon rejoined us with his shoulders slumped in defeat.

"Well, follow the yellow brick road, folks... " Tate advised some five minutes later, a bloated garbage bag slung over one shoulder. "We'd better be on our way... won't be that hard to commandeer a ride along the way."

Ben stumbled up, toting an even larger, bulkier load. Squinting upward as the intensity of the downfall seemed to increase with each passing minute, he then playfully bumped Tate with the bag.

"Oh yeah, no sweat, Sergeant Rock*head*. This here is perfect hitchin' weather. Pick and choose the most comfy ride for sure. Personally, I'm holdin' out for the first stretch limo that rides by... with a built-in wet bar, of course."

While Tate ignored the comments save a wry grin, Cas followed up with a hard clap to Ben's left shoulder.

"Aw, quit your bitchin' and lead the way, Thomason. For motivational purposes, just pretend there are hookers and free shots of Tequila at the end of the rainbow."

Turning on her with a cocked brow, Benjamin Thomason shook his head vehemently.

"Hookers? Not on your life, sister. After all, I'm an unhappily married man, ya know. As for the south of the border paralyzer ya mentioned... "

The big man paused for obvious dramatic effect.

"I'd gladly pound down a boatload if I thought it'd make me forget the last twenty-four hours."

To that, I heard Jake Owens whisper a hearty, "Amen," as the five of us walked slowly eastward, the hastily falling snow soon piling ankle-deep on the unused roadway. Despite the potential hardship in hoofing through tundralike conditions, I'd never experienced a stronger sense of relief in my relatively short life. In comparison to the hell on earth we'd somewhat managed to survive (not to mention alter so dramatically), such a challenging, potentially treacherous march was more akin to a tranquil walk in the park.

***

I'd never been one to believe in miracles. Thus, when a yellow bus with the words *Boulder Valley County School District* pulled up alongside our ranks barely fifteen minutes into the trek, I initially figured it for a fatigue-induced hallucination. This particular theory grew increasingly valid with the appearance of none other than Eugene Walker, Good Samaritan at large, parked behind the wheel. Yes indeed, the same Gene Walker who had, in some warped alternate universe, died such a tragic, gruesome death after transporting a half-dozen survivors to the post via his county school bus.

"Hop in, folks... I got plenty of room." He'd grinned, not even batting a suspicious eye as Ben and Tate had loaded aboard carrying overstuffed garbage bags that reeked of burnt alien flesh.

Twenty-five minutes later, we arrived at the post alongside several other familiar faces who'd also been caught adrift in what the locals were calling the latest *Storm of the Century*.

In the hours that followed, I'd briefed Burt Hanover and the rest of the staff concerning the plane crash and subsequent site investigation which had resulted in a shocking confrontation with what appeared to be potential terrorists. Tragically, I'd also passed on the news of Deputy Randall Jeffries' death, along with all five supposed terrorists. Being that neither Burt, Doc Gonzales, Jay or Jessica had any memory of what had transpired in that aforementioned alternate realm (though each had appeared a bit dazed and complained of splitting headaches), there was no reason to delve into further detail. Tate had suggested we keep all information regarding William Konrad to ourselves and allow the feds to handle the case from there. It goes without saying, but who in their right mind would've believed us anyhow?

Not surprising to the few of us secretly privy to the information, Burt had passed on some tragic news of his own. Mere hours before our arrival in

Gene Walker's bus, Nick Parione had been discovered lying face down at the bottom of the stairs entering the generator room. Doc Gonazles concluded the young man had passed of a sudden, massive coronary. *Note of interest:* an autopsy performed some three days later would reveal that Nick's internal organs and portions of his brain had mysteriously deteriorated to that of a man four to five decades older than his listed age. Talk about your strange side effects. The man had literally grown old in a matter of seconds, from the *inside out*.

Of the lot of us, Cassie easily gave the best performance in terms of acting both shocked and saddened by the news, though, like the rest of us, the latter of these two emotions wasn't at all hard to dredge up. Why, even tough as nails Ben Thomason appeared on the verge of welling up upon hearing the 'official' word on Dejà vu's death. Despite the fact we'd all known it was coming, the jolt was still considerable. After all, you hardly forget or take likely the deeds of the man who saved your life. Nick had understood the price for his heroics long before carrying out the deed. He and I had discussed the limitations of his power on several occasions. More than once he'd confessed to not having the courage to test those limits, stating he'd probably go to his grave never knowing. Lord, the irony of it all. In discussing it later in secret group sessions, all had agreed in speculating that deep down, Nick had probably always known he had the capability to back up time for longer than mere minutes or hours, but had also instinctively realized the possible consequences of attempting a lengthier duration. In the end, facing an almost certain death, he simply threw out all the stops and tested his powers to the breaking point. The grim reality was, he knew dying in that cold, stony generator room was a given. He could either perish alongside those he'd tried to protect, ripped apart by the same beast we all seemed fated to fall victim to, or attempt to save the lot of us with one final, albeit personally desperate, measure. Regardless, from a survivor's standpoint, it's hard not to view such a selfless act as anything but astonishingly brave. As Ben had so eloquently put it, "Looks like I misjudged his character... big-time. Kid was a warrior after all."

Always the unique phrase-turner, Cas added (a bit teary, I might add) "Yeah, I guess his arrogant, loudmouth punk act was just that. Lucky for us. Lucky for a *lot* of people."

Tate added, "From a military standpoint, Parione deserves a posthumous medal of honor... times ten. Damned shame, really... he didn't have a blessed clue of the power he wielded."

Nickolaus Parione's body would be transported to DC for proper burial some twenty-four hours after our arrival back at the post. We had, of course, been snowed in during that time, and I was forced to share space with folks I'd previously seen die. In many cases, I'd witnessed said deaths. To state the obvious, it was a strange feeling. Almost dreamlike, like much of what had transpired between those two distinctly different worlds we'd recently inhabited.

For local records, Deputy Randall Jeffries' death would be listed as accidental, the cruiser he'd steered sliding out of control and smashing into the snowplow driven by Tate Fletcher. Jeffries was touted a local hero for his part in capturing the would-be terrorists, and a plaque bearing his name and grainy black-and-white photo from his graduation from the Sheriff's Academy would soon adorn the walls of city hall for all to see.

As for the legacy of hate and death behind one William Konrad, it would have to be properly sorted out by the government, as Tate, Ben and Cassie had stated they would all file official reports of the top secret variety once proper officials arrived on post.

In his taped manifest, previously procured by Tate Fletcher and one of two physical objects to have inexplicably made the transformation from one time-space continuum to the other (unlike the similarly procured black box pulled from the downed craft), Konrad had revealed his hatred for the U.S Government in no uncertain terms. Ranting and raving in true fascist form, spittle flying from his lips in frothy gobs, he claimed to have been a loyal government employee (specifics not given but it sounded like a rather prestigious, military-based bio-engineering gig of some type) who was blackballed and subsequently fired over some illegal experimentation in the areas of human growth hormones, methamphetamines and beta radiation. Obviously, the man had gone off the deep end, to the extreme of turning said experiments on himself. Though we had originally thought the terrorism plot to be aimed at the presidential visit in Las Vegas, Konrad had revealed Phoenix, Arizona as the target city, as he meant to dump the vat of elixir into that city's reservoir and study the eventual effects. It was later learned he and his band of infidels (all associated with elements of Al Queda...

no shock there) had hijacked the plane from a National Guard site just north of San Diego, killing six and wounding three others and then confiscating uniforms for disguise purposes before their landing in Corvallis.

Exactly how Konrad had managed to infect Jake Owens and Randall Jeffries with the same poisonous mix will likely remain a mystery, or exactly how he was able to regain human form and back again (explaining the pitifully baggy wardrobe he'd obviously stolen from a victim's home). Then again, considering that it never really happened... I guess it matters little in the grand scheme. Lord, it's just so hard to dismiss all that transpired before Nick was able to magically rewind the timetable. As far as surrealism goes, there's nothing quite like passing the time of day with someone you watched die right before your eyes (my most vivid memory is meeting Mayor Bowen on the street a week or so after the incident and thinking, *He looks much better with his head attached*).

What no one has yet to decipher from even a semilogical standpoint is why the Twin Cities as a whole suffered from a case of mass amnesia in the aftermath of Dejà vu's rewind while a chosen few, including yours truly, could recall even the most minute details of what transpired (or should I say, 'didn't transpire?'). Even stranger were those citizens trapped and ultimately slaughtered on the post grounds, none of whom seem to have the slightest inkling that nearly two days of their lives had been lived and subsequently relived, though with dramatically altered results. As for me, I seemed to be blessed (perhaps *cursed* is more apt a word) with an almost photographic recall of said nonevents, right down to the very moment Nick had begun the historic rewind in that frigid generator room. I could recount every word spoken by or to me, while Ben, Tate and Cassie confessed to many blacked-out segments which would forever remain unaccounted for. Meanwhile, it was Sheriff Jake Owens whose thought process appeared the most jumbled. In the months that followed, I often noticed the man wearing a dazed expression, as if he were struggling mightily to regain a memory or image just out of reach. If in fact these were memories tied to that bloodthirsty being he'd been forced to share a body with, I'd speculate such losses as a true blessing.

***

There's little doubt Doctor Konrad would never have settled for the Twin Cities for his little experiment if not for the crash (and subsequent spillage of the filled vat), not to mention the virtual impossibility of finding a suitable water source in which to dump the chemical. If what transpired with Jake and Randy were any indication, he'd definitely had a winner on his hands. I could only imagine (though I truly prefer not to) what kind of chaos might've ensued if that mix had gotten released in a major city. It is mind boggling and truly what such apocalyptic nightmares are made of. What a relief to know that (hopefully) the formula has died with the man responsible. We can only pray Konrad alone was privy to whatever formula created such a witch's brew.

As for as our remaining trio of heroes, each

remained on post for the duration of their individual treatment, departing as a graduating class some six weeks following the incident, just as temperatures began to rise to tolerable levels and the surrounding grounds were no longer being blanketed by daily snowfall.

Of course, each was required to meet with a group of visiting feds concerning the terrorist attack, and most notably what, if anything, they'd learned in facing Doctor William Konrad. I cannot say for sure whether or not Tate, Ben or Cassie attempted to fill in the federal boys on the time-travel segment, and I never bothered to ask them. For some reason, I just didn't feel it was my place. As for myself, I kept mum on the subject for fear of being led to the nearest padded cell. There was a moment during my interview with the agents, both of whom so reminded me of the *Mr. Smith* character from the *Matrix* films of my youth, that I seriously considered spilling my guts for no other reason than a bit of soul cleansing. There was, after all, the issue of the faux line badges (obviously used to gain access to the stolen plane), the second of such items to have successfully made the time jump. I'd originally confiscated them from Jake Owens' shredded blue jacket-the badge showcasing Konrad's photo ID eventually aiding us in marking him as a fraud. In the end, I stuck with the terrorist plot and left it at that, handing the badges over to Tate to do what he deemed fit.

As far as potential aftereffects from what we'd experienced in that alternate realm, no one walked away completely unscathed. Each had his or her own personal manifestation to come to grips with, be it mentally or physically. Ben, for example, showcased a wide (approximately as wide as a number two pencil), lengthy scar that circled the whole of his upper right shoulder, curving directly beneath his armpit and meeting back up on the opposite side. From a distance it might've resembled one of those razor wire tattoos that had become so popular of late amongst professional athletes and the like. When Ben showed it to me during one of our last sessions together, he said it sometimes itched like mad, as if it were birthed from a fairly recent wound. Being that I'd seen Ben's right arm cut off and had subsequently studied the bloodied stump in the aftermath, there was no doubting the scar ran the same exact pattern. Talk about chilling, I recall the hair on my neck standing out like quills at the very sight.

Similarly, Tate possessed a scar that ran from his lower abdomen to his breastbone in a slightly crooked line. That said, the man owned two dozen such marks on every conceivable part of his body, so one would think nothing special of this particular addition. That is, until the man himself pointed it out as a 'new arrival' he'd accidentally ran across while studying himself in a long mirror just days after our return to the post. Again, I'd seen the man's chest ripped open in that... other zone, and this appeared still another supernatural aftereffect of said wound.

Not surprisingly for Cassie and Cassandra as well, their scarring was more of the emotional type. I noted during our sessions how each struggled so mightily to maintain control, where normally it took a sudden burst of anger to trigger the change. It made me wonder which personality had been dominant in that one faithful moment when death had come knocking. Logically, one would've assumed that in battling the beast, Jekyll-ene would've been holding the mantle. I thought about pushing the subject but quickly abandoned that notion due to the fragile psyche involved. The sisters definitely had enough on their plate without me gumming up the works even more. Instead, I tried to focus on the positive aspects of each personality and how perhaps they could better learn to coexist if playing superheroine was indeed what they'd chosen as their life's calling, and in truth, what alternatives really existed for such an enigmatic, strong-willed cast of characters? It wasn't as if getting married, raising a family and playing homemaker were a realistic option. The woman was a multipersonality with mutant characteristics, and though she was undeniably attractive from a physical standpoint, I can't see there being many takers on *Cupid.com* for one prone to *breaking* house in lieu of cleaning it.

Cassandra would always be the pessimistic thinker; Cas the rowdy, raucous brawler, and 'Mama J' the mindless She-Hulk birthed in primal rage. I could only hope she'd learn to cope with whatever additional torment had been added to the mix as a result of death and the subsequent rebirth that followed. As hungover and disjointed as the time trek had made me feel, at least I'd been spared the inner-mind's eye view of being so brutally gutted... god bless and thank you once again, Nickolaus Parione. As for personal aftereffects, there is occasionally a dull ache near my right ankle that seems wholly unjustified save the severe fracture it had endured within that bizarre realm of unreality. As it stands, I continue to fail miserably in attempts to pass this phantom pain off as some strange coincidence.

So vividly I recall my final words to each of our heroes as they departed the post that fine pre-spring morning.

"It's been a real experience, Counselor," said Tate Fletcher with a cocked brow. "Watch out for those low-flying planes now, you hear? And if one just happens to crash in the nearby vicinity, do me a favor and... (he paused to wink, leaning over to give me a gentle nudge) lose my number."

I'd shook the veteran soldier's extended hand (nonbionic to avoid future soreness) and assured him that if such a situation did arise, I'd surely pass him by in a streaking blur headed for parts unknown.

While Cassandra had shaken my hand politely and said simply, "Be well," a brief glimpse of Cas had magically emerged a few moments later, practically hugging the stuffing out of me and planting a big, wet kiss on my right cheek.

"See you down the line, cutie. You know, you've got brass balls for a paper-pusher." She beamed before reverting back to Cassandra mode. Thinking back, it was indeed fortunate I didn't return the kiss as I'd temporarily intended.

As for Ben Thomason, grumpy, stubborn, tough as nails but also one of the most charismatic individuals I'd ever run across before or since, we'd shared several cups of coffee in the mostly abandoned mess hall the morning of his departure.

"Gotta give credit where credit is due, Darrin... " he'd said between noisy sips. "You did good... on both ends of the time spectrum. Hell, if you had even a shred of superpower about ya, I'd surely recruit you as a junior CO at my place of employment."

"Don't overshoot my worth, Ben. It was all reflex... reflex fueled by fear. Lord knows my spine is probably a permanent shade of jaundice after all I've seen... what we... went through."

Leaning back with a sigh, Ben regarded me through squinted eyes, speaking in a deliberately soft tone as he temporarily fell completely out of character.

"No shit, I ain't just blowin' smoke here. Most civvies woulda curled up and startin' suckin' their thumbs at some of the trauma you witnessed firsthand. Ya handled the whole shebang like a real trooper. If I was to vote, I'd place you a close second to Sir Nickolaus Parione as most valuable player throughout the whole shebang."

"Well, I can't... I mean... I didn't really do anything but get in the way... " I babbled, feeling my face grow hot.

"Not only that, ya seem sincerely devoted to helping people. Ain't easy for a man to find his callin' in this life. Nobody knows that better than me. You're good at dealin' with cracked eggs... don't ever let 'em tell ya different. You can make a difference here, just as I hope to get back to doin' what I do best and rededicate myself to it."

"And your marriage?" I asked hesitantly, unsure as to whether or not I was treading on sacred ground.

"Bingo! That's exactly what I'm talkin' about. Right to the meat of the issue... a real pro, yes sir," he said with renewed sparkle, that familiar gleam of mischief flashing from both eyes.

"About that... I realize what a horse's ass I've been of late. I'm gonna try like hell to get Leah back... to make her believe in me again. Besides, it's damned obvious I'm a lost cause otherwise. That Asian princess is the best thing that ever happened to this old warhorse, for certain."

Leaning in to speak confidentially, though the room and perhaps the entire wing was more than likely empty save the two of us, Benjamin once again reverted to serious mode.

"Ya know, Doc, I felt her there with me... when I was layin' there bleedin' out in that frozen dome," he half-whispered, looking past me with a deep, thoughtful gaze I knew the man rarely exhibited. "Leah was leanin' over me, tellin' me everything was gonna be alright. I could even... *smell* her perfume, ya know? The one she wears on those rare occasions when we'd toss off the spandex and hit the town as regular folk... well, as regular as you can be for a guy with dozer-mitts for hands.

"Lord knows I probably don't deserve another shot with that woman, but I'm gonna risk it regardless. I can only hope she misses me a third as much as I do her."

"How 'bout the drinking, Ben? You willing to give it up for Lent?"

Raising his coffee mug toward mine (his massive mitt making it resemble a miniature teacup), Ben grinned and proposed a toast.

"Don't know Jack about Lent 'cept what's

collectin' in my belly button, but I will make a declaration right here and now with *you*, Counselor Jackson, as my sole witness... "

I steered my cup shakily towards his, as his 'lint' remark had me about to split a gut in hysterics.

"From this here day forward, no more boozin' or brawlin just for boozin' and brawlin's sake... " he bellowed, though concluding the declaration in a muted whisper, "meanin', such behavior is gonna have to be at least *partially* justified... "

"Amen, brother," I managed between snorts, unable to refrain from spilling a third of the steaming liquid onto the tabletop in the process.

"You're a good Joe, Counselor," Ben replied with a nod. "I do believe I'm cured."

The morning we as a staff watched those three depart our midst was indeed a somber one, though much more so for the young counselor with whom they'd shared so much tragedy and triumph. None but those who lived through it could truly appreciate its impact, and there was no denying the secret link the four of us shared. There had been, of course, a fifth link to the chain, and easily the strongest of all. Not one but two cities, and perhaps the planet as a whole, owed their very existence to Nickolaus Parione, AKA Dejà vu, but were blissfully ignorant of such a cold, hard fact, and sadly would remain that way.

In the days and months that followed, I'd witness petty arguments and the usual complaints of the locals concerning the weather, gas and food prices and the like.

Usually, such common human behavior had no effect on my personal feelings or daily outlook.

That said, there were times I wanted to scream at the individuals responsible and shake a fist in their faces to make them understand how fortunate they were to still be alive and residing in the Twin Cities. Twin Cities that, in an alternate universe which bore the same name and citizenry, came frighteningly close to being obliterated off the map. I so wanted to tell them of a group of outsiders who went by such over the top code names as Force, Scar, and Jekyll-ene. Outsiders who had saved the entire community's collective bacon.

But even more, I wanted to sit them down and tell them of a cocky young man named Parione, who, unlike the rest, wasn't able to walk away to make new memories, but instead sacrificed all to ensure they would.

***

Two years and three months after the fact, and though relocated to the East Coast for a full nine months, the people and events of the Jasper Outpost rarely escape my daily thoughts. Having completed my major in the social sciences, I currently serve as head counselor for the chemical dependent at a small clinic in Charleston, South Carolina.

Though my days are full, usually of the ten to twelve hour variety six days a week, a grueling schedule that hardly befits a man so recently married, I do find time to keep in occasional contact with several of the principal players from the Outpost assignment via e and sometimes snail mail. Recently renamed the *Twin Cities Outreach Center*, Burt Hanover remains the man in charge, while Doc

Gonzales continues to chat up a storm as the post sawbones. Counselors, of course, have come and gone since my departure, and I hear Jay Peterson and Jessica Lewis have since moved on to greener pastures; Denver and San Diego, if memory serves, with the latter having gone on to pursue a career in child psychology.

As for the trio I've come to think of as the 'Outpost Three', I've maintained a two to three emails a month correspondence with Cassie Wilkes, who has long since hung up her superhero tights (resigning from the *Alpha-Dames* supergroup almost immediately upon her arrival back in Miami) and instead works, suitably enough, as a combination lecturer/administrative assistant at a Miami hospital specializing in multiple-personality disorders. A year earlier, under the supervision of a team of hypnotists first introduced to her by the Avengers' Scarlet Witch, it was determined that Cas, not Cassandra, was indeed the dominant personality. Since that time, Cassandra rarely makes an appearance, while the ultraviolent older sister once known as Jekyll-ene has vanished from her psyche altogether. Less than three weeks ago, she emailed to tell me of her engagement to one of the doctors on staff, a British chap named, I kid you not, Billy Conrad. That's... William... *blessed...* Conrad. The irony of it all is to laugh... hysterically.

According to his last snail mail, Tate 'Scar' Fletcher is no longer an active government employee, but second-in-command of a newly formed Supergroup that makes its headquarters in the desert climes just outside Flagstaff, Arizona. He sent along a recent group photo of the proudly posing foursome that calls itself *Brute Force*. It seems the other three members of the group were once former teammates of a late 20th, early 21st century team named *The Revenge Squad.*

The first, a tall, muscular black male wearing a dark crimson cowl, bright yellow tights and black combat boots is identified as *The Guardsman*. Standing a bit distant to Tate's left is a strikingly gorgeous female of obvious Asian descent, her silky, pitch-black hair wound into a tight ponytail that hangs snakelike and ever so seductively over her right shoulder. The woman code named *Marvella* wears no cowl of any type to hide her exquisitely chiseled facial features and piercing brown, naturally slanted eyes, but does don formfitting red tights (fitting a very fine form, I must say) and a pitch-black silken cape along with calf-high, sharp-tipped boots. There is a familiar hand resting atop her right shoulder-familiar mostly due to its shovel-sized appearance. Ben *Force* Thomason has changed little save the fact that his Fu Manchu mustache has gone mostly gray beneath his dark blue cowl. Though he does appear a bit bulkier through the upper torso, that might possibly be the result of the skintight, sleeveless camouflage shirt that appeared two sizes too snug for his barrel-shaped chest. With each wrist adorned with spiked bands, the remainder of his costume, as it were, consisted merely of blue jeans and spit-shined black combat boots. The big guy never was the fashion plate sort, and I couldn't help but snicker at the sight of his oval-shaped belt buckle with its dark blue shading and shiny silver skull and crossbones at the center. I could only imagine the anguish with which

Leah, whom he'd mentioned had also worked as a fashion designer, had endured from her husband's rather unique costume choices.

I recall Ben once telling me he'd estimated that in over twenty-five years of random combat, he'd suffered at least a thousand separate broken bones, insisting that his left wrist alone had endured at least three dozen such snaps, while a close second in the body-fracture sweepstakes was his right clavicle or perhaps the bridge of his slightly crooked nose. In terms of life cycles, one might speculate the hero-type's expectancy to be dramatically shorter than that of your ordinary average Joe, obviously due to the high danger aspect of their chosen field. Oppositely, it could be argued that if one possessed the quick-healing, instant rejuvenation powers such as Ben's, natural longevity might possibly be the result.

The photo had obviously been a PR flyer of some type, and even advertised a website entitled *BruteForce.com* which I wasted little time in perusing. A flashy, professionally maintained site, it featured a separate page for each member which included a detailed bio.

It seems that both Ben and Tate, along with this Guardsman fellow, had resigned from their respective government gigs a few months previously to devote themselves full-time to the group, while Leah had obviously put the fashion career on hold. The site provided a contact number and email address for anyone contemplating hiring out for their service, the team motto listed as 'no mission is too large or small for those requiring *Brute Force*.' Oh, how the hero business had changed with the times. I could almost hear Ben cursing aloud how they'd all become whores to the masses, though it was fairly obvious he'd decided to retire from the corrections field after all, as had his old friend The Guardsman.

The page I'd enjoyed the most conveyed a personal message only a select few could truly appreciate or understand, that being the special dedication page to the late Nickolaus Parione, along with several other former teammates of the Revenge Squad who had perished in action (including such names as *Johnny Reb* and *Darkclaw*). Again, it featured bios for each fallen hero, and I couldn't help but linger a tad on Nick's particular entry. My god, the powers that young man possessed! The untapped potential of which truly boggled the mind. Therein lay the problem, perhaps, and deep down Nick might even have known it to some extent. Perhaps it was fate he perished so young, as possessing the ability to alter history should never be placed atop the shoulders of a mere mortal. Regardless, his final use of said powers, to stretch their limitations under such powerful duress, could not have been more selfless. Often I cannot help but wonder about Nickolaus' final moments as he initiated the rewind. I hope he felt no pain. I hope he somehow understood the lives he was saving and that his sacrifice was not to be in vain. I hope he understands and feels the appreciation of those who know. I hope to see him in a better place, and thank him personally for the life he gave... returned to me.

Along with the photo, Tate had included a short letter, to which he politely wished me luck on my new job and invited me to of course stay in touch.

At the bottom of the letter's second and final page, Ben had scribbled out a brief message that instantly brought forth a wide smile while simultaneously warming my insides with as good a feeling as I'd had in quite some time.

Take a look, Hoss... finally got my priorities straight. Leah says hey and thanks you for helping to save my leathery hide. Like I told her, Counselor, you're a good Joe... a damned good Joe.

I read and reread that letter a half-dozen times, pausing only to reexamine the photo ad nauseam.

It didn't hit me until hours later, while casually brushing my teeth in front of the bathroom mirror, and I could barely refrain from spitting forth a mouthful of toothpaste at the comical irony of it all.

Tate and Ben in the desert... Cas residing in Miami... my taking up permanent residence in the humid climes of South Carolina.

Though it might not have been a conscious decision on any of our parts, I had the distinct feeling we were doing our dead-letter best to avoid *frozen* precipitation at any and all costs.

Personally, I'd had my bones chilled but good atop the Jasper Outpost all those many months ago, and hoped to spend the rest of my days in permanent thaw out mode.

Somewhere in the vast distance, I can almost hear the *Outpost Three* bark out a unanimous 'amen'.

[illegible]

By The Author

Bloodlines – Legacies of Madness
Bug-Stompers of the 21st Century
Creeping Dead
Damned Grounds
Desolation Island
Desolation Outpost
Gauntlet
Mr. Hate
Passports To Hell
Recluses
The Dead Effect
Yellow Fever

www.ingramcontent.com/pod-product-compliance
Lightning Source LLC
LaVergne TN
LVHW030907080826
845145LV00010B/2796

* 9 7 8 1 7 8 6 9 5 5 0 9 8 *